1

"A sweet, touching view of the

"Coming-of-age novels are always interesting, but this novel puts a new spin on it."
—*RT Book Reviews* (four stars)

"What a generous, big-hearted book this is. McLaren explores her subjects—friendship, regret, rebirth, the irresistible pull of place—with such tenderness that you'll find yourself wishing you could be a Firelight Girl, too."
—Marisa de los Santos

"Touching, brilliantly insightful, and deeply compassionate ..."
—Amy Hill Hearth

PRAISE FOR
How I Came to Sparkle Again

"A gem of a novel. I loved the fresh setting and quirky, endearing cast of characters. This novel is like a perfect run down a black diamond slope—fun and fast-moving and invigorating."
—Kristin Hannah

"Warmhearted and funny ... Quick with the quips and repartee, the dialogue is a pleasure to read, as McLaren shows her readers how even the brokenhearted can get their sparkle back."
—*The Seattle Times*

"McLaren's intimate portrait of a seasonal town and its colorful characters makes for an entertaining ride."
—*Publishers Weekly*

"A delightful novel of life, lessons, and growth for a plethora of characters ... *How I Came to Sparkle Again* is [a] soul-satisfying treat for these long winter months!"
—*Romance Reviews Today*

"Sad and funny and so much fun to read! ... *Sparkle* is both entertaining and wise!"
—Nancy Thayer

"This warm, satisfying novel is a treat."
—Sarah Pekkanen

"This novel is filled with all of my favorite things: characters who are so real you want to reach out and give them a hug; a magical setting; enough surprises to keep the pages turning; heartbreak, laughter, crying, and sighing. Not to be missed!"
—Susan Wiggs

"McLaren weaves a wonderfully tender story ... A true page-turner, *How I Came to Sparkle Again* reads as fast as a run down the slopes!"
—Susan Gregg Gilmore

"A generous and endearing novel of loss and reconnection, of friendship and love and finding your way home to a small town called Sparkle, where the ski bums have big hearts and name their dogs after beer, and just the right number of people grow up into adults."
—Erica Bauermeister

The Road
to Enchantment

Kaya McLaren

St. Martin's Griffin
New York

THE ROAD TO ENCHANTMENT. Copyright © 2017 by Kaya McLaren. All rights reserved. Printed in the United States of America. For information, address St. Martin's Press, 175 Fifth Avenue, New York, N.Y. 10010.

www.stmartins.com

Designed by Jonathan Bennett

The Library of Congress Cataloging-in-Publication Data is available upon request.

ISBN 978-1-250-05822-5 (trade paperback)
ISBN 978-1-4668-6227-2 (e-book)

Our books may be purchased in bulk for promotional, educational, or business use. Please contact your local bookseller or the Macmillan Corporate and Premium Sales Department at 1-800-221-7945, extension 5442, or by e-mail at MacmillanSpecialMarkets@macmillan.com.

First Edition: January 2017

10 9 8 7 6 5 4 3 2 1

To my parents. It's not easy to raise a spirited child without breaking her spirit. Good job. Thanks for your love, acceptance, encouragement, and faith in me.

ACKNOWLEDGMENTS

I want to acknowledge my Apache friends, former students, and other people in the Jicarilla community who I didn't know well enough to call friends, but who I deeply admired. I spent three years living and teaching on the Jicarilla Apache Reservation and I feel so grateful for that experience. I feel like I got to experience a part of America few ever get to see. I was always treated with kindness and respect. I expected to experience racism, but unless it was so subtle that I didn't notice, I never did. My intention of setting my story there was to share the richness of that place and to break down the walls that sometimes divide people, but I recognize that this is delicate. I am not an expert on Apache culture by any means. There is so much I will never know or understand. There is so much that is none of my business. It was difficult for me to untangle what is mine and what is not mine to write about. Apache culture, particularly anything that is sacred, is not mine to write about or profit from. But three years of my life history are mine. In the end, I wasn't able to untangle it completely. It's my hope that my Apache friends and former students will see my good intentions and forgive me if I overstepped my boundaries in any way or for anything they feel is a misrepresentation. It's my hope that they will feel that I did not make generalizations, that I neither glamorized nor painted a negative picture of life on the rez, but that I treated characters as individuals. I hope that they will allow me creative license because this is, after all, very much a work of fiction. I fictionalized the name of the Apache tribe and of the town in which they lived in this story to avoid confusion, unintentional misrepresentation, and invasion of privacy.

I'd like to thank David Velarde, Jr., and Ina Montoya, for answering some questions about the Abaachi language, and I'd like to thank Maureen White and Cleo, who taught Abaachi at the elementary school where I worked. Each morning, Cleo's voice would come on the radio with the "Abaachi of the Day," a phrase to learn. I remember coming to school and trying my new phrase out on them, and they laughed and laughed and said it sounded like I was speaking French–Abaachi, and that I sounded like that cartoon skunk. They were great.

I'd like to thank Cox Canyon Winery, for letting me tag along during a harvest day and for explaining the finer details. Thank you for the great conversation about terroir! I also want to thank David Arnold from the Wines of the San Juan, and both Jerry Burd and Karl Johnson from the Black Mesa Winery, all of whom were so generous with their time and knowledge about wine-making and grape growing in northern New Mexico. And I'd like to thank Dennis Rak from Double A Vineyards, for information about winter-hardy hybrids. Information on the Web, from the University of Minnesota, Cornell, the Finger Lakes Wine Society, Small Farm Central, and by Bruce Bordelon of Purdue, was useful to me as well.

Thank you to painter and treasured friend, Mary Hoeksema, for all kinds of goat ranch and cheese-making details, and for inspiration always.

When I was really struggling with Willow's story line, Deborah Peña, who lived in Dulce twenty-seven years, told me about the wide range of experiences her children had going to school in Dulce—one who was picked on and won't return to this day and one who was picked on and then protected—and came to belong so completely that when a group of kids from the school was going to go to Costa Rica, and funding from the tribe was only offered to the Native American kids, the Native American kids said they weren't going to go unless Debbie's son was funded and could go as well.

When I had questions about probate and tax problems, attorneys Daniel Farr, Kate Fitzgibbon, and Jill Kinyon came to my rescue. Tobi Goering offered helpful information, too.

I'd like to thank Kara Hunnicut, for teaching me not just how to play the cello, but the joy of playing the cello.

When I thought I was done, Tess Haddon and Carmen Quall dropped everything and read for the next two days, giving me feedback that helped me take it to a new level. Their clarity was like a miracle to me.

This book went through some radical changes since its first draft. Many people gave me their valuable time and helpful information that ended up in story lines that were cut or changed, but I want to thank them: Dr. Sarah Lesko, Connie Celuska, Leslie Lehr, and Denika Kleinmann.

I am truly, truly blessed to have agents that I call my fairy godmothers—Christina Hogrebe and Meg Ruley, and for the support of the whole team at the Jane Rotrosen Agency. And I'm equally blessed to have Jennifer Enderlin as my truly masterful editor, mentor, and coach. Thank you also to Caitlin Dareff, Katie Bassel, and everyone at St. Martin's Press, for everything you do.

1

Maybe it was the fact my feet hadn't touched real dirt in so long that I suddenly became aware of them when they did. Sure, they had been in sand not that long ago, but sand lets all things pass through it—water, crabs, and people. Clay doesn't. Clay holds what lands on it. This thought terrified me. I never did like this place and I sure didn't want to get stuck here.

Glittery glass shards from broken bottles littered the side of the remote dirt road. I stood outside the gate and looked over into my mom's world, into my past. Some things were exactly the same. For example, the old 1953 pink Cadillac still poked out of an arroyo in the bull's pasture like a fossilized dinosaur unearthed by the elements. And by "pasture" I did simply mean a large fenced-in area full of sage and not much else.

Señor Clackers, my mom's Toro Bravo Spanish fighting bull, had been her answer to a security system, a way to keep the drunks and thieves out, and he had just noticed me, so I knew I had only seconds to make my move. He was roughly fifteen hundred pounds of pure muscle that rippled under his shiny black fur when he moved, but at the moment he stood still, his head held high, sniffing the air, his regal horns reaching clear up to the sky. My mom had installed a system of gates so that the bull blocked a narrow section of the driveway when she wanted protection, but kept the bull out of the driveway when she wanted to welcome a visitor or go in or out herself. I quickly crawled over one metal gate and pushed another gate shut, blocking the bull from the driveway and allowing me to walk through safely. Curious, he trotted over to me, his massive testicles swinging back and forth as he did, the characteristic for which Mom had named him. Bull testicles were something I hadn't seen in my twenty-one years of city life and now struck me as somewhat obscene even though rationally I knew that was ridiculous. I took a step back, lacking complete confidence in my mom's aging fencing. Señor Clackers's long horns hooked forward as he snorted through the fence.

Mom's two dogs, Mr. Lickers and Slobber Dog, noticed us and began to bark and run toward me jubilantly, as if they had mistaken me for my mom, and I wondered what similarity they saw that caused them confusion—our frame? Our posture? Our walk? As they neared, they balked, as if they realized I was not my mom after all. The dogs and I had met twice before, but still, I spoke to them calmly, wondering how protective of my mom's estate they would be.

"Estate" was actually a word far too fancy for what lay before me.

I bent down to see which dog was male and which one wasn't, so I could remember which was Mr. Lickers and which was Slobber Dog. They were siblings and looked remarkably alike, built much like blue heelers, with four colors of fur all mixed in together, white paws, white stars on their chests, and white stripes down their noses. I let them smell my hand and then pet each one before I continued my slow walk up the driveway.

I didn't know how I was going to find homes for all of my mom's animals. In addition to the bull and the dogs, there were the horses, the donkey, the llama, and the guinea fowl. The livestock would be a pain to sell, but the dogs . . . No one around here needed two more dogs. I looked down at their sad faces and wondered whether the Vigils farther up the road would take them back.

I scanned the nearly three hundred acres, wondering where exactly Mom had fallen off her horse and why. Maybe a rattlesnake had spooked it. Maybe coyotes or a cougar. Maybe it had been stung by a wasp or a bee. I would never know.

As I continued to walk toward the house I had once shared with my mom, the guinea fowl ran to get out of the way, eventually flying up to low branches on a nearby juniper. Their black feathers with little white polka dots littered the gravel. I picked one up and admired its elegance. Was I really going to catch all of these birds? No. Maybe I could advertise that I would give them away to anyone who would come out and catch them.

Since I had been here last, Mom had built a structure into the side of a hill on the other side of the barn. She had told me about it, but I had never seen it. The front was stucco with wooden timbers that poked out above the windows, and a hand-painted sign above the door that read, "The De Vine Winery." Behind it, the five acres of grapes Mom and I had planted had filled out, now striping the nearby hillsides with bold green lines where only small green circles had dotted the landscape not that long ago.

A white vinyl couch sat facing the large arroyo where coyotes used to hide, and next to the couch, sun shone through the green glass of an empty wine bottle.

And to my left was the house and garage, something between artistic and ramshackle that a friend of my mother's old friend had built out of straw bales, stucco, and salvaged materials. It looked boxy, even with solar panels sitting on the flat roof. The walls were fat with deep windowsills that I had loved to sit in, soaking up sunshine while I did my homework on cold winter days. Over the door was a stained-glass window he had salvaged from a church that had burned down, a window depicting the Nativity. It had been damaged so he'd had to cut off Joseph and the wise men, leaving Mary and her baby alone with the livestock and the Angel of the Lord. He had built a large frame around it before he had set it into the wall. Turquoise paint peeled from the wooden door and window frames. Near the door grew oregano, black-eyed Susans, and hollyhocks, an odd combination of survivors.

In every direction it seemed there was a doorway I was afraid to walk through, not wanting to see the archaeology of my mother's last day—the rag she'd used to disinfect the bags of the goats she had milked that morning, the rake she had used to pick stalls, the pans and buckets that were undoubtedly still in the drying rack, the clothes she hadn't laundered, her hair in the shower drain.

At once, a momentary wave of fever and weakness washed over me as my stomach turned. I dropped down on all fours and abruptly threw up. I had been doing this for the last two days and chalked it up to grief.

I sat back on my knees, looked up at the front door of the home where my mother's absence felt so wrong, where it was finally real in a way it hadn't been until that very moment. Then overcome by weakness, I laid down on the gravel, rolled over, and looked up at the sky above. It was clear and blue with only one cloud in it—a large bear that floated in the southeast over the Vigil place. A bear. My old best friend, Darrel. The sky seemed to be telling me he was coming, and so I shut my eyes and waited.

2

I was thirteen the first and only day I had ever seen a cloud shaped like a cougar in the sky, an animal that sneaks up on you from behind and attacks before you ever see it coming. I had seen it as I rode my bicycle home from the old brick junior high school through the maze of old neighborhoods and into progressively newer ones.

Only after I had turned a corner did I notice the very large plume of black smoke coming from the vicinity of my house. As I neared, I could see my mother in the driveway, sitting in a lawn chair roasting something over a flaming mattress. Neighbors peeked out of their suburban ranch homes to monitor the situation, and in the distance I heard a siren.

My mom had an extra lawn chair and marshmallow stick waiting for me when I pulled up on my bike. On the chair sat a bag of Peeps, those marshmallow chicks Mom put in my Easter basket every year even though for years now I had been way too old to be playing along with the Easter Bunny. Mom had speared one of the Peeps and something about it was a disturbing and grotesque sight roasting over the mattress fire.

"Hi, baby," Mom said as she pulled the bright yellow marshmallow off her stick, and washed it down with a swig of cheap Chardonnay. Then she put a hot dog on her stick and offered one to me.

I shook my head as I assessed the situation. To be honest, I wasn't sure whether Mom had finally slipped right over the edge. I decided to begin gently. "I'm sorry you had such a bad day," I said calmly.

"Your father has a new girlfriend. Surprise," she replied.

Seven words seem far too few to completely turn a person's life upside down, and yet they did. "What?" I asked, stunned. "Is he leaving us?"

"Yeah, he's leaving us, baby."

While I didn't want to inflame an already critical situation, I was furious and couldn't stop myself from saying, "You should have been nicer to him."

"Did you ever see me be mean or disrespectful to him? No. So don't be mad at me. He's the one who left. And I'm the one who wouldn't leave you for all the tea in China."

Unsure of what to do or say next, I scanned the neighbors' windows to see who was watching as I listened to the sirens of the fire truck get louder and louder, and waited for the inevitable scene. Just then, Ms. Nunnalee, my social studies teacher, drove up to her house across the street. On a normal day, she stopped at her house quickly to let her dog out before going back to school to coach whatever sport the girls were playing that quarter, but on this day she looked at my mom with wide eyes and kept driving. God. How horrifying.

Even though I was sure the engine was racing through town, everything seemed as if it was in slow motion. After what seemed like an eternity of embarrassment, the fire engine finally arrived. My mom's wiener was only half roasted.

"Hi, Monica," the oldest of the four men said delicately, while the others went to hook a hose to the nearest hydrant.

"Hi, Dave," Mom replied. "Hot dog?"

"Um . . . Actually I just ate. Perhaps another time," said Dave diplomatically. "Um, Monica . . . You know we have to put this out, right?"

"Yeah, I know." With that, she picked up her lawn chair and walked into the garage, resigned.

"Sorry about my mom. Apparently my dad has a new girlfriend," I explained to them, as if that would make everything okay. Still stunned, I picked up my lawn chair too and followed Mom into the garage, where she then shut the automatic garage door behind us.

She began to riffle through an old box on the shelf, and near the top, found what she had been looking for: an old poster of Sam Elliott. She grabbed the hammer and some nails, along with her bottle of Chardonnay, and walked purposely to her room where she tacked Sam on the wall behind where my parents' bed had been. She took a long swig, then lay down in the pile of blankets and rolled herself up. "God, I smell him everywhere," she muttered to herself. "This whole damn house stinks of him." She fell asleep or passed out next. I wasn't sure which.

The next morning was foggy. Foggy in spring? Fog was typically an autumn phenomenon in western Washington, so this struck me as a very bad thing. And I knew what it meant—it meant that I could not see what was coming at all. But this much I knew about fog—it was never a good sign. No, fog never foretold good things, like surprise birthday parties. Fog was always creepy.

But after enduring a whole day of school being the target of all the day's—and probably the week's gossip—I wished the fog hadn't burned off so I could just disappear right into it. I hopped on my bike after the final bell and got out of there just as fast as I could, angry about the damage my crazy mother had done to my social life.

When I returned home, my mom was standing outside of the house next to a green pickup truck, all loaded high with boxes, wearing the overalls she always wore when she was doing a big job, and a red bandana tied around her head to keep her hair out of her face.

"Hi, baby. Get in," she said, like nothing was unusual or downright wrong. She took my bike and loaded it into the pile in the back of the green Ford pickup, and then with a rope, tied it to the heaping mound of our other selected belongings. "I traded in our station wagon today."

I took a deep breath and looked up at the truck. I had not seen this coming—no, not at all, but I figured we were simply moving across town to a different house—one that didn't smell like my dad.

Above the pickup floated two clouds shaped like geese. *Geese fly south*. For better or worse, I accepted moving was my destiny, opened the door, and stepped into the truck.

When Mom first pulled away, I simply felt numb. I didn't panic too much right away, figuring that my parents likely needed to sell the house and each get smaller, less expensive places. But then Mom turned right instead of left, and we began to drive in the wrong direction.

"May I ask where we're going?" I asked.

"New Mexico," Mom answered.

Shocked, I had to verify that I had indeed heard correctly. "New Mexico?"

"A friend of an old friend of mine bought some cheap land there long ago, and built a small house on it that's off the grid. Do you know what that means? It means no power lines or phone lines go to it. It has solar power. How about that? We're going to be completely self-reliant. Anyway, now that guy is on to other things so he offered to sell it to me for a song and carry the contract, which is great because I would never qualify for a loan."

"New Mexico?"

"It's beautiful. I've seen pictures. Georgia O'Keeffe country."

"Am I going to see Dad again?"

"Of course. He'll fly out and visit you. Or maybe he'll send you plane tickets so you can fly back and visit him."

"So, wait. I'm going from seeing Dad every day to seeing him what—once or twice a year?"

"We both are," Mom answered plainly.

"And there's no phone so I can't even talk to him?"

"Nope. Sorry. Maybe he'll send you a phone card so you can call him from a pay phone sometimes. Write him a letter and suggest that."

Panic rose up in my chest through my throat, but I tempered it in my mouth because I always got further with Mom when I used a calm, big-girl voice. "I can't believe you're taking me this far from him."

"I can't believe he didn't value his family enough to keep it in his pants," she retorted.

I buried my face in my hands. This couldn't really be happening. It made no sense—except that when I looked at my mother, it kind of did. She would not be an easy person to live with. After all, she didn't seem to care very much about what other people wanted and she definitely drank too much. "You drove him away. You're the reason he left me."

My mother turned and looked at me, at first angry, and then she softened a little bit—enough to go back to looking at the road anyway. She didn't reply. We drove in silence, with the exception of Mom occasionally asking me whether I needed her to pull over at a rest stop or whether I was hungry. I would answer with a nod or by shaking my head.

As each hour passed, I felt the growing distance acutely. My sense of severing overwhelmed me. Sometimes tears would escape as I looked out the passenger-side window. After I wiped them away, my mother would look over as if to say, "Stop it," and it fueled my silence.

The green forests and pastures along the I-5 corridor in Washington led south to Oregon. And the cliffs of the Columbia River Gorge gave way to open desert and golden wheat country. We passed the Blue Mountains and the Wallowas of northeast Oregon, drove over the Snake River and into farmlands of Idaho. Each change in topography was one more world apart I was from my home, my dad, and my friends.

Somewhere around midnight, we pulled into a Motel 6 in Boise, brushed our teeth, and fell asleep in silence.

And the next day, no apologies or comfort were offered either. Farmland turned to ranchland. Little junipers sprung up in the high country between Idaho and Utah. Then, on our left, the Wasatch Mountains towered above the Great Salt Lake on our right.

As the afternoon crept on, we crossed the mountains and entered a land completely alien to me. Eastern Utah stretched out before us, so vast I could see all the way across it to Colorado. The mesas with their flat tops rose over carved canyons, and the whole country seemed painted in shades of tan, pink, gray, and orange. It appeared as if almost nothing lived there. *Such lonely country,* I thought. As we drove south to Moab, the rocks and cliffs actually glowed like amber coals.

New Mexico wasn't what I expected—at least the part we were in, the north. It didn't look barren like eastern Utah. Hills and mesas in sandy tans poked out from behind forests of small junipers and pines. And the largest elk I'd ever seen fed on grass in the lowlands.

We entered the Cestero Apache Reservation, but for miles and miles and miles, there was no one.

It was twilight when we dropped into Sweetwater, and in the dark, it looked like a quaint mountain village tucked in against the mesas and mountains. Upon closer inspection, I noticed bars on the windows of businesses, and buildings in disrepair. We passed through as quickly as we had driven in—so quickly that if we had blinked twice we would have missed it, and just a mile beyond

Sweetwater, we left the reservation and entered Coalton, which looked even poorer.

After a few more miles, my mother turned south into Monero Canyon, our new home. The dirt road was badly rutted, and a flooding creek threatened to wash out the little wooden bridge that my mother fearlessly drove over. Farther and farther we drove into the dark canyon, until finally our headlights shone on a little house on the left. I could not believe how far out in the middle of nowhere we were.

Mom pulled in, parked, and pulled a flashlight out of her purse. I followed her as she walked up to the little house, pondering the irony of feeling both so hidden and so exposed all at once. Anything could happen to us here. Anyone could drive up to our house, and we would be defenseless. Being off the grid meant we could not call the police—if there were any police out here. The windows had been boarded up, making it seem even less friendly, and there were actual bullet holes in the door—bullet holes! I pointed to them and, alarmed, asked, "You're kidding me, right? We're going to live in a place with bullet holes in the door?"

"Now that we're here, no one will shoot. Someone was just shooting at a vacant house. That's all."

" 'That's all'? Does Dad know you're endangering me like this?"

"Stop being dramatic."

Incredulous, I simply shook my head.

"It's been a long day. Help me unpack until we find the boxes with our blankets and sheets, and let's get some sleep. Tomorrow everything will look better."

Only the next day, it didn't look better at all. It looked like a dump. I wasn't sure who to be angrier at—my mother or simply at life in general. I looked to the sky for clues that somehow it would all be okay, but saw nothing but blue. The sky was only smiling—not talking at all.

3

This time, it was me who was dumped the day before I arrived.

At first, it had seemed a pretty normal day, except that I was still excited about the news that Ross, the producer of the studio where I worked, had given me yesterday—that in addition to four emerging indie artists I was really excited to work with this month, Steven Silver was going to be recording a solo acoustic CD here, and he wanted my cello tracks on it. *Steven Silver* wanted *my* cello tracks on *his* CD. *Mine.* In my book, there was Paul Simon, Sting, Peter Gabriel, and Steven Silver. My dream was for all of them to make a CD together, but short of that, it was my dream to record with any of those guys. And it was happening.

So, I was excited about that, but still, it was a pretty normal day. I sat with my cello between my knees waiting for Ross to be ready for the next song. I looked over at Ian sitting behind his drums. Although sexy in his white T-shirt that showed off his muscular arms, his face reflected the inner conflict he'd been having since he had turned forty-three weeks ago. As I put a birthday cake in front of him then and lit the candles, he had said, "I'm running out of time to make my wishes come true. I need to do more than blow out candles." I hated to see him like that. So, when I caught his eye, I glanced at the singer and rolled my eyes, attempting to make him smile, and Ian answered by pretending to scratch his head, but really making a pretend gun with his hand that he held to his temple before he pulled the trigger. This was something we did regularly.

The singer the label had sent into the studio was even more annoying than many. Ever since Carrie Underwood won season four of *American Idol* in 2005 and went on to have a very successful recording career with another label, it seemed our label was set on finding someone who could rival her. They sent us singer after singer who screeched at the top of her range. It was my job to create and play a simple cello part in all of their songs—something that followed the melody pretty closely so that it would add the depth and richness their voices lacked. Depth and richness had been cast aside to make room for the high note. Like many others, the singer of the day had won some glorified karaoke contest by hitting the high note, but today she couldn't quite hit it and no amount of cello was going to cover that up. Ross clearly hoped that several tries would warm her up, but instead, it seemed to be shutting her down. I wasn't sure how much more I could take. Being unable to eat that morning had left me weak in both strength and tolerance. The whole day was torture, but still within the realm of normal.

Sometimes I got lucky and was called in after the singer had recorded all of his or her tracks, and then I could lay down my part of the song pretty quickly and painlessly, but today Ross was hoping for "synergy"—basically, that a room full of musicians would fill the singer with so much happiness that she would wax melodic.

Like I did nearly every day, I thought about my cello teacher, Marta Sandoval, who had given me lessons twice a month for two years for something close to free simply because she saw something in me, and on days like this, I found myself feeling like I had wasted all those precious hours of her life. To make matters worse, as I slipped into the corporate music scene, I had gotten lazy about keeping in touch. My last Christmas card had been returned. I didn't know where she was. But each passing year left me with a greater urgency about finding her again. There were things I wanted to ask her now—things about how to be a musician with authenticity when I basically spent my days making music for The Man, when my music was often dictated to me, when sometimes the noises I made with my cello hardly struck me as music at all, but something closer to background-filler noise within songs—just something to make a song sound fuller and richer, something so subtle that no one consciously noticed it or could identify it. I just felt like Marta would be able to lead me back to my authenticity. I kicked myself for the complacency or perhaps the shame that had caused me to lose her.

After work, Ian and I met at the door to walk home together as we always did. It was my favorite part of most days. Our seven-block walk through the underbelly of Hollywood back to our cheap apartment provided us with a little exercise, time to decompress and laugh, and exquisite people watching as well.

For the first time in a long time, I had an idea for a song that I wanted to write and so I carried my cello home that day. That was the first unusual thing about a day that had been normal up until that point. Suddenly, I was feeling creative again.

I kept waiting for Ian to carry my cello for me, but he didn't, and that was also unusual. Ever since he had joined his new band, he had been kind of a princess about his wrists and hands. I figured that was likely the reason for his lack of chivalry.

"I know I've said it before," said Ian, "but those talent—er, glorified karaoke shows—are ruining rock and roll." That was a normal thing for him to say. We'd had this conversation many times and agreed that desperately seeking approval was the anti–rock and roll, and anti-art in general.

I replied, "Today while I was waiting for Ross to finish telling that singer something, I found myself imagining what Woodstock would have been like if, you know, Jimi Hendrix waited for Crosby, Stills, and Nash to critique his performance, and then begged the audience for votes that would save him." I knew that would make Ian laugh, and it did.

"The degree to which that is ridiculous is approximately the degree to which rock and roll is off course." He was quiet for a moment and then added, "And that's why when you were in the bathroom this morning, I gave Ross my two-weeks' notice."

I knew it was a defining moment for our relationship and that I would lose him if I didn't hide my fear, but I wondered how he was going to pay his half of the rent because I sure couldn't cover it all. My meager savings had been wiped out after having to pay for a new—actually, rebuilt—alternator for my car. Even though Ian had talked quite a bit recently about leaving his steady but boring studio musician job and striking out with his new band, I didn't think he would do it so soon. After all, his band didn't even have a complete set to play yet and had zero gigs booked.

"Wow," I said with a fake smile, hoping it was convincing. "So it was just time, huh?"

"Yeah, it was just time."

Since I didn't know what else to say, I tried to make a joke. "But now, the next time you're stuck in traffic and some jackass next to you is singing along with some karaoke contest winner on the radio with the windows down, trying to hit that high note only he or she can't hit it or anything close, you'll miss that moment of satisfaction that comes with knowing you helped create that source of torture for everyone in a four-car radius."

"Yes," Ian said with mock seriousness. "That will be sad." Then, looking up, he pointed to our favorite Thai restaurant. "Hey, we should celebrate!"

I felt a gag rise in my throat. Thai food was unthinkable. I put a hand on my belly. "I can't do it," I said, wincing. Not only was the thought of Thai food enough to turn my stomach, so was the idea of spending money when he didn't know where his future paychecks were going to come from.

"Your stomach's still weird, huh?" he asked, distant and distracted.

"Regrettably."

"That's okay. You can rest and I can go celebrate with the band." In my head, I was calculating the money he'd likely spend on food and drinks. As if reading my mind, he asked, "How are we going to pay next month's rent?"

I shook my head. "I don't know."

He was quiet for a moment as we continued to walk, but not long enough for me to think it was an idea he had just thought of when he said, "If we broke up for a while, I could move into Ty's closet for just a hundred bucks a month."

My eyebrows rose along with the bile in my throat, but I managed to hold it down, along with all the things I wanted to scream. Five hundred and twenty-five dollars was his half of the rent, so four hundred twenty-five dollars would be his monthly savings. That was the dollar amount that exceeded my value after almost three years together.

My rational mind whispered that this was a blessing, that I was being offered an out just in the nick of time. After all, I had seen what happened to men in bands—the poverty, the traveling, the other women, an addiction or two, and then the inevitable band drama and band breakup. If I stayed with him, all of it would eventually turn my life into a living hell. But my rational mind only whispered, while my heart screamed because I had spent the last three years imagining growing old with him, and I wanted that.

I wanted back what I had thought I'd had just ten minutes ago.

That life. That boyfriend. But it was gone and I knew it. There was nothing I could say to change where this was going. He had clearly already decided what he wanted and it wasn't me. The only thing I got to choose at this point was how much dignity I wanted to keep.

"Aren't you going to say anything?" he asked.

"I can't believe you're doing this, but far be it from me to stand in the way of your destiny."

Although I had said it tongue-in-cheek, that was lost on Ian. "Thanks, babe. I knew you'd understand. I mean, you don't want to be a shitty studio cellist the rest of your life either, right?"

A shitty studio cellist. As if choosing four hundred and twenty-five dollars a month over me wasn't insulting enough. "If I'm so shitty, why does Steven Silver want my tracks on his CD?" I asked.

"You know that's not what I meant. I just meant there's a difference between making music for other people and making it for yourself." He paused to see if I understood, but I was still seeing red. "It's just for a little while. Just until the band starts making money. Then you and I can move back in together."

Before I could tell him what he could do to himself and that I would never go back with a man who abandoned me because I wasn't worth four hundred and twenty-five dollars a month, my phone rang. Darrel's name appeared on the screen and I picked it up just to be rude to Ian, just to let him know his presence didn't matter to me. "Hey, Darrel!" I said cheerfully.

"Willow, your mom . . ." Darrel began.

Instantly by the tone of his voice, I knew something was very wrong and a chill ran through me.

"I noticed her horse running around with a bridle with a broken rein and so I went looking for her, but Willow . . ." Darrel began to cry. I'd never heard or seen him cry before. "I was too late."

I stopped in my tracks and the look on my face stopped Ian too. Everything slowed down. As my stomach sank, I lowered myself to the ground with it. Ian was clearly uncomfortable with the space I was taking up on the sidewalk as people walked around me, but I didn't care. "Are you saying what I think you're saying?"

"Yes. I think she had been there a couple days."

I laid all the way down on the sidewalk next to my cello, looking up at the sky for some sign that a mistake had been made, that the woman he had found hadn't really been my mother, for any sign that my world wasn't crumbling under me. Nothing. I knew there were logistical things I had to figure out, but I couldn't think of what they were. I couldn't think clearly about anything at all. All I could think was *My mom is dead.* For a moment, I dared to hope I had fallen asleep at work and was simply having a nightmare, but I ran my fingertips over the bumpy surface of the sidewalk and knew I wouldn't dream in that level of detail. "Um . . . um . . ." I stammered.

"Are you alone?" he asked.

"No, Ian is with me," I replied. Sensing his celebration plans had just been ruined, Ian tried to mask his dread with a look of concern.

"Oh, good. Listen, I called the sheriff. He'll probably call you soon, but I wanted to tell you myself. I didn't want you to hear it from the sheriff."

"Um, thanks," I said. My mom. She had driven me nuts. Our relationship had been tumultuous to say the least. But she was my mom and I did love her. It might not have looked like it, but I did. I wondered if she knew that, and regretted not taking my last opportunity to tell her. My mistake was permanent now. There would be no do-overs, no reconciliation. My chest felt so very heavy, as if the spaces between the broken pieces of my heart were filled with lead buckshot, the small pellets rattling around.

"Willow, I know that your people sometimes like to see the body before you let it go, but I want to strongly encourage you not to do this."

"Okay," I said, trying to imagine my mother's body too gruesome or too disturbing for me to see, wondering how bad it could be after just a few days. "When the sheriff calls, I'll tell him to send her body directly to the funeral home for . . . I don't know. Cremation, I guess. She never liked funerals. God, I can't believe we're having this conversation."

"I know," he said.

"Well, I'll leave here right away and get there . . . I don't know . . . the day after tomorrow I guess."

"Okay, um, I'll feed the animals until you can get here, and then I'll help you any way I can. You're not alone."

"Thanks, Darrel."

"Willow, I'm so sorry."

"Thanks, Darrel. I love you."

"I love you too."

I hung up and then looked at Ian, who was waiting for an explanation. I could hardly say the words. They came out in a whisper. "My mom died."

He took me in his arms, but I was too shocked to cry. "I'm sorry," he said. "I'm so sorry." And we stood like that for a long minute or maybe two, until his phone vibrated, and with one hand, he pulled it out of his pocket and checked the text message that had just come in.

"Did you really just do that?" I asked.

"What?" he asked innocently.

"Did you really just check your message one minute after I told you my mom died?"

Sensing that things were about to explode, he took his time trying to think of the right answer. "I'm sorry?" he eventually asked, not as if he really was sorry, but as if he was asking whether those were the magic words.

I shook my head. "Despite the fact you just broke up with me, leaving me with an apartment I can't afford by myself, I thought that after almost three years, we were at least better friends than that."

"Willow—"

"You know what, Ian? Just . . . go. Just go . . ." I was going to add *to hell,* but those two extra words seemed like a lot of effort and unnecessary drama, so I kept it simple.

He stood on the sidewalk, befuddled, as if I had just been the one to break up with him, but I saw his relief under his act.

He went out to celebrate with the band, and in a state of shock and despair, I packed my things. There wasn't time to get a storage unit, and even if there was, all of our secondhand furniture combined was worth less than what it would cost to rent one of those storage units for one month. My clothes fit in two boxes, my shoes in another. My collection of mismatched china and a few small kitchen gadgets fit in two small boxes, and in one more small box, the few books I had been intending to read for the last three years but hadn't, a few books of sheet music I had picked up with the intention of continuing to develop myself as a musician (but I hadn't done that either), and a small bundle of my very favorite letters from my mom—the ones that were just so classic that I had kept them to enjoy long after she left this world, having no idea that day would come so soon. I had a jewelry box, a small painting of a cellist playing in the streets of Paris, a wool blanket I liked and another handwoven one—a souvenir of someone's trip to another country that I had found in a thrift store. I had a wooden box with home-office supplies in it and records I'd need to do my taxes in a few months, and a small crate of things I kept in the bathroom. All of it fit in my 1979 Volvo wagon along with my cello.

I left before Ian came home. I just went.

As I drove east to New Mexico, my mind was full of the resolutions I was not going to have and the happy endings I was not going to get. I thought about how Mom and I had tried to make things kind of normal again through our letters after my last somewhat destructive visit, but that was as far as we got. And I thought about Ian, wondering how I had wasted three years of my life with him. What had I seen in him?

I supposed that for starters, he wasn't completely drunk or high all the dang time. That was huge, because for the last twenty years, I'd been trying to meet a man who loved me enough to quit his vices and had, with the help of my elderly dear friend Betty, only four years ago recognized I was doing that and accepted that the outcome I was hoping for was never actually going to happen. It had left me feeling hopeless, because I was too old to be making mistakes like that. I should have known better by then. Clearly, I was unable to select a good man. Add that to my list, I had thought, because I had also been unable to select good bands to join (my experiences there pretty much paralleled my experiences in romance), and I had been unable to find a truly acceptable place to live. I was barely able to stretch a paycheck all month. In all ways, I had thought I'd have my life together much more than that by then. I had lost faith in men and music, but worst of all, in myself. And then Ian came along and suddenly I believed again.

I remembered one night during the first couple weeks we were together, when we went to see La Santa Cecilia play at the bar down the block. They had fused their Mexican roots with their love of 80's New Wave, mixing Nortena sounds and Cumbia,

Spanish, and English, and coming up with something uniquely contemporary. The lead singer had a strong presence, a strong sense of style, and an even stronger voice. She wore a crazy purple tutu dress, striped leggings, and cat's-eye glasses, and belted out lyrics in two languages with passion.

The moment we walked in, I shouted to Ian over the loud music, "They're already blowing my mind! I love them!"

"Any band with two drummers has already won my heart!" he shouted back.

"And that guy with the accordion . . . How many people can rock an accordion . . . *and* white pants while he's at it?"

Ian laughed. He got my humor, my eye for the slightly absurd or the unexpected in everyday life.

And as I stood there on his arm, I noticed people were looking at us. Maybe they were trying to figure out what he saw in me or maybe in his glow they were finally able to see the beauty in me that they usually missed. Or maybe next to Ian, I radiated so much love that it changed my appearance.

Only then, after I was on Ian's arm where I felt the difference between invisibility and visibility did I realize that I had been invisible most of my life. I thought back to the second grade, to seeing mouse clouds or bunny clouds and trying to be as invisible as them—a creature only seen in between hiding places. And then when Mom had moved us next to the Cestero Apache Rez, eye contact was rude so no one looked at me. Although it was even more than that. We were poor and dumpy and white so no one *wanted* to look at me even if it hadn't been rude, which it was. My reprieve from my invisible years on the rez had been moving to Los Angeles, or so I thought. But very soon I discovered there was California beautiful and there was everybody else. I was included in the *everybody else* category. We didn't get noticed. Normal people can't compete with California beautiful. That, combined with the fact that people in big cities didn't look at each other, had left me relatively invisible here as well.

But there I was with Ian anyway. He saw something in me, and now suddenly everybody else seemed to as well. Invisibility was something not afforded to anyone on Ian's arm. He had that kind of charisma. It could have been the change in my confidence that allowed everyone else to see me because he did have that effect on me. Not that I wasn't pretty—I was pretty. Not beautiful, but pretty. My face was pretty ordinary, pretty blue eyes, a pretty okay nose, lips that were pretty small to be considered sexy, and features that were too soft to be striking, but were pretty nice. My hair was long and blond, but not particularly styled. Not polished. I definitely did not look polished like the California beautiful girls.

Maybe Ian had been burned too many times by the girls who were California beautiful, or maybe he just found them to be too much work. I had observed firsthand that he seemed to react with some level of disgust toward them. There was eye rolling and usually a comment about mindless conformity, commercialism, or plastic surgery, which he called "mutilation." I suppose I had to give him that. While we were together, he did make me feel like the prettiest, most authentic, hip, and artistic woman in Hollywood. Pretty. It was very different from California beautiful.

Normally Ian was more of a listener than a dancer, but that night he couldn't help himself. He took me in his arms and danced me around the floor, twirling me and dunking me, his own silly mix of what he knew and everything he made up to fill in what he didn't know. We laughed and laughed. And when the music slowed down, we danced slower and closer, the sexual chemistry between us smoldering as he held my eyes with his own.

Out there on the dance floor with Ian, I believed in it all. I believed in him. I believed in music. I believed it wasn't too late for me after all—that I might still create something radically different and yet relatable. I had been pretty locked up creatively since I had come to Los Angeles. I made up parts to other people's songs, and then I listened to other people's music, and I talked about the day I would create something of my own, but I never got around to it. It was embarrassing to admit it, but musically, I had been in a rut for almost twenty years. Perhaps it was because at the end of a work day, I didn't want to play more cello, or perhaps it was because I didn't have the right synergy with anyone. It could have been that I wasn't inspired by my surroundings or my life, but I suspect it was simply less risky to talk about it and dream about it without ever actually going for it. Trying meant risking failure. But when Ian walked into my life, I started to believe in the words I spoke about my dream. I thought it was finally going to happen—that I had finally met the first member of my new band, a member with whom I felt tremendous synergy.

Only later did he tell me that he had no intention of making music with me outside of the studio. I realized one day that it took more than a cellist and a drummer to make a good band, and not wanting to waste more time, I suggested that we find two or three more people to round us out, and that was when I learned that the music he dreamed of making didn't involve a cellist at all. Or a woman. He wanted to be in a band with other dudes—his word, "dudes." He thought dudes created less drama and would likely stay together longer. I wondered at the time how anyone could create less drama than me, because after all, I was usually invisible. By then I was so in love with him and so blinded by my hormones that I didn't step back and look more closely at my situation. I let it go and just enjoyed being in his energy—the energy of vague possibility. And I enjoyed feeling seen—even if it was just a shallow sort of way of being seen.

In retrospect, I think his real reasons for choosing to be with me as long as he did was that he knew I would never begrudge him the things he did and would choose to do in order to further his musical career. I'm sure it didn't hurt that at times I was kind of his mommy or his maid. I was the one who cleaned the apartment, did the laundry, and cooked meals most of the time. Economically, it made a lot of sense to stay together too. Neither one of us made enough money to live alone, really. Maybe that was the real reason he stayed with me as long as he did.

And maybe that's what had made it too inconvenient for me to look closely at the truth as well. I had to own that. In our three years together, he had been a real dick more than once. I had enough invested in our life together that I didn't want to see the truth of who he was. I wanted to believe instead that we could work out anything, that we would grow, that we were destined to spend our lives together, that no one would understand the musical side of me like he did, and that I would never ever again have to live in a nasty studio apartment like the one I'd lived in before we moved in together.

He got his laundry cleaned and folded and I got to surf the swells of his confidence, and we both got to live in a nicer apartment than we would have alone. I supposed it was fair enough.

4

The gravel dug into my back. I stayed where I was for one more minute, appreciating the depth of the blue of the sky at seven-thousand-feet of elevation before I stood and walked toward the white vinyl couch.

At least sixty white goats roamed the pasture behind the barn. I wasn't sure if they were the Saanens that Mom had started goat ranching with long ago or the Cashmeres that she had been switching over to. The difference wasn't obvious to me. They looked at me somewhat alarmed, assessed the danger, and decided it would be best to run behind Monster the llama and Paco the donkey. Annoyed, Monster charged them, scattering them in all directions. Had I been a coyote, he would have just made my job significantly easier. I shook my head. Why my mom hadn't gotten rid of him long ago, I couldn't begin to guess. He was an ugly thing, white with black spots like a Dalmatian, with his long fur tangled into dreadlocks since he wouldn't let anyone near him—especially with a brush. Maybe on some level Mom had appreciated the entertainment. Or maybe she had been *that* lonely.

Some of the guinea fowl sat on the top of the barn, while others pecked at the ground, and while I could not deny that they had been an improvement over the Bantam chickens we used to have, I found the noise they made annoying. Some chirped one note repeatedly, occasionally rising in volume to a screech, while others sang a two note squeaky song that bordered on honking. I predicted that the situational stress combined with this noise would surely cause me to go out of my mind in approximately ten minutes.

On my right was an old train container that my mother had turned into her milking barn, and next to that was the hay barn in which, presently and historically, Mom had always had a pet skunk. She never sought it out; rather, it found its own way there, but she sang to it while she fed it cat food every day.

Two horse stalls opened out into paddocks on the far side of the hay barn, where two horses nibbled on each other's withers over the fence, an Appaloosa named Spot and a bay I knew only through my mother's letters. I wasn't sure which one had been the one she had been riding when she'd had the accident that took her life, and for a moment I wondered if I wanted to. I had ridden the Appaloosa on my last visit here and he had seemed trusty enough. I hated to think it might have been him. The bay was new. At a gas station, Mom had pulled him off one of the many trucks that carted horses from this region over the Mexican border ever since horse slaughter in the U.S. was made illegal. Although Mom was no stranger to slaughtering, we both had heard nightmarish stories of what happened in those facilities—facilities without regulation and far less humane than what had been in our own country, and I suppose her heartstrings had been tugged. She had said she thought he looked good, although I knew she didn't really know enough about horses to make that assessment and most of the horses on those trucks were lame and unlikely to ever get better, but before I could say so, she said she had hoped that the next time I visited, we could ride together. That pulled on my heartstrings because our relationship had never been an easy one, and I could see she was reaching out to me. It seemed more likely that bay horse had been the one she'd had the accident on, and I wondered whether I would put him back on a truck bound for Mexico, or whether I would find him a new home and risk him doing the same thing to someone else, or whether I was going to lead him somewhere far enough where I wouldn't smell him and shoot him myself. I couldn't imagine doing any of those things, to be honest, and I sure wasn't going to get on him, although I knew even good horses occasionally spooked. It didn't mean that he was a bad horse. Sometimes accidents just happened. A spook in the wrong place could go terribly wrong.

I made it to the couch, laid on it, and looked up. The blue was so deep, it was almost violet, and I wished I could float right up in it instead of having to be here with this unbearable emptiness, and all of these animals I was now responsible for.

I pulled my mom's most recent letter out of my pocket, studying her script on the envelope, the way she affixed the stamp without care to its evenness. Mom was a lover of old-fashioned letters. She said she needed reason to hope for something good or she would never pick up her mail. I had been annoyed by this laborious means of communication—the procurement of paper and stamps, the effort of writing instead of typing, remembering to take the letter out the door so I could drop it in one of the few remaining big blue collection boxes on my way to work, and then the waiting. But now that I held her letter in my hand, I understood something about what it held that an e-mail did not. It was physical. The smell of one's home sometimes infused the paper. Mom's paper smelled like dirt and goat cheese. Mine smelled like incense. The personality that came out in a person's unique handwriting . . . the places where her hesitation was evident, the places where she changed her mind and chose a different word. The stamp and the postmark, the anticipation of opening it. All of these things made this letter seem like a small work of art—much more than simple narration and communication. I took the letter out of its envelope and read it for what might have been the twentieth time.

Dear Willow,

It's one of those days where I find myself standing back and observing the humor and the joy in my everyday life, so it seemed like a good day to write you a letter about it and genuflect.

I have six new baby goats at this time, two of which are black in my otherwise white herd. It happens sometimes. I had to spend a few nights in the barn making sure they were able to nurse when they were hungry because their mothers just sort of look at them as if asking, "What have I done?" They look at the other goats as if to apologize. Goats are racist bastards. But it seems the mamas are adjusting to the parameters of their new reality and so last night I was able to return to my own comfortable bed in the house.

After a conversation with another woman who has milk goats, I began to experiment with music, keeping a log of different music I played during milking and the output of milk. Peter, Paul and Mary was by far their favorite—to be specific, "Puff the Magic Dragon," followed by James Taylor, a close second, "Shower the People." They really like it when I sing along. Peter, Paul and Mary makes sense to me because if I listen to them in the right state of mind, I can hear a goatlike quality to their sound, but James Taylor doesn't sound like a goat, so that's interesting to me. Perhaps it's my voice that adds the goatlike quality to his music. Regardless, I am getting burned out on both of these songs and need to find some alternatives.

When I finished milking, it was time to feed, which meant going into the hay barn where Stinky the skunk lives, and like all the others before her, I sing "Everyone knows it's Stinky" to the tune of "Windy" as I sprinkle cat food in her dish. Say what you will, but I'm the only person I know who has never found a snake in her barn, and let me tell you, when I was sleeping out there to help with the baby goats, that brought me considerable comfort.

When the goats have eaten, the dogs and I move them out of the corral and into the pasture. Mr. Lickers gets overly excited and sometimes just begins to run a very frantic circle around them, freaking them all out. I figured out that, "No, Mr. Lickers!" sounds like "Go, Mr. Lickers!" and so now I shout, "Poor goats! Poor, poor goats!" and sometimes the sorrow in my voice stops him. And sometimes getting kicked by Monster the llama or Paco the donkey does. Monster and Paco have been useless in protecting the goats from the coyotes as far as I can tell, but they do help with Mr. Lickers. Still, I'm selling Monster because he scares the goats, causing them to pig pile in the corner, and sometimes by the time I break it up, a baby has suffocated on the bottom. He has killed more goats than the coyotes. I've been entertaining the idea of putting him in with Señor Clackers but I can't really afford another mouth to feed if he doesn't serve a purpose.

Señor Clackers has mellowed out since your last visit, but thank God the locals don't know that. They still talk about how he gored that crazy fugitive that was hiding out this canyon years ago. Yes, Señor Clackers is still a hero. I've been wanting to try to ride him lately, but I know if anyone saw that, my security system would no longer be respected. Still, I think I could do it, and as an eccentric New Mexican woman, I am almost obligated to try, am I not? I love that bull. I don't know what I'm going to do when he crosses over the rainbow bridge. Surely there's no way I could liberate another like him.

Slobber Dog has been into hunting for eggs and can now fit two in her mouth, which I personally find amazing. Fortunately, the eggs the guinea fowl lay have really hard shells. I've even seen the teeth marks of rodents on them. Yes, even varmints can't get through those shells. The guinea fowl are so much better than those chickens we used to have. Remember how we used to have to off the roosters right away because they were so violent? With the guinea fowl, you can hardly tell the roosters from the hens. They are substantially gentler in their lovemaking, and they mate for life. I love finding their black-and-white polka-dotted feathers all over the place too. Someday I'm going to do something really cool with those feathers. I just don't know what yet. Oh, but I digress. Slobber Dog saves me the trouble of egg hunting. She really derives satisfaction out of it. At first, I thought it was a little gross eating an egg that had been in a dog's mouth, but when I really thought through the other place it had been, a dog's mouth didn't seem so bad. So I make myself an egg breakfast about this time . . .

Willow, honey, how many pages is this and I'm only now getting to breakfast? The rest will have to wait for another day. It's time to make cheese, top barrels, and milk again. Did I tell you that my cheese has been a big hit with the wine tasters? I've been selling four ounces for five dollars—a better price than people can get goat cheese for anywhere else, and a better quality too, since I started adding Cashmeres to the herd. That Cashmere milk is rich, I tell you. Just full of fat.

Well, I know it's hard to get time off from work and even harder to live without the pay. I know you're happy there with Ian and this pleases me immensely. I'd come to you, but I can't leave the animals. You know how it is. But I really miss you. It's been how many years? Three? Four? I don't even know. I wish I was in a position to offer you a plane ticket, but things have been tight since I built the winery (I can't wait for you to see it!). I do *have an extra horse now, so when you do come, we can ride together. Anyway, I sure do love your letters in the meantime, so please do keep them coming. They're like little psresents in the mail. I love you, baby.*

Love, Mom

Ouch. I cried imagining my mother singing along to "Shower the People" while she milked goats out here all by herself. And then I cried because she was just so funny and wacky and quirky, my mom and her pet skunk and this bull that she stole. There would never be another one like her. Not anything close. My mom was one of a kind. But the end of the letter . . . that end when I read how she missed me terribly . . . knowing I did not somehow find a way to get away and visit . . . that I had instead stayed with a man who just chose to move out and live in someone's closet, a man who checked his text message just seconds after I told him my mom had died. I missed the opportunity to visit my mom one last time because I chose a bozo over her. It hit me like a punch in the gut, and again fever washed over me until I leaned over the side of the couch and threw up again.

Just then, I heard tires on gravel and sat up to see Darrel's black pickup come racing up the driveway. The dogs ran toward his truck, barking excitedly. As he stepped out, I waved and called out, "I'm over here!"

He had slimmed down since I had seen him last, but still Darrel was what a person would call "big-boned." That he was nearly six-five made him seem massive, but despite his size, there was always a softness and a gentleness about him. He had a broad, round face that reminded me of the man on the moon, and almond eyes more reminiscent of his Samoan heritage than his Apache heritage. He had grown his hair out to his shoulders, no small accomplishment since he had not only inherited his mother's eyes, but her curls as well.

"*Daanzho, choni,*" I said. *Hello, friend.* How long had it been since I had spoken his language?

"*Daanzho, choni,*" he replied, walking over to me. "Are you okay?"

"A little nauseated," I said. "Watch your step."

He looked at my nearby puddle of vomit and made a face. "That's normal," he said.

"Really?" I asked. I had no idea it was normal for grieving people to throw up, but since he was a nurse, I figured he knew what he was talking about.

"Yeah," he said, as if everyone knew this. "Be sure you're drinking enough water."

He sat down next to me and we just looked at each other for a long moment, saying everything we had to say with our eyes before we said them again with words.

"How is your heart? Are you okay?"

I shook my head and tears streamed out of my eyes. "Until a few moments ago, none of this seemed real. And then I read her letter and it just hit me that she's not here and . . . she missed me, Darrel, and I didn't come to see her one more time."

Even more sadness filled his eyes.

"I'm so sorry that it had to be you to find her, Darrel. I wish you could unsee whatever you saw."

"I'm sorry I didn't find her in time," he said quietly.

I looked at his beautiful face—his high cheekbones, his gentle eyes. "Oh, Darrel. Not once did I think that. Not once."

We were quiet for a few moments, and then said in unison, "I missed you."

"Have you heard from Quentin?" I asked. Darrel and Quentin had been together since high school graduation, but nearly a year ago, Quentin won big at the casino, and had been traveling the world ever since.

Darrel shrugged sadly. "Now and then I get a postcard. It's been a little while."

"Darrel, I'm so sorry." I could see his heartbreak. Time hadn't healed this wound.

"How's Ian?"

"He dumped me so he could live in a friend's closet and save four hundred and twenty-five dollars a month."

"Under these circumstances?"

I thought he meant my mom dying. "Yeah," I said.

Just then, Slobber Dog accidentally knocked over my mom's mostly empty wine bottle. Darrel's eyes widened. "Oh my God, Willow, you didn't drink that, did you?"

"No," I said, wondering what was wrong with my mother's wine. Did she ferment incorrectly and poison some people with botulism? Was that the real reason she came off her horse? Did her own wine kill her? Was it possible the coroner's report came back already and I somehow didn't see it first? No, that made no sense. "Why?" I finally asked.

"Because, you know, you're pregnant."

5

Darrel's very first words to me back in 1989 were, "It's going to be okay."

Mom and I had both slept in our first morning in our new home here in New Mexico. It wasn't a deep, restful sleep-in. It was the type of sleeping in where I woke up angry and tired and kept trying to hit the reset button by going back to sleep, but my brain knew something was not right and it just wouldn't rest. My brain knew the light didn't filter into this room the way the light filtered into my room at home. My brain knew this house smelled all wrong. My brain was aware of the little scratchy sounds of at least one mouse somewhere in the house. The best I could do was doze and have weird dreams. Eventually, both Mom and I surrendered to the stress of our new surroundings, got out of our unfamiliar beds, and coped with the remaining contents of the pickup truck.

Although it was a school day, Mom had let me have the day to settle in a little bit. I had cleaned the mouse droppings out of my dresser and then put some of my clothes neatly inside, more neatly than I had ever done before, in retrospect because it was one of the few things I could control. The rest of my clothes I kept in a box, so

I could be ready faster when I figured out a way of leaving this place. I had put a couple things on my wall just so my mom wouldn't suspect that secretly I was planning to escape. Yes, I had planned to escape, although that plan had not one single detail to it at that moment.

She was in the kitchen, cleaning mouse droppings out of drawers and putting away spatulas and wooden spoons when I slipped out with a quick, "I'm going for a walk," without allowing any time for a reply. I was still unspeakably angry at her for this unilateral decision that had ruined my life.

As I walked down the driveway, hoping to find some clue to a secret way out of here and back to my old life, I began to think about everyone I had left behind—my dad, and my best friend Jennifer, other friends as well. I wouldn't be part of their lives anymore. Even if we still communicated, it wasn't the same as continuing to create common history. I didn't think of it exactly in those terms then. I thought of it more like getting kicked off a school bus that was headed to a really fun field trip, a moment like that where you knew all the kids were going to return talking about what fun they'd had and all you'd be able to do is listen and nod as you faked a smile. No amount of hearing about it would make you part of the memory.

At the same time, being here also felt like getting off the bus at the wrong stop and wondering how on earth you were going to get home, knowing the whole time that people who loved you were worried about you.

I kicked rocks angrily, not caring when big ones hurt my toes, and when I reached the gate, I let my arms hang on the other side and dropped my head too, just sort of hanging on this thing that kept me in my new life against my will. Eventually I dropped to the ground and leaned against the gate as I looked longingly out, until even that hurt too much and then I just buried my face in my folded arms that rested on my knees.

I heard his footsteps first, and opened my eyes, to watch him walk up the road. Judging from the time of day and the books in his arms, he must have been walking home from the school bus. He seemed far too tall to be my age, and although his skin was brown, his black hair was curly so I wasn't sure if he was Apache or not. He was fat enough that I guessed he had likely experienced a fair amount of teasing in his life. I dared to hope he hadn't noticed me down there and from the blank look on his face, I couldn't tell, but as he neared, he looked at me and said, "You're going to be okay."

At first, I didn't know what to say, but then I asked, "How do you know?"

He replied, "My dad ran off, and my mom dropped me off here at his parents' house when I was four so she could go pursue her wrestling career in Vegas. I had never even met my grandparents before. I thought I was going to die at first too."

"That's awful," I said. It was. I mean, I wished my mom had dropped me off at my grandma's house instead of bringing me here, but I knew my grandma, so that was different.

I was able to judge the situation well enough not to say anything.

He shrugged. "My grandparents are great. I'm happy here now. You'll be okay," he said again.

I watched him walk on down the road, this hulk of a kid with a walk that appeared slow even though it wasn't. Somehow he managed to cover some ground without appearing to be in a rush. And I supposed that somehow I could see in his walk this journey he had taken from loneliness to acceptance. It seemed he accepted where he was as he took each step. It seemed he was comfortable with his own company.

A part of me envied that he had made that transition, but the other part of me didn't ever want to accept my own new circumstances.

I lay on my back there in the driveway for some time, looking for clouds, looking for any sign from the heavens that things would be okay, but there were no clouds—none. And it occurred to me only then that living out here might not only cut off my relationship to my dad and to my best friend, but to God or whatever benevolent force it was that communicated with me through the clouds. It was one thing for my mom to cut off my relationships with people, but it was quite another to cut off my relationship with God.

But just as I was beginning to equate this cloudless place with being a godless place, Darrel interrupted that thought and prevented it from taking root. He had come back up the road on a bay horse, ponying a palomino behind him, and my heart leaped because I had always wanted to ride a horse, but so far in my life my experiences had been limited to the pony ring at the King County Fair when I was six and seven. I sat up and watched him approach, not wanting to look too eager, but not wanting to look unfriendly, and certainly not wanting to miss a thing.

"Come on," Darrel said. "This will help."

I stood. "You mean ride a horse?"

He nodded.

My smile gave away how much I would have loved to, but at the same time I confessed, "I don't know how."

"You can just sit on it. It will follow my horse. If you need to hang onto something, hold onto its mane. We'll just walk today. You'll get the hang of it."

I looked back at the house, decided I didn't care whether my mom knew or approved or not, and let Darrel give me a leg up onto the palomino's bare back. Then to my surprise he opened the gate, hopped back on his horse, and led me back up the driveway so I could check with my mom, despite my protests that it wasn't necessary.

I tried not to look happy, there on the horse's back. I tried my very best to continue to look mad at her, but she could tell. "Wait just a minute," she had said and rushed back into the house, returning with a camera and snapping our photo, not knowing she was breaching etiquette by not asking first if she could take his picture. Luckily, Darrel didn't mind, and only later would I come to know how unintentionally rude she had been.

As the horse I was on followed his horse back down the driveway, I asked, "So, your mom's a wrestler, huh?"

"Yeah. She sent me a VCR and some tapes of some of her matches so I could watch her. Are you a wrestling fan?"

"No," I confessed.

"Me neither. No one likes to watch their mom get beat up."

"Where did you live before you lived here?" I changed the subject.

"Los Angeles. My mom grew up there. She's Samoan," he said, as if that explained it all. I had never heard of Samoa or anything from it, but figured I would ask my mom later instead of risking Darrel thinking I was ignorant.

"Did you like it in Los Angeles?" I asked.

"I think so. I don't really remember that much. Where are you from?"

"Enumclaw, Washington."

"Rain," he said plainly.

"Yes. Lots."

"Rain is good," he said, much in the way a person might say, "Some people like liver."

It was our first day. We made small talk until I came to relax into the horse's gait, and we rode until I had almost forgotten all I had left behind in my old life, until the sound of horse hooves leisurely clapping on the resonant moist clay slowed the pace of my inner panic into something more manageable, until the astringent scent of sage became the smell of friendship and adventure. It was our first day, and Darrel told me I would be okay, and by the end of the ride, I believed that, well, there would at least be moments when I was.

6

Terror. Terror was the right word for how I felt the first time I walked into the Mid-High in Sweetwater. It didn't help that it was day four without a shower. The rainwater collection system at our new house had malfunctioned, and so my mom needed to buy a water tank for the back of our pickup so she could bring water back from town, but she hadn't gotten to that yet. So there I was with my mom, who had put on her finest hippie-wear just for the occasion—an embroidered peasant skirt that had been in style twenty years before, coupled with cowboy boots and a Davy Crockett jacket. Both of us had our greasy blond hair pulled back—my mom's in a braid and mine in a ponytail.

As we walked into the school, I saw one small cloud in the sky—a wasp. Its body was segmented, with wispy legs hanging down, and its wings seemed to move in slow motion as the cloud passed by. Wasps. When a wasp stings a person, it scent marks them as an enemy so all the other wasps know to attack. And unlike bees, wasps can sting more than once. They can sting over and over and over. I was justifiably terrified.

I waited in the counselor's office with my mom while the counselor tried to find equivalent classes and resolve as many scheduling conflicts as possible to make them all fit. By the time she was done, I had missed first-period algebra. With assurances that she would help guide me to the right bus after school, the counselor sent Mom on her way. And since I was still mad at her, our goodbye was unceremonious, but I thought I saw a tiny flash of concern as she wished me good luck.

Walking through the empty halls to my second-period English class with the counselor wasn't so bad, but walking into it in front of everyone was horrifying. I avoided eye contact as I took an empty desk, and jumped into the day's lesson on prepositional phrases, which I already knew. I felt the stares on me, but never saw them. Whenever I glanced up, people appeared to be looking at other things. Mostly I kept my eyes on my paper, hoping to avoid trouble, which seemed to work. At first. But when the class ended, I realized just how much I'd been thrown to the wolves.

First, there was the experience of walking through the halls, knowing that everyone could see how out of place I felt because the fact that I did not belong there was uncomfortably obvious. The crowded halls were full of beautiful girls with their clean, shiny black hair. They were all so much prettier than me with my greasy blond ponytail, and everyone knew it. In the Wild Kingdom hierarchy of kids, I knew what place was mine—omega, the bottom rank.

New Mexico state history was my next class, and in it, I was totally lost. How would I ever catch up on a subject that was completely new when the school year was already three quarters of the way over? There was a Mexican-American War? This was news to me. Over Texas? Why would anyone fight over Texas? Being from the Northwest, this made no sense to me. Sure, there was oil there, but certainly that wasn't known in 1846. Hopelessly, I looked at the questions in the back of the chapter, and flipped back through the pages, scanning for answers.

The girl next to me took pity on me, and pointed to a paragraph where the first answer could be found. I smiled gratefully. A couple more times she helped me like that, and then when the bell rang, I was once again swallowed into the mass of brown skin and black hair where I stood out painfully. I didn't have to look directly at the sea of kids to see them. Some had sweet or timid faces, and greeted their friends with shy smiles. A few looked at me much like a cat looks at a mouse, as if entertainment was about to begin. But the scariest kids of all were those whose faces were already hardened in a way I had never seen before, and it struck me that some kids here must be living a life so much harder than I was capable of imagining—a life so much worse than mine, which was undeniably pretty bad. In their cold, angry eyes, I saw no hint of kindness or compassion—no space for it at all.

I noticed two other white kids in the hall, but neither made eye contact with me.

P.E. was my least favorite class in my own school, but here it was even worse. First, there was the horror of the locker room. Then, there was the horror of knowing that I hadn't showered in four days and might stink, which was not a good way to make friends at all. Finally, there was the horror of having to play basketball when I was no good at it.

It was pure misfortune that the ball came directly at me after the tip-off. I attempted to dribble, but knowing how stupid I must have looked, I stopped, and searched for a teammate to throw it to. Everyone looked so mean. As I passed the ball, a girl from the other team jumped in and intercepted. I looked at the floor. I'd failed. For the rest of the class, I made an effort to follow the pack as they ran up and down the court so that it would look like I was participating but I stayed far enough away from the action to avoid being on the spot again.

"Guard your person!" One of my teammates snapped at me. She

had one of those hardened faces that scared me so. Who was I supposed to guard? I looked around and saw a huge girl on the opposite team receive a pass and make a basket. "Her!" said the mean
teammate and then seemed to gesture with her lips toward the
big girl. *Oh no. No, no, no, no, no,* I thought, as I pointed at the big
girl and asked my teammate, "Her?"

"The new girl just pointed at you," my mean teammate said to
the big girl, who turned and glared at me.

What was that about? I wondered. I made an attempt to fake it a
little better—to look like I was trying, without actually pissing off
the big girl. Fortunately, my proximity to the big girl kept most
people from passing the ball to me. I felt grateful for that.

But then the ball got knocked out of someone else's hands and
went bouncing across the court, wild and loose right for me. I had
no choice but to do something, so I intercepted it, and began to
dribble toward my team's basket. Right as I was about to shoot, the
big girl came careening over, jumped in front of me, and elbowed
me in the face while reaching for the ball.

I saw stars and went down. Although I sensed it was an important moment not to cry, it wasn't my choice.

"Oh, she's crying," my mean teammate announced with mock
sympathy, as the other girls gathered around to watch.

"Shyla, stop it," the teacher said firmly, and then she turned to
the big girl. "Ramona?" the teacher asked, waiting for an explanation.

"It was an accident," the big girl said to the teacher. I wasn't
convinced.

As my teacher helped me up, I knew I had a choice, the consequences of which were of extreme importance. I could continue
to try to avoid trouble, and hope they moved on to targeting someone else, or I could get back in the game and fight back, no matter
what the consequences were. I had no idea which choice, if either,

would result in making it most likely that the mean girl, Shyla, and the big girl, Ramona, would leave me alone.

But there were immediate consequences to take into consideration. I had the opportunity to go to the nurse's office right then. Not only would it get me out of the rest of class, out of this situation I hated, but I would be able to put an ice pack on my throbbing cheekbone, and slow the swelling I was beginning to feel around my eye. It seemed like the best choice. I was sure there would still be the opportunity to fight later, but truthfully, I didn't have much fight in me, if any at all.

"Ramona, since you're the one who accidentally hurt her, you take her to the nurse's office," the teacher said.

I could tell Ramona was not happy at all about that so I said, "That's okay, really. I can find it."

"No, Ramona will take you," the teacher said.

So, together we walked toward the office. "Now my team is going to lose," Ramona said angrily.

"I'm sorry," I said, unsure of why a P.E. basketball game meant so much to her.

"You better be. If you ever point at me again, I'll knock you out."

"I'm . . . I'm really sorry. I didn't know that pointing was not okay."

"Only witches point. Everyone knows that, witch."

"Truly, I didn't know. I'm from Washington State. I didn't know."

"I don't care where you're from."

As we walked around a corner, Ramona intentionally bumped into me, pushing me into the sharp corner of a row of lockers. My face hit the edge right where she had elbowed me before. I yelped and covered my eye with my hand.

"That was an accident, and if you make up any story about it being on purpose, I will kill you," she said.

Bewildered, I kept walking until I reached the safe harbor of the office, where the secretary gave me an ice pack. I looked at the clock. The end of the school day seemed like an eternity away. I still had to go back to the locker room to change my clothes, face the horror of the cafeteria to eat lunch, and find my next class. All of it seemed impossible. And there were still three more classes to go and a school bus ride home, and my eye was swelling more and more by the second.

The school bus would have been every bit as terrifying as I had anticipated, but Darrel sat in the seat behind me.

"What happened to you?" he asked.

I didn't know whether or not to tell him the truth. "I fell," I finally said. I didn't want to talk about it—especially where other kids would overhear. A few had stopped their conversations, waiting for my answer.

When the bus dropped us off at Monero Canyon Road, Mom was waiting in the green pickup truck. Never in my life did I think I'd be so glad to see her, but I was—at first . . . until I saw her optimistic and expectant smile as if she had really thought that I might get off the bus with a big smile and say I loved my first day of my new school, as if that was ever even a remote possibility. Any normal person would have known there was no chance in hell things were going to go well for me there and would have spared me that experience. But not my mom. Her denial infuriated me.

"Do you want a ride to our driveway?" I asked Darrel.

He shook his head. "I'll walk. I need the exercise." I think he knew Mom and I needed to talk.

As I neared the truck, Mom's expression changed from hope to concern. "What happened?" she asked as I slid into the passenger seat.

I could not find words to describe what I had experienced. I could only turn and let her see my swollen eye and my traumatized expression. And then I cried.

"Who did this to you?" my mother asked, enraged.

I did not want her to come to school and make things worse, and so I said, "A girl in my P.E. class elbowed me in the face and said it was an accident."

"Then explain that mark that's like a line. That doesn't look like an elbow."

"The teacher made her walk me to the nurse's office. She accidentally bumped into me and I fell into the corner of some lockers."

My mother stared at me. She could tell I wasn't telling the whole truth.

And the next morning, just like I feared, she came to school to talk to the principal and the P.E. teacher.

And just as promised, later that morning when I was focused on remembering my new locker combination and spinning the dial just right, Ramona slammed my face into my locker door. I turned around to look for a way to escape, but a crowd had already formed around me, blocking my way out. I tried to read the expressions of those who watched. Were they compassionate? Would they help me? Or did they hate me as much as Ramona and Shyla, but were just quiet about it? I couldn't tell. They simply watched.

"I warned you, *Mangani*," Ramona said. Although I didn't know at the time what *Mangani* meant, I could tell by the tone of her voice that it wasn't a compliment.

"You look creepy, *Mangani*," said Shyla. "Like a ghost. You've got creepy ghost eyes."

Please God, I need a miracle, I pleaded silently.

Ramona laughed sadistically as she cocked back her big fist, but just as she was about to hit to me, Darrel stepped between us and took the punch in his hand. He looked at Ramona and shook his head. Ramona was huge, but Darrel was at least 30 percent larger.

"Get out of the way, Samoan!" said Ramona. "This isn't your business."

"Would you like Uncle Walt to follow you around school?"

Although I did not understand what was being asked, I noticed fear flash across Ramona's eyes. She stared me down for another minute before she said, "Watch your back, *Mangani*."

"Is that a yes?" asked Darrel. "I'll tell him."

Ramona held up her hands. "It's cool," she said as she walked away with Shyla.

Darrel watched the new welt on my forehead grow and said, "Assholes come in every color."

I nodded as I struggled not to cry. "Thank you. You saved me."

"This could have happened to any new kid in any new school, so please don't think it's an Apache thing. Most people are good. Most Apaches are good."

"They're in my P.E. class. I didn't know not to point and I'm not good at basketball."

His wince was almost undetectable but I saw it. "A few kids give me a bad time because my mother is Samoan, but I think they're just jealous of my disease resistance. Mutts have better disease resistance than purebreds." He smiled. His expression was deeply compassionate, and it touched me. "Come on," he said as he led me to the office. "Let's go see the counselor and get you out of that P.E. class."

To my amazement, the counselor listened to Darrel as he adamantly expressed his safety concerns for me and got my schedule changed so I had every class with him. That way, it would be no problem for him to walk near me or with me between each class.

Since we were neighbors, I wouldn't even have to be on the bus without him.

I hated to inconvenience him like that and felt the urge to argue that all of that wasn't necessary, but the pressure on my swollen eye and forehead told me that it was, and so I said nothing.

There was no P.E. class we could take together, and Darrel convinced the counselor that the girls' locker room was a very dangerous place for me, so the counselor agreed to let us walk two blocks down the hill to the pool each day to take independent study swimming, provided we were willing to eat our lunch as we walked back to compensate for travel time. I was not only relieved to get out of conventional P.E., but was every bit relieved to get out of lunch too. This Darrel, it seemed to me, had performed a miracle.

As we walked out of the office, he looked over at me. "Everything's going to be okay."

And even though there was every reason to believe that was the biggest lie ever told, I believed him.

7

"I'm pregnant?"

"Yeah. Everybody knows that."

"What? Darrel, whatever you heard—it's just a rumor. I'm not pregnant."

He nodded. "I'm pretty sure you are. Grandpa had a dream."

I froze in my tracks. Oh shit. Everybody knew you could take Darrel's grandpa's dreams to the bank.

"He already told everybody. Sorry about that. He was just so excited about you coming back and having a baby and he figured you knew by now."

I sat back down on the white vinyl couch. The puking. The crying. I looked up at the sky that had been completely clear moments before. "Look at that cloud," I said to Darrel. "Look at that stupid cloud."

He looked up and smiled. "A bunny."

Yes, a goddamned bunny cloud floated above us.

Despite the clear evidence of Grandpa Luis's dream and the bunny cloud, I did not want to believe it and insisted on the formality of a pregnancy test before accepting this breaking news as fact.

Darrel and I had barely gotten out of my mom's pickup in the Cestero Shopping Mart parking lot when Roberta Gomez, my art teacher, became the first to express her condolences and congratulate me. "Willow, oh, I'm sorry to hear about your mother." Her hair had become much more silver since I had seen her last, but her round happy face was more or less unchanged. She reached out and hugged me, and that made me cry. "But I understand that you also have something to look forward to. Congratulations about that . . ."

"Um, well, thanks," I replied as I pulled back from her embrace. "But as far as your congratulations go, Grandpa Vigil just had a dream. As far as I know I'm not pregnant."

"Oh, well . . ." she said with a tone that said, *he's never been wrong.* "Okay, well, I wish you the best always," she said diplomatically. Maybe she could tell I was freaked out and not ready to accept the news.

"Again, very sorry," Darrel said as we made our way into the store. "Grandpa assumed you knew by now."

"By now?"

"Well, it's been about a month. Surely you'd notice."

"I just figured it was stress from losing my mom."

"Hey! Look who's back!" called out Felicity Ortiz, who had been in some of my classes in high school.

"Hey, Felicity," I said warmly.

She hugged me too. "I heard about your mom. I'm so, so sorry."

"Yeah, thanks," I said tearing up all over again. I couldn't even speak.

"I hear you're going to be a mom soon, though. That's good, right?"

Collecting myself bought me an extra minute to think of my response. "Felicity," I said, as if she was being ridiculous. "Do I look pregnant to you?"

Her expression changed to grave concern. I wondered what kind of faces Darrel might be making behind me to tell her to cool it. She just shook her head. "You in town for a while?" she asked, perhaps to change the subject.

"No, I'm just here to settle my mom's affairs."

"Oh," she said sadly. "I'm so sorry to hear that."

"Yeah, well . . ."

Neither of us knew what to say next, so she said, "Well, see you around."

"See you," I said, and she walked off.

Darrel pushed the cart for me toward the produce aisle and while I picked out cheap produce—bananas, celery, carrots, potatoes, onion, garlic, zucchini, two more people I didn't recognize but who must have remembered me or have known my mom expressed their condolences and then suggested eating ginger for morning sickness. Darrel gave them a nod and a *Daanzho* as we passed.

I was freaking out more by the second. I didn't want the whole town to know I was pregnant because I didn't know what I wanted to do about it if I was, and I didn't want the whole town to know if I opted out of this situation. I supposed I could just say I lost the baby, but I have never been a good liar. These things were just nobody's business. Not at this point.

As I selected Saltine crackers and pretzels—the only two foods I thought I might have a chance at being able to hold down in the near future, an old man in a cowboy hat said, "Oh, morning sickness?"

"Uh . . ." I stammered.

He smiled knowingly and said, "It gets better," as he moved on.

As I made my way to the aisle with the split peas, lentils, and rice, a lady around my mom's age with two long braids and thick glasses, and then a grandmother with a tight perm and a limp also expressed their condolences and then congratulated me on my pregnancy.

51

Selecting the cheapest oatmeal, I vowed that the moment I left this store I would never come back. I'd go to Chama or even Pagosa if I needed anything else. I wanted to hide in a cave and never come out, or better yet, lose myself in the anonymity of a big city.

Just as I was selecting a generic pregnancy test, Kiana Montoya, another old friend, spotted me. I'd have recognized her kind face and smiling eyes anywhere. She had put on a little weight, but it only made her face prettier. Her long black hair was pulled back in a beautiful red beaded barrette. "Willow, I was so sad to hear about your mom. She was always so full of life."

"Oh, thank you, Kiana," I replied.

"The cycle of life, huh? When one life goes, how comforting that another life arrives."

"Well, it's not official yet," I said pointing to the pregnancy test in my basket.

"But your grandfather dreamed it, right?" she said, looking at Darrel, who nodded.

Kiana looked back and forth between us, as if trying to get the rest of the picture.

"Yes, at this point it's just a dream," I said.

"Who's the father?" she asked.

"Uh . . ." I wasn't sure what to say because to answer that question would be to admit to being pregnant. "Well, again, we don't know if there's any baby. I've been living with someone for the last three years out in L.A. so, it's not Darrel's if that's what you're wondering."

She laughed. "No, I know it's not Darrel's."

"Okay, well, I've . . . I've got a lot to do, so we have to be going, but good to see you again," I said.

"Yeah, good luck with everything," she replied.

"We have got to get out of here," I whispered to Darrel, practically hyperventilating.

But the clerk at the checkout counter had known my mom and wanted me to know how sorry he was to hear about what happened. And then as he scanned my pregnancy test, he asked, "Isn't this just a waste of money?" and like Kiana, he looked at Darrel and asked, "Your grandfather dreamed it, right?"

Darrel nodded slightly, but looked down at me in such a way to suggest that I didn't know yet, or wasn't taking the news well.

"Okay, well . . ." the clerk said awkwardly. "Um, have a good day."

"Thanks. You too," I replied before taking my bag and practically running out of there, leaving Darrel behind to catch up.

But before I reached the pickup, Mr. Pesata, my old high school principal, recognized me and said, "Willow. I was so sorry to hear about your mother. She was a very nice lady." I looked at his shoulder, as was the custom in Apache tradition, eye contact being considered rude—especially to elders. His thick light-sensitive glasses had turned a dark enough shade that I couldn't really see his eyes with my peripheral vision, but I noticed he had many more wrinkles than he did when I had seen him last. It had been over twenty years.

"Thank you, Mr. Pesata," I replied. "Good to see you. How are you?"

"Oh, good," he answered. And then he cut to the chase like he always did. "Willow, you're too skinny. Are you throwing up your food or do you have worms?" He wasn't joking or being mean. He was genuinely concerned.

"Um, neither," I answered, caught off guard and a bit offended. "People just eat less in Los Angeles, and you know, I haven't felt like eating since I got the news about my mom."

Just then Darrel caught up. Mr. Pesata looked at him and said, "Well, you make sure she eats, all right? The baby needs food."

I looked at the sky as Mr. Pesata walked off toward the store, and then jumped in my mom's pickup before anyone else could congratulate me, buried my face in my hands, and said, "Oh God, Darrel, what am I going to do?"

"Maybe go to the post office to pick up your mom's mail, and then drive home and make some soup," he said. That was his answer.

8

When I stepped off of the airplane and through the gate in Sea-Tac Airport, I didn't have to scan the crowd for more than two seconds before I spotted my dad who had spotted me and was running up to meet me. Ms. Nunnalee was behind him holding up a sign that read, "Welcome Home, Willow!" in big, bright glittery letters, as if I would forget she was the reason I was gone in the first place if only she used enough glitter. Enhanced or perhaps even exaggerated by her summery maternity top, I could see her protruding belly and I grimaced.

"Willow!" called Dad. I ran into his big arms. He held my sides and stood up straight, lifting me a few inches off the ground as he hugged me. *I'm safe. I'm finally safe,* I thought at first, but as I watched Ms. Nunnalee catch up with him, her perky sign still in her hand, my sense of safety drained out of me. Sensing her presence next to him, Dad let go of me.

"Hi, Willow!" she said. "Welcome home!" She held out her arms for a hug, and as I hesitated and glanced at my dad, her hopeful smile fell into a fake smile. I stepped forward and gave her a little hug even though I didn't want to, just to make my dad happy and not ruin the moment, but truth be told, I fantasized about pushing her out of an empty gate where she would fall and crack her head open on the pavement below.

Together we walked to the baggage claim where we waited for my suitcase to be spit out of the chute and onto the conveyer belt.

"Well," Ms. Nunnalee began in an attempt to ease the awkwardness. "The morning of the wedding, you're going to come with me and my friends to Bev's Beauty Parlor to get our hair, nails, and makeup done!" The way she paused and waited made me think that I was supposed to squeal with excitement about this. I wondered how long I could not say it—how long I could not say, "Did it ever occur to you that I might not be one tiny ounce of happy about these new developments in my family?"

Dad nudged me and so I said, "I haven't had my hair cut in a long time. That will be nice." That was the truth. Coalton was so tiny that it didn't even have its own post office. It had a Catholic church, a small Catholic school, and a smattering of houses. That was all. And since the Cestero Apaches weren't big into haircuts, there were no hair salons in Sweetwater either. There was a hair salon in the nearby town of Chama, but it never seemed to be open on those rare occasions that we ventured the thirty miles there. My bangs had grown down to my chin, shaggy and terrible, and so I had pulled them back with a rolled-up bandana that served as a headband. On the reservation, flat hair seemed silky, sleek, and normal, but it was 1989, and that, coupled with considerably more moisture in the air meant that I was back in the land of fluffy, wavy, curly hair. I looked at the women around me and admired one in particular who had long dark hair that tumbled down her back in small spirals. As I did, I flushed with self-consciousness. I had become dumpy, and Ms. Nunnalee saw it. That's why she had told me about the beauty parlor plan. She wanted me to know she would be my salvation from this indignity. I turned away to hide my disgust for her and for myself and for the whole situation.

Dad took my hand and gave it a squeeze. "We have to go to the doctor tomorrow morning to make sure everything with the baby is fine," said Dad, "but after that, we're going to go to Ocean Shores!"

My imagination had trouble keeping up with the words coming at me, but I pictured sitting alone in the clinic waiting room, looking at well-worn copies of *Good Housekeeping* and *Sunset* while Dad and Ms. Nunnalee excitedly looked at their new baby on a sonogram screen, Dad holding her hand and smiling while she wiped emotional tears from her eyes. I imagined both of them brainstorming baby names throughout the whole two-hour drive to Ocean Shores, pausing only to hammer out some unresolved detail of the wedding they were having next week now that my parents' divorce was final. And then things were harder to imagine. Ocean Shores was where our family had gone together—my dad, and me, and my mom. Mom. Not Ms. Nunnalee.

Suitcases began to tumble down the ramp to the circular belt, and finally I spotted mine, a gift from Grandma Mildred. Dad reached out and grabbed it, and then carried it as the three of us walked down the corridor that was essentially an enclosed bridge over the traffic below. I had thought it would feel so good to be back where I belonged, but as I crossed that bridge back into the land that had always been home, I realized I didn't completely belong there anymore. The pieces of that old world had shifted, and the space I had inhabited was now infringed upon by Ms. Nunnalee and the baby who grew inside of her.

When we reached the car, Ms. Nunnalee asked, "Would you like to sit up front so you can visit with your dad on the way home?"

Home. We weren't going home. We were going to her house

across the street from *home,* where I would be staying in *the guest room.* I shook my head, trying to imagine her folding up small enough to fit in the backseat. I didn't like her, but I wasn't a person that would squish any pregnant lady into the back seat of a car. "No, thank you, Ms. Nunnalee. You're sitting for two," I sort of joked.

She smiled gratefully at me and said, "Willow, call me Sarah."

I took my place in the backseat, out of view and unable to hear much of the conversation between Dad and Ms. Nunnalee, who I would never call "Sarah" as if she was something more to me than my old social studies teacher. She wasn't.

Two weeks. I would spend two weeks with my dad this year. That was all. He was getting married and going on his honeymoon, and when that happened, I would be shipped off to Grandma Mildred's. It appeared to me that he had clearly already had a honeymoon of sorts that had knocked up Ms. Nunnalee and didn't need to abandon me a second time to have another. Even though I was excited to spend extra time with Grandma Mildred, I was keenly aware this custody or visitation alteration was indicative of my new second-class status.

I could tell by the happy look in his eyes that I saw in the rearview mirror that he naïvely thought he could have this new family in addition to me, that in that moment, he thought he could have it all. But he was wrong. Sometimes you could only have one thing at a time. Sometimes life makes a person choose. A new woman or your old family. An extra day at the beach with your daughter or a doctor's appointment to check up on your new child. A honeymoon or your kid. At every juncture, he chose them.

9

A varmint of some kind had built its nest in the engine of my mother's pickup truck that first year we lived here. The nest had clogged the fan and caused the engine to overheat, warping the engine head, blowing a head gasket, and cracking the battery. For reasons that were unclear to my mom, the alternator also went shortly thereafter. I do recall that the repairs were in excess of a thousand dollars and that was if my mother did all the labor, which she did, with my help.

Each auto-repair session began with me getting into the cab, popping the hood, and then slamming it to scare out whatever varmint it was that had done the damage. Mom, meanwhile, lay on her belly a few yards away, pointing a .22 in my general direction, hoping to get a good shot at it, but much to her disappointment, she never saw anything run out of the bottom of the pickup.

If she was a surgeon, I was her nurse, handing her tools and shining the flashlight here and there. Together, we stopped sometimes to study the Chilton's auto-repair manual and come to some kind of consensus about what was what, or ask each other why that particular bolt wasn't pictured.

"Aren't you glad you're learning to be independent now? You'll never need a man to do these things for you and you'll never be left up a creek without a paddle when he leaves if you know how to make your own paddles."

It did feel good to be capable but *when he leaves* was what echoed in my mind. I fought it at first, and then I thought, well, if my own dad left me, why would any other man stay? My dad was supposed to love me more than anyone, right?

And it wasn't that he didn't love me. I knew that he did. He did not endorse my mother's plan to bring me all the way here and at some point threatened legal action, but settled for spending four weeks with me every mid-July to mid-August, during which he'd try to squeeze in a year's worth of parenting. But each visit only made it more and more apparent that he had moved on to his new family where I was a guest, and in their modest home, somewhat of an imposition.

When he leaves. Mom was right.

But then I happened to look far up the canyon, toward the Vigil place where Darrel lived with his grandparents. Darrel never left me. Grandpa Luis never left either.

10

Darrel walked into the house with me when we returned from the grocery store. I stood in the doorway for a moment with my cello in my hand while he set the groceries on the counter. In the kitchen, Mom's milking bucket and a mug sat upside down on the drying rack. I wondered what she had drunk out of that mug, whether she had splurged on coffee, or found cheap tea, but it seemed most likely she had simply drunk raw goat's milk.

Burnt and discolored pans hung from hooks on the side of the kitchen cabinets, which had begun to peel their orange and turquoise paint. I picked one flake of paint off and put it in the garbage. On the terra-cotta tiled countertop, a few mismatched glass canisters that contained or had contained various cheap and nutritious carbohydrates were empty or nearly empty. Two potatoes and an onion sat in the old cookie jar, safe from mice.

I opened the energy-efficient refrigerator that looked more like a freezer to find very little food—goat milk, goat cheese, goat meat, and two eggs. I couldn't guess when the last time was that she had eaten something different and indulgent—a salmon filet or asparagus, a chocolate dessert, cow dairy cream or cheese. Perhaps prior to our relocation here in 1989.

The small propane two-burner stove and oven, both scrapped from a travel trailer, still appeared to be working after all these years.

Two wooden stools sat on this side of the counter. This was where Mom and I had eaten all of our meals together.

Slowly, I took a couple steps into the house. A threadbare Mexican blanket covered the secondhand couch. Apple crates full of books served as end tables. On top of one sat a fat copy of *Solar Storms* by Linda Hogan, a hand-woven bookmark peeking out of the top. The cushions Mom and I had made for the deep window-sills twenty-five years ago from eggshell foam and thrift store table-cloths now had holes in them. The mismatched pillows that sat on the cushions were faring only a little better. Two piles of tattered blankets served as dog beds and sat next to each other in the corner of the room farthest from the kitchen. The walls were bare—plaster and straw bale being a too-risky thing to drive a nail into, but during the day and even on nights when the moon shone brightly, the scenery outside filled the windows like fine art. Mom had taken the curtains down long ago so the views could be better framed by the walls.

In a box on the counter sat her mail, most unopened. I leafed through it and picked up a delinquent notice from the county. She had made a few inconsequential payments, but ultimately was about three years behind in her taxes. *Oh, Mom.* I shook my head, exhaled, and held up the notice for Darrel to see. Other envelopes from the county with "Urgent" printed in big red letters were unopened. I looked more closely at the numbers—a grand total of $3,141. Since it was a working ranch, her taxes were about half of what they would otherwise be, thank goodness. This number was not impossible.

I dug a little deeper into the box and found a hand-written letter from Jerry Schlaich that read:

August 1, 2014

Dear Ms. Davis,

I'm so glad that all these years you have enjoyed the home I built, and I am sorry for the financial turmoil that you've been experiencing, but you have kind of backed me into a corner. I recently checked with the county and learned that you have not paid your taxes, resulting in a lien being placed on the property. This becomes a problem for me. It's not my wish to kick anyone out of their home, Ms. Davis, but I'm not in a position to gift you this property. I have granted you extension after extension for almost three years now. I've been more than nice. I rely on your payments as part of my income. You owe $4,500 in back payments and need another $4,500 to pay off the remainder of the loan. This letter is to inform you of my intent to foreclose if you do not bring your account current by September 1.

Jerry Schlaich

"Oh, no," I said, and handed the letter to Darrel. It was now the seventh. Digging through her basket, I found a notice to appear in court for . . . September 8 at two p.m. Tomorrow! "Oh my God, oh my God, oh my God," I said as I handed Darrel the notice. "What a nightmare! How am I supposed to magically produce nine thousand dollars by tomorrow? Wait, twelve thousand including her taxes. Oh, wait, fifteen thousand dollars with the cost of her cremation. I need to sell this place to pay her debts, but I need to pay her debts before I sell this place! What a mess."

I picked up the pregnancy test. "Well, as long as we're dealing with bad news . . ." I said, walking off to the bathroom.

"A baby isn't bad news, Willow," he called out to me. "There's more to life than just making money."

"There's more to life than just making babies," I called back. "Steven Silver wants me to record with him next month!"

"Wow!" said Darrel. "But you don't have to choose between a baby and that," he said.

I didn't answer. Instead, I picked at the pink-and-blue box, wondering what percentage of pregnancy-test purchases were made by a woman who hoped she was pregnant, and what percentage were made by women like me who hoped like hell they weren't. It was such a happy box. Pink and blue, the colors of nurseries. I opened it, took a big breath, and removed the test.

Even though the test said to wait for two minutes, a pink plus instantly appeared on the stick. I thought, well, surely the directions wouldn't say to wait for two minutes if accurate results were instant, so I put the stick on the bathroom counter, washed my hands, walked out back into the kitchen and living room, and hoped to God that pink plus would turn into a blue minus in the allotted time.

"How much is a goat worth?" I asked Darrel.

"About a hundred dollars for meat. Her Cashmeres are worth more. Depends on their age too."

"About sixty goats, about a hundred dollars a goat . . . that would solve half of the problem right there. The llama?"

"Since you can't touch him, maybe a hundred. Maybe two."

"Hmm."

I looked at the horses. "Which one was it?" I asked.

Darrel, understanding what I was asking, replied, "The bay."

"What do you know about him? Did he have problems or did he just have one of those freak moments?"

"Your mom rode him a lot, so I think it was a freak moment."

It could have been. It could have been a freak moment. But given the foreclosure, the fact her winery hadn't become the raging success she always dreamed it would be, and the fact that I hadn't visited her in years, I wondered. I wondered if it was an accident. Had she been depressed and in a state of hopeless despair? But Mom would have made sure all of her animals had good homes first. That was the thing—she would not have just left her animals to fend for themselves—especially the dogs. It had to have been an accident. I kept my moment of doubt to myself.

But I did think about the mostly empty wine bottle by the couch and I wondered if she had been under the influence while riding.

That the bay was a horse she had ridden a lot was a relief to me. I didn't have to shoot him or put him on a meat truck. "Since I don't know much about him, maybe ask nine hundred and take seven?"

Darrel nodded, as if that sounded fair.

"A couple thousand for the Appaloosa maybe? I wonder how old he is. He could be worth more."

"He's a good horse. You should keep him," said Darrel.

"In Los Angeles? Impossible." Darrel, having not been there since he was four, had no idea.

"Keep him until the last minute so you and I can ride."

I smiled, remembering our rides. "Those were good times," I said.

"Yeah," he agreed.

"The truck . . . maybe fifteen hundred?"

Darrel shrugged in noncommittal agreement.

"Señor Clackers. Ugh. How can I sell Señor Clackers? He's so much more than hamburger."

"He's a hero," said Darrel. "He can live with me if you're willing to give him away."

"Thanks!" I said. "Done! He's yours! What about the guinea fowl . . ."

"You'll never catch them," said Darrel.

"Not even with a blanket?"

"Unlikely."

"I could sell them at rock-bottom prices to anyone who could catch them."

He shrugged. "Wouldn't hurt to try."

"The donkey."

"There's not a big demand for donkeys."

"The hay."

"Maybe five dollars a bale because you can't deliver. Maybe six."

"I wonder how much she has." We walked out to the barn. Mom was actually running low. She hadn't bought new hay for the up-coming winter yet. There were maybe thirty bales left—not enough to even bother selling. It was possible I would use it all in the next month if the animals didn't sell fast. I wondered how she ever thought she was going to stay afloat in this sinking ship. What did she think she was going to do?

Darrel and I both looked around the barn. There was nothing of value in it. One beat-up saddle, probably not even worth fifty bucks.

"Her wine-making equipment," I said, beginning to walk that way.

"You need the key," said Darrel.

So we walked back to the house first. I paused in the doorway, remembering my test, took a deep breath, and exhaled.

Darrel patted my shoulder. "Go get your answer. I'll find the key."

I felt the hot wave wash over me and my stomach tie up in knots, and knowing what was coming, made haste to the bathroom, gathered my long blond hair into a ponytail and then a bun to keep it clean, threw up, and then reached up for the pregnancy test before I came to rest on the cool bathroom floor. The pink plus had not turned to a blue minus. "Son of a bitch," I muttered. I threw the test in the garbage, stood at the sink, washed my face, and then just rested my elbows on the counter, holding my face in my hands. How was I going to handle all of this? I had to be pragmatic. That's all there was to it. I couldn't afford a baby. End of story.

I didn't have to ask myself how this had happened. I knew. Ian and I had spontaneously been invited up to Topanga Canyon to hear a band play at the estate of a friend of Ross's. It *was* a great band. I'll say that. Along with the standard guitar and bass, it had a Cuban drummer and a Persian drummer, a lyrical female singer and an edgy female rapper, a mandolin player who sometimes whipped out an electric fiddle, and two more people who played trombone and accordion. It was the first entirely fresh sound we had heard in well over a year and likely more, and we had danced and danced like we had that first week or two we were together. In retrospect, maybe Ian had already decided then that our days were numbered so he might as well enjoy them to the fullest. After working ourselves into a sweaty frenzy on the dance floor, we snuck off into the woods and made love without any regard to precautions. I had figured that thirty-nine-year-old women didn't get pregnant without fertility interventions and that if by some chance I was wrong, well, Ian and I were surely going to get married eventually, so there was nothing to worry about. Clearly, I'd had a little to drink when all of this made sense to me. It may have been the best sex we'd ever had—definitely the best we'd had in a long time . . . urgent, passionate, carnal. Ugh. While it was hard to regret that experience, I sure regretted the end result.

It felt almost as if I had come into this bathroom one woman in one reality and now I was leaving the bathroom as someone else in someone else's life, as if the bathroom itself had been some kind of bad sci-fi portal.

When I walked out, Darrel was smiling. "We're going to have a baby!"

How could I tell him I had no intention of seeing this pregnancy through? I was broke. Broke. Almost as broke as my mother. I was having to take time off work to deal with an estate that was not likely going to put money in my pocket. I had no place to live, so when I returned, I'd have to somehow find an apartment I could afford with first, last, and damage deposit. It would be something close to a miracle to break even every month after that. I sure couldn't afford medical bills from a pregnancy and the expense of day care. Not in a million years. There was no way I could do it. I shook my head slowly.

Confused, he asked, "You're not pregnant?"

"I didn't say that. I just said I'm not having a baby." I was filled with shame just saying it. No one wanted to be in this position. No one.

"Willow—"

Tears filled my eyes. "I don't want to talk about it."

We just stared at each other for a long moment, each one of us keenly aware of the fragility of the situation, each of us needing time to think more carefully before we said one more word about it.

11

Back in 1991, three large Tupperware totes sat on the kitchen counter, holding fermenting crushed grapes, the sum total of my mom's harvest for the year. It was the first time she'd had grapes to harvest at all.

"God, it stinks in here," I said. It did. I waved my hand through the cloud of tiny fruit flies. "Gross."

But Mom, with the first little taste of her dream actually coming true, was in a state of bliss that even a fifteen-year-old daughter couldn't touch. "This isn't gross! This is alchemy! This is magic! Rain falls from the sky and it soaks into the ground, solubilizing the nutrients as it percolates through the minerals. And then the roots of these grape vines suck it up and produce these fruits with that very same water. Did you know grape vines can have roots twenty-five feet deep? Imagine how much more character the water would pick up from the soil at that depth! That's the magic of wine—how all the very essence of a place gets captured in the fruits. And there's this thing called Xnia . . ." she pronounced it like *Enya,* ". . . which is how other nearby plants affect the grapes. While these grapes were still blossoms, the wind carried sage pollen to the flowers where it didn't fertilize the ovum, but influenced it. It made an impression, so that my wine will have hints of sage . . ."

"That sounds gross," I said, making a face, and feigning disinterest as I looked in the fridge for something to eat that didn't involve goats or goat milk. I found nothing and shut the door.

"No, Willow, it's not gross; it's magic. The unique way the sun hits the ground here will be captured, the way the cold nights bring out the sugars. This is a special place and my wine will reflect that. People will sip it and immediately get images of Georgia O'Keeffe hiking all over these hills—even into her nineties. The terroir will transport them here. This land radiates strength."

"It radiates the fallout from the nuclear testing in the forties," I said, trying my best to rain on her parade.

My mom was unfazed. "No, the moment I saw this land, I knew it had strength. I knew my wine would have excellent terroir. And I knew my daughter would too."

"Tare-wah?" I asked.

"Terroir," my mom answered. "It's a French word to describe the uniqueness of place. The De Vine Winery and Goat Ranch has excellent terroir."

"What about animals? Will your grapes have hints of goat odor?"

Instead of receiving the insult, she merely said, "I don't think so."

"I hope to God this place doesn't influence me or impress upon me," I said.

"God, I really hope it does," she replied.

She saw something in this country that I did not see. I saw lack. Lack of clouds. Lack of water. Lack of opportunities and possibilities. Lack of belonging. And I saw extremes. Extremely harsh sun, extremely cold temperatures. Extreme poverty. Extreme lightning storms. Extreme dust storms. To me, it was a harsh land.

As I listened to the words coming out of my mouth I supposed

I could see the ways that the harshness of this place had already impressed upon me, making me harsher, harsh like the way high altitude sun burns skin, harsh like the dry soil that deprives the plants that live in it. My words directed at my mother were undeniably harsh, and the fact she had been right about the influence of this place on me only made me madder.

Here is what I wanted: peaches. I wanted peaches, and misty rain. I wanted to smell the soil in the forests of western Washington where we had come from, the soil that smelled like blackberries and felt soft under your feet. I wanted my dad—not the one I visited now, but the dad he was to me back when we were his only family. I wanted to be with my grandma, put on fancy clothes, and go to the symphony or the ballet with her. I wanted to hear seagulls before a storm, and I wanted to eat something we didn't have to kill ourselves . . . salmon. Salmon and strawberry ice cream. And I wanted to go to a school where it took more than one glance to know I didn't belong. I wanted to belong, deeply belong—not just belong in the way I had come to belong here, that way where after almost two and a half years, people tolerated me and were nice enough. That was superficial. I wanted to really belong. Never in a million years was that going to happen here.

Mom poured the cheese curds through a cloth and collected the whey to drizzle on the dogs' food later. Then she knotted the cheese cloth and hung it on a hook by the sink, moving the whey container with it, and she washed the bowl in which the milk had curdled.

"Since you're so angry at the whole damn world, why don't you put it to good use and go chop some more wood?" Mom had traded a goat for a cord of wood and had been lamenting her decision ever since. She should have traded the goat for a chainsaw, she realized after the fact.

Without a word, I went outside to the pile of wood and began attacking piece by piece with a splitting maul and then an ax. In uncoordinated moments, I'd miss and take another chip out of the handle, but I didn't care. I didn't care about anything. Except Darrel. I cared about Darrel. And my horse, Ruby. They were the only good things in my life. The only good things. And the dogs. But that was it.

For a moment, I imagined that my mom was dead and I had to go live with my dad. Maybe if I was there full time, I'd feel like his daughter again. But then I thought of how it was when I was there just a month or so ago. My baby half-sister, Hailey, was learning to walk and all my dad did when he was home was chase her around. He'd try to have a conversation with me, but it was impossible, because at some point Hailey would mimic a word he said, and then the whole conversation would come to a screeching halt as he and Ms. Nunnalee celebrated with high-pitched fawning.

But maybe I'd be allowed to live with my grandma, who took her special china out of the hutch when I came to visit because it was such a special occasion. Two weeks in the middle of every summer now, my dad drove me to the Greyhound bus station in Seattle where I caught a bus to Leavenworth to visit her. Both this last summer and the one before, Grandma and I walked downtown to the German bakery for cream cheese Danishes and fresh-pressed apple cider before she took me shopping for a new summer dress and shoes to go with it. Later, in her large picnic basket, we'd pack a chilled bottle of sparkling apple cider in two layers of dishcloths so it would stay cold, sandwiches with the crust cut off, fruit salad dressed in cream and sugar, and peach scones we had made ourselves. I'd put on my new dress and shoes, and she let me wear her pearl earrings. Then, with the basket and a blanket, we'd drive to the outdoor theater to watch a local production of *The Sound of Music*. Last year, we even drove up to Chelan to listen to some of the Bach Festival too. All of it had been so elegant, so beautifully civilized.

I sunk the maul deep into a round of pine where it stopped at the first of several knotholes. Lifting the maul with the round of pine stuck to the blade, I slammed it down on the chopping block, sinking the maul deeper.

I thought about the ways my mom might die. If she traded a goat for a chainsaw next time, she might accidentally kill herself with that. Or maybe a serial killer would get her while she was cutting wood in the woods. Probably not—because she could fight back with a chainsaw, and besides, I wasn't sure New Mexico had serial killers like Washington did. So I pictured various chainsaw accidents, and recoiled at my own imagination. Even though I kind of hated my mom, I didn't really want anything bad to happen to her.

I finished splitting that piece of wood, set the maul down, split each half with an ax, and added those pieces to the woodpile. Even though she ruined my life, I guess I still kind of cared about my mom. Kind of. Only kind of.

12

It was in silence for the most part that Darrel and I made vegetable soup and ate it, and it reminded me of the early days here with my mom when so little understanding existed between us. I finished my soup first, and washed my dish in the sink when I was done. Darrel brought his over to wash as well, but I took it and washed it too.

"Come on," he said. He picked up a blanket and led me outside. "You need to feel the earth supporting you."

He spread the blanket on the ground near the house, and there we lay, staring at the night sky, my head resting on his arm.

"I forgot about this," I said.

"About stars, or about lying next to me?" he asked.

"About stars," I replied. "I remember you well. Remember that time we cut class, climbed up Sweetwater Rock, took a nap, and dreamed the same dream?"

"Which time?"

"The first time."

"Yeah," Darrel said. "We dreamed about a polar bear and a grizzly bear sleeping in a den." He smiled. "That was a good dream. Peaceful."

"Was that dream about us? Am I a polar bear? I never thought of myself as a bear."

"When you showed up, you were a mouse." He laughed.

"That's just mean," I replied.

"Okay, a frightened deer."

"Ugh, I suppose you're right."

"You run big circles around things that scare you. Like now."

I had to admit, he was right. "I do."

"Grandma thought you were a whale. Musical. Not a fighter. Belongs on the coast."

"Hmm. I can see that."

"You might be a polar bear. You carry me and my grandparents in your heart. It makes you see things differently. It makes you a little bit Apache. You could be a bear. A white one from the north. But I don't know."

"No one has talked to me about animals since you," I said. "It's so nice."

"Not even when you tell them about the clouds?"

"I don't tell anyone about the clouds."

He put his hand on my shoulder and pulled me in a little closer. "Oh. That must be lonely."

I let his words sink in. "It is," I replied. At once I realized that living here had been nice in that way—even a godsend.

"How could I have forgotten about all these stars?" I asked.

Darrel squeezed my hand. "Welcome home."

As I looked at the stars, I had the sense of possibilities, but I couldn't see any individual one clearly.

"Give thanks," Darrel said. "You're almost forty. This almost didn't happen for you. How many thirty-nine-year-olds get pregnant without intervention? How wonderful!"

"It's not that easy," I replied. And while I had no interest in embarking on single motherhood, it did make me sad to think that given my age, this would likely be the last time I was pregnant. This was likely my only chance to be a mother. And it was impossible.

"It could be that easy," he said.

I felt frustrated at his lack of understanding. He had to know me well enough to know the solution I was going to need was only a solution I would seek in extremely desperate circumstances. "Not all of us get dividends and tribal housing," I said, thinking of the mean things I'd heard and internalized in my life about welfare mothers, since for a while my mother was one of them. While other societies understood that mothers needed help, our society shamed mothers that needed help. I didn't know if my words were a low blow. They weren't intended to be, but as they hung in the air, they sounded harsh. Darrel didn't understand. While sure, there was corruption and embezzlement that happened from time to time within the tribe, ultimately the tribe shared the profits from the oil on their land. He had a safety net that I didn't.

"You don't need dividends and tribal housing," he said. "You have this place."

I nearly exploded, but our friendship hadn't had much maintenance in the years since I'd left and I knew it couldn't take an explosion. Instead I took a deep breath. "We both know this place will be repossessed and I'll never see a penny. I mean, I'm going to try to liquidate all of her assets, pay her taxes, and give the man carrying the contract some back pay in hopes of buying myself a little more time, but . . . we've got to be real. This is no time to dream."

"No, Willow," he said, squeezing me with the arm I was laying on. "This is a critical time to dream."

13

Darrel handed me a ball of kite string in the library one morning, and excitedly I thanked him and hugged him. He had been with me when I had seen it in the grocery store and asked Mom to buy it for me, but it was a dollar and forty-nine cents, approximately the cost of a bunch of celery. We could not afford both. The celery won.

"It's from Grandpa," he said, deferring my thanks. "He wants to know the results."

Three days before, I had stumbled upon a kite book there in the library where Darrel and I hung out every morning before the bell.

On my third day of school, Darrel had brought me here because his aunt Sara was the librarian and therefore he had it on good authority that Ramona and Shyla never stepped foot in the library. Sure enough in the month that had passed since that day, we had not seen them in there once.

When I first saw the kite book, I simply thought that would be a fun project I could do for almost free, a way to amuse myself after chores and homework on weekends, but then it occurred to me that maybe I could talk back to the clouds or whatever benevolent force controlled them.

As I checked out the book, I asked his aunt Sara if it was okay for me to take the old newspapers that were in her wastebasket. She gladly gave them to me.

Later that night in the privacy of my room, I took the book and the newspapers out of my backpack, and retrieved the two branches I'd snapped off earlier from the willows that grew on the edge of the dry creek across the road from our house. I knew the Scotch tape was sacred, so I didn't take that from the junk drawer in our kitchen. Instead, I took a small bottle of Elmer's Glue-All, which I was sure was meant to last us for the next decade, but seemed less likely to be missed. Following the directions carefully, I constructed my very own kite.

I then found a blue ballpoint pen and began to write in my tiniest script, a letter to God in the white spaces between lines of text. I wrote about the injustice of my situation, about how angry I was at my mom for essentially kidnapping me and taking me here, and about Dad essentially abandoning me for a new-and-improved kid. I wrote about how much I hated standing out, hated being a blonde on an Indian reservation, about how I hated being poor, about how much I missed delicious food, and my friends, and my grandma, and the way things used to be.

But I had only a short length of string I had found in the junk drawer—not enough to fly a kite. And the next day, when I asked Mom for some at the grocery store, she wouldn't buy it for me, informing me that a dollar forty-nine could buy enough oatmeal to feed us for a month. So when Darrel gave it to me two days later, I felt hope, like maybe now God or whatever was up there controlling the clouds would finally hear me and maybe send me back to where I belonged, although I didn't specifically know where that was. Maybe with my grandmother. That ball of string in my backpack felt like Dorothy's magic ruby slippers, a ticket back to my old life. If it worked. I didn't know whether it would work.

Eagerly, I took my kite on a test flight the minute I finished my chores that night. I went to the highest hill on the property to make sure my kite would get as close to the clouds as possible, but there was not enough wind.

The day after that, the wind was perfect, and I let all the string out, let it go as high as it would. I watched it floating above me. At first, I was just stunned that it really did fly. And then as I focused on the delivery of my cry for help, I became almost hypnotized by the movements of the kite as it sailed. Soon, a good feeling flooded me, giving me the sense that my message had been received.

Three days later, I received a letter from my grandma telling me that she had worked it out with my father and after I spent my four weeks with him, I would be spending two weeks with her this summer and every summer after. She detailed the fun things we would do—make jam from her raspberries to put on the scones we baked. And then we'd get dressed up and take our scones in a picnic basket to the amphitheater and watch a play. It would be grand, she said. And it felt like a life raft to me, this dream or this promise of an extra special day with my grandma. It was something to hold onto.

Or maybe it was her holding onto me. Perhaps she was the person and I was the kite, and come July, she would reel me safely in.

Either way, it gave me faith that the kite had worked.

And like I promised Darrel, I told Grandpa Luis all about it, but I left out the part about how much I hated it here and anything else that I thought would hurt his feelings.

"Time with your grandma," he said thoughtfully. "That is a good thing to pray for."

14

Through the windows I watched Darrel leave. He had insisted I have dinner with him and his grandparents the next night. They missed me, he said, and had been expecting me for months. Grandpa Luis wanted a long-overdue cloud report. Grandma simply wanted to embrace me.

The dark night shining through the large picture windows looked like the emptiness I felt inside of me without my mom. I paced restlessly through the house, disoriented and grieving, up and down the short hallway and around the couch in the living room, the dogs following me, every bit as confused. I tried to think of an action plan, a way to prioritize every impossible task, but I couldn't seem to get past my inability to believe what was happening.

I wanted to tell my mom I was pregnant. I wanted to just sit on the edge of her bed and spill the beans. She had been imperfect in many ways, and maybe it was because of that very truth that the one thing I could always count on with her was that mistakes would be forgiven.

I remembered spilling a bucket of milk all over the kitchen floor while Mom was searching through cupboards for something. I stared up at her, horrified, waiting for her to react, but although she had heard the splash, she waited a couple extra seconds before she turned around and looked at the mess. "That happens," she had said plainly. "There are rags and a mop in the closet next to the hot-water heater." That was it. What would she say now? Would she drive me to a clinic to terminate this pregnancy? Would she help me see a way not to? I needed her so much in this moment. I wanted to tell her all about how my mother died as if it had happened to someone else.

On my next lap down the hall, I turned into her room instead of passing it. The dogs trotted in through the open door, their toe-nails clicking on the concrete floor. They slipped into my mother's room around my legs, and then stood in front of me, as if blocking me from entering sacred space, as if they didn't want me to change one more tiny thing when far too much had already been changed. But I walked around them and sat on the end of her bed.

"Mom, I'm pregnant," I said and waited just in case somehow I would feel her response. "Ian left me. I'm alone and pregnant and you're gone, and I don't know what to do about anything. Everything . . . looks . . . so . . . hopeless . . ." I bent over, held my head in my hands, and cried. This deeply upset Slobber Dog, who sat at my feet and whined.

Maybe I imagined the feeling of my mom's hand rubbing my back. Maybe I just remembered how it felt. Or maybe she was with me somehow. "Any help you can offer would be greatly appreciated."

Mr. Lickers jumped up on Mom's bed, causing a book to slide off and slap the floor. I walked over, reached down, and picked it up. It was a pretty book with two glasses of red wine in front of a vineyard. *From Vines to Wines,* by Jeff Cox. *Oh, Mom,* I thought, shaking my head. *Your relentless pursuit of this dream is what sunk this place.* Instead of putting it back on the bed, I put it on top of the small pile of books on her nightstand.

At some point I was going to have to clean this room out, but tonight I wasn't ready. I wasn't ready to move the things she had left from the places she had left them. I wasn't ready to erase her . . . erase the evidence that she had ever existed here. But I picked up her dirty laundry on the floor and put it in a basket. I looked back at her bed, at the places her body had left its impression on her sheets, and I left it that way. I wasn't ready. I had loved that body. I had reached for it as a little child. There were layers inside of me to which my mom's body would always mean safety, and those layers still wanted their mommy. My mommy. Not my mom—my mommy. There was a difference.

Instead I tidied up her night table—the copies of *High Tide in Tucson, Pieces of White Shell,* and *Woman Hollering Creek* all bookmarked in different places, these books she would not finish now, her reading glasses, a glass of water. I took it to the kitchen. It was a start. The books, the glasses . . . what was I supposed to do with them? Maybe one day I would read the books. Maybe one day I would wear her reading glasses. How was I ever going to get through the house with so much attachment to ordinary things? They were just things. This copy of *High Tide in Tucson* wasn't anointed in any way just because she had touched it. Her reading glasses weren't going to miraculously heal my eyes when that day came. She likely hadn't even picked them out because she liked them best. They were likely simply the least expensive ones she could find. Mom cared about function more than form.

There was so much to figure out, so much to do. I'd had such a long drive and such a long day, and I was so tired. It was time to just surrender, to put it all on hold until tomorrow, to crawl into my bed and cry myself to sleep.

I walked past the bathroom and didn't even bother to change into pajamas or brush my teeth. I just turned out the light and crawled into bed, into the sheets that were likely the same ones I had put on the bed the last time I had left. The dogs jumped up and nestled beside my legs as I lay back, reminding me of the times that Mom had come in at bedtime, sat on the edge of my bed, kissed my forehead, and wished me good night.

Was I going to be this sad for the rest of my life? I wondered.

I sat up and reached to pet the dogs where they lay next to my legs, all of us lost and adrift, looking for some direction, some purpose, some structure to our lives, some reason to believe that everything would be okay. When I laid back down, Mr. Lickers crawled up closer to my heart, snuggled up in my armpit, and rested his blocky head on my shoulder. With my other hand, I stroked his head, and as I synchronized petting the dog with my breathing, I managed to calm myself enough to sleep.

15

My sense that I was in a foreign country took on new heights when during my fourth-period English class, I heard native songs just outside our window, and turned to see five men in traditional buckskin clothes, holding eagle feathers as they sang. I did not know what to make of this. What was going on? And why? Was this something that happened on a regular basis? No one else was looking out the window or acknowledging that it was happening. At one point, I wondered if I was actually the only person seeing or hearing this.

As Darrel and I walked from English to algebra, he could tell I was wondering but didn't know if it was okay to ask, so he volunteered, "Trolls."

"Trolls?"

He nodded. "Trolls. When they built the new gym, they dug up the earth. Trolls live down there. Now there's trolls running wild all over the community, causing problems."

"Problems?"

"Yeah, like what happened with Shyla and Ramona. A troll probably told them to do that. The singers have come here just in case. At the elementary school, some kid was finger painting with his own poop in the bathroom. He said a troll told him to do it. They've been having lots of behavior problems at the elementary school. The singers went there first."

Was he joking? He didn't seem to be joking. No one else was laughing.

"So the singers were getting rid of trolls?"

"That's the simplest answer," he said.

"So that I won't get beat up anymore."

"Yes. One of the singers is my uncle Walt. He doesn't want you to get beat up anymore."

I didn't know whether to feel self-conscious about that or grateful. "Is this what you meant when you asked Ramona if she wanted you to get Uncle Walt?"

"No. Uncle Walt is a sacred clown. He's part Taos. If someone in the tribe is acting like a jerk, it's his job to follow them around and mimic them so they can see how they appear to others, and you know, to make being a jerk more inconvenient. This is how he keeps peace in the tribe under extreme circumstances."

That struck me as pure genius.

But I couldn't get past the trolls. I mean, certainly my ancestors in the U.K. had their stories about trolls. I didn't know exactly what they were. I think trolls and leprechauns got blended in my mind. Did trolls live under bridges? Were they meaner than leprechauns? I didn't really know. Had people in the U.K. historically tried to eradicate trolls? I don't remember hearing anything about that. Here though, trolls seemed to be a bigger problem and getting rid of them was clearly complicated.

"Do trolls live everywhere or just here?" I asked, trying to figure out more about this new reality I now had to function in.

"Everywhere. In the earth."

"No one I know has ever had a problem with them before," I said, hoping I sounded neutral and not challenging.

"That's because white people can't see them."

"White people can't see them? Why? Because of blue eyes?"

"No. White people can't see them because they don't believe in them."

"Then isn't the answer not to believe in them?"

"You can't not believe in something you've seen."

That's when Mr. Lopez, the school custodian who had been walking behind us chimed in. "Those weren't trolls under the bleachers. Those were Mr. Nelson's Chihuahuas."

"I'm not talking about that," Darrel said to him.

Mr. Lopez was Spanish and from Coalton, not Apache, and I could see Darrel didn't welcome his input.

"Everyone says they saw trolls at the basketball game last Friday night, but I went under the bleachers because I'm not afraid of trolls and all I saw were Mr. Nelson's Chihuahuas."

"Good to know," Darrel said in a way that was intended to end the conversation.

I said nothing. I could not afford to offend Darrel with my white ignorance or arrogance. I needed him. So I was about to let it drop, but then it occurred to me that perhaps I needed more information. "What should I do if I see one?" I asked.

"Maybe pretend you don't see him. He won't expect you to see him because you're white, so he'll probably move on."

Suddenly it occurred to me that if trolls were believed to be here, perhaps there were other entities I needed to know about also. "Is there anything else I should look out for?"

"Skin walkers, witches, aliens, and the Goat Man, but mostly just rez dogs. They pack up and get pretty vicious sometimes."

I wasn't sure where to start with that. "Um . . . ?"

But we reached algebra class before he could explain. "I'll tell you later," he said.

And he did. Later that afternoon, while we rode horses, he explained that sometimes someone does something so hideous that they are no longer a full person—like if he kills a family member or rapes his daughter. Then that person can become a witch, and some witches become skin walkers so they can turn into any animal they want when they need to. "Look out for anyone wearing fur," he told me. That was a sign. "And don't make eye contact with people. You'll freeze if you make eye contact with a witch or a skin walker."

Our horses walked on through the sage and the grass. I looked up at the cliffs at the top of the mesas, their striations crisscrossing like lace, and the talus below them fanning out like the rippled tulle of tutus. With his chin and his lips, Darrel gestured toward Archuleta Mountain. Apparently, that was how people pointed here since pointing with fingers or hands was something only witches did.

"People say the aliens are living under that mountain. Hunters get stopped all the time by men in black suits who drive around in black Suburbans. People say the aliens kidnap people—mostly women and children, and they kidnap animals too and then they breed the humans and animals to make new creatures like the Goat Man."

I wanted to say, "You know that's genetically impossible, right?" but it struck me that there was really no point in saying anything. Alien abductions and beasts like the Goat Man were accepted facts here.

I was going to have to find common ground to operate in this reality. In Washington, we had serial killers and our reaction to them was similar. The bogeyman took a lot of forms. I just looked at it like that. In this world, there were some real nut jobs, so stories were created to explain the danger and how to avoid it. Would avoiding eye contact with a serial killer help a person not be a target? Maybe. Worth a shot. So maybe that was a good rule to follow.

As for the aliens, when I shared this bit of information with my mom at dinner that night, she had military-conspiracy theories that were equally far out. My takeaway was that there were forces out there bigger than me—whatever they were—and that with luck, I would escape unscathed.

Ghostbusters had just come out a few years prior, and so I could not help but to imagine Darrel's uncle Walt and the singers singing "Trollbusters" to the same tune. That wasn't the common ground that was needed.

Suddenly my world seemed like a very dangerous place—not because of skin walkers, witches, trolls, aliens, and the Goat Man, but because of how different the assumptions were that we were all operating under. I felt doomed for social disaster and suspected I was going to get beat up again whether Darrel was next to me or not.

16

I didn't know where I was in those seconds before I opened my eyes when I first woke up to silence. Where were the cars? Where were the people? And then when I opened my eyes, I felt disoriented in time. How old was I? Then I remembered, rolled over, buried my face in a pillow, and cried for a minute before summoning the resolve to begin to handle some problems despite my grief. My stomach was already gearing up for its morning routine, but wasn't at a crisis level yet. The sooner I terminated this pregnancy the better, I thought.

For a moment, I sat on my bed and surveyed my surroundings in that room and the archaeology of my teenage years, preparing myself to take most of it to the dump. If I had lived without it since I was eighteen, I probably didn't need it. I opened a drawer to my nightstand, looked at my assortment of bookmarks and pencils, and a tablet on which I had outlined my goals and plans. Page one only contained a list of things I would pack when I left.

I stood and picked the old photo of my first horse ride with Darrel out of the frame of the mirror that rested on a desk against the wall. I studied it, remembering thinking on that ride that I obviously had not been completely forsaken by God if God loved me enough to send me Darrel.

After I finished throwing up, I sat on the stone bench in front of the fireplace and surveyed everything in front of me. There was so much stuff. It all had to be sorted through. The few things worth keeping needed to be kept. And the things not worth keeping needed to be released. But after being forced to release my mom, I really wasn't up for releasing more. Still, it had to be done. What could be sold needed to be sold. If I could somehow bring her accounts current, I could sell this place for hundreds of thousands of dollars, and then I'd have some choices.

Actually, with money like that in my pocket, being a mother might actually be a choice.

But the time to terminate this pregnancy was now, very soon, or never. The odds of being able to pay what my mom owed were microscopic. Dreaming like that was really just a cruel thing to do to myself. This was simply going to be a month where I did what needed to be done and where I lost a lot of things I didn't want to lose. This was just going to be the worst month of my life, but the sooner I dealt with it, the sooner I could get on with the next chapter.

Pulling a tablet and pen out of a drawer near the counter, I tried to strategize, to come up with some kind of list of priorities for how to attack this huge and heartbreaking job, but despite the pep talk I had just given myself about doing what needed to be done, I felt absolutely paralyzed.

The first thing it seemed to me that needed to be done was . . . I didn't know. I didn't know what to do. I knew I needed to go to the county courthouse, show up on behalf of my mother in court, but I had no idea what to expect. Would they give me a few days to move some personal things out of there?

Next, I supposed I needed to list her herd of goats on craigslist, as well as the donkey, the llama, the horses, her pickup, her piece of junk tractor, and the saddle. Señor Clackers needed to be transported somehow to Darrel's place.

And while I sold livestock, I still needed to clean out my mom's things. What would happen if the court wanted me out today and didn't allow me to go back for anything? I supposed I'd put her dogs and any pictures I could find in my car when I went to court just in case.

Only then it struck me that I might be taking my mom's dogs back to the city, so I'd need to find an apartment to rent that I could afford that would take two dogs, and I'd need to cough up first and last month's rent and a damage deposit and I still needed to be able to pay for an abortion.

That word. I said it to myself. It was such an ugly word to me. I was so uncomfortable even just thinking it.

And Darrel was right. This was likely the last time I'd ever be pregnant. This was likely my last chance to go down this road.

But the reality was that if I couldn't afford an abortion, I sure couldn't afford a baby.

I fed the animals as if two decades had not passed since this was part of my daily routine, putting hay in the wheelbarrow and carting it to the different pastures. Then with my phone, I carefully photographed all of the things I intended to sell. The morning light was good, casting a warm glow on the white goats especially.

When I first heard tires hit the gravel in the driveway, I stepped out from the other side of the barn and I saw a woman I didn't recognize.

As she stepped out of an old white Dodge pickup, I noticed she was lean and muscular in that way women are when they buck hay and drive fence posts day after day. She wore a man's undershirt with overalls like my mom always did, and her long silver-streaked hair hung down her back in two braids.

"Hi," she called out. "You must be Willow. You look so much like your mother. I was talking to Sara Vigil last night and she told me that you were back in town. Do you remember her? She was your librarian at school . . ."

"Of course," I said, smiling. How could I forget? I had spent every morning in the sanctuary she provided. "Boy, word travels fast."

"Even faster than you think!" As she approached, she held out her hand. "I'm Paula Rhyning. I moved out here from Ohio four years ago and met your mom at a book club meeting. She was a kindred spirit. I feel lost without her. How are you doing?"

Maybe because she sort of reminded me of my mom, I stopped myself before saying I was okay. "I'm struggling," I said.

"Oh, honey." She reached out and gave me a hug that was more awkward than it had been intended simply due to the newness of our acquaintance.

"Thanks," I said, mostly to give her permission to let go.

In her hand, she held a sandwich bag with a few photographs. "I wanted to share something with you. I love to take pictures, and your mother's face, you know, she had a lot of character. That winning smile she'd shoot when she was amused . . . It cracked me up every time. And other times she was so deeply introspective as she looked out in the distance that I'd get a glimpse of her vulnerability or . . . I don't know, something like that."

Vulnerability was not a word I ever would have used in the same sentence as my mother. In all our years together, I never saw it. But Paula handed me three pictures, and as I studied one, I did see it. Was it age that brought this out—that awareness that not a single one of us escapes death? Was it me? Did I break her heart by staying away so long? Or was she merely thinking about the coyotes getting her goat kids?

"These were my favorites," Paula said. "You can have them if you want. I figured you might not have many pictures of her."

I bristled. Was that a dig? I might not have many pictures of her because I never came around with a camera? Is that what she was saying? But when I looked at her face, all I saw were the purest of intentions. She simply knew I didn't have any recent pictures and she was giving me three.

"That's really nice of you," I said. "Do you remember what she was talking about when you took this photo?" I held up the picture where I could see vulnerability or something like it.

"The impermanence of all things."

I nodded, and my eyes watered.

She put her hand on my shoulder.

"I thought I would have more time," I said.

"We all think that."

"I wasn't a very good daughter."

"She didn't think she had been a very good mother."

I looked up at Paula's face as I searched for an answer I knew didn't exist. "It can't be fixed now."

Taking a deep breath and exhaling first, she chose her words carefully. "I don't believe that," she said. "Souls are eternal and souls bond. There is something that still connects your souls. You can heal it on a soul level. You just can't over-intellectualize it. You have to distill it down to love just as much as you can. Just love her. She'll feel it. And then be open to feeling it when she loves you back. Love is the truth. Everything else is just bullshit at this point. Guilt and regrets . . . she's got no use for any of that where she is now. Those things can't even reach her."

I wanted her words to sink into me, but they stayed on the surface like an oil slick—even when I was quiet for a moment, waiting for them to take root.

I flipped through the pictures again. In one, Mom was riding the Appaloosa bareback, its gray coat matching her silver hair in stark contrast to the brilliant clear blue sky behind them. Her skinny legs dangled off each side, and if I blurred my eyes, I could almost see her as she might have been when she was a kid—wild and free like that, riding horses bareback and barefoot through the woods.

She paused and looked around. "So you're putting it on the market?"

I shook my head. "It's being foreclosed. I don't know how this works. I just found a letter from the man who is carrying the contract and the court summons for today. She hadn't paid her taxes or house payments in almost three years."

"Oh, no."

I winced and nodded. "Do you know how any of this works?"

"Did she have a will?"

I wanted to make a joke about whether she had ever met my mother, but instead I simply said, "No."

"You need to go to the courthouse and write something like, 'My mother was single and I am the only daughter and beneficiary. Her property is in the county. I request to be named her personal representative.' It would probably be best to do that before the foreclosure court. I could be wrong, but I don't think they can foreclose on a dead person. I think they'll give you a little time to deal with her estate."

"But I don't even have her death certificate yet," I said. This was all so surreal. It was a surreal conversation to be having.

"You can say that you'll submit it or copies of it when it's available."

"Okay."

"And then you can legally start selling her stuff."

"Yeah, I'm going to put her livestock on craigslist this morning, but even if I sold all of the animals, her truck, and her tractor for the best price, it's still only a little more than half of what I'd need to bring her accounts current and pay for her cremation." Cremation. I was talking about my mother's cremation. This was unreal.

"Are you going to have a service?"

"A service? . . . Oh my God, I haven't even thought about that. I mean, she was always such a loner, you know? It was always just me and her."

"We'd come—her book group. In fact, if you just want to sprinkle her ashes here, we could bring some food by and maybe share a couple bottles of wine and tell stories, and . . . just be together. The three of us would do everything, except . . ." Paula smiled as if she had just remembered something.

"What?" I asked.

Paula's demeanor was apologetic as she broke the news to me. "Okay, well, she knew you would hate this, but she used to say that at her funeral or memorial service or whatever, she wanted you to play 'The Sound of Music' and she wanted everyone to dance."

"Are you kidding me?" I asked, dropping my head in resignation. Then I lifted it up to the sky, exasperated, as if I was now asking my mom, "Are you kidding me?"

"She knew you would hate it, but she loved that moment so much."

Somehow this felt like the final insult to me, as if it wasn't bad enough that she'd abandoned me when I was pregnant and left me with fifteen thousand dollars' worth of bills to cover and no way to cover them. How was it in her imagination that she never considered that maybe in my moment of greatest grief that I might not want to relive in any way the most humiliating moment of my life. I mean, wouldn't a good mom think about her daughter grieving and want to make life easier for her? "Final wishes, huh?" I asked, just sort of accepting that not one single thing about this moment in time was going to go easily.

"Final wishes."

"Okay, well, I'll let you know when her ashes are ready, and we can go from there," I said. "With any luck, we'll be able to do it here before the foreclosure."

"Let me know if I can help you. I remember cleaning out my parents' house. It was brutal. Sometimes it just helps to have someone else with you to keep you moving forward. If you need any help at all—especially with her bedroom, because trust me, that's the hardest—please don't hesitate to call on me. Promise me you won't hesitate."

"I promise," I said.

"I'll take a load to the thrift store for you whenever you're done sorting through it all. Let me know if I need to hitch up a horse trailer. That will just leave you with a trip to the dump and the things you want to keep. Let me or someone else help you with any heavy lifting." She wrote her phone number on the back of an old receipt, and handed it to me.

I studied her face to see if she knew, but if she did, she was polite enough to hide it. "Is there anything of hers that you want?" I asked.

With a little shrug she said, "I'll find a thing or two in your thrift-store pile."

"Thanks," I said. "And thank you so much for the pictures." I held them up before slipping them into my back pocket. Then I walked her to her pickup where she gave me another hug, this one much less awkward. I waved as she drove down the driveway.

17

"You should be able to be happy wherever you are," my mother had once said to me near the end of our first year here. "Happiness comes from inside you, not from outside of you."

"Well, then, why couldn't you have been happy in Enumclaw?" I had retorted.

"I'm trying to create something here—something new, a new beginning, a new life." My mother was clearly frustrated that I couldn't see her grand vision and that I didn't seem to want any part of it.

I found my mother's inability to see other people's points of view utterly stunning. "So if happiness can come from a new life, isn't it also fair to say unhappiness can come from a new life?"

"People are unhappy because they *want* to be unhappy." Insensitivity frosted with shame, my mother's specialty.

Angry, I had said, "Believing that frees you of all responsibility for how your choices have affected other people."

"Did your father teach you to say that? He liked being unhappy. It made him feel alive."

"Wow." I shook my head in disbelief. "You really believe that."

"I really believe that," my mother said without flinching. "*I choose to be happy.*"

"But not in our old house," I added.

"I choose to expand my horizons and try new things," seethed my mother. "You really ought to try it."

"And *you* really ought to try being a junior high school student at *my* new school." I stormed out and slammed the door behind me before my mother could say one more stupid, know-it-all thing.

I cut through the fields, crossed the road, and began climbing up out of Monero Canyon. I climbed and climbed and climbed until I reached the top of Monero Mountain, the tallest peak around. From there, I looked down—at my new home on one side, and Coalton a couple miles away on the other side, and I realized the openness of this country afforded no privacy. Distance wasn't satisfying. It was not possible to get far enough from problems and people out here where no matter where I went, I could still see them. They did not disappear from view.

It was then and there I made the decision.

When I finally returned to the house, Mom looked up from whatever she was doing in the kitchen and I announced, "The day after graduation, I'm leaving here and I'm never looking back."

Mom didn't flinch. "Well, that's kind of what young adults are supposed to do," she said.

"Not look back?" I challenged.

She shrugged. "Sometimes it takes some momentum to launch. You'll figure it out."

She was supposed to be sad. She was supposed to beg for a conversation about how to make this a more livable situation for me. In the moment, it looked to me like she didn't care at all and I deepened my vow to myself that I would. I would leave one day and never look back.

18

Since I had no idea how long it would take to become my mother's legal personal representative, I left much too early. As I drove, my thoughts would wander off to the future, trying to solve problems that I couldn't even see clearly yet, and then I'd have these other moments where I became fully present again and admired the mesas that gracefully towered above a stretch of the highway. Trees grew in impossible places near the edge or along parts of the loose slope that dropped off dramatically. Giant boulders sat on the precipice, threatening to fall, but the trees grew anyway. That was the thing about life, it seemed. Life was pretty tenacious—most of the time anyway.

Here was this little embryo inside of me growing during an impossible time. The stress alone of this situation, of my mom's death, of the breakup, of the foreclosure, of needing a place to live and not having the money to get into a place to live—all of this should have been enough stress to cause me to miscarry on my own. Still, the life force inside of this little group of cells was tenacious enough to hold onto my uterine wall. If I had the luxury of a choice, I would respect it for that. It was funny, I thought, that pro-choice was associated with protecting a woman's access to abortion, but I just couldn't imagine a woman choosing this path unless she in fact, like me, felt she had no choice at all.

Other times, as the scenery rushed by, I seemed to travel back to the past, but in a really fragmented way, almost like a slide show full of memories I thought I had long forgotten. A Raggedy Ann birthday cake she had made for my sixth birthday with red licorice for hair. Seeing her walk through the door of the school nurse's office after I had fallen off the jungle gym and cut my head pretty badly at school. A time she had joined my class on a field trip to the zoo and when another mother had spanked her daughter in front of everybody, Mom said, "You just taught her to be violent any time she's frustrated. Way to go." Mom was ahead of her time. I thought that other mother was going to lunge at Mom and attack her, but it seemed that as the other woman sized Mom up and assessed the risk, she understood the truth, which was that my mom would have taken her down. At seven, I hadn't understood exactly what was going on, but I did understand that my mom was in some way defending my classmate, and I was proud of her. In that moment, she seemed like a superhero to me—even the way she stood, chest out, hands on her hips.

More and more houses began to appear and before I blinked, I was in the middle of Tierra Amarilla, the county seat. Less than a half-dozen cars were parked in the parking lot of the county courthouse, so parking was easy, but walking in was not. I feared I wouldn't be able to hold it together for the duration of all that needed to be done here today.

I asked a clerk about what words I needed to use to petition the court to appoint me as my mother's representative, and she kindly helped me. I wrote the words that seemed so unreal to me—that my mom had died and I was the only one left. I was it. And suddenly I felt very, very alone—even more alone than I had on Friday, which was saying a lot.

"I'm very sorry for your loss," said the clerk, and looking through her thick glasses up into her eyes, I could see that she was sorry, and I wondered if people like her had any idea just how much they made the world a better place. Bringing compassion and humanity into an otherwise pretty sterile institution was huge. How many people did she help through this process each month? Plenty, I was sure. And still, she hadn't grown insensitive.

I still had two hours before Mom's court date, so I walked outside and looked down the road. There was a café that looked nice, so I went there, bought a muffin, and used their wi-fi to create ads on craigslist for all of my mom's assets that I hoped to sell. This killed the better part of an hour.

After that, I checked my e-mail. Word had spread around the music studio, not only about my mom, but about Ian leaving me too, and a half-dozen work friends wrote to express their condolences.

Court came and went in less than five minutes.

Jerry Schlaich looked a bit like Mick Jagger's younger and less attractive brother. He was from the generation that had partied hard—the one just after the Vietnam generation, the one that always seemed a little lost to me, as if they had been gearing up to be like their righteous older siblings only to find themselves in the mid-seventies with no cause to fight for, and nothing to do but drugs. I could tell he was none too pleased about how my mom's death had just made his situation more complicated.

The judge called me forward and looked at my copy of the petition I had submitted a couple hours ago, and he told me he wanted to see a death certificate when it was available. Then he gave me thirty days to pay her taxes and pay off the house to Mr. Schlaich plus interest and his attorney fees, which added nearly two thousand more dollars to the grand total. The situation kept getting more and more impossible.

With that, the judge smacked his gavel and we were dismissed.

I caught Mr. Schlaich's eye as we made our way toward the center aisle and said, "I'm really sorry my mom left you in such a bad position, and I really am going to do everything in my power to fix that."

He shrugged. "If you can't, that's fine. I can turn around and sell it for three times as much today as I sold it for back then." He was hoping for that outcome. I could see it in his eyes and slight smile. On top of that, he did not even have the courtesy to express his condolences. Even though he had been remarkably lenient with my mom, I didn't like him.

Distracted, I drove right through Chama on my way back to Coalton without stopping to buy a gift to take to the Vigils', where I was due for dinner in less than two hours. Technically, I did have time to turn around and drive the half hour back to Chama to shop there, but I looked at my gas gauge and thought about the gasoline I would burn going there and back—at least four gallons. That was at least twelve dollars. Twelve dollars was a lot of money to me now. And there was a lot of work to do and not a lot of time in which to do it. I needed to clean out the house and get back to work in L.A. I didn't have paid leave, so every day I spent here was costing me money. There really wasn't time to waste. I needed to just suck it up and go to the grocery store in Sweetwater again, even though I had promised myself I wouldn't.

The mere thought of everything in the grocery store nauseated me and I didn't have time to prepare anything. I thought, well, I could bring a fruit tray, or better yet, just a fruit basket, and looked through my mom's cupboard for an empty basket until I found one.

Voilà. No preparation required. Fruit. I'd be in and out of the store in two to three minutes.

I parked as close as I could, took a deep breath, waited for a clearing in the parking lot, and then rushed in. I didn't look at anyone as I grabbed a basket and went straight for the produce aisle to select fruit as fast as I could.

Only one man, one I didn't know but assumed was a friend of Grandpa Luis's, expressed his condolences and then congratulated me. I held back my tears this time, said thank-you, and made it back to the checkout counter in less than thirty seconds.

"Emotional?" the clerk asked, the same one who'd suggested my pregnancy test was a waste of money. "My wife got really emotional when she was pregnant. I was pretty sure she was going to kill me."

I was pretty sure I understood why, but I said nothing.

He began to take my fruit out of the basket, put it on the scale, and type in codes at the speed of light. "Cravings too? Fruit is good. My wife craved french fries. That was not so good."

"It's a gift," I said.

"Oh, are you visiting the Vigils? They'll like this."

"Yep," I said, handing him my money, and helping to bag a couple kiwis and oranges while he made change.

I thanked him and hustled out to the parking lot where the woman who had worked at the post office since forever and a woman police officer paused their conversation near the grocery cart return in order to express their condolences and then congratulate me. I fought my raw emotions, said thanks, and got in my mom's truck as fast as I could without drawing any more attention to myself. I rested my arms on the steering wheel and laid my head down on them while I collected myself. *Be strong, be strong, be strong,* I told myself. Be strong. There were so many problems on my plate that I could not likely solve in a day. But there was one that I could.

As I took my phone back out, I put my hand on my belly and whispered, "I'm sorry." Then I went to a Web browser page, typed in, "Santa Fe abortion clinic," waited for my choices to come up, picked one, and dialed.

Friday. In four days, this part of my nightmare would be over. I shut my eyes and put my hand back on my belly. Somewhere in there was a group of cells no bigger than a jelly bean—just a clump of cells, I told myself. But I didn't believe it. "I'm sorry," I whispered again.

19

Even though I was only thirteen that Christmas before we moved to New Mexico, I had been astute enough to observe that understanding skips generations. Grandma had come over on the twenty-third to join my mom in starting all the cooking that would carry us through the next few days. For me, time with Grandma had always been a way of being transported into a more elegant world where everything was just a little bit finer, but I could see that was not true for my mom.

"Monica, you can't just dump flour into that like that. You need to sift it. Do you want chunks of flour in your crust?"

"That's ridiculous, Mom. I'm just going to mash butter and shortening down on all of the flour and compact it again. It makes no difference."

For a short while, they were quiet, and then they made small talk about something agreeable, but then my grandma launched in again.

"I can't believe you keep your knives on your counter," my grandma said soon after that. "Just because someone breaks into your house doesn't mean you have to arm them."

"How many times has someone broken into your house, Mom? How many times has someone broken into mine?"

"See, we're both overdue," said Grandma.

There was more silence, and then more small talk, and then more tension.

"Did you set a timer?"

"No, Mom, I can look at a clock. Also, I can smell it when it's finished."

"Right, because who needs to listen to that amateur Betty Crocker? Clearly she doesn't know what she's doing."

Each time, my mom would make a face as she took a deep breath in and let that deep breath out, a face that said she wasn't sure how she was going to get through the next four days without blowing her stack.

"Just because you're in your own house doesn't mean it's okay not to wear a bra," said my grandma. "Company could come over. I'm company. Aren't I worth a little effort?"

"Mom, my boobs are so small you can't even see them—certainly not under this apron. I think you're operating on an assumption."

"No, I can tell."

"Then don't look so hard."

"Is your bralessness under that apron a covert feminist statement? Cooking is not a weakness, Monica. She who cooks has all the power."

My mom shut her eyes, trying to block out my grandmother before her anger boiled to the surface.

"Did you see where some women have stopped wearing stockings and are walking around in bare legs with their dresses?" This was my grandma's way of saying the world was going to hell. "You know what I always say . . ."

Mom joined Grandma in reciting what she always said. "Stockings are the difference between wearing a dress and wearing a nightgown."

I was starting to wonder how my mom was going to endure the holidays as well. I had never really looked at my grandma through my mom's eyes.

"Have you thought about cutting your hair? As a woman gets close to forty, all that hair just drags her face down."

And another part of me thought that there was nothing wrong with the ritual of sifting the flour, keeping knives out of view (there was something sort of ugly and violent about them), wearing bras and stockings, and getting a flattering haircut. In my mind, all of those things were what it looked like to live with style and flair, but I could see how all of those things constricted my mom. And even though I was the last to feel sorry for my mom, even I started to have impulses to defend her. Fortunately or unfortunately, she started drinking wine to cope with her mom and I lost all of those impulses.

I didn't know how to define drunk and not drunk. That word really didn't have a lot of meaning to me. I saw it more like a color-coded scale, like the sign outside the Forest Service Office that showed where the fire danger was that day. Green would be when Mom wasn't drinking. Yellow was when she was drinking but only into her first glass and a half and feeling happy. Orange was when she started telling people exactly what she thought. Red would be for when she got so mad that she vacuumed angrily and every-one had better get out of her way. And burgundy would be when she simply locked herself in her room and cried. I had thought about making a sign like the Forest Service's for Dad, so I could move the pointer on it each afternoon, and he could understand what he was walking into before he opened the door from the garage to the laundry room. Sometimes things went from orange to burgundy in a heartbeat—too fast to pause and vacuum, and I feared that would be the case today.

Hours passed, Dad came home, and seeing that no one felt like cooking one more thing, he ordered a pizza. Pies cooled on the stove, and a turkey defrosted in a large pan of cold water. *Jeopardy* was on and Grandma was fired up about how it was the fifth day in a row that the winning contestant had worn horizontal stripes. "How come someone hasn't told her not to wear horizontal stripes? Horizontal stripes look horrible on everyone!"

"Not those French guys in their black-and-white shirts and berets," said my mom just to be feisty.

"Horizontal stripes even make them look fat," insisted my grandmother.

"Brawny," corrected my mom. "Nothing wrong with that. Women don't want a skinny man."

I didn't dare look directly at my dad when Mom said that, so I pretended to look at something on the table while I noticed that insult hit my dad. His shoulders rounded and his head dropped ever so slightly but I caught it. In that moment, I hated my mom for her carelessness and the harm she did when she was in level orange.

I carefully set the table, knowing Grandma would see no reason it couldn't still be a special dinner even though it was pizza, and Grandma joined me in the kitchen to make a salad. But when the pizza arrived, my mom defiantly put it on the table, looking directly at my grandma, challenging her to say something. We all knew that one of Grandma's commandments was "No labels on the table," and this was a mighty big label. Still, I hoped to God that Grandma didn't take the bait.

To my surprise, she didn't. She looked at the pizza box, looked at my mom with one eyebrow raised, and said nothing.

"What, Mom?" my mom baited. "Say it. You know you're dying to say it."

In the long pause that followed, time seemed to slow down and everything became very still. And then my grandmother said something much greater than what anyone has expected. "Have you considered going to A.A.?"

Burgundy! Code burgundy!

"Happy holidays!" my dad said with a mix of sarcasm and ironic cheer, as he loaded slices of pizza on a plate and took them down to the bedroom he and Mom shared.

Grandma served us slices of pizza and then moved the box onto the kitchen counter so that the table was once again pristine. We sat down together. After I put some salad on my plate, I spooned some blue cheese salad dressing on it from a small crystal serving dish. Even from the dining table, we could hear Mom crying and the murmurs of Dad as he tried to make things better.

"She needs to get her act together," Grandma whispered.

A part of me agreed with her and another part of me saw that they brought out the absolute worst in one another.

20

I don't remember a time when I didn't look at the clouds and see animals. I believe I must have done it as a baby even. But I do remember fragments of piecing it together that the clouds had meaning. The first time it had clicked, I had been at recess in first grade, and from the playground I had seen a bird with its beak open as if it was singing. Later that same day, our class went to music where Mrs. Osborn taught us a new song I loved so much that I didn't stop singing it for the next two months. As I walked down the hallway after music back to our regular classroom knowing I needed to be quiet but unable to silence that glorious song inside of me, I hummed quietly enough that no one else could hear and thought about how that singing-bird cloud and I had something in common. But I didn't know it was more than an isolated incident.

I saw a dog cloud on the morning before Jennifer showed up at our school in February that same year. She would become my best and loyal friend. It only made sense in hindsight. At the time, I was literal and the symbolism of animals was lost on me.

In second grade, I saw an alligator with its mouth open, teeth showing, on the way to a dentist appointment once—an appointment where a tooth was pulled. I remember thinking the cloud had teeth and my day involved teeth. And I remember thinking alligators were scary and the dentist's office was scary. I had pointed out the cloud to my mom as she was driving. She glanced up and replied that she couldn't see it and needed to keep her eyes on the road.

That was the year my mom started drinking wine earlier and earlier in the afternoon. As I walked home from school, sometimes I'd see a cloud of an animal that hid or ran, or protected itself some other way, and only after I walked into a volatile situation would I realize that I should have protected myself like a turtle, or hidden like a mouse, or ran like a deer. For instance, if Mom was expressing her anger by vacuuming, slamming the vacuum into walls and doors, it was best to run like a deer. If I had left toys all over my bedroom floor and on that particular day she couldn't stand it anymore and was ready to rant "I'm not a maid!" for a good long several minutes, running or hiding weren't options. I had to be like a turtle and not let her words penetrate my skin. If she was upset and on the phone, a wineglass and bottle nearby, I knew, thanks to the clouds, to go hide in my room like a mouse. Of course I didn't tell anyone about those clouds. To tell about the clouds would have been to say things out loud about my mom that I somehow knew I wasn't supposed to speak about—not even to Grandma Mildred, my favorite person in this whole world. After all, Grandma Mildred was my mother's mom and by then I knew I wasn't supposed to tattle on people.

Grandma gave me a diary for Christmas when I was in fourth grade. On one page, I'd sketch the cloud I had seen, and on the next, I had written what happened later that day. I was collecting data.

Until my mom read it. She didn't know what the pictures were of, but she was mad as hell that most of my entries had something to do with her and the effects of wine. Mad as hell. She vacuumed every day for week.

And I hadn't written or spoken about clouds since.

21

"You are *Kos Ch'eekee,* the Cloud Girl," Darrel's grandfather, Luis Vigil, had said to me on my third day in New Mexico.

Inside, Grandma Anita was folding rags, dipping them in a tea she had made, and packing these compresses up for me to take home to use on my bruised and swollen eye.

"Pardon me?" I asked, and looked at Darrel, confused, for I hadn't told him about the clouds.

"I've been waiting for three months to meet you," Grandpa Luis said.

"Grandpa Luis has dreams about things," said Darrel's grandma Anita as she walked outside and handed me the bag. "They don't always make sense at the time."

I thanked her.

"You were in a sky full of clouds shaped like animals. I have something for you." I waited with Darrel next to the horses while Luis went inside the small blue house and retrieved a little box of animal crackers. "When I saw them in the store, they reminded me of the clouds."

"Thank you," I said, opening them to share with everybody.

There was something comforting about animal crackers. They transported me back to a simpler time in my life, a time when I had a whole family.

"So tell me about the clouds," said Grandpa Luis, excited, never faltering in the faith he had in his own dreams.

"Sometimes I see an animal in the sky and it tells me something about what's going to happen," I said, surprised to hear myself say it out loud. But if Grandpa Luis was having dreams about the future and no one seemed to think too much of it, it seemed okay to tell him about the clouds.

He laughed and clapped his hands, not as if he was laughing at me, but as if he was applauding the accuracy of his own dream. "Very good!" he said, and for the first time, I felt proud of my secret. "Tell me more!"

Darrel turned to me and said, "I can't remember the last time I saw Grandpa so excited."

Outside the Vigils' house were about a dozen cow dogs chasing each other around a dozen broken-down cars with their hoods open. In a fenced area next to the house, birds still searched for the sunflower seeds and corn that had been left on the dead stalks, and picked at the soil below them now that the season had thawed it again.

I wasn't sure what to tell him. "Well, uh, the day before I moved here, I saw a cougar in the sky."

"Oh, so you weren't expecting this move," he said. "It surprised you and knocked you down and made you think you were going to die."

He understood. I couldn't believe I didn't have to explain the rest. He just understood. My eyes must have bulged a little as I said, "Yes," because he laughed again.

Grandma Anita said, "Grandpa Luis is very good at animal interpretation."

"And then the next day as we began to drive down here, I saw two geese in the sky."

"Of course. They fly south," said Grandpa Luis. "But you know something else about geese—they take turns being the lead bird so the other birds in the back can follow in their wind shadow and rest. So, sometimes you will need to work very hard and allow your mother a rest."

While I didn't like his message, I was impressed with the depth of his interpretation and fascinated just to be having this conversation.

"I saw a wasp before I walked into the school yesterday," I said.

"You must have been terrified," he said sympathetically.

"Put those compresses in the refrigerator so they get nice and cold and put them on your eye for ten minutes every hour at least," said Grandma Anita. "They will make you all better fast."

With a smile, Grandpa Luis said, "Well, you be sure to tell me about any clouds you see from now on. I want to know about them."

He took the now-empty box of animal crackers from me, gave me a leg up, and then he reached down and picked up two puppies that were wrestling in the dirt at his feet. "Here. Put these in your coat and take them home. They're lucky dogs. A girl in a new school can always use a little luck. They will grow up and protect your home."

There was no way to politely refuse the puppies, and so I unzipped my coat partway and he handed me one and then the other, and I put one in each side of the front of my coat, hoping the elastic at the bottom of it would be enough to hold them in, and that I wouldn't fall off the horse at any point and crush them. "Um, thank you," I said, sure my mother would have a fit.

As if reading my mind, Grandpa Luis said, "Tell her they were a gift, and she has to accept a gift."

I laughed. "Okay."

Grandma Anita said, "You probably don't have any dog food at your house, do you? Hey, do you have mice in your house up there?"

"No pet food, plenty of mice," I replied as she shuffled back into her house. She came out with two little bags of food and two kittens, which she handed to Darrel.

Darrel smiled as he put the kittens and the food into his coat, wincing as they dug their claws into his shirt.

The puppies in my coat, meanwhile, were settling down into the warmth and comfort of our togetherness.

Darrel said good-bye and we started off.

"Come back soon, *Kos Ch'eekee,* Cloud Girl!" called Grandpa Luis after me, so I turned back and waved one last time.

To this day when I think of the happiest moment of my life—not happy in that euphoric way like the excitement of sun in the spring finally, but happy in that contented way, happy like the warmth of September sun, I think of that day, riding with a coat full of puppies lulled to sleep by the rhythm of the horse, my secret out and safe with those who understood it and even appreciated it. I had found my other family.

22

The door flew open when I pulled up, causing the half-dozen or so dogs in the yard to scatter a bit. Darrel and his grandparents stood in the warm light of their home, expectant and eager with anticipation, waiting for me to come inside. Grandma Anita and Grandpa Luis looked shorter and older, and fragile enough that a stiff wind could just blow them away.

I quickly made my way up the path and the three small stairs to the door, set the fruit basket down, and embraced Grandma Anita who felt like a delicate little bird, all bones and feathers, and then Grandpa Luis, who had a little more substance to him. Before I hugged Darrel, I handed the fruit basket to Grandpa Luis, who admired it approvingly. I had done well. It was a good gift.

"Are you okay?" Darrel whispered in my ear as he held me in his arms.

"No," I whispered back, certain that the elders no longer had the ability to hear that volume.

"You're in the right place," he whispered back and guided me to the living room. He then returned to the kitchen to finish the final details of dinner, leaving me to visit with his grandparents.

"It's so nice to see you both again, it's hard not to stare."

Grandpa Luis laughed. "Only snakes trying to hypnotize their prey stare."

So, like I did with Mr. Pesata, I picked a point on their shoulders to look at when I spoke to them and looked at their faces only with my peripheral vision and quick glances, and in this way, they studied me too.

"You don't look so good," Grandpa Luis said directly.

I looked down, my closed lips spreading across my face into something like an apology or an admission that he was correct.

"Yeah, I don't feel so good. I'm going through a tough time," I said when I could see that they were waiting for some kind of explanation.

"So, tell me about the clouds you've seen lately," Grandpa Luis asked eagerly, setting a box of animal crackers before me, which made me smile.

I politely took one and discovered that it tasted really good to me. "Oh my goodness," I said, fighting my urges to act like Cookie Monster on *Sesame Street,* "This is the first thing that has tasted really good to me in days!"

Grandpa Luis laughed and looked concerned at the same time.

"Well, when I first arrived here, I saw a bear over your house."

"A bear!" exclaimed Grandma Anita, clasping her hands together.

"That's good," said Grandpa Luis. The Apaches identified themselves with bears. Bears, they claimed, were their brothers.

"And before I got the news on the day I left, I saw a salmon cloud in the sky."

Grandpa Luis nodded. "That makes perfect sense. When it's time to go home, it's time to go home."

They seemed to be waiting for me to announce that I was pregnant, but even though I now knew it to be true, I didn't want to talk about it with anyone. I didn't tell Grandpa Luis about the bunny cloud. Maybe Darrel already had.

We made it to dinner, avoiding the subject, but then Grandma Anita put a bowl of vegetarian Apache stew in front of me and said, "Darrel said you don't eat meat anymore so I separated this from the pot before I added the meat."

"Oh, thank you," I said.

Grandpa Luis looked in my direction sternly and shook his spoon at me. "You should eat meat—especially in your condition."

Darrel gave me an apologetic glance and then reached under the table and took my hand.

"Luis, we promised Darrel we weren't going to talk about it," scolded Anita.

He turned back to her. "Well, she looks terrible. Both she and that baby need protein."

I wanted to run, but that was not an option. Love stays even when it wants to run. Love is not running. That's what love is. And I loved them. I kept my eyes down and ate my stew.

"I don't understand why we can't talk about this," said Grandpa Luis. "We've always talked about everything."

Tears began to roll down my face. I felt so much shame for so many reasons. Shame for choosing that option that women only chose when they could not imagine how anything else could possibly work out. Shame for being alone and pregnant—for not having looked out for myself better, for not having chosen a better, more generous, more capable man—a man who had loved me more. Yes, I felt shame for being unloved. I felt shame for being weak in this moment, for tears I couldn't stop, for mental clarity I couldn't achieve. I felt shame for not telling the whole truth, for holding back on someone I loved so much, someone who had always understood me and supported me.

Out of the corner of his eye, Grandpa Luis watched me cry into my stew, continuing to eat. "You stayed away so long that it appears you forgot you're our family. That baby is our family, too. He belongs to everybody. He belongs to the world. He is going to be a great musician. Many people will be touched by his music. I had a dream about this child. Manganis believe in separateness. They call it independence, but it's separateness. Apaches believe in togetherness."

Grandma Anita reached across the table for my hand that held a spoon, and she took it in hers. "I can see you feel alone, Willow, but you are not alone. This feeling is blinding you. I am right in front of you. I am right here. Look at me, *ts'iyii*. I love you very much."

All of the things that had been hurting bubbled to the surface: this sense of being alone in the world without my mother, of wanting her back so badly. My regrets. The fear that Ian hadn't kept me because I wasn't worth keeping, or if I was, I feared no one would ever see that. This sense of far too much responsibility on my too-small shoulders, a life that was difficult enough to afford without the burden of a child. The fact that the difficult nature of our unkind and ungenerous world caused me to see a child as a burden. It was all overwhelming.

Darrel released my hand and put his arm around me instead, as if trying to save me from a raging river of fears, as if he could pull me safely ashore where it could pass by in front of my feet instead of carrying me away.

Grandma Anita walked around and cradled my head against her heart. "She's coming back to us," Grandma Anita assured Grandpa Luis. "She's a little lost right now, but she's finding her way back to us."

I let them hold me here, here on the surface of the earth, here on the Cestero Apache land, here in this little house that had always felt like a hug with its crocheted afghans and savory stews that

119

I let them hold me here until I remembered I wasn't
_membered this feeling of being loved and remem-
was.

_u then I thanked them, and assured them I was okay. We ate
the rest of our dinner in that feeling like after the rain of a summer
thunderstorm finally begins and the temperature drops ten degrees,
that gentle relief.

23

My little half-sister, Hailey, was three the summer between my junior and senior year, the last summer I would be required to spend with my dad, and that meant she was old enough to begin swimming lessons, ballet, and gymnastics. Dad worked during the week, so that left me with the woman who would always be Ms. Nunnalee to me, my social studies teacher, in one of those three places watching the illustrious Hailey roll over, or blow bubbles under water, or do knee bends with sweeping arm movements.

"I'm sorry you get stuck with me during my visitation," I said to Ms. Nunnalee as we sat on the bleachers next to the pool on the last day of Hailey's swimming lessons.

"Oh, it's no problem," she replied cheerfully.

No problem. No problem. I chewed on those two words for a while. Those two little words actually summed it up. I was no problem. I wasn't a blessing. I wasn't an important member of the family. I was no problem.

"Oh, look at her now! Isn't she cute?"

I had just four weeks a year with my dad and it seemed I spent every minute of them being roped into some conversation about how wonderful my little sister was. It had gotten to the point where I didn't even want to be there anymore, where if I had to have one more conversation about how wonderful Hailey was, I was going to snap.

The four of us went out to dinner at a family restaurant that night to celebrate Hailey's big swimming success, just like we had gone out to dinner to celebrate her big gymnastics success the week before, and just like we would in two weeks after her dance recital.

"I'm the best," Hailey said, looking up at me sitting next to her in the big red vinyl booth that bounced with her every movement.

"Clearly," I had replied. I was almost eighteen—old enough to blow it off, old enough not to compete with a three-year-old, old enough to be generous enough to let her have her moment of glory, old enough to be a loving big sister. But instead, I added, "I can totally see why Dad dumped me for you." Then I got up and walked quickly in the direction of the restrooms, where I slipped out the back door.

I remember hearing Ms. Nunnalee say, "Uh-oh," and Dad say, "Hey," in that tone that was both stern and caring, and as I rounded the corner, hearing the vinyl booth squeak as Ms. Nunnalee got up to let Dad out. I'm sure there was a discussion about whether to send her into the restroom to get me, and then perhaps there was the moment she didn't find me. Maybe Dad looked outside for me, or maybe he stayed in his seat as if he was in control, as if his steadfastness would be enough to pull me back into that red vinyl booth. Maybe they were afraid to leave the restaurant in case I came back.

In any case, I had time to run the eleven blocks home, pack my meager belongings into my canvas duffel bag, and walk another half mile to the nearest bus stop, where I hid behind a bush until I saw the bus coming. I hopped out, waved it down, paid my fifty-five cents, and rode to the Seattle train station. There, I presented the ticket that wasn't good for another two weeks, paid a twenty dollar fee to change the date with Christmas money I hadn't spent, and hoped my dad wouldn't find me before the next train.

He didn't.

It was very late when the train pulled into Leavenworth, just over Stevens Pass from Seattle. I walked from the train station to Grandma's house, wondering whether it would scare her if I woke her up, wondering whether it would be kinder and more polite to sleep in her backyard. But when I rounded the corner, I could see her silhouette in the front window. She was on the phone, possibly watching for me. Suddenly, it occurred to me that I might be in big trouble, that this time I might have put her in a terrible position and she might not be on my side.

But to my relief, she hung up the phone, walked outside even though she was in her nightgown and housecoat, and embraced me. And even though I was a solid four inches taller than her by then, I rested my head on her shoulder, felt the terry cloth of her robe under my cheek, and breathed in her Ivory soap scent. It was a smell that made me feel safe. "Most people can't or won't see me," I said. "Dad, Mom, almost everyone in my community, Ms. Nunnalee— no one sees me. But you see me. And Darrel sees me. And the Vigils see me. I just don't want to be with people who can't or won't see me anymore." I felt so weary.

Looking deep into my eyes, she said, "I see you. I see you." Then she took my hand and led me inside.

As I lay in bed that night, I heard her talking to my dad. "Give her a little time to cool down. She'll call you. She loves you."

Did I? Did I still love him? I closed my eyes. I wasn't sure.

24

After dinner, Darrel ushered me out of their house to see his, which he had begun building after he had graduated from nursing school and returned to the rez. It was a small adobe house with one bedroom, one bathroom, a living room and kitchen, and a lot of soul. For years, he had built it in his spare time, making each adobe brick by hand from the earth around him. The first time I had visited, it was nothing but a foundation, and the second time, his walls had been almost three feet high.

"Wow, Darrel. It's beautiful," I said, and it was. From the outside, it blended in with the landscape so well it would have been easy to miss it.

Inside, it was cozy. He had handwoven rugs on the floor and an almost abstract painting of a horse in a canyon by his cousin, Darren Vigil-Gray.

"Wow!" I said, admiring it. Darren Vigil-Gray was a big deal. He even had a painting in the Smithsonian.

"Graduation present," Darrel replied proudly. "It reminds me of riding with you."

"Aw," I said, touched that after all these years, I still had such a special place in his heart.

His furniture had been reupholstered with Pendleton blankets, primarily in red, a color considered lucky. On an end table sat a picture of Darrel and Quentin with their arms around each other. I picked it up, studied it, and then looked up to see the expression on Darrel's face. The part of him that was Apache hid his feelings well, but his Samoan eyes sometimes revealed more, and in them now, I saw heartbreak. "He will come back," I assured him. Darrel had written me almost a year ago when Quentin had first left on his big trip.

Darrel shrugged and handed me a small stack of picture postcards—pyramids in Mexico, Machu Picchu in Peru, penguins in Argentina, hot springs in Iceland, a mosque in Morocco, the canals of Venice in Italy, a lion standing before Kilimanjaro in Tanzania, the Sphinx in Egypt, rock formations along the coast of Thailand, villagers with ponies outside their yurt in Mongolia, the Maori in New Zealand, a Haida village in Canada. "Wow, he wasn't kidding about wanting to see the world."

"He got one of those round-the-world tickets."

"Did he invite you to join him for all or part of it?"

"He did, but he knew I wouldn't leave my grandparents at this point in their lives."

I held up the last postcard. "Canada. He's almost home." I wanted to read the backs, but Quentin hadn't written those words for me, so I handed them back.

Again, Darrel just shrugged. "Maybe." He leafed through the postcards. "But even if he came back, would he still be the person I knew and loved? Surely the world has changed him. It's been almost a year. A year is long enough to change everything."

In high school, Darrel and Quentin had loved each other from afar, too shy to ever actually talk about their attraction. There was a time when Darrel had been Quentin's dream. My heart sank. "We both were left by people who had other dreams to pursue," I said simply.

He paused to consider that and then replied, "And we're both going to be okay no matter what happens."

Slowly I shook my head. I didn't know. "It's too bad he couldn't have waited for you."

"He thinks my grandparents will live forever. Plus, I don't feel called out to other places like both of you. I like it here."

"Did he say anything about missing you in his postcards?"

"He said he wished I was there. Is that the same thing?"

I considered it. "I think so."

Maybe a hint of a smile crossed his face, but I could have imagined it. It seemed he had no hope. But then Darrel showed me the rest of his tiny house where there were still vacant spaces in Quentin's side of the closet and on Quentin's side of the bed. That was hope.

25

In math class our senior year, Quentin asked me if Darrel and I would come to his parents' church and listen to him sing at the Christmas service. I was so honored, I said yes without thinking twice. I thought Darrel would be reluctant, but when I extended the secondhand invitation, he seemed excited.

We wore our Sunday best—for Darrel, a nice black suit, and for me, last year's summer dress that Grandma bought for me, paired with a sweater, tights, and some cowboy boots that were risky to wear because they were slick in the snow. Darrel drove us in his grandparents' pickup truck, despite their disapproval. Quentin's dad had preached against some of the traditional ways, and everyone in the tribe knew about it. Some agreed and some did not. The Vigils did not.

Greeters shook our hands when we entered, and we took a seat near the back and to the side. Once the service began, Quentin turned around from where he was sitting in the first pew, spotted us, and smiled. It seemed to me that he was smiling more at Darrel than at me, but that made no sense because I was his friend from math class—not Darrel, and so I figured maybe I had judged it wrong or maybe Darrel's hair looked funny on the other side and Quentin took an extra split second to make sense of it.

Quentin's dad preached about the miracle of Christ and about how we'd all be damned if King Herod had succeeded in killing him. From here, he segued into sin and all the ways we were potentially damning ourselves, despite Jesus' best efforts to save us. False idols. Other gods. Drinking. Violence. Infidelity. Homosexuality. Every time I regretted coming, Quentin would turn around and check on us, and I could see on his face how much it meant to him that we were here.

Eventually, he stood at the front of the church and waited as the piano player plinked notes on the out-of-tune piano to accompany him. Quentin looked delicate to me in that moment—his small frame, his hair cut extra short for the occasion, his wire-framed glasses, his little movements that showed his nervousness. When the introduction was through, he opened his mouth and sang "Silent Night" with all his heart. What he lacked in pitch, he made up for in earnestness, and Darrel appeared captivated by it. Yes, he appeared to be beaming. And it appeared that Quentin was singing right to him at times. Being naïve, I figured this was because Darrel was touched by the music. Music was powerful, after all. When the song ended, Quentin looked right at Darrel once more, and then took his seat. Once Quentin was facing the front of the church again, it seemed to me that Darrel deflated a little bit. And still, I didn't put two and two together. I had no clue that Quentin was gay.

When the service was over, Darrel and I stood and waited as people filed out of the church. A handful of worshippers were gathered around Quentin, surely complimenting him, and so I gave him a wave and a thumbs-up when I caught his eye and then we turned to go.

Once we were outside, I said, "I'm sorry you had to hear some of those harsh words, Darrel."

Darrel shrugged. "I don't believe any of them. Apaches and Navajos used to believe that people like me were extra powerful because we had both male and female power. Sometimes we're called two-spirit people. We're more likely to be healers. We serve our community in powerful ways. That's what *T'soye* and *Cho* taught me. I think it's the truth and how it should be. I'm going to follow that path—become a nurse, heal people, serve my community." He looked back at the church. "White people are so quick to banish anyone who doesn't fit the mold. It's such a waste. We didn't do that—at least not before the missionaries arrived. We looked hard for each person's strengths and for ways that each person could share them."

Just then, Quentin came rushing out of the church looking for us.

"That was good," said Darrel, nodding his approval.

"I enjoyed it very much," I added.

Suddenly Quentin seemed shy. "Thanks," he said, self-consciously.

"We're going to Chama for about an hour and a half," I said. "You want to come?"

"Let me go ask," he replied and left us again.

"I don't know if that's a good idea," said Darrel. "If you or I get caught, our parents will see the humor in it. His won't. His will beat him."

We had a tube of black acrylic paint, and had prepared a jar of watered-down brown acrylic paint as well, and every intention of racially correcting all the plastic light-up Jesuses we could find, since there was a zero percent chance that a man with white skin and golden brown hair was born in Israel at that time.

"Well, we could skip our art project and just go to Dairy Queen."

Darrel nodded.

So that's what we did. The three of us slid into a booth in our Sunday best, ate Peanut Buster Parfaits, and celebrated. I thought we were celebrating Quentin's performance or the holiday season itself, but Darrel and Quentin were celebrating finding each other. Darrel told me after graduation that Quentin had invited us to that service so that we not only would see him sing with his soul wide open, but that we would also see that he came from a world that wasn't going to understand or tolerate his two-spirit nature . . . so that we would understand how important it was not to be outed one minute before he was ready. All of that had gone above my head, but not Darrel's. He knew he had met the one, he said when he told the story now, and he knew the outcome all depended on patience, choosing the right moment very carefully, and not breathing a word of any of it until that moment came.

26

A slight breeze was blowing when I left Darrel's house, and so I stopped along the way home to snap off a couple of willow branches near the dry creek where they grew next to the road. When I reached home, I opened my box of mismatched china still in the back of my car and removed one piece of crumpled-up newspaper.

Inside, I found my kite string in the bottom of the dresser drawer in my old room, and with it I lashed together the two willows. Then I notched the ends of the willows and ran a string around what would be the perimeter of the kite. I laid that on the piece on newspaper, and folded the edges over the string, gluing and taping them.

While the glue dried, I brushed and flossed my teeth, changed into my flannel pajama bottoms and a T-shirt I had worn way back in high school, and fed the dogs a bedtime snack. Slobber Dog did not begin eating right away, so I held out my hand and she dropped a beautiful, small, slightly speckled brown egg into it. I patted her on the head while she began to eat her kibble, and then put the egg in the fridge.

The kite lay on the counter before me, the counter where Mom and I used to eat together. I looked at all the white lines between the print, grateful that there was so much room to write because I needed so much help. I picked up a blue ballpoint pen and began writing.

> *Great Spirit and Benevolent Forces, with every fiber of my being I am asking for your help. Please guide me in all that I do. I have never felt more lost. I don't know what to do about anything. I feel trapped and hopeless. Please show me the way. I need so many miracles. Please help me prevent my mom's home from being foreclosed. Please. Please somehow give me the power to meet all of her financial obligations. Let me finish her business with integrity. Any money I walk away with will be a miracle to me. I need to start over. God, this pregnancy breaks my heart. This is not a situation I ever thought I'd be in. I thought Ian and I would stay together forever and that if this day ever came, we would go forward with being a family. It breaks my heart to think this might be my last chance to be a mother because I'm not ready for motherhood. I'm not finan- cially ready, I'm not in a relationship, and I'm essentially home- less at the moment. Nothing is in good order. God, you know it's not in my heart to harm or kill any living thing. I don't eat meat, I don't kill spiders, I used to cry during goat castration. What I'm about to do doesn't sit well with me at all, and if I could see another way, I would choose it, but I just can't. So I ask for your forgiveness.*

I put the pen down, rested my hand on my belly, and cried. I grieved not only for my mom and for the time I thought I had left with her, but I grieved for Ian and for the life I would not have. He was not going to be the husband that I thought he would be. I grieved for the motherhood I would not experience, for the family

I would not be part of, and even for the person I was before I was put in this impossible situation. And then I picked up my pen and finished.

> *God, please go before me and show me the way. Please. When I return to Los Angeles, I need to find a place to live that I can afford near work. This seems impossible to me—especially with dogs, but I'm told that with you all things are possible, so if that's true, please guide me to it. God, I don't know how it all works—how much of our lives are in our own hands and how much are in yours. Is it a waste of energy to attempt to change the things that appear not to be within the realm of my control? Are the outcomes already destined? I wish you could explain it all to me, because none of it makes any sense to me right now. I know I need to do something, but I don't know what to do. Show me the way. Please, show me the way. And please say hi to my mom for me and tell her I love her and that I'm so sorry I didn't spend more time with her. Looking back, I feel like I let her down my whole life, like she wanted a daughter who was a pistol like her but instead she got a great big crybaby. Please tell her I'm sorry. I need some strength, God—always, but especially in this moment. Strength and guidance, strength and guidance, strength and guidance. Please, please, please, please give me plenty of strength and guidance.*

When I was done, I put on my mom's heavy wool coat, carried the kite up the rustic ladder to the roof. The solar panel took up most of the space up there, and Mom had taken my old chair down. Surely after twenty-two years, it had grown too rickety to trust. She had replaced it with another old wooden chair. So, there wasn't much space. I couldn't run to launch the kite up there. I had to wait quite a little while for a gust strong enough. When it came, I released the kite as fast as I could while still maintaining tension, and to my relief, it made it all the way up. I sat cross-legged up there, looking at my prayers floating in front of the almost-full moon and all of those stars. I hoped that something was out there, that someone was listening, and that I wasn't as truly alone in all of this as I felt.

My eyelids became heavy and the temperature of the night air plummeted. It was time to go to bed, but I wasn't ready to take my desperate prayers down. As ridiculous as I knew it was, that kite was my only source of hope. So, I tied the end of the string around the chimney and left it flying up there before I walked down the ladder and into the house my mom and I had shared.

27

On that first summer visitation with my dad, we had gone to Ocean Shores. While Ms. Nunnalee slept, Dad took me to the kite shop where we picked out two kites and then went to the beach to fly them. It was the best day, the last day of its kind. Soon after, Hailey was born and my dad moved on.

I had written just one thing on that kite, very small in ballpoint pen. "Please let this day last forever," I knew wasn't a reasonable prayer, and didn't expect it to be answered. I simply wanted my wish to be known.

It wasn't that our conversation had been riveting—it's that it had been easy. I think we talked about how the pull of the moon created the tides, and how the color of sand varied from place to place. The reliable August sun had been shining brightly. Even though I had been wearing sunblock, fearing I would burn, he put his UW baseball hat on me and let me keep it. I felt like his girl in that hat. He helped me launch my kite in the stiff wind and then he launched his own, and we stood out there on the beach not too close but not too far away either, smiling at each other as we let more and more string out, seeing whose could climb highest. Watching that kite was meditative. Time seemed to stand still in a way like I imagined time was in heaven, not the way it stood still in math class. I was happy.

I brought the kite home with me on the plane. When the clumsy Southern couple next to me put their large carry-on suitcases in there and then gave them an extra shove, I feared they had broken this souvenir of the last day I would ever have my dad to myself, but remarkably, the kite, all disassembled and wrapped tightly, survived. Mom looked at it and scowled when she picked me up, resentful I suppose that he got to be the parent who took me on a vacation while she got to be my parent during the less glamorous daily life.

On days when I missed my dad terribly, I flew that kite from the top of a hill, staring at it against the blue sky, losing myself in its freedom. It was not a super fancy kite—not one of those box kites or trick kites, but it wasn't one of those paper kites with the American flag on it either. It was plastic and looked like an eagle, and I loved it. Sometimes clouds with a message would float behind the kite, but usually not. Usually the clouds just let me watch my kite without distraction, losing myself in the dance between that which I had control over (the string) and that which I had no control over (the wind). Sometimes I could even lose myself so much watching the kite that I could believe I was back on the beach with my dad.

28

The next morning, I stepped outside to look at the sky. Nothing. No prayers answered. No signs that everything would be okay. Oftentimes clouds built over the day, I knew, so maybe I just needed to be patient.

While I saw no clouds, I did see Darrel riding this way on a giant draft horse cross, so I slipped back into the house, dressed quickly, braided my long hair, fed the animals, and was brushing out Spot, the Appaloosa, when Darrel finally arrived. I slipped through the paddock fence into the barnyard to greet him and his horse.

"Grandma says you shouldn't ride in your condition, but I told her that we would stay on the road and walk."

Although it was terrible, I sort of hoped that riding would cause me to miscarry and spare me the appointment that was just three days away now and absolve me of the responsibility of that decision. Instantly I felt guilty for thinking such a thing. I said nothing, nodded, and greeted his horse by petting its nose. "What's his name?"

"*Ntsaii*," said Darrel.

"*Ntsaii?* You named your horse 'Big'?"

"I named my horse 'Huge.'" Darrel smiled proudly.

I laughed as I slipped a bridle on Spot and led him to a mounting block Mom had built out of two tires and a piece of plywood. Although Spot was quite tall, he was still dwarfed by Darrel's giant horse.

"Wow," I said from Spot's back. "I forgot how far up it is up here." How many years had it been since I'd been on a horse's back? Four?

"Well, he's taller than Ruby was."

"Oh, Ruby. What a sweetheart she was," I said as we began to walk down my driveway, followed by Mr. Lickers and Slobber Dog, who barked excitedly at first, but then, distracted, darted into the sage to chase things or pretend to chase things.

The clear sky was a color of blue I never saw in California, the deep, almost violet blue seen only in the Rockies.

"This is nice," I said, the rocking motion of the horse walking already soothing me.

"Yeah," Darrel said. "Together again."

I smiled. "We sure had a lot of good rides out here. Life doesn't get much better than riding with you, *shi chonii*." *My friend.*

"Life doesn't get *any* better than riding with me and you know it," he said with a smile.

"You know, you may be right," I conceded.

"I'm always right," he joked.

We rode in silence for a long time, a comfortable silence, much like the way a dog doesn't have to speak to be your best friend.

We kept Darrel's promise to Grandma Anita and stayed on the road, but we took a spur that slowly climbed a hillside. As we rose higher and higher, the view opened up so I could admire aspen groves in the early stages of their autumn glory on nearby mountainsides.

"I haven't seen autumn in a long time," I said.

"Oh," Darrel replied as if I'd just told him the saddest story he'd ever heard.

I inhaled the autumn air deeply, feeling its chill on my face and in my lungs, the scent of sage mixed in perhaps making it seem even cooler.

Horse hooves clapped pleasantly on clay like drums occasionally punctuated by the cymbal-like sound of a hoof hitting a rock. I thought about Grandpa Luis telling me the child inside of me was going to be a great musician and wondered what it would be like to have a child that heard music in everything the way I did.

Grandpa Luis's words haunted me. *That baby is our family, too. He belongs to everybody. He belongs to the world.* Tragically, though, everybody in the world was not going to help me when I needed help. They were not going to feed and clothe and shelter us. That would be my full responsibility. And I wasn't strong enough to carry all of that alone. *He is going to be a great musician. Many people will be touched by his music.* That one was harder for me. Maybe I needed to consider adoption. Was I capable of that? Capable of carrying a baby to term and then turning around and giving him away—especially when he was likely the only baby I would ever have? It was unthinkable. The grief would be more than I could bear. But even more than that, as my belly grew, mutual friends of both Ian and me would see and say something to him about it. I couldn't predict how that would go, but I could not imagine it going well.

Only when we reached the top and stopped did I silence my thoughts enough to fully realize where I was. I was on horseback with my old best friend. I was in the center of a several-mile perimeter with not another human soul in it. I was in stillness and silence. I was where I could look down on the little worlds below the way the clouds might. Things that had seemed so big an hour ago seemed tiny up here.

And conversely, things that seemed tiny down there seemed really big up here. Like a clump of cells. A clump of cells that would become a musician and would touch a lot of people. I took a big breath and let it out slowly.

"It's going to be okay," said Darrel.

I turned and looked at him, wanting to believe. "How do you know?" I asked.

He smiled broadly and declared with full confidence, "Love is stronger than fear."

Was it? Was love stronger than fear? Did Ian not just leave me because he was afraid his dream wasn't going to come true? Was I not about to terminate a pregnancy because I was afraid I couldn't provide for and take care of this baby? Had I not neglected to visit my mom because I was afraid I couldn't afford to? It seemed to me that fear was 3–0.

"Do you mind if I take a picture of us up here?" I asked Darrel.

He shook his head, so I pulled out my phone and turned it on. A text from Ian popped up right away, and Darrel noticed my expression change. "What is it?" he asked.

"Text from Ian. *Just checking on you.*" I deleted it.

"That's nice," Darrel said. "Maybe even hopeful."

I shook my head. "Texts are what people do when they want to avoid intimacy or any contact really, but look like they're not."

I had wanted to capture the moment before Ian intruded, and now that moment was gone, but I snapped a selfie anyway with Darrel and Ntsaii in the background, and another of just them, but with Spot's ears in the bottom of the shot.

"I should check whether anyone responded to my ads on craigslist while I have reception up here," I said as I did. "Someone is interested in Monster. Wants to come out today to see him. Fingers crossed," I said as I responded back. "Someone else wants ten cashmere goats but not the whole herd. Still, that's something." I wrote back to that person as well. "Another person wants a couple meat goats. I don't know if I can do that, and I don't know if I'm in a position not to," knowing as I said it that the truth was the latter. Someone was going to eat the meat goats. I could make money to pay off my mom's accounts or not make money, but either way, someone was going to eat them.

"You can think about it," said Darrel, but I had already responded.

"Okay, thanks for your patience. Sorry about that. But hey, it sounds like I could make two thousand, four hundred dollars today!"

"That would be a blessing," he replied.

"It would be a good start." I looked at the sky. Still no clouds, but an answered ad was an answered prayer.

29

"I will be home soon," said Mom's note on the kitchen counter when I came home from school one day in my sophomore year. Outside, I noticed some of the young male goats were missing and figured she had gone to sell them.

I sat at the kitchen counter and had begun my algebra homework when I heard her truck coming up the driveway. I didn't bother to look up until I heard her calling, "Willow! Come outside! I have something to show you!"

She was backing a sorrel horse out of the back of a trailer when I opened the door. "I got you something," my mom said.

I got you something. Those four words changed my life. Looking back, that horse's conformation left something to be desired. She was twenty-one years old, after all. And her head was not particularly elegant, but in that moment she was the most beautiful thing I had ever seen. Her fur was a lustrous copper that actually shimmered in the sunlight, and her eyes were soft and gentle. I could not believe that she was mine.

"Her name is Ruby," said Mom. "I traded some goats for her."

The horse of Darrel's that I used to ride had died about a month prior, and since then Darrel and I rode double on his horse once and then we hadn't ridden at all. Darrel was such a big guy that asking a horse to carry me as well as him had seemed inhumane.

In a state of disbelief, I stroked her neck and her face, and said hello. Then I hugged my mom, who watched my reaction, smiling from ear to ear.

"The woman who I got her from suggested letting her settle in and get used to her new surroundings tonight and then riding her tomorrow," said Mom.

That seemed reasonable to me, and so that night I walked her all over the property, talking to her about things I had noticed here or there, telling her about Darrel and the rides we would take. I often stopped to hug her, wrapping my arms around her neck, inhaling her horse scent deeply. It was the smell of a girl's dreams coming true.

That horse and I were inseparable for almost two years. Every day after school, Darrel and I rode. For this beautiful hour or two, I wasn't in a school where I didn't belong and almost no one talked to me. I wasn't at home where I failed to have the pioneer spirit that Mom wanted me to have. I was in this completely neutral other world where I didn't come up short. Darrel, Chonii, me, and Ruby. We were our own sanctuary.

Sometimes later in the night when I had finished my homework and chores, I'd go back outside and sit on her back, lean over and drape my arms around her neck, bury my face in her mane, and let her keep my legs and seat warm. I'd just hug her like that for what seemed like forever, for this beautiful, suspended, perfect moment.

Each day before I left for the bus stop, I'd pause by her corral, and she'd walk over and gently touch her velvety nose to mine through the fence. And I knew that no matter what bad moments might lie before me that day, that I would be okay, because for that one moment before it all, I had this little bit of much-needed tenderness, of total acceptance, and I knew when the school day was over, Ruby would be waiting for me. She'd offer me peace and sanctuary. She would make life good again.

During my senior year, a week came where Ruby seemed to be in pain. Her ears would flatten as she looked back at her flank. Her belly seemed a little larger and I wondered if she was foundering or simply had some bad gas pain. Walking her seemed like an obvious solution to most problems, and so I did. But on our last ride, she often stopped and looked back at her left flank. I thought if I could just get her to the hill that she loved to run up, she would work that gas out and be okay. She stopped four more times before that hill, and then bless her heart, somehow found it in her to run up it. At the top, breathing hard, she stopped again and looked at her flank. She was in pain. I apologized, got off of her back, and walked her home.

Mom called a vet out, a visit we really couldn't afford, and Dr. Hayden did a belly tap, a needle draw from the abdomen to see if there was fluid where there shouldn't be fluid. When he pulled the needle out, blood gushed out of her with great force. I knew right then I was losing her, and even though I wanted to be a calm and assuring presence for her, I sobbed. She likely had a hemorrhaging tumor, the vet said.

There was no denying she was in pain. I could tell what the right thing to do was by the apologetic looks on Mom's and Dr. Hayden's faces. "I know," I said, and hugged Ruby one last time. She rested her heavy head on my shoulder. I didn't want to upset her with my grief, and so I told her thank you, thank you so much, thank you for everything, a million times thank you. I told her I loved her. And then I walked to Darrel's house like Mom had suggested while she fired up the tractor. If a horse that had been euthanized with an injection was buried on land, the neurotoxin would eventually leach out of her body and poison the earth and the water. Instead, they had to sit in a field until a rendering truck rolled through town, but no rendering trucks came out this way, the vet said. And so Dr. Hayden led Ruby into an arroyo and shot her behind the ear. I heard the shot. Then I saw the dust cloud behind Dr. Hayden's truck as he drove away, and I heard the tractor as my mom buried my precious friend. I never made it to Darrel's house. I just sat on the side of the road with my head in my hands and cried and cried and cried.

Mom didn't ask me to be tough that day. She didn't even think of asking me to help. No, she did that difficult task to spare me the experience of it. On that day she was my mommy. The day she gave me that horse and the day she helped that horse go to heaven, those were the two best days in her career as my mother. They were greatest gifts she ever gave me.

30

After I felt the dead bolt snap into the open position, I paused for only a minute before turning the handle. This winery is what had done it. This is what had sunk her. She had built it about three years ago, about the time she stopped making house payments and tax payments. I was hopeful there would be some assets in here I could liquidate as well—the crusher, the press, some barrels, and maybe even the picking and fermenting bins. If Mom hadn't been in debt, I'd keep the equipment in here to entice the next sucker who dreamed of owning a winery, but as it was, I was willing to sell anything I could get my hands on.

I pushed the door open and walked in. It was beautiful. Obviously, Mom had thought this gamble would pay off in a big way. I could see from the lengths she had gone to that she had imagined people would come all the way out here to taste and buy. I ran my hand over her beautiful wooden counter, above which a rack of wineglasses hung for tasting. Mom's capacity for positive thinking to the point of self-delusion had always driven me nuts, but looking at all of her work and care in here . . . at the pride she obviously took in this place, instead of driving me completely nuts, it mostly just broke my heart this time. It was as if she had no concept of where she was in space, no idea that she was way, way too remote for people to come all the way to sample her wine. Not only was this place a solid two hours from Santa Fe, the road usually wasn't fit for cars.

Slowly, I wandered back to her workspace where she crushed, pressed, fermented, barreled, and bottled. Except for one glass drying upside down on a towel, it was immaculate. Twenty-five barrels lined the back wall. I knocked on them. Some were empty and some were full. Along one side wall, shelves shaped like diamonds were filled to capacity with thousands of bottles of wine, each section holding a different blend and vintage—all reds because her one solar panel didn't generate enough electricity for the slow refrigerated fermentation that whites required. I pulled bottles out, examining the labels. On each was a picture of the stained-glass window in our house. "The De Vine Winery, Coalton, NM," was printed in plain black letters below it. She had different names for her different blends—"Passion," "Salvation," and "Absolution," and I had to give her credit for that. They were clever. And her labels were attractive.

I paused to count the bottles. Five sections up, twenty sections across. One hundred sections. Each section held about twenty bottles of wine. She had about two thousand bottles of wine. On the floor, the overstock sat piled high in boxes. Holy moly. If it was swill, which it probably was, each bottle could sell for ten dollars simply because it had a great label and would make a great gift. The bottle alone had surely cost my mom ten dollars. If I sold it all, that would be twenty thousand dollars—more than enough to solve my problem here. And if it wasn't swill, it could possibly sell for more.

Since I was only going to be pregnant for a few more days, I opened a bottle of "Absolution," poured a little into a glass, and swirled it around and around, allowing it to breathe. I had to know.

Since her wines were not made from the grapes of *Vitis vinifera,* the traditional European varieties, but instead made from cold-resistant hybrids, connoisseurs would always consider her wines to be inferior. I remembered one particular rant of hers out in the vineyard where she had picked up a handful of earth and smelled it. "God! This place has such great terroir! It's not fair that most of these hybrids are grown in places with shitty terroir! Most people will never know what these vines can produce . . . how great this wine can be!" My mom definitely lived in her own world. She suffered from very high self-esteem.

I sniffed deeply as I brought the glass to my lips and took a sip. Black currants, lavender, oak, earth, maybe sage. It was different from the California wines I was used to. I had to give her that—it was different. I let it sit in my mouth for a minute and swished it around. It was not overly tannic, which was something I appreciated. I never liked wines that were reminiscent of lighter fluid. With each passing second, I liked it more. It was definitely not swill. Fifteen dollars for a bottle of this wine seemed very reasonable to me.

And then for some reason, I spit the wine back out instead of swallowing it. Maybe my body knew my stomach couldn't take it. Or maybe I wasn't as fully committed to my plan on Friday as I thought I was. I kept thinking of Grandpa Luis telling me that this child belonged to everybody, that his music would touch a lot of people. I rubbed my brow, and forced myself to redirect my attention back to the task at hand.

Next, I pulled the cork on a bottle of "Passion." Cherries, blackberries, oak, roses, leather. *Yes,* I thought. It was good, very good—different and a little dangerous tasting. Well-rounded and complex. Mom had done a really nice job on that one. As wines went, this one was sexy. It seemed reasonable to ask around twenty dollars for this particular wine.

"Salvation" was an easier wine to drink, a table wine I'd call it. It was not particularly demanding or complex. Fruit first, not overly oaked, it lacked in the lower tones. "Salvation" was a ten dollar bottle of wine.

Thirty thousand dollars was the approximate value of all the wine on the shelves, plus a little more with the wine in the boxes. The very thing that sunk her could also save the day. Somehow, I had to get these bottles into restaurants and stores—fast. But I had no idea how.

31

Our first year here, Mom dried out quite a bit. We were living on a shoestring. That spring, we planted the Cab Franc, and the following winter, it died back to the roots. That bought her another year of sobriety. She learned about hybrids then, and so our second and third spring, we planted two acres of Baco Noir. It took about three years for them to reach maturity, and so with very meager harvests, Mom was mostly sober for almost two more years.

But the fall of my junior year, some of the Baco Noir had yielded fruit. The production of her grapes had timed out pretty well for her, being close to my sixteenth birthday and all. This meant that Mom had both a wine in the style of Beaujolais Nouveau, and a designated driver.

That was the same year Darrel and I had decided to try band. Neither one of us could afford instruments, and so our choices were shaped by the surplus instruments left in the band teacher's storeroom. There was a tuba, a French horn, and a trumpet, all of which were dented. Neither one of us wanted to carry a tuba home from the bus stop, and so that left Darrel with the French horn and me with the trumpet.

I won't say that I could have been a great trumpet player if only my mother had stayed in her seat during my first Christmas concert. That would be untrue. Playing the trumpet felt painful and dangerous from day one, my cheeks held to my face by muscles that I knew would one day fail. When that day came, my cheeks would herniate, maybe tear, definitely get stretch marks, and never go back to the way they were. I had seen pictures of Dizzy Gillespie, so I knew the complete destruction of my cheeks was somewhere between possible and inevitable.

And so maybe I owe my mother a great big thank-you for the traumatizing moment that inspired me to transfer out of band and take home ec instead. Sure, at the time it seemed my life was ruined, but twenty-three years later, I'd have to choose the integrity of my face over my pride at the Christmas concert of 1991. While it would be untrue to say no one remembers that now, it *is* true to say it doesn't really matter now, and that I can almost look back and see the humor or perhaps even the beauty in it. Almost. Not quite.

The grapes produced enough that my mom could begin what she had called her learning curve, and what I called her descent into her second round of alcoholism because a learning curve would mean learning something about how aging affected that particular wine, and I don't think any of those bottles lasted through the end of January. And so there I was, just five weeks into my sixteenth year of life, sitting in the second row of the Sweetwater High Beginning Band at the Christmas concert, enduring the inherent humiliation of a beginning band performance. Our performance would be followed by the regular band and then the jazz band, just in case there was any question about how bad the beginning band had been. I thought it couldn't get more embarrassing than that.

Until my mom got up during our clumsy version of "The Sound of Music" and spread her arms open wide like Julie Andrews on the mountaintop as she spun her way down the aisle to the front where she started dancing. She made hand gestures for other people to join her, but seconds ticked by and no one did. Stunned, my ability to think became impaired. I had this thought that if I got up and ran, everyone would know for sure that she was my mom, and so I was better off just remaining in my chair. Only later, after half my brain wasn't being used to read music and remember what that meant for my fingers, did I realize that there was never any question. She was white and I was the only white kid in beginning band.

Mom began to move like a child taking ballet lessons—clumsy and unrefined, but with a complete lack of awareness with regard to the discrepancy between herself and a professional ballerina. Sweeping her arms in arcs, her hands flowing behind them, she was also oblivious to my horror. When the song reached the crescendo of the next chorus, she leaped, and her denim prairie skirt rose up her legs to heights I considered indecent. A murmur of stifled chuckles rose up from the audience.

I noticed the sideways glances from my classmates. Tears of shame welled up in my eyes, but no amount of blinking kept them in for long. The moment they spilled out was the moment Grandma Anita and Grandpa Luis got up and waltzed to the music. His cowboy boots slid across the surface of the gym floor as her skirt swayed with the music. They were trying to take the focus off my mother, trying to normalize her behavior, and I loved them so much for it that I began to merely fake playing the trumpet while I pulled my long, greasy hair out of its ponytail to hide my face and cry right there on stage—ugly cry, where my nostrils flared while the rest of my face contorted in strange ways. And this was when more and more couples came to the front of the stage and danced, and when Darrel's uncle Walt approached my mom. I was terrified as I watched long, lean Uncle Walt put on his black cowboy hat and walk over to her, expecting him to imitate her, knowing no amount of mockery would shed any light on the situation for her, for the very thing she wanted was for others to join her. But instead, he took her in his arms, and led her in a nice conservative waltz. Never before had I seen or even heard about Uncle Walt making a bad situation better by being nice.

It was the year the community danced at the Christmas concert. They had so much fun, in fact, that they danced through the regular band and the jazz band as well, pushing chairs aside, turning the gymnasium floor into a dance floor. My mother was so proud of her work. In her mind, she had freed the masses from their own self-conscious oppression and limited paradigms of social appropriateness. She never apologized. Not once.

Facts are irrefutable, but truth is as malleable as clay. Truth is in the eye of the beholder. And her truth and mine could not have been further apart.

32

It had been over a week since I had done laundry in L.A., but since I wasn't wearing my L.A. clothes out here (except for my underwear, which I was about out of), it wasn't my highest priority. I had been dreading the chore because I knew it would be appropriate to wash the clothes in my mother's basket and something about that felt like erasing her. But when I had some "morning sickness" in the middle of the night last night, I had gotten some vomit on my sheets. There was no postponing my trip to the Laundromat any longer. Some things could not sit. Plus, I figured it would be good to have clean L.A. clothes to wear when I attempted to sell my mom's wine. It would help give a hip image to the brand. I still had a few hours before the interested people came to look at the livestock, so I stuffed my sheets and my other laundry into pillowcases, and set off.

I turned on the radio as I drove into town and listened to the local station, the only one we received out here, just in time to hear Mrs. White say the Apache Phrase of the Day. "*Danndei.* Sit down. *Danndei.*" She was a friend of Darrel's grandmother and sometimes had come to my high school social studies class to try to teach the language to kids before the language died. She had a very gentle demeanor and I always liked her.

She and Mrs. Velarde, my old home ec teacher, were both at the Laundromat waiting for their clothes when I walked in. Mrs. Velarde was knitting, and Mrs. White was beading a small piece of leather. I lit up when I saw them. "*Daanzho!*" I said, and to Mrs. White I added, "I just heard you on the radio!"

"Well then, *Danndei*," she said, laughing, so I set the plastic laundry basket down and took a seat next to them.

"I'm so sorry to hear your sad news," Mrs. Velarde said, and Mrs. White nodded in agreement. They were traditional, and it was traditional not to mention the names of those who had passed on, or do anything that might call them back in any way. Death was somewhat of a taboo subject but grief was a common and shared experience. It was nice, really, to be with women who knew how to express their sympathy with almost no words at all. Nonetheless, each time someone mentioned my mom directly or indirectly, I had to fight back tears.

When the moment passed, Mrs. Velarde added, "I also understand congratulations are in order." Her knitting needles clacked rhythmically.

I tried to smile but my eyes wouldn't lie. I had never been any good at hiding my feelings the way so many people here were. My face was as transparent and expressive as a face could be.

"Oh, what's wrong? Do you miss your mother?" asked Mrs. Velarde.

Mrs. White sympathetically added, "It's nice to have your mother around for your first pregnancy."

I could have just let them believe that was all, that was it, but I was never any good at lying, and I needed some motherly advice or assurance.

"My boyfriend and I broke up," I confessed. "He wanted to save money by moving out of our apartment and into his friend's closet. He just quit his job so he could be in a band."

"Oh," Mrs. White said, concerned.

Mrs. Velarde looked concerned too, and then she broke into a smile. "I've heard of people coming out of the closet but not going in."

Mrs. White laughed and then turned serious again. "You are scared to do it on your own."

I nodded.

"I see," she said.

Mrs. Velarde cast off her final row and tied the yarn. "But you're not alone," she said, taking the pastel green baby bootie she had just finished knitting, pairing it with another she had finished earlier, and then handing them to me. "I made these for you when I heard you were back in town," she explained.

And that is when I lost my battle to hold back my tears. They rubbed my back and let me cry on their shoulders and said, "Oh," and, "It will be okay."

"It really will be okay," said Mrs. White. "We women stick together."

"You will have what you need," Mrs. Velarde said with such certainty that I believed her. "Our mother, *Niigoszaan,* Mother Earth, provides for her children the way you will provide for your child. You are not alone. *Niigoszaan* will help you."

"Are you going to stay here on your mother's land?" asked Mrs. White.

I shook my head. "It looks like it will probably be foreclosed. I'm trying to save it, but it will take a miracle. And anyway, my job is out in L.A.," I answered. "That's where I can make a living."

They seemed concerned about that. "*Niigoszaan* will have a harder time providing for you in an apartment in the city," said Mrs. Velarde.

"Maybe think about it," advised Mrs. White. "Your mother wasn't rich, but she never went hungry and neither did you. It would be good if you could have her earth here. You have a community of women here. Think about it."

Their advice fell on more or less deaf ears, but their kindness sunk as deep into my bones as the September sunshine. "*Eheedn,*" I said. *Thank you.* And then I held up the booties and said, "*Eheedn,*" again.

"You remembered," said Mrs. White. "You always were very sharp."

"*Aoo, nzhugo,*" said Mrs. Velarde. *You're welcome.*

Two buzzers went off simultaneously, and the women stood to move their clothes from washing machines to the dryers. I put my mom's things into a washing machine as quickly as I could, quick so I would not think about it, added soap, inserted coins, and pressed the button.

"Did you check your pockets, Jolene?" Mrs. White asked.

Mrs. Velarde giggled. "Yes, Marian, and you?"

"I do it before I leave the house." Then Mrs. White pointed to a sign, an amused smile on her face, and read it to me. "Please remember to take bullets out of pockets before putting clothes into the dryer."

"One day Mr. Ramirez forgot," said Mrs. Velarde. "It was bad."

"It was bad?" I asked, hoping she would say more.

"It was bad," she simply repeated.

When their clothes were in the dryers and my mom's laundry was in the washer, we all returned to our chairs again. Mrs. Velarde cast on a new project on her knitting needle, and Mrs. White resumed beading. And I sat between them, leafing through a *Family Circle* magazine, looking at women who appeared so happy to be mopping floors or cleaning ovens, women with whom I shared nothing in common at all. I looked at recipes for back-to-school snacks for the whole class, at diet tips, and simple exercises I could do in order to stay attractive to my husband, and then finally, I just put the magazine down, closed my eyes, and listened to the rhythm of the machines, of Mrs. Velarde's knitting needles, of my own breathing. I felt the warmth of their arms on either side of me, the strength of women who had walked through plenty of family hardships, and I felt the truth, which was that in this moment, I already did have everything I needed. I had friends and community. I had shelter. I had a piece of earth with grapes. I had baby booties. I didn't know if all of that would be true in five minutes or five hours, five days, five months, or five years, but in this moment, it was something. It was something I could hold onto.

33

My sex talk had occurred in the book aisle of the Barkin' Basement Thrift Shop where my mom searched for cookbooks that might tell her how to make lentils that did not taste like cardboard. We had been eating a lot of them because they were a cheap source of protein, but truth be told, after six months of eating them pretty consistently, we both were growing to hate them. A few steps away, I browsed the fiction section, which seemed to be either romances or mystery thrillers. In all of that, I managed to find a book written for teen girls, a book that appeared to have a romantic storyline. As I plucked it off the shelf, Mom looked over. Apparently that was her cue.

"Allow me to do you a big favor and demystify sex and love for you." She picked a romance off the shelf and held it up for the world to see. It featured a bare-chested man holding a woman who was spilling out of the top of her dress. "This book would have you believe that at first you hate him and then your smoldering hatred becomes passionate love. If you hate somebody, Willow, chances are there is a good reason, so don't let hormones cloud your judgment, because trust me, they can and then one day when the thrill wears off, and it will, you'll wake up next to somebody that you hate."

"Noted," I said, looking around to see who else might be listening. I guessed that there were five shoppers, all women, who might be listening, but they were polite enough to pretend they weren't. I thought I saw tiny hints of smiles on two of their faces.

"I'm not going to lie. Some good foreplay with the right person is fun. But sex itself is kind of a nuisance. You kind of get squished and pounded on and oftentimes your urethra gets a little beat up causing you to feel like you have to pee all the time for the next two days even if you don't get a urinary tract infection, which is common, by the way. Movies have a way of making this look like it's fun, but in reality your legs start to feel like they're going to snap right out of their hip sockets and usually somewhere in this you get a bad chiropractic adjustment. When it's all over, you're sticky and messy and stinky, and usually not nearly as satisfied as if you had just given yourself an orgasm."

On a scale of one to ten measuring how horrified I was at this point, I'd have to say I was an eighty-seven. My mom had just said "orgasm" among other choice words for anyone within earshot to hear. "Okay, Mom, I get it," I said in hopes of getting her to stop, but she was a freight train of sexual information and there was no stopping it.

"No, Willow, you haven't begun to get it. That's not even the worst part. The worst part is when Mr. Wonderful rolls over and begins to doubt everything he said to convince you this was love so that you would be his living blow-up doll. A blow-up doll is an inflatable toy shaped like a somewhat anatomically correct woman that a lonely man can have sex with, but I digress. The thrill of the hunt will be over for him. You'll no longer be that six-point elk he would chase through the woods for days. You will be as boring as ground beef in a Styrofoam tray all wrapped in cellophane at

the grocery store. It doesn't matter that ground beef is more delicious that tough, gamey elk. It's about the hunt, not the product.
Meanwhile you'll feel invested and vulnerable. You'll be looking
for reassurance, and this will cause him to feel trapped. He will
leave you about then, all heartbroken and stinky and sticky and feeling like you have to pee all the time and needing a good trip to
the chiropractor. And if you're really unfortunate, you will be pregnant or have a sexually transmitted disease. Young men aren't capable of real love, Willow. Remember that. Young men are just
looking for a place to stick their dicks. They will say anything to
accomplish this. They will say things they don't mean. If some man
ever says the word 'forever' to you, just punch him in his lying
face."

"Okay, Mom, I'll punch him," I said, desperately hoping she
would stop.

"Good girl," she said, but she didn't stop. "These books are written for women who don't understand that they only have those
feelings of lust and longing so that our species doesn't go extinct.
Those are just instincts. They have nothing to do with rational
decision-making or what is best for you. Ignore those instincts just
as long as you can because I promise you, they are a greased skid
straight to your own personal hell on earth."

She pointed to my book and then to the book in her hand. "This
leads to this. And it's really not good for you. These books only
make you more vulnerable to being a place for a man to stick his
dick, and they will only leave you confused when he doesn't follow the script."

She paused to see if her words had taken root, and unsure,
quizzed me. "What is the only thing a man wants?" she asked.

"A place to stick his dick," I whispered, wishing I could melt
right into the ground and disappear.

She nodded. "Don't ever forget it. Don't ever, ever forget it."

I would have told you that I was far too traumatized to remember any of the wisdom she tried to impart, but now as I took her cookbooks off the shelf in the kitchen and it all came back to me, I realized that no, her words did eventually sink in. Too late, but they did.

Her intention was good. She wanted to spare me the painful experience of being used and heartbroken and pregnant—pretty much the experience I was having now. She had tried to be up-front and honest. And bless her heart because most moms would have been too uncomfortable to deliver such a soliloquy. But I wished . . . well, I wished a couple things. I wished she could have made the sex talk much, much less embarrassing to hear, and I wished I didn't carry that same shame with me today. I wished she could have told me something about real love, about good marriages, and about how to achieve that because good marriages did appear to exist for a lucky few.

Did it matter that I didn't save sex for a man who wanted to marry me? Maybe. Married women were not immune to being abandoned. Husbands left wives all the time. But maybe getting married cut a woman's chances of abandonment in half at least. It seemed to me that anytime a woman like me settled for a man who wasn't marriage material, the outcome of abandonment was certain instead of possible.

Ultimately, I hated to admit it, but my mom had been right. It appeared I had just given my future to a man who had only been looking for a place to stick his dick.

34

Linda and her husband, Buck, rolled in pulling a stock trailer, all smiles. I put on my happy face and smiled back.

"Hello!" Linda called as she stepped out of the huge red Dodge pickup with extra chrome. They clearly had money. "I can't wait to meet the goats!"

We all shook hands and then Linda showed me the soft cashmere hat she had just finished knitting on the drive up here from Los Alamos. I gave it proper admiration, and then led them to the goat pen where they handpicked their ten Cashmere goats. Linda gushed on and on about how excited she was to card and spin fine wool, and then knit all kinds of wonderful things. She had visions of knitting herself a cardigan sweater.

Buck was pretty good about hiding his excitement, but I could still see it. Making his wife so happy filled him with satisfaction. They were somewhere in their mid to late fifties, and portly in that way people are after decades of eating home-cooked meat-and-potatoes dinners together. Life had been good to them. They were sweet. I couldn't help but to study Buck and wonder if there were other men still like that in this world, men who got so much satisfaction out of making their wives happy. He was the opposite of the men in my world, the men who saw women as hindrances to their success as rock stars. I wondered if Buck had ever been sexy. Because he was so kind and generous, he was attractive, but sexy was another matter. Ian, on the other hand, was sexy, but because of his resolve to live in a closet, he was no longer attractive.

I helped rope the ten goats Linda chose and led them one by one into the stock trailer behind Buck's big, shiny truck, and then Buck gave me a money order for two grand, and we were done. As far as Mom's taxes went, I was almost two-thirds of the way there.

While I waited for the woman to arrive who was interested in Monster and the man who was going to buy two meat goats, I loaded as many cases of wine as I could into the back of my 1979 Volvo station wagon and a few more in the passenger seat. Later, I would drive down the dirt road until I had good reception, and there I'd research restaurants and wine shops in Santa Fe that seemed most likely to be interested in my mom's wine and attempt to make appointments to meet with their buyers. Tomorrow morning, I would drive to Santa Fe and do my best to make something happen. At the very least, I would be able to deliver the money from the livestock directly to the tax office as I drove through Tierra Amarilla on the two-hour drive to Santa Fe. I would accomplish at least that.

Four hours of driving. That was a lot of gas. It occurred to me that I could bring my cello and once my sales appointments or sales attempts were over, I could play in the plaza for change to offset some of the fuel costs. Every dollar counted. Every single dollar.

35

I was fourteen when the Cab Franc vines my mother had planted the year before had completely died back to the root. New shoots had sprung from the roots, but no flowers and no fruit.

That's when Mom decided to solve our problems by getting twenty Saanen milk goats, and one disgusting male she named "Hugh Hefner." At first, I was purely fascinated by them all—by the process of pregnancy and birth, but everything after that was tough. First, weaning—listening to the young goats cry out desperately for their mothers. All night, night after night, I listened to their cries.

But it was when Mom enlisted my help castrating the young males that I reached a new breaking point.

I had been eating oatmeal. Mom had a list of Top Eight Cheap and Nutritious Foods (oatmeal, rice, beans, bananas, celery, carrots, onion, and whole wheat flour) and while nearly every meal we ate was made exclusively with ingredients from this list, oatmeal was the one we ate every day without fail. I missed Cheerios. Such a simple thing. Cheerios. I missed their smell, their initial crunch, the way they absorbed the sugary milk, and the gray sugar on the bottom of my bowl. And yet as I looked out on the fruitless grapevines, I knew I should be grateful for any food at all.

"I'm going to need your help castrating goats today," Mom had said like it was no big deal.

I froze. Finally I said, "You're kidding, right?"

"You just need to hold them. I'll cut off their balls."

"You want me to hold goats while you cut their balls off?" I wondered if my mother had just met me.

"If we don't castrate the young males, their meat will get all tough."

"So what?"

"We can't have that."

"I'm not doing it."

"Yes, you are. We are in this together."

"No, we're not in this together. I am essentially being held hostage in a place I hate and now you're putting a gun to my head to help you mutilate goats. Where is the togetherness in any of that?"

Mom, unfazed, said, "On farms, kids help. That's how it goes. Step up. It's going to take both of us to keep food on the table. You like eating, don't you?"

"I want to go live with Grandma Mildred. I hate this. I hate you."

"Bummer for you. You're holding the goats."

I began to cry as I picked at my oatmeal, stalling for time, trying to think of a way to run away from this. The world outside the border of the ranch was even scarier than the world inside its borders, and time and time again, this kept me from running away.

"Come on," my mother finally said. "Enough of this. Let's just get it over with."

"No!" I shouted through sobs that were getting more hysterical.

"Knock it off. I need you to be strong."

"But I'm not strong!"

"Willow, I'm serious. Pull it together and do your part. Quit crying."

But I couldn't. And Mom, frustrated by her own set of challenges, snapped and slapped me across the face.

For a moment, we just stared at each other, neither of us quite believing how things had escalated to this point, neither of us quite understanding how the other had failed to see their needs and failed to care about them.

My mother was too angry for remorse. "Pull. It. Together," she seethed.

"I hate you," I almost whispered. "You can beat me until I'm dead and I'm still not going to help you mutilate and torture goats."

But it was as if my mother didn't hear me at all. Anger hears nothing.

Right then, Darrel riding toward our house caught my eye, and I bolted out the door and ran into his arms, crying about goat castration and my mom hitting me. He whispered that I could go hide and he would do it.

And he did. While I ran for the hills, he held the screaming goats as my mother castrated them. Even from a quarter mile away, I could hear the crying goats, and I cried and cried for them and for myself and for all the meek who suffered in this cruel, cruel world at the hands of heartless people.

36

I figured I had just a few days to figure out "The Sound of Music," and so that night I took my cello out of its case, tuned it up, and began to experiment with the melody. In the process, I made some interesting mistakes—mistakes that had the potential to become their own melodies. I paused to dig through the boxes I had packed until I found blank tab paper so I could write down the little riffs that I might want to work with later.

Then I plugged away at the melody, writing it down as I went. I played it over and over, making the same little mistakes in the same places, pausing to replay those musical phrases over and over and over until my fingers remembered.

Each time I played the song through, I remembered that performance. The first time I played it through, my emotional memory of it was acute and painful, as if it was happening now. The next time I played it, it felt as if it had just happened yesterday. But as I continued playing the song over and over, it was as if each time I floated a little further above my sixteen-year-old self, higher and higher until finally I was watching the memory from the ceiling of the gym. I could see my sixteen-year-old self and feel deep compassion for her. But from the ceiling, I could see something true and earnest in my mother in her uninhibited state. I could see how proud she was of me, how moved she was by our music even though it was so bad. She heard the best in it. She heard the best in me. This is what overtook her.

The cello has always had the power to transform my heart. The top of the body rested right there on my chest. Right there the sound waves went right in. I imagined those sound waves massaging my heart, softening it.

Each time I played the song through, I knew a little deeper that there was nothing really to forgive my mother for. There had been times when she had been so clueless, so self-absorbed that she hadn't been able to hear the music around her at all, but that night with her inhibitions down, she heard it and it was beautiful to her. My almost-forty-year-old self could appreciate that.

37

By my mid-thirties, I'd had eight lovers or boyfriends or romantic disasters—whatever you wanted to call them. It was my elderly friend Betty that pointed out to me that all of them had had an alcohol problem. She'd only met four of them, but each week I'd have Sunday dinner with her. The irony was that since so many of her friends were in the wine business, we nearly always discussed this over a glass of wine. But see, that was the difference. *A* glass of wine. One. I was fortunate that I didn't crave more and more the way so many people did, but instead was happy with one glass.

Betty would ask how things were going with the man in my life or the man most recently out of my life and I'd tell. One day after my eighth had broken it off with me because I couldn't *just accept him,* Betty simply had said, "You want all of these damaged people to stop drinking to prove that you're worth that sacrifice, but Willow, what you don't seem to get is that it's not about you at all. It's much larger than you, sweetie. You've got to let it go. You're not going to get resolution with your mom by dating these bozos." Bozos.

I didn't know for sure whether she was right-on about me trying to get resolution with my mom this way or whether these bozos had simply felt like home to me, but still, enough of what she had said resonated. I desperately wanted to be freed of this pattern, and so I went home. I went home with the intention of seeing whether I could somehow slay this dragon. It was the fall before I met Ian, and the grapes were ready for harvest. So I spent the four days of my long weekend helping Mom pick, crush, press, and barrel. And though I kept waiting for the opportunity to hash something out, instead the hard work seemed to diffuse my frustration at my own life and the forces that had created it, and I tempered into acceptance.

But on the last night, Mom had some celebratory drinks and then wanted to go for a walk with me. As we walked past the stock pond, now mostly dried out except for some shallow water in the middle and gooey clay mud around the edges, Mom exclaimed, "Let's see if that's quicksand!" and went running out there, followed by the dogs who had the good sense to stop at the edge. This was something that drove me nuts about her. She'd done the same thing years ago as she ran out onto the stock pond in the middle of winter one year, shouting, "Let's see if the ice breaks!" Another time she hit the brakes on an icy road, sending us into a slide just to see if that was black ice. To her, this level of abandon was fun. To me, it was terrifying.

It was not quicksand, but she fell anyway and the sticky mud held her down. She struggled to get up, but her arms slid out from under her and her face went down into the muddy water. Alarmed, the dogs barked and I ran toward her, but she managed to get her face up before I reached her. She sat back on her knees, laughing, then held up her arms, growled, and roared, "I'm the creature from the stock pond! I bet you didn't know all these years that something so scary lurked out here!"

"By that do you mean your alcoholism?" I had snapped. "Yeah,

I was well aware that lurked out here. Jesus, Mom, you're going to do something stupid like this one day and die." But she didn't hear that last part. She was deeply hurt by the zinger I'd launched about her alcoholism.

"I am not an alcoholic," she said.

"Really," I replied, not buying it.

"Alcoholics cannot manage their lives. I manage my life just fine. Was there ever a day I failed to take care of your basic needs? No. All of my animals are cared for every day too. So don't give me any shit about this, Willow. I work hard, and if I want to have a little wine, I think I'm entitled to it."

I said nothing. It seemed pointless. She wasn't going to change.

But then she added, "I wish I had a different relationship with you—one where I felt safe." She paused for a minute to let her words soak in, but I wasn't thinking about anything I did to make her feel *unsafe*. I was thinking about how all of my alcoholic exes always spun things around so they were the victim. They were all so attached to their victim-ness, to the *poor me* stories they told themselves. "You villainize me in your memory and I don't know why because all I ever did was love you. You don't remember things correctly. You twist everything."

"Let me get this straight. I'm the one who is always sober . . ." I began, "but *my* memory is the one that is twisted? And you're the one that danced in front of my whole school at my Christmas concert but *you* wish you felt safe with *me*? *You* want a different relationship? Well, get in line, Mom, because I want something different too. I want a sober mom."

She started to cry. It was the first time I had seen my mom cry like that, and neither of us knew what to do. We each took a few steps toward the house, but then she turned to me and said, "I want to be left alone."

And so I walked back to the house a little ways behind her, hoping that if she tripped or something I could get to her fast enough. An amorphous cloud in the sky took the shape of a horse and I had wondered what it meant. Maybe it meant something about freedom. Maybe it meant something about the fragility of a herd animal running solo. Maybe it had something to do with power. I couldn't make sense of it the way I normally did with clouds. In retrospect, maybe it was telling me about the fatal accident she would have one day.

Mom was in the shower when I came into the house so I simply went to my room, shut my door, and packed. Through the door, I could hear her go into her room and shut her door as well.

I expected that the truth would set me free, but instead, it felt like punching a wall. *What are the rules?* I wondered. Isn't truth an important part of any authentic relationship? So why didn't speaking it feel any better than not speaking it?

The answer came to me immediately. *Because I hadn't spoken it in love.* I had spoken it in anger.

This wasn't how I wanted to leave things. But I also couldn't resolve anything right then. Nothing can be resolved when someone is drunk. I wished Mom hadn't been emotionally incapacitated in that moment, but she was. And so I imagined the winds of heaven blowing between us, clearing out the negativity.

And the next morning, we did our best to pretend it hadn't happened, but our best wasn't very good. We spent three hours in the pickup in the uncomfortable aftermath of the truth not told in love, trying to make things appear normal in the small ways we knew how. And when we said good-bye, she didn't hug me and I didn't hug her. Serious damage had been done.

That was the last time I saw her.

Surely the truth was a really important part of any authentic relationship. But so was acceptance, and I hadn't known how to balance those two things. I still didn't.

Maybe the only thing a person could really do in this life was just accept everyone exactly as they were and just love them the best she could.

38

"I'll be right back," my mother had said, darting into a shop that sold local goods. She had come to Santa Fe to explore the possibility of different stores carrying her wine, which I thought was a little premature being that we had only brought in a tiny harvest that year and at the very least, it needed two years to age. I found my mother's pitches embarrassing, and asked whether I could wander around the plaza instead.

At first, I heard only fragments of a few isolated notes, but something about their tone called to me, so I jumped off of the sidewalk where local Pueblo and Navajo artists sat on lawn chairs and sold their silver and turquoise jewelry on colorful blankets. Normally, I paused to admire the "needlepoint" style of the Zuni jewelers, appreciating the delicateness of their work. But on that day, I looked in the other direction, toward the plaza. In the sky above, the trees that grew there were two small clouds shaped like songbirds. I had not encountered clouds like those before, but had a vague positive feeling about them.

I crossed the street and entered the park, following the rich sound of the music. At the American Indian War Memorial sat a woman playing the cello, notes as low and sad as I felt. Each one resonated deep in my chest. The notes had been strung together so that the sadness had transformed into something beautiful and whole, something that made sense, something people could hear and understand. All of it welled up inside of me—my fears, my frustrations, my endless loneliness in all the places Darrel did not inhabit . . . even the degree of loneliness I still felt when I was with him. The notes stretched on like each interminable day I had experienced since moving to Monero . . . slow . . . slow like wind erosion. The cello was like one lonely voice. Finally, my soul had a song. I felt my face involuntarily contort, and knowing that something was happening that I could not stop, I closed my eyes so the world could not see my soul break open. Still, I felt the chill of tears streaking down my cheeks in the slight breeze.

"Well, that was fast," my mother's discouraged voice said from behind me. "They don't have a liquor license so they can't sell wine."

Of course. Of course my mother would talk over the music of my soul so that it could not be heard. Of course she would show no reverence for its beauty, or give any indication that she'd heard it at all. I would have expected nothing less. I turned and looked at her, opening my eyes, revealing my experience.

"What's wrong?" she asked, concerned.

"Nothing. I just love this music," I answered.

After a short pause, Mom asked, "Are you premenstrual?"

I shook my head in exasperation. "Jesus, Mom. Are you that incapable of listening?"

I turned my attention back to the cellist, whose long gray hair seemed to reflect what I heard in the music—wisdom . . . something very natural and organic . . . notes that stretched much further than most people would dare to take them . . . patience. Well-worn cowboy boots poked out of a black tiered skirt on either side of her cello.

As the song ended, the cellist stared back at me.

"All right, let's go," my mother said, turning to leave.

"Excuse me," said the cellist.

"Mom," I said, reaching out to touch her arm. "She's talking to you."

My mother turned back around.

"I want to teach her," the cellist said, looking at me.

"Oh, do you have a music school? I'm sorry, I can't afford it."

"No," the cellist replied. "I'm the principal cellist in the Santa Fe Symphony. I make my living doing that. She would be my only student."

"I'm sorry. I don't have any extra money. We barely get by."

The cellist asked, "Well, what do you have?"

"Goat cheese," my mother answered defiantly.

"I like goat cheese," said the cellist. "Do you also have goat manure?"

"I have plenty of goat manure," replied Mom.

"I need compost for new garden beds I'm building."

"I can't afford to buy her a cello."

"I have an old one she can borrow for as long as she needs to."

"I couldn't afford the gas to bring her all the way down here each week."

"I will meet you halfway. In Abiquiu, at Ghost Ranch where Georgia O'Keeffe lived. Every two weeks for sixteen ounces of goat cheese and a Hefty bag of goat manure."

I could not believe my ears. A miracle was being offered to me. I held my breath, suspense paralyzing me. I couldn't remember ever wanting anything so badly in my life. I looked at my mother, pleading with my eyes but not daring to say a word.

After a long pause, my mother finally said, "Deal."

"Monday, high noon, starting next week," said the cellist.

"Thank you!" I gushed.

She held out her hand, and I shook it. "I'm Marta Sandoval," said my new teacher, "and I'm going to change your life."

39

My usual rough start the next day was even rougher because my legs were so sore from horseback riding that I could barely walk. I cried out with every step as I made my way to the bathroom, alarming the dogs.

As he had the last two mornings, Mr. Lickers attempted to lick my feet while I threw up, while Slobber Dog began frantically looking for things to bring me—a pair of socks, a throw pillow, a boot, as if one of these things would cure what ailed me. I had meant to remember to shut the bathroom door behind me this morning, but I forgot. When my stomach was empty, I reached up for a bath towel, laid it on the bathroom floor, and lay on it for a minute while I waited for my strength to return. I wrapped a corner around my feet to block Mr. Lickers, who then turned his attention onto himself, giving himself a bath. The throw pillow Slobber Dog had brought me did feel nice under my head at that point.

Slobber Dog lay down near my head, where she stared at me. I stared back. She looked mostly blue heeler, but she had inherited a stockier body, and a blockier face from a pit bull ancestor, as well as fur that was mostly the color of honey. She had patches of gray and white on her chest and face, and the very tip of her tail was white too. I had never seen a dog quite like her. The more I studied her, the more I found her exquisitely beautiful. Perhaps it was the intelligent and caring look in her eyes.

I shifted my glance down toward Mr. Lickers, who stopped licking his leg for a minute to look back. His coat was dappled blue-gray with many small black spots and larger black patches. In places, some tan or white showed through. He had a white star on his chest that reminded me of a sheriff's badge, which seemed fitting given the way he policed the ranch. His two front feet were white as well, reminding me of men's dress shoes from the seventies or maybe golf shoes. His mostly black face had a white stripe running up his nose. Older now, he was gray around his muzzle. Satisfied I had no requests of him, he resumed licking his leg.

When I felt strong enough to get off of the bathroom floor, I made some mint tea, and then sat in my favorite sunny windowsill where I ate some soda crackers and massaged my legs. *I missed this sunny spot,* I found myself thinking. When I was a teenager, one or both cats always joined me up here. Grandma had sent me a lap desk for a birthday present one year, so I could sit in this windowsill and write her letters. I loved this spot. Mom and I had each had our windows. This one had been mine.

After I fed the animals, showered, and applied makeup for the first time in nearly a week, I searched through my box of clothes for something professional and hip—jeans, boots, and an off-white silk shirt. In keeping with the De Vine Winery theme, I accessorized with a collection of beads and crosses. However, my jeans were already unpleasantly tight, so I traded them out for a soft, stretchy, gray, crocheted skirt. The silk shirt didn't look right with that, so I traded that out for a plain white T-shirt. I now looked more hip than professional, but things were pretty casual out in these parts, so I went with it. It was time to go get 'em—to make something happen. I put my cello on top of the cases of wine and set off.

My phone calls to prospective wine buyers yesterday afternoon had not gone especially well. I had found only two wine stores, one bar, and one bistro that had been reluctantly willing to meet with me today, but I maintained a good attitude anyway. Realistically, four meetings were all I had time for today. Nearly all of the restaurants explained that they had already printed their wine menu and didn't want to have to print another. The bistro, however, used a big chalkboard, so they had the ability to change, and they prided themselves on featuring local meats, produce, cheeses, wines, and beers. I was hopeful about that one.

I couldn't remember taking this drive when it wasn't to have a cello lesson. I associated every mile of this road with Marta. Over the years, I had lost touch with her, as unthinkable as that was. L.A. life was so fast. I always meant to write back, but it seemed I was always on my way to somewhere. Months went by between letters and then years, and then one day I guess I didn't answer at all. Part of it was that I was busy, but to be honest, the other part of it was that I thought Marta had always hoped I would create something new and radical musically if I wasn't going to play in a symphony. She never said that directly. That was my own projection. But still, I felt a little like maybe I'd let her down. Furthermore, a lot of my studio work involved playing the same three notes over and over for the duration of a song. Technically, it wasn't anything to be proud of, and I didn't want to say that I had wasted this gift Marta had given me. I couldn't bring myself to lie and I couldn't bring myself to tell the truth. That left silence as my only option. But I owed her more than that, and more importantly, I loved her more than that. Last year I had sent her a Christmas card, but it had been returned. When the urgency of my circumstances passed, I figured

I should make an effort to find her. I hoped I wasn't too late. After all, who knew if Marta was even still alive? She had been older than my mom by about ten years, so she wouldn't be terribly old, but still, things happened. People died. It happened all the time. Clearly.

In Abiquiu, just after Ghost Ranch where Georgia O'Keeffe had lived and painted, I stopped at Bode's Market on the way because I had always loved that store. From the street, it looked just like a gas-station convenience store, and indeed they did have some groceries that were typical of that, but in other ways it was anything but typical. It was bigger than most, which was good because it contained its own deli, books, an assortment of New Mexico souvenirs, outdoor gear, and a wall of silly novelty gifts like Jesus flashlights and votive candles with saints that may or may not have been fake, and vintage-style metal lunch boxes. But most importantly, they had a huge wine section and sometimes they even had wine tastings here—definitely much hipper than a typical gas station general store. Not surprisingly, the wine buyer wasn't in, but I left a bottle of each kind of wine along with a note for her in hopes that something might happen there later. Mom's wine would be a good fit there. I bought a blueberry muffin for the road and carried on.

Santa Fe was like a really confusing maze, with most roads coming out from the center of town in small segments interrupted by other city blocks. It didn't help that so many landmarks were the same shade of sienna adobe and looked similar. Eventually, though, I found the first wine store. It didn't take much convincing. The buyer had local wines featured in their own section, and was happy about possibly offering another choice. After tasting the three wines, he wrote me a $1,080 check for two cases of each.

The other wine store was on the far end of town near Whole Foods and Trader Joe's. Whole Foods and Trader Joe's . . . I wondered what it took to get into those. I left a bottle of each of my mom's wines along with a note at those stores as well even though it was a long shot. At this point, I had six bottles of wine to lose and everything to gain.

The second wine store was smaller with less shelf space. The buyer there only wanted Passion and Absolution. I couldn't say I blamed him. Salvation really wasn't that great. He bought two cases of each and wrote me a check for $840.

I couldn't believe it! After just two stops, I had made almost two thousand dollars!

My next two stops were in the plaza, where parking was something close to impossible. My first appointment at the bistro was in less than a half hour, but my second appointment at the bar wasn't until the early afternoon. I'd have time to play some music in the plaza in between and hopefully earn a little money for my travels.

After parking under some trees near the government buildings, I packed three bottles of wine and a bottle opener in a canvas bag and walked toward the cathedral, stopping to appreciate its beauty for a moment. I paused and settled back into this place that was both familiar and wildly exotic to me. It did feel like returning home.

The wine buyer at the Taste of Santa Fe Bistro was bubbly and wildly enthusiastic about my mom's wine—especially after she tasted it. Like the last store, she opted out of Salvation, but said she would really push the others. She bought four cases of each. One thousand, six hundred, eighty dollars just like that. Holy smokes! I was up to three thousand, six hundred dollars . . . plus the two thousand, three hundred dollars from the livestock . . . Mentally, I added it up. Five thousand, nine hundred dollars. Enough to pay off my mom's taxes with . . . two thousand seven hundred and something left over to put toward paying off her cremation. The huge debt owed for the De Vine Winery and Goat Ranch still loomed, but there was reason to hope. The enthusiasm of the bistro's buyer and her confidence in my mom's product was really affirming, and gave me heart.

I returned to my car, drove to the alley behind the bistro, delivered their order, and then found a new parking place in the shade, which was much more difficult than it sounded. I put my cello on my back and walked on toward the Palace of the Governors where the Native American artists sold their wares on the sidewalk. There, I paused to admire the jewelry. I especially liked the silver buttons on hair ties that made a plain ponytail look fancier. One with a piece of black onyx in the middle caught my eye. It looked just like the one my mom had given me for my eighteenth birthday, the one that had fallen out of my hair at a big outdoor concert once without me knowing it until it was too late, much to my devastation. I knew what a big deal it had been for my mother to buy me something new and silver. Although it wouldn't be the same, exactly, I really wanted to replace it, so even though I was in no position to splurge twenty dollars on something that frivolous, I did it anyway.

And that's when I heard a cellist playing something contemporary—maybe even something original—nothing like the classical pieces Marta used to play. My heart dropped as I realized my niche had been taken and I would not be earning any gas money in the next hour or two. Still, always curious about what other musicians were doing—especially someone doing something contemporary with the cello of all instruments, I continued toward the source of the music.

I wound my way around businesspeople on lunch break and large families enjoying themselves until at last I reached the center. And there on the bench that encircled the memorial, sat an old woman with long silver hair and cowboy boots that peeked out from under a long printed prairie skirt, pulling a bow over the strings of a beautiful blond cello. Marta! Her fingers had become somewhat gnarled and knotted, leaving me to wonder whether the slow piece she was playing had been chosen to accommodate an ability that was changing. Even if that was the case, the quality of her notes and tone was nothing short of magnificent. Her eyes were closed as she played and I wondered whether she was just making up the music as she went along.

Marta. I had found her. Here. Here where it all began. For the first time in decades, music moved me to tears as I listened. Had it been the cello I had loved or Marta, this kindred spirit? The answer was both. The cello alone had not been enough. I had needed Marta to bring it to life and keep it alive.

When Marta opened her eyes, there I was with tears streaming down my face, just as I had so many years ago. "It's you," she said. She carefully set down her beloved cello and embraced me for the longest time. It felt like coming home.

"May I join you?" I asked, and when she nodded, I took my cello out of its case, took a seat next to her on the bench, and tuned my instrument. Then with a big smile, I gave Martha a nod. "Ready."

She smiled back at me, blinked back tears, and looked to the sky as if she was saying thank you to God for this incredible moment.

I listened intently, and then joined in, creating my own harmonious part. After a few minutes, Marta slowed her notes down, drawing each one out like a flower opening and blooming. She wanted me to make up a melody and run with it. She wanted to give me a chance to shine, or perhaps this was simply the way Marta asked: Who are you today? What is the song in your heart? Are you happy or are you sad? Do you keep things simple or are you very busy? Marta had often said that whatever a person created was created from their essence, be it a song or their life. Either would be an expression of essentially the same thing. And so I took care in answering, beginning with a melody hopeful and exuberant, then slowing, slowing, slowing down into something more discordant, something that sounded like the same loneliness I'd experienced when I had first moved to New Mexico, but even lonelier because I had realized after I moved to L.A. that it wasn't location—it was me. Finally, with no particular rhythm, I played discordant notes, down, down, down, down past getting dumped by Ian, down past discovering I was pregnant, lower, lower, lower, down to the grief I felt about the loss of my mom and the probable foreclosure of her estate. I played all the way down to this moment in my life.

Marta's face was pained as she played harmonies, a gesture of extreme and genuine empathy. She felt my despair, and she staggered her notes so that it seemed nothing was coming together, so that the music did not flow.

Yes, I nodded, and then I held a low C so long and resonant that surely humpback whales off the coast of California heard and breached. It was Marta's turn to take the melody. She started by playing parts of classical pieces I recognized well enough to add a sporadic note. And then the music became very modern. It flowed. I imagined a yoga class listening to it while they balanced and stretched. Had Marta quit the symphony and all things traditional? Had she discovered yoga or adopted a new paradigm with which to approach life? Then Marta's music took on a shy, vulnerable quality as she played a happy tune which built and built and built into something glorious and euphoric. Had Marta fallen in love?

Both of us slowed now, and looked at one another. It was time to play about this moment. I played six happy notes and then held a long one while Marta played six happy notes. Back and forth we went like chatter: I'm so happy to see you! I'm so happy to see you too! Can you believe what a miracle this moment is? I know—it is nothing short of a glorious miracle! This moment makes me think my life had significance! This moment makes me believe I have not been forsaken by God! You have grown up to be lovely and soulful! You are my touchstone, my rock, my anchor, my inspiration. All of these things were said clearly and unmistakably with music.

When at last, our conversation stopped, listeners erupted into applause. Both of us seemed almost alarmed by this. It felt as if I had walked out of a confession booth and realized everyone in line had heard my private story.

It was by far the most authentic music I had made in my life. There had been times I had wondered whether I was even capable of creating anything truly authentic, whether I had anything at all to say to the world with my music, or whether all I could do anymore was play it safe and collect a paycheck. But in Marta's presence, I had found it or rediscovered it—my authentic "voice."

"We have to create music together," Marta said.

She was right.

40

The day Ian was hired, I could hardly breathe. I was taken with him from the moment he stepped through the door. Despite the fact his hair was reddish, he didn't have that delicate china-doll appearance that most red-haired men had to me. He was tan from all the time he spent in the surf break off Hermosa Beach and all of him—his skin, his hair, his aura just seemed golden to me. Maybe I knew he was my destiny or maybe I was just superficial. It's easy to get confused.

He was the kind of guy who didn't have to try hard to be cool. In a plain white T-shirt, jeans, and blue Converse low-tops, he was sexy. Lean and muscular from drumming and surfing, I found myself more sympathetic to every man who had ever talked to my chest instead of my face, because I wanted to talk to Ian's chest too. When Ross introduced us all, I forced myself to look up at his face, noticing that his tan skin was darker than his sun-bleached eyebrows, making them almost invisible.

It seemed to me that Ian held my gaze longer than he had with the other studio musicians when he said hello and repeated my name, but it might have simply been that time slowed down the same way it does when a person has a car accident or witnesses a violent crime.

But I think what really stole my heart was the way he drummed, heavy on the toms, light on the snare and symbols. It reminded me of the songs that floated through the New Mexico air, especially in summer when families held feasts to celebrate their maturing girls. Sometimes Darrel and I rode all the way to Sweetwater on our horses and then up onto a long ridge that eventually reached the tall mesa above town. We didn't ride all the way up it though—just far enough that we could hear all the songs floating above town like butterflies, drum beats like flapping wings.

That's what Ian's drumming reminded me of. At the end of the day when I commented about his drumming style, he explained that his very first LP was *Genesis,* as if that explained everything, which it did.

I was on my way out the door when he told me his friends' band was playing at a club down that street later on, and asked me if I wanted to go. He could have asked me if I wanted to go get a root canal or a pap smear and I would have said yes. I'm pretty sure I would have followed him anywhere.

He seemed not quite excited, not quite surprised, but something close. He seemed pleased. So when he offered to make me dinner that night, I could not adhere to my rule about staying out of the dwellings of men I barely knew. I could not resist.

I followed him to his place seven blocks away, lost in conversation about music and musical influences, about passion and musical moments so profoundly beautiful that nothing ever looked or sounded the same afterward, about hopes and dreams and goals. He just *got* me. And I *got* him. How long had it been since anyone had just simply *gotten* me? That level of understanding was rare, and that level of understanding combined with that insane level of sexual chemistry had to be destiny, right? That's what I had thought.

He led me up the staircase to his apartment, and as he unlocked the door, I remember thinking that when I walked through it, I would be walking into a new era of my life. I knew it that fast.

Ian made grilled chicken with mango salsa, and a green salad with papaya dressing. It was not pretentious food, but definitely made with ingredients not found on my mother's list of Top Ten Cheap and Nutritious Foods. The novelty of food not found on that list has never worn off for me. I loved mangos. I loved papayas. I fell in love with that dinner he made me. It did not help my judgment.

He plugged speakers into his computer and played me songs with great drums that had influenced him along the way—songs from Led Zeppelin, Cheap Trick, Lenny Kravitz, and Joe Strummer—both during and after The Clash, Grant Lee Buffalo, and Rusted Root. He handed me an extra pair of drumsticks and we drummed along on empty boxes he had used in his recent move, until we were both sweaty and laughing.

It seemed like the thing I had been waiting for. It really seemed that way.

Only now did I look back and realize I never played him the songs that had influenced me—songs from Damien Rice, Nirvana, Ben Howard, Matthew Schoening, and Zoë Keating. No, we stayed in his world. We never visited mine.

That night at the bar we drank enough that when he walked me home and kissed me good night, we could both pretend that it hadn't meant as much as it had—to me, anyway. But as time went on, and we kept making dinner together and going out to listen to bands, it made less sense to live alone and more sense to live together.

And so, four or five months later, I climbed the stairwell with my first box of things. I looked at the door once more—old, creaky, painted chocolate brown, a round brass doorknob embellished with tiny engravings of flowers around the edge—and I knew that when I walked through that door, I'd be starting an even more profound chapter of my life, the chapter where love deepens with commitment and commitment deepens with love, the chapter where two people agree to create their future together. That is what I had thought.

But looking back, I just felt stupid. I was a buddy before I moved in and I was a buddy after I moved in. Here is what I did not know then: people vary widely in their capacity for love and in their capacity to love, and his capacity was far, far smaller than mine. And nothing I could have done would have changed that.

41

Driving home from Santa Fe, I felt something like cautious hope.

Marta and I had played a few more songs and then gone out for lunch with the money in her case and caught up. I told her about Mom and about her last request, and Marta said she wanted to honor the woman who had shared her daughter and her goat cheese, and come to the service and play "The Sound of Music" with me. I was deeply touched.

And I told her about getting to record with Steven Silver next month, and I could see that she was proud of me—even if I wasn't always.

She was composing music to tell the story of Georgia O'Keeffe's life and had visions of playing it at Ghost Ranch next summer. She wanted to know whether I was back for good, whether I'd be around, whether I wanted to compose and perform with her. She had no idea how much I wanted to work with her. But I couldn't be in Los Angeles and Santa Fe at the same time and I certainly couldn't afford to travel back and forth. Still, before I had to leave for my last appointment, she gave me her phone number in case I had time to play music with her again.

As I walked back to my car with my cello on my back, Ian's words haunted me. *You don't want to be a shitty studio cellist your whole life* . . . Marta was giving me the opportunity to do more, to be more, to maybe create something of significance. Argh! There I went dreaming again. And anyway, what was I doing listening to someone who lived in a closet? Why would I give his opinions any power at all? Making a living as a musician was something to be proud of—regardless of in what capacity.

The manager of the bar I met with after lunch agreed to try a case of Salvation and see how it sold. If people liked it, the owner said, they would offer our other blends as well. I wasn't all that optimistic about that happening. Salvation wasn't going to make a lot of people fall in love with the De Vine Winery, but still I couldn't call it a loss. It was one hundred and twenty more dollars I had in which to solve problems with. I supposed Salvation would be a fun wine to order though—just to say it out loud, so who knew. Maybe it would do better than I thought.

I still had twenty-nine days left. With just four more days like this one, I could pay off Mom's winery and ranch. I could. It did not seem like quite the long shot it had seemed this morning. While more opportunities in Santa Fe might exist, I could still try Taos, Farmington, and maybe Los Alamos. I could even make a trip all the way down to Albuquerque. I could go north to Pagosa Springs and Durango.

It was possible. And then I had to ask myself, if I knew that I would be able to save and sell Mom's estate, would I go through with the procedure on Friday? The price I could get for her place could buy a lot of child care. It would certainly make my circumstances significantly less desperate.

I needed more time to figure it out, to see whether this momentum and reason to hope would last.

After I stopped in Tierra Amarilla to pay Mom's taxes on my way back through, I called the clinic and postponed. Or canceled. I wasn't sure which.

42

The night before my grandma drove me back over the mountains, I had heard her voice downstairs, so I slinked down to the landing to see who she was talking to. She held a phone receiver in her hand, which made more sense that time of night.

"It doesn't really matter who should apologize," she said sternly into the phone. "You're the adult and you're losing her . . . She's hurting, and you need to show her you care." It was obviously Dad. As I crept back up the stairs, I heard my grandmother continue, "Well, since she flies out early the morning after, we'll be staying at the Double Tree in Tukwila tomorrow night and I intend to take her next door to Farrell's in Southcenter Mall for dinner at six, so you know where to find us . . ."

I poured myself a hot bath so that I had reason to lock a door and keep it locked, and I sat in the steamy water sifting through all of my memories. Suddenly, my relationship with Dad seemed like something that I had thought was durable clear plastic but was really fragile glass . . . and like I hadn't realized it until the glass shattered and it was irreparably broken. It wasn't just him losing me anymore.

I was losing him too. And now that I knew Grandma had reached out and put the ball in his court, I was no longer the rejecter. It was now within his power to out-and-out reject me. For the first time, I wasn't just grieving or confused or mad. I was scared.

The next night, I didn't pretend to be surprised when Grandma asked for a table for three or four. I didn't pretend to be happy or pretend to be mad.

And to my dad's credit, he showed, and without his new, improved family. He held his arms open and I walked into them and whispered that I was sorry. He whispered that he was too. I held on an extra moment while I fought back my tears. I didn't want to cry in front of him, and I sure didn't want to cry in a restaurant.

We sat down and made small talk about the things my grandmother and I had done, and about my trip home the next day. We ate our burgers, and we ate our sundaes, talking about everything except what I think we both wanted to know. Are we still dad and daughter?

When dinner was over and the waitress had returned with the change from our check, we all stood to leave, and I hugged my dad again. "Are you still my dad?" I whispered.

"I will always be your dad," he whispered back.

"Everything has changed."

"I know. It's hard," he replied.

Neither of us knew how to do any better.

Finally he said, "Well, kiddo, have a decent trip tomorrow and write me when you get home. I'll be waiting to hear from you."

I said okay and put on my brave face and walked away from him for the next year or even longer even though really, I just wanted to go back to Ocean Shores, just him and me, and fly kites again like we did before Hailey was born.

———

Mom and I were waiting for my baggage at the Albuquerque airport when I flat-out asked her, "Why did you and Dad ever get
married? I mean, you're both so different from each other."

"Yeah, that was the whole point," she replied.

My suitcase tumbled down the chute to the carousel and I stepped
forward to grab it. As we walked toward the parking lot together,
she said, "I was young and working at a bar in Spokane. Every
Monday your dad would come in, watch football with his friends
from the bank, and ask me out, and every Monday I declined. Until
about a month after I had slept with the guitarist of some really
good band that had played there the month before. Leonard or
Larry or maybe it was Barry. He was really good."

"In bed or at music?" I asked.

"Well, both, but I meant music. The whole band was. Paisley
Velvet or Velvet Paisley . . . I don't know—something like that. I
thought he was my soul mate and he thought I was a one-night
stand. Broke my heart. And so after that, vanilla started looked
much more appetizing to me, so the next time your dad asked me
out, I said yes. I knew he would treat me well, and I wouldn't end
up feeling used and heartbroken."

"Did you ever love him?"

"Well . . . sure. Maybe not in the way a person hopes to be
loved . . . But he was a good man and a good father to you and I
loved him for that. I'm just sorry you didn't get five more years with
him before it all went to shit."

And in that moment, I forgave Dad for leaving mom to actually
experience real love. I had to stop thinking of Ms. Nunnalee as this
floozy that broke up my family. She was his do-over, his real love.
And I didn't really know where that put me.

In that moment, I could see that Mom had missed out on true
love too. And now that she lived way out in the middle of nowhere
in New Mexico, she was unlikely to find it and it was unlikely to

find her. Dad got a do-over with true love, but Mom didn't. I suppose that softened me toward her a little bit. "I love you," I had said to her in that moment, just because I was sure she hadn't heard it in a long time.

43

I went across the street to the little general store and bought a card with a picture of the Chama Narrow Gauge Train on it, took it to the picnic table outside, and wrote:

Dear Dad,

I don't know exactly what to say because I know your history and Mom's is complicated, but since there was a time when you loved her and were her family, I thought you should know she died last week in a horse accident. I'm back at her place in New Mexico handling her affairs the best I can. Anyway, I just thought you should know.

Love, Willow

I sealed, addressed, and stamped the envelope, and slipped it into the blue mail bin outside of the store. It would have been more appropriate to call him, I knew, but I wasn't up for hearing the degree to which he might not care. Inside of me there was still a little girl who wanted her whole family back the way it was in the seventies.

The rest of the week was a blur of phone calls, driving, and selling wine. On Thursday, I visited two bars and a wine store Taos and I returned to Abiquiu when the wine buyer at Bode's called back, selling just a little more than two thousand dollars' worth of wine, and on Friday, I traveled to Pagosa and Durango. I had no takers in Pagosa, but two restaurants and a store in Durango bought nearly three thousand dollars' worth of wine. Minus the three thousand for Mom's cremation, I now had about four thousand toward paying off her home. Since the judge had added on interest and attorney's fees, that left me with about seven thousand more to go. It wouldn't be easy, but it was possible.

On Sunday, someone was coming to look at the bay horse. That would be seven to nine hundred dollars more.

I was cautiously hopeful I could sell enough wine in Los Alamos, Farmington, and Albuquerque in the next week to pay off the rest of the debt. With any luck, I would be out of New Mexico before the end of the week. I still did not know what I was going to do with the dogs or the rest of the livestock. The livestock I could probably give away, but the dogs?

In preparation for departing, I had called Paula and taken her up on her offer to help me clean out Mom's house on Saturday— tomorrow. I was in high gear, getting it done. Staying focused on just the most critical tasks kept me thinking about the less urgent and more difficult things. Accomplishing these tasks gave me a sense of control. I needed that.

And then on my way home from Durango late Friday afternoon, the funeral home in Pagosa called to tell me Mom's ashes were ready to pick up. Suddenly it was real again. I tried to stay in my achievement mind as I parked in front of the funeral home, went inside, settled up, and left with an urn full of what remained of my mother. My mother. The arms that had held me when I was a baby—they were in this vessel. The lap I crawled into was in this vessel. The hands that bathed me and braided my hair—in the vessel. Confronted with the physicality of her death, it was so real to me in a way that it hadn't been an hour before.

I put the heavy urn on my lap as I drove back to her house. I blinked extra hard or extra much throughout the trip to see the road better. I really was in no condition to drive, but by the grace of God, whatever that was, I made it home, where I threw hay in the different pastures and then took my mom's urn and crawled into her bed with it.

People survived this. Rationally I knew this. I knew people lost their parents every day. I just couldn't comprehend it. I couldn't comprehend that many people feeling this badly. Add to that people going through any loss—a death or a breakup, and suddenly the world just seemed intolerable. There was too much pain in it. Way too much pain in it.

I rolled over on my side and pulled the covers over my head like a hood, with only my face sticking out so I could breathe. If my mother's smell could be detected, I was too congested to smell it. Mr. Lickers jumped up behind me and lay down, while Slobber Dog lay in front of me. Sandwiched between them, if I closed my eyes, I could almost believe my mom was there with her arm wrapped around me.

I was in such a rush to get back to my job in Los Angeles that I kept forgetting about the part where Ian would eventually discover I was pregnant. Was I going to hand my baby over to a man who lived in a closet so he could take him to band rehearsal, expose him to whatever the guys were smoking that day, and to decibels of noise that were far too much for his little ears? No, I was not. So what was I going to do? Move to Austin? Move to Nashville? Neither of those music cities cranked out the volume of cello-enhanced music that we did in L.A. What if I returned and denied the baby was his? God, I didn't want to do that. I didn't want to act like a *Jerry*

Springer Show guest with lots of drama around the identity of this child's father. I wanted better for my child. Was I being too over-protective and overcontrolling? Did Ian deserve a chance to be not just a father but an actual dad to this child? Could I count on him not to break this child's heart the way he had broken mine?

I could always go back to L.A. and then leave once I started to show. It would put food in my mouth while Mom's estate sold. That part made sense. I could endure Los Angeles for four more months. But wait. It was going to be difficult to find a place to live for just four months and by the time I paid for that, my job might not put food in my mouth. Maybe it didn't make sense.

It wasn't a moment when I had a lot in me.

During my sophomore year, Grandma Anita had been working on some beautiful new moccasins. Day after day she beaded the top with red roses, and when she finished those, she began to fill in the background with pearly white beads, until she received news that her favorite aunt had died. She put the moccasin project away as I watched and said, "We Apaches believe you must never create when you are grieving or depressed or feeling negative in any way. Your energy gets into the things you create."

I always thought of that when I had to work with some angry or whiney music someone wrote. It made sense to me that music and all forms of art, really, could be cathartic, but then it never made sense to me why anyone seeking to move through something would keep it. That seemed no different to me than keeping vomit after throwing up. The same arguments could be made about its worth. I mean, it could have been argued that everyone vomits and therefore everyone relates to vomit, and that it might actually help someone else vomit. Other artists didn't seem to be trying to work through anything, but instead appeared to be reveling in their whiny victim-thinking. The Apaches had it right on this one, I had thought for years. White people didn't realize that they solidified negativity by creating when they were in that space. Why would anyone want artifacts of sadness or anger? Why would anyone want to keep their vomit, or stranger still, sell it to someone else?

But anyway, this made me think about the wisdom of creating a new life while I was grieving and heartbroken and so very terrified. What kind of new life could it possibly be when created with those feelings? Maybe that was reason enough to go back to my old life in Los Angeles. It was going to take energy and radiance for good opportunities to be magnetically attracted to me in a new place.

I didn't know. I didn't know what I was going to do. I just knew I couldn't be still. There was no pause button for life—no matter how much I wished there was. Since I didn't know, the best course of action seemed to simply be prepared for anything, and I was already on track for that.

Tomorrow Paula and I would clean all of this personal stuff out of here and get the house ready for the next owner. This week I had made it a commercially viable winery thereby increasing its value by at least another 25 percent at least. It could work. Next week sometime, I would return to L.A. unless I came up with a new plan before then because I needed to work and I had a job there.

I couldn't imagine what exactly my future might look like, but I closed my eyes anyway. Maybe tomorrow the clouds would tell me something. At the moment, starting a new life seemed overwhelming. I pulled the covers over my head a little more, as if I could block out my confusion with them. I wanted my mom to tell me everything was going to be okay. I listened, but all I heard was the breathing of dogs.

44

I don't much remember those times when as a very little girl I crawled into bed with my parents. I know I did, but I don't really remember.

What I do remember is when Mom and I would drive over the mountains to Grandma and Grandpa's house where we would stay in my mom's old room, the two of us snuggled up together in a twin bed. Grandma would make us Ovaltine and let us drink it in bed—even after we had brushed our teeth, and then she'd sit in a chair next to my side of the bed and read a story my mom had loved when she was a girl. During the extra good parts, I'd look behind me at my mom and see the recognition and the happiness in her eyes, as if the book itself was a dear old friend and this was a glorious reunion.

Grandma passed away in the middle of my senior year. While Mom was shopping at the big grocery store in Pagosa after we got the news, I took three dollars of my precious savings and I bought Ovaltine. That night and the next, before Mom returned to Leavenworth for the service, I made us both mugs of Ovaltine, and brought them here into her room where we drank them in this bed. Nobody read us a story. We took turns looking at each other as if to ask, "Are we going to be okay?" and we took turns looking back at the other as if to answer, "Yes. We are going to be okay." When we thought the other was asleep, we cried as quietly as we could, and when we were aware of the other person's tears, we put our arms around her. This bed was our soft place.

45

Like every day, my morning started off rough with morning sickness, but this morning was even worse waking up with my mom's ashes on the pillow next to me in her bed. In the light of day, I could recognize this wasn't especially good for my mental health. I got myself out of that bed, and on with my morning. There was so much to do, and getting it done was the only thing that gave me hope.

When I felt better, I pushed the furniture in the living room to the side, rolled up the rug, and started making the to-keep pile and the to-give-away pile. The to-throw-away pile was a big black trash bag by the front door. I was determined to take no prisoners since I had been there six nights. It was already Saturday and time to get down to business—no matter how difficult.

When I looked out the window where I could see the end of the driveway, I noticed Darrel had left me a pile of boxes when he had come home from his shift at the nursing home early that morning. I drove down to the end of the driveway and picked them up, brought them back to the house, and began to fill them with books, CDs, and old vinyl LPs. I wasn't sure what pile to put them in. I looked at the pillows in the windowsills and decided to keep them there for the time being. It seemed smart to keep the kitchen clear and full of everything I needed to prepare food, so I left that alone for the time being too.

In the hall closet, I found, among other things, a hat fashioned out of white goat fur. It was a simple hat—more or less a big cylinder, reminiscent of something she might have seen in *Doctor Zhivago,* a movie she had loved. My mom had clearly made the hat. Inside, it appeared it had been sewn with white unwaxed dental floss. At first, I wondered if I had known the goat from whom this fur had come, but then I put it on. It was soft and warm. Upon closer inspection, she had made matching mitts to go with it. I couldn't quite call them mittens. They were more like oven mitts. Big. Almost as big, it seemed to me, as a baseball mitt. And almost as thick too. But on those days and nights when it got to be ten below, I could not deny these would be the tools for the job. Although I didn't expect I'd be living somewhere with temperatures like that, they were too funny, too quirky, too *Mom* to discard. I expected I would have to keep them.

She had a small collection of coats that had been out of date for decades—a long red plaid wool coat, a denim jacket, a puffy ski coat that was short enough that there would surely be back exposure every time the wearer bent over, a long down coat that reminded me of wearing something that belonged on a bed, her well-worn brown Carhartt coat, and a pair of Carhartt coveralls for those very cold days. I put on the red plaid wool coat. It didn't smell like Mom. She probably never wore it. I liked it and put it in the to-keep pile. I kept the Carhartt jacket and overalls in the closet to wear during the week when I did chores. The other coats could go.

She had rubber boots, cowboy boots, running shoes that looked too clean to have been worn much, a pair of factory-made moccasins that had fringe around the ankle, and a pair of Birkenstocks that she surely found at a thrift store. I examined the well-worn sandals and hoped they had been new or close to new when they had been donated, because otherwise that situation would have simply been gross. I put them in the big trash bag, and the running shoes in the to-give-away pile. I tried on the cowboy boots and the moccasins. I might have kept them, but they were too snug. I kept the rubber boots in the closet for wearing in the barn.

My closet seemed like the easiest thing to attack next because lord knew there was nothing in there I wanted. Inside was a treasure trove of ugly garments that other people had discarded for a reason. But as I took each piece out, it seemed I remembered something about my mom.

This blue acrylic sweater, for instance. I had picked it off the rack at the secondhand store and held it up to my chest to check the length and look for holes. Mom happened to look over at just that moment from the other side of the circular rack next to me. "That color is beautiful with your eyes," she had said, but it was the way she had looked at me that I really remembered. It was almost as if she was seeing me for the first time in a long time and noticing how I had grown, noticing the emerging beauty I sure did not see. She had looked at me with such love in that moment, and I remember looking back at her, at her blue eyes, the ones she had given to me, and for this brief moment I felt the beauty in me she saw. Or at the very least, I had been able to believe I had beautiful blue eyes.

And these jeans that were not Levi's like I had wanted. I'd had an idea when I had found them on the boys' rack and tried them on about how I could taper the legs by running them through the sewing machine. I cut off the very bottom hem and let them denim turn to fringe. And then I embroidered some subtle patterns into the back pocket and added a few small seed beads. Pleased with the result, I had modeled them for my mom.

"Cool!" she had said, and I could tell she was sincere. "You are so artistic and clever." What I could appreciate now perhaps even more than I did then was that she had really meant it. To this day, I still had the confidence to buy an article of clothing at a second-hand store and turn it into some idea or another I'd had about what I wanted to wear.

This black tiered prairie skirt. "Timeless," my mom had said. "Very New Mexico. Georgia O'Keeffe had one just like it." It went without saying Mom and I loved everything Georgia O'Keeffe had done, and the fact she had lived less than an hour away from where we did caused her to become something like our patron saint of independent-free-spirit-artistic-feminist living. I paused and looked at two poster prints of Georgia O'Keeffe paintings that Mom had managed to find and had given me for birthdays.

And now, only after living in Los Angeles, in that city that seemed to always be striving to shrink women, making them smaller and smaller, making the acceptable spectrum of behaviors and appearances smaller and smaller, was I able to open my eyes and see this Georgia O'Keeffe country, this place where a woman could run through the sage barefoot, wild and free, unseen and not judged, the sole evaluator of her beauty and worth. And I understood on a deeper level what my mother had wanted for me.

I was cleaning out my dresser drawers when I heard Paula's tires in the driveway. I had been noticing that my clothes were folded more neatly than I had ever folded clothes in my life, and I imagined my mom slowly and carefully folding them and putting them away after I had gone. Surely she had grieved. I hadn't thought too much about that at the time. I had been too busy figuring out how to survive on my own. But now in this stillness when I was dealing with what she had left behind, I could picture her here dealing with what I had left behind.

As I walked out to greet Paula, I put everything in the give-away pile, knowing that these days a lot of old clothes were ground up to make stuffing for furniture and things like that. I wouldn't have wished those clothes on anyone.

Paula paused for just a moment after she stepped out of her truck. She looked at the house and took a big breath. Her expression seemed to say, "We will get through this," and I found that reassuring, because I wasn't sure I would've alone. And I knew she loved my mother as much as I did and that, combined with the fact she had done this for her own mother gave me confidence that she would have the reverence this task required.

"Here we go," I said, my dread causing the words to come out heavy like lead.

"Here we go," she repeated. This wasn't going to be easy for her either.

Inside, she tried on Mom's cowboy boots and her moccasins. They fit, so she put them by the door. It shouldn't have mattered, but nonetheless it pleased me that she wanted these things.

I carried a big box into Mom's room and opened her closet doors. I took one piece out of her closet at a time and together we considered it and shared our own memories of Mom that it triggered. Sometimes Paula nodded and then reached out. I would hand her whatever was in my hand and she would hold it up against her body and consider it further. Slowly we folded clothes and put them in the large box—a blazer with padded shoulders from the late eighties, a long narrow denim skirt with a high slit from the early nineties, a shirt that needed ironing but hadn't been ironed since we moved here—clothes my mother never wore, but for whatever reason left her feeling prepared for any occasion, no matter how unlikely.

We went through her belts and her purses, through her drawers of socks and underwear, T-shirts and overalls, a bathing suit with elastic that crumbled when I stretched it, a pair of cutoff Levi's for a hot day. We filled another box and a big trash bag. Then we went through her jewelry box, weeding out cheap junk from the seventies and eighties—gigantic colorful earrings I couldn't believe she had ever worn, a thick gold chain, a long strand of plastic pearls. And we admired the good pieces, pieces that might have been gifts from my dad, pieces that might have been my grandmother's. A strand of pearls, a pearl bracelet, and a set of pearl earrings. A diamond engagement ring. A gold ring with a possible sapphire in it—we weren't sure. Earrings that might have been diamonds or might have been cubic zirconium. A pair of Black Hills Gold earrings and a matching ring with leaves in three shades of gold—a silvery shade, a brassier shade, and a classic gold color. A beautiful opal ring that I fell in love with right away and slipped on my finger. These treasures I put back in her wooden box lined with velvet and engraved with flowers and I carried them out to my to-keep pile.

I picked up the books in the pile next to her bed.

"Except for the one about wine making, those are the books we read in our short-attention-span book club," said Paula.

"Short-attention-span book club?"

"You don't have to read prior to the meeting. We just read a short story or essay at the meeting and discuss."

"I love it," I said, and flipped through her copy of *Woman Hollering Creek,* and a piece of paper fell out. "Thanks for last night.— R," it read. "Who's R?" I asked Paula, showing her the note.

"Oh, Ramon. He's this dirtbag sheriff that came out here after Señor Clackers gored that fugitive. He wooed her and brought over his girlfriend's pet goat to get bred by your mom's male goat. She didn't know he had a girlfriend and promptly left that goat tied up to the sheriff's headquarters in Tierra Amarilla with a sign around its neck telling him to eff off."

"She never got to experience the kind of love I wished for her."

"No, she never did," said Paula. "But mostly she was happy here anyway."

"I want to crawl in her bed one more time," I said, and did. I crawled right into the side where she slept, disturbing all of the wrinkles that her body had left behind, and I rested my head on her pillow.

"Can I join you?" asked Paula. She was sad too.

"Sure," I said.

So she crawled into the other side of my mom's bed and curled up to face me. "We did a good job today," she said, tears slipping out of her eyes like they slipped out of mine.

"She would have been proud of us for doing what we had to do," I said.

"Yeah," Paula agreed. "She would have."

"Thank you," I said.

"It was an honor," she replied.

I pointed to the urn on the nightstand. "I picked them up yesterday." I fell apart just saying it.

I could see it impacted Paula similarly. And I could see her question.

"Tomorrow some people are coming out to look at livestock. Monday I'm going to go to Albuquerque . . . How about Tuesday?"

"Tuesday is fine. I'll tell the others." She gave me a little smile. "Your mom would be mighty proud of you, you know—getting her wine into stores and restaurants. I don't know for sure why she never did it. She said it was too difficult to leave the ranch—she had milking. And she said she didn't want to give forty percent to whatever business was going to do her distribution for her. But I think maybe she was afraid people would reject her wine, and after she put so much into it, I think that was a position she just couldn't put herself in. I could be wrong."

I wanted so badly to talk to Paula about this pregnancy. I needed my mom to tell me whether this was a moment to be pragmatic or whether this was a moment to have faith that everything would work out. Paula was the closest thing I had to her. "I need some advice," I told her.

"Yeah?"

"I'm pregnant. It wasn't planned. My boyfriend dumped me the day I drove out here. He's broke and would be of no help financially and he's selfish so he would be of no help emotionally or logistically either. I'm broke as well. That was the main reason I made an appointment scheduled for yesterday to have an abortion, but I canceled it or postponed it . . . I'm not sure which. When I started to believe I might be able to save this farm, sell it, and have enough money to solve some problems, I needed time to reexamine my reasons for doing whatever I decide to do. But you know, this place is unlikely to sell quickly. I need a job. I have one in L.A.—one where I actually get to record with Steven Silver next month so I absolutely have to go back for that. But if I return and stay there more than four months, eventually our mutual friends will see my growing belly and tell Ian, the father. He'll have rights and my life will revolve around them. Worse, this child's rights will. I don't want to have to hand this baby over to my ex. I was thinking about moving to a new music city. I still am. But landing in a new place with no job or place to live . . . I don't know how fast things would work out or what I'd do in the meantime. And I know this is really selfish, but I'm worried that no man will ever love me again . . . or at least not for a long time, because babies really complicate new relationships, you know? I'm worried that being a single mother will be really, really lonely in that way. And if I can't go to bars after work and listen to the latest bands, will I fall out of the musician scene? A lot of networking happens there. Will I lose all my friends? I'm worried I'm not strong enough to endure it. I just . . . um . . . I just can't seem to get clarity about any of it."

Paula didn't speak right away, and her pause made me nervous. Maybe she was very pro-life and I had just picked the wrong person to help me weigh it all.

"Do you think I'm a bad person for considering terminating this pregnancy?"

She shook her head. "No. I was just thinking about what is left of my friend, you know? This is Monica's grandchild. It makes me sad he might never exist, and it makes me sad that if he will, Monica will never know him. I was seeing it through my biased eyes. So I was quiet for a moment because that's not what you need. You don't need my stuff, my grief, my attachment. You need someone to help you listen to your own inner voice."

But maybe what she had said was what I had needed to hear to get clarity. She was right. This baby was part of my mom, and I wanted to keep that. "I think maybe you just did. I hadn't thought about it that way."

"You're going to keep him?" She smiled hopefully. *Him.* She had obviously heard what Grandpa Vigil had predicted.

I nodded. "But make no mistake. I'm terrified."

"I would be too. Willow, I'm not you, so take this for what it's worth, because we clearly want different things out of life. I just mean I chose to live here and you chose to leave here. But if I were you, I would save this place and then I would stay—at least for the first several years. You have me and the Vigils here. We're not going to let anything happen to you or your baby. You have a home here, with room for a child to run. And although it's not your career of choice, you have a winery here that is now getting regional distribution and becoming financially viable. If you change professions and run the winery, you don't have to put your baby in day care. When you have to make trips to the city to sell wine, I'll take him.

To a large degree, this land can feed you. You know that. Maybe we can get you one of those geodesic-dome greenhouses they make up in Pagosa so you could extend your growing season and have plenty of vegetables. I know none of that is the same as music, and I know music means a lot to you. If you stay, you can decide if and when to tell the father. And when you're done raising your child, or at least further along in the process, you can always return to being a full-time musician."

All of those things bounced around in my mind like Ping-Pong balls in a lottery machine. I couldn't focus on one long enough to really think anything through, but one small thought was an obvious roadblock. "I don't know how to blend her wines."

"I do," she said. "I used to hang out with your mom when she was working her magic in there. She has a book of notes hidden."

"You know what's in Passion?"

"I know what's in Passion."

"She did a really nice job on that wine."

Paula rolled over onto her back and folded her hands behind her head. "Yeah. She did."

"Thanks for your advice," I said. She had made some good points, but I was still too attached to my L.A. musician lifestyle to see my options clearly.

"It wasn't really advice, Willow. Again, no one knows what's right for another person. It was just my random thoughts about what would be right for me in that situation. That's all."

"It was useful to get out of my own head and get feedback from another person."

"You're going to be okay, you know—no matter where you decide to live."

46

Two years ago or so, I had received the sad news that my elderly friend Betty had passed. She had been my dear friend who had taken me in when I had first moved to Los Angeles and felt so overwhelmed and so lost. I made the mistake of thinking going out with Ian to listen to a new band at a club the night I received the news would be better than wallowing in sadness. We stayed out too late, and consequently by the time I crawled into bed, I had already gone to Cuckooville. Maybe that is too harsh. Let's just say my resilience was long gone. I started thinking about what a good friend Betty had been, feeling regretful that I hadn't made time to go over to her apartment in the assisted-living facility where she had moved seven years prior, and I couldn't hold back my tears any longer. I was facing away from Ian on my side, knowing he wasn't really a dependable source of comfort, and so I was surprised when I felt his hand on my back. In retrospect, maybe my crying shook the bed or maybe I was louder than I thought and he figured comforting me might be the fastest way to get me to fall asleep so he could fall asleep.

Seeing what I wanted to see, I turned over, rested my head on his chest, and gratefully let him hold me.

But after a minute, I felt one arm lift off of me, and then I saw the telltale glow of a cell phone light shining on the wall. "You're texting?" I asked.

"No, I'm playing a video game."

"Nice," I said, getting up.

Ian had tried to hang on with his free hand. "No, Willow," he said as if I was stupid and oversensitive. "Come on. Don't be like that."

I walked to the bathroom, locked the door behind me, lit a candle, and drew a hot bath. Sitting down, I hugged myself. The hot water embraced me. I submerged myself deeper into it and cried as quietly as I could, and when I was done crying, I sat cross-legged sideways in the tub, leaned forward to rest my forehead on a towel on the side, and let the steam clear my sinuses. I stayed in until I was sure he was asleep and then I slipped into bed beside him. He did not roll over and hold me. If he came out of sleep at all, he hid it well.

Money was not the only way Ian had been miserly.

47

After Paula drove away with a horse trailer full of things to take to the thrift store, I walked over to Señor Clackers' fence, rested my arms on top of it, and wondered whether he would live out the rest of his days at Darrel's or in fact here.

I figured he must have been getting close to twenty—ancient for a bull. He had been rather fiery back when Mom had first brought him home, a sleek, black, rippling mass of muscle pacing the perimeter of his enclosure, snorting at everyone, pawing at the ground, and waving his long pointed horns as if to say, "I am about to mess you up!" And just five years ago or so he did mess up Ray Kovash, thank God. What a nut. Kovash had been driving through the rez when a cop attempted to pull him over for having a taillight out. There ensued a high-speed chase that ended out here in Monero Canyon. Ray had reached into the back of his van and pulled out just a few pieces of his extensive high-powered arsenal and then shot at the cops who had pulled into the canyon behind him. He managed to sneak out of there, probably in an arroyo, and for five days a large-scale manhunt was on. The cops discovered the rest of his high-powered arsenal cache in his van and a background check revealed that he belonged to an online group that hated cops and intended to go to war with them.

Mom claimed she wasn't afraid of him because Kovash hated cops, not her. She thought he probably had come to her property because he desperately needed water. She wrote me a letter about how the dogs began acting weird, and then the goats. She sat outside in the dark and listened, and at some point heard bullet shells hitting the gravel. Maybe his gun had jammed—I don't know. I can't think of any reason why Kovash hadn't shot Señor Clackers when he heard him running toward him. It appeared as though Kovash had been running away from the bull when Señor Clackers gored him in the back. Mom said from where she was it appeared that Kovash was impaled and stuck to the bull's head until Señor Clackers scraped him off on a fence post and then crushed him under his hooves. The sheriff had deputized the bull.

While everyone made a big to-do over what a hero he was, my mom wrote about Señor Clackers having a traumatic past, about how she thought he'd had a flashback much like the flashbacks the men in her generation had sometimes after returning from Vietnam. And she saw this event as unfortunate and traumatizing for the bull. When I read her letter detailing all of this, mostly I was struck that while she'd had little or no problem traumatizing me by throwing me into a new school where I didn't belong and then had ideas about making me castrate goats with her, the bull was an entirely different matter. The bull, for some reason, deserved the compassion that I hadn't.

For weeks, Mom reported an unsettling number of looky-loos coming out to gawk at him, which stressed him further. For a while, she put Monster the llama in with the bull so he could spit big green loogies on anyone who thought about getting too close. Eventually the looky-loos went away, and Monero Canyon returned to peace.

There was no denying Señor Clackers had protected my mom well. He had been a good friend. And there was no denying my mother had loved him. She must have loved him from the moment she had stolen him to have taken the risks involved with that. I always thought she would eventually tell me that story, but I would never know the details now.

"Hola, Senor," I said to the bull who lumbered slowly my way. He reached his nose over the fence as if he knew this was the side of the pasture where the good people were, or the people with food as the case may have been. I went to the barn and returned with two flakes of hay—two slices of a bale about as thick as my hand was wide—in my arms. I dropped them over the fence and then sat near him as he ate. He looked at me with one large eye, and seemed far too gentle to have ever killed anyone.

The dogs began to bark and so I looked over to see Darrel galloping up the driveway on his horse. "Hey," I said, standing up to greet him.

"Hay is for horses," he said with mock seriousness. I could tell that something was up though. "Grandma needs you tomorrow at three."

"Oh? Is she okay?"

"Yeah, she just needs you tomorrow at three."

I squinted my eyes. "Does she need help?"

"Something like that."

"But you can't help her?"

"I'll be at work. Plus, it's a woman thing."

"Okay. That should work. I have some people coming out to look at livestock tomorrow, but they should be gone by then."

I was puzzled. But before I could ask more questions, Darrel said, "I got a postcard from Seattle from Quentin today. He wrote it a week ago. He said he was taking the train back here on Thursday and that it would take two days if the train was on schedule! That means he could be here tonight!" He exhaled nervously. "I'm kind of freaking out."

"Whoa," I said.

"I wonder if I should drive down to Santa Fe and see if I can find him at the train station. I know he'll need to hitchhike to get back here, but I don't know what train he's on and . . ." Darrel paused. "I know it's stupid, but I don't want to look too eager."

"Did he say anything else?" I asked.

"He said he doesn't expect things to be the same. He doesn't expect me to feel the same. He doesn't feel like the same person, and he knows we'll have to go through the process of getting to know each other again." Darrel bit his lip.

"Well," I said while I thought about it, "that actually seems really respectful."

"What if after seeing the world, I'm not enough for him anymore?"

I sort of shrugged and said, "What if after seeing the world, he's even more acutely aware of what a gem you are?"

He nodded slightly as he breathed in.

"I think if he felt you weren't enough for him anymore, he wouldn't have shown any interest in going through the getting-to-know-you process again."

Darrel smiled gratefully. "Yeah," he said, convinced of a better scenario than he had been imagining.

"How nerve-wracking to wonder when and where he's going to show up."

Darrel nodded. "I have to go to work in an hour. I've got the night shift tonight. He might be sleeping on the couch or the bed when I get home tomorrow morning. Do you think I should leave a note?"

I shook my head. "I don't know."

"I am *really* nervous," he said.

I stood next to his horse and patted Darrel's leg. "It's going to be okay. There's even reason to believe it will go well, but whatever happens, it's going to be okay."

He smiled appreciatively and then his expression shifted and he hesitated.

"What?" I asked.

"I want to be an uncle to your baby. I know you're figuring out a lot of things, but I just want you to know, I really want to be an uncle to your baby."

I put a hand on my heart as it melted. "Oh," I said as I felt the tears begin to rise. "Darrel, you can't say those things to me when I'm this emotional," I joked.

But Darrel was serious. "It's important you know."

I rested my cheek on his leg like a faithful dog, and then gave it one more pat before I stepped back.

"Okay, I have to go take a shower before my shift. No one wants a nurse that smells like horse."

"I love you, Darrel," I said, wishing my love was enough to cocoon him and keep him safe from any more heartbreak.

"I love you too," he replied, and I could tell he wished the same.

48

In my memory, the moment was in slow motion. We all had thrown our caps in the air, hugged our neighbors, and then spilled out into the aisles to meet our friends and family. My mom was near the top of the bleachers and was sober enough to make it down without falling, but unlikely to make it all the way down soon in the thick crowd, so I had time to hug Darrel first, which I couldn't wait to do. After all, Darrel was the reason I had made it to gradation, and making it to graduation had been a huge accomplishment.

He was not difficult to find in the crowd, towering above everyone else and taking up the space of two people. He was looking in the other direction, and so I shouted, "Piggyback!" and ran up behind him, jumping on his back, and then I kissed his cheek. "We made it! It's over!"

And only then did I see what Darrel had been looking at. Quentin, who had sat next to me in Algebra III all that year and helped me beyond measure, had been approaching Darrel, but I watched as the resolve on his face turned to heartbreak, and he turned and ran. All of a sudden, I thought of all the times Quentin had asked me questions about Darrel, or all the times Darrel had asked me questions about Quentin. I had never put two and two together. But I felt Darrel deflate under me and knew the expression on his face had to be the same as Quentin's.

"Oh, no," I said, resting my cheek on Darrel's shoulder as I slid off his back. "I'll fix this." I took off running after Quentin, who bolted through the back door—the one that took him directly to the packed parking lot.

I stood in the doorway looking for him, scanning in all directions for any part of any person who might appear to be running away. Seeing nothing, I race-walked through the aisles in the shoes my grandma had bought me on my visit last summer. They had a little heel, which I still hadn't learned to walk in, so running was definitely clumsy and precarious. My heart sank more and more as I realized Quentin surely must have gone by now. And then someone inside a red 1978 Honda Civic with a yellow passenger-side door caught my eye. Quentin.

I opened the passenger-side door much to his horror and slid in. "He's like a brother to me," I said. "I'm like a sister to him. He likes boys."

Quentin smiled through his tears. "Really? I mean, I thought so, but . . ."

"He likes you. I didn't realize it until just a minute ago."

Quentin looked at me as if he didn't dare believe something he wanted so much was true.

I touched his arm. "Everything is okay. Nothing is broken."

"I told my parents I was gay before graduation tonight."

I let that sink in, and noticed two duffel bags, a school backpack, and a box in his backseat.

"I can't go back," he said with remarkable calmness. "They've disowned me."

"I'd invite you to stay at my house, but I don't know whether my mom will be drinking later. I'm leaving for L.A. tomorrow, so it seems likely that things could blow up," I said.

"I understand," Quentin replied. "I figured I could go ahead and move to Albuquerque. Darrel is going to go to UNM too, right?"

"Yeah," I said.

He smiled. "It will work out," he said optimistically.

"Darrel is probably worried that his chances with you were just ruined. Are you ready to go back in there now or do you need a minute?"

"I'm ready," he replied.

"Okay," I said and squeezed his hand before I got out of the car.

When I returned to the gym, Mom was congratulating Darrel. He looked over her at Quentin hopefully. I gave him the okay sign and he smiled.

The next morning, Quentin and Darrel rode out on horses to say good-bye to me as I put my final things in my car. It was reasonable to assume he had stayed with Darrel at the Vigils', but I didn't ask. To a great extent, it was none of my business. It certainly wasn't my mom's business, and she was standing right there.

Darrel and I didn't know how to say good-bye to each other—and certainly not with an audience. And I didn't know how to say good-bye to my mother either, despite all the reasons it should have been easy.

It was a moment when honesty would have been overwhelming, and so we all held back as we hugged and said I love you and I'll miss you. We looked at our shoes instead of each other, knowing we would break if we actually looked in each other's eyes. I got into my car either too soon or too late—I couldn't tell. I could only tell the timing felt clumsy and awkward. The small toot of my horn as I drove down the driveway sounded far too happy for how

I really felt. All those years I spent wishing for this very moment, and here it was. It was nothing like I dreamed it would be. In the rearview mirror, I saw my mom wipe her eyes, and Darrel pat her shoulder while Quentin held the horses. I saw my dogs pace back and forth in front of my mother, agitated by her emotional state. I saw a place with wide open spaces I would never live in again, and land with which I was familiar.

But I had talked about it so long that I could not change my mind now. I turned the wheel, pressed down on the gas pedal, and drove toward the highway that would take me far away. I looked back over my shoulder once, concerned about leaving my mother there all alone, and comforted that Darrel had Quentin.

And when my tires hit the pavement, I took a deep breath and looked at the cello in the passenger seat. It was time to make Marta proud, time to look forward instead of back. But still, I couldn't help but look back. For hundreds of miles, I looked back.

49

I probably shouldn't have been climbing a ladder with a cello on my back all alone in the middle of nowhere at night, but I really wanted to play on the roof under the stars like I used to do. The roof had been my sanctuary. And on this night, a waxing moon poked out from behind some clouds that seemed to be coming from the eastern horizon, barely blocking out any of the millions and millions of stars above.

Once on the roof, I paused for a moment to look at those scattered clouds. They didn't really look like anything to me. "Barnacles" popped into my mind. I supposed the clouds looked like barnacles. Maybe that's what they were intended to be, or maybe I was grasping.

Barnacles stick. Barnacles stay. Or barnacles stick themselves to something that is moving and go with it—a boat, or maybe a whale. And so, if the message was barnacles, it wasn't very helpful.

I took my cello out of its case and opted to sit on the new wooden chair up there instead of my travel stool all folded up in the case. Then, still looking at the sky, I began to practice "The Sound of

Music" without reading the music I had so diligently written down a few nights ago.

I practiced that until it was effortless and smooth, and then I began to experiment with the little riffs I had liked, building on one as I thought about my baby . . . It was so strange to even think those two words—"my baby" . . . building and building until those few notes grew into a song. A few cells become a baby. A few notes become a song. The song itself, although it had no words, was just that, I supposed—a song about becoming something. It was a wish and a lullaby. I would call it Happy Growing.

I don't know where songs come from. Sometimes they seem to come right out of the ether. Sometimes I entertained the idea that they were presents given to us from heaven, little energetic entities that come to us through us, not unlike the souls of children I supposed.

I played it again and again and again, solidifying it in my somatic memory, but still resolute to write it down when I went back inside. Wherever songs came from—whether from heaven or my own imagination, I knew that this song was a gift to my baby. I knew I would play it for him one day.

I thought about Darrel's words: *This almost didn't happen for you,* and they sunk in a little deeper. As I little by little let go of all of my ideas of how I thought my life would be or even my ideas of who I thought I was, I had tiny moments when I realized he was right and that I was lucky. Those moments didn't last long before I spun into anxiety, but when they did occur, they felt like truth.

I played my lullaby again, imagining the sound waves going into my body and tickling that baby.

50

In March of my senior year, my final scholarship rejection letter had come. It didn't matter that I'd been accepted into both New Mexico State and the University of New Mexico—I couldn't afford to go to either of them without a scholarship, and music scholarships were hard to come by and extremely competitive. Marta had encouraged me to apply to some music programs in Nebraska, Wyoming, and the Dakotas—places where there would have been less competition, and I could see in retrospect that I should have done that. At the time, all I could think of was that every application was a lot of work when I was already overloaded with homework and chores. Mom and I had planted another acre of cold-hardy hybrids. An acre was roughly the size of a football field. With pickaxes, we dug countless holes in that rocky, hard clay soil, so I had been justifiably very tired.

Also, I had been a little snob who had been unable to get excited about living in any of those quiet, out-of-the-way places that I had actually considered to be a step down from where I was. But as I read the last rejection letter, my fate sank like a stone in my stomach.

"Well?" Mom paused in my doorway as she walked back from the closet where she had just dropped off another bowl of milk to curdle.

I shook my head.

"Oh," she said, disappointed.

The way things had been left after my last visit with Dad had left me feeling like I wasn't entitled to any help with college from him, but regardless, the Enumclaw First National Bank where dad had been assistant manager had just merged with Bank of America, and he was out of a job. Even if he wanted to help, I knew it wasn't within his ability now.

As if I hadn't already been envious enough of the culture and heritage of my Apache neighbors, I soon realized that any native kids who wanted to go to college would have financial assistance from the tribe. Since the Cesteros had oil on their land, they were richer than many tribes and could help their youth like that. Darrel had his college plans in place, and was excited to go.

It was a long, quiet drive to Santa Fe with Mom for my cello lesson later that afternoon, with our disappointment and our sense of failure sinking in. I would have liked to have been a more competitive candidate, someone people believed in, but I wasn't. And I knew Mom would have liked to have been able to afford to send me to college whether or not I received scholarships, but she couldn't. I think she probably knew that the farmwork had affected the efforts I had put into creating a future involving college. Our hearts were heavy. I could feel it. It wasn't just me.

Cello was the only thing I loved—the only thing I wanted to do for the rest of my life. And now it was a dead end. A person didn't just waltz into paid symphony positions. A person had to study hard and practice diligently to get those opportunities. Marta had told me that.

Marta. She had invested so much in me. She was wrong to have believed in me. It turned out that I had been a huge waste of her time. I couldn't imagine telling her and I couldn't imagine not telling her.

When Mom pulled up to her house, I sat for an extra five seconds before getting out, feeling like I was going to cry, staring straight ahead as I gathered up my courage. Mom, bless her heart, didn't tell me that everything was okay or that everything would be okay. I would have either blown up or cried if she had.

Marta knew when she looked at me. I didn't have to say anything. "Oh," she said, feeling my disappointment. "You got a mailbox full of no's."

I nodded.

"It's really hard to get yeses in this field."

"I feel like I wasted your time," I said.

"You didn't waste my time."

"It's highly unlikely I'll play in a symphony now."

She shrugged. "There are smaller symphonies in smaller cities. They don't pay, or pay much, but you can still bring the songs to life to share with many people. And you know, your future is not set in stone. You could work for a year and then apply to more places next year." She thought for a moment. "Okay. Many kids who don't go to college go to trade school. Today's lesson is going to be trade school."

We walked into the room where I always had my lessons. Her small adobe house had the elegance of a concert hall to me—a chandelier hanging from a rough-hewn dark beam, a handwoven rug on the hardwood floor, a grand piano, white lace curtains. In the room where I had my lessons, there were four windows that reached from floor to ceiling. We usually pointed our music stands so that we were facing outside as we played, and in the winter when the sun was low enough to duck under her little wisteria arbor, we could sometimes feel the sun on our faces.

"I swore I never wanted to hear this song again, and so when you were learning, I intentionally kept it hidden, but now this song is going to put food in your mouth. You can make a little money playing at weddings." With that, she put down a piece of music before me—Johann Pachelbel's Canon in D. "It's generally about five minutes and fifteen seconds—the perfect amount of time for a bride's processional. I'm not going to lie. You will grow to hate this song, and it's sad when it happens because it really is a beautiful song. But love it or hate it, it feeds you."

So, for the next half hour, we worked on it.

And then she slipped that sheet music into my cello case, and walked to her stereo, flipped on the radio, and found a station playing some pop love ballad I didn't much care for. "This is the other thing that will put food in your mouth. You have to listen for the opportunity in the song, listen for what's missing . . ." She picked up her cello and began to play along with the melody. "Is the melody missing? No. So you don't play that, not unless the singer is really bad and either can't stay on pitch or has a voice that lacks warmth." Then she began to play the bass line. "Is the bass line missing? No. Stay off the bass line. But be aware of the bass line because that's usually a good place to build from. This is intuitive. There are no rules. I can't really help you much with words, but if we play with the radio enough, you might get better at hearing the opportunities in the music. This is what studio musicians do. It pays all right, but jobs are pretty rare. Still, you don't know. You could even end up playing with a band and doing this."

We played along with Richard Marx and Lionel Richie, and then she turned the channel and we played along with Talking Heads and The Psychedelic Furs. When she turned the channel again, we played along with The Rolling Stones, Guns N' Roses, and Def Leppard. We just made up our own parts in the song and played along. "It doesn't matter what you like or don't like. You have to be willing to hear the opportunity in anything," said Marta.

Then she stood and walked to the stereo once more. She turned off the radio, and popped in a cassette tape. "In the same way you have to look for the opportunity for what to play in a song—even a song you don't like, you also have to look for the opportunity in life—even in a set of circumstances you don't like. Here's the truth. Sometimes I'm playing symphonies that are profoundly beautiful, symphonies that elevate my heart, symphonies so clear and true that I feel passionately that they be preserved forever and brought to life regularly. And sometimes I play symphonies I don't like— symphonies that are discordant and abstract, noises meant to be interesting but not elevating. But all the time I am keenly aware that none of those symphonies were written by women.

"The other day one of my opera singer friends gave me this." She pressed play and "Aikea-Guinea" by the Cocteau Twins poured through the speakers.

I had never heard anything like it. Someone had taken some very beautiful, lyrical, classical elements and blended them with rock, New Wave, and punk. This musician or musicians had built a bridge from the past to the present, giving something operatic in nature an edge and new relevance. And in that moment, some kind of dream was born for me. Some kind of new possibility opened up.

Marta could tell I loved it and when the song ended she said, "I know. It blew my mind and my friend's mind too. And at rehearsals ever since, we've wondered what we might have created if we had put our energies into creating instead of mastering. I mean, we need masters. We need technicians so skilled that they can play anything that has ever been written and with soul. I have a significant place in this world. But I keep thinking, has everything been done? As I listen to this, I think: no, there's a lot of room for completely new, unique, and uplifting sounds. I haven't been thinking big enough. So my point is that there is more than one track for musicians. Who knows what you will create. And therefore, who are you to tell me that I wasted my time with you? You don't even know yet what is possible."

I don't think there had ever been a moment when I hadn't wanted to make Marta proud, but in that moment, I was determined. Right then, I decided that I was going to go to L.A. and I was going to play wherever I could for whatever I could until I found the group of people with whom I could create something of some kind of significance—something that would make Marta proud of me.

I think she was proud of me for making a living doing what I loved, and I think she was happy to have given a poor kid a skill that allowed her to do that, but as each year ticked by, I felt worse and worse about not creating anything that blew her mind the way the Cocteau Twins had.

51

I donned my mother's overalls for the outside work I intended to do. There had been times I felt embarrassed about these very overalls, which she had worn every day and everywhere. I had felt hick enough, and on those rare trips to Santa Fe or Durango, there had been this tiny window of opportunity to slip out of our life here with the constant milking and manure management and simply be a normal person—a person who bought milk at the grocery store and who didn't get so dirty every day. But by wearing those overalls, Mom brought the goat ranch with us. Now, though, I found them incredibly comfortable. I wasn't showing. I had no baby bump. But I was retaining more water. I was filling out. Relieved to be out of pants that were on the uncomfortable side of snug, I looked at my reflection in the mirror mounted to the back of my bedroom door. Studying my reflection, I worked my hair into two long braids like my mother used to wear, and studied it some more. I could see her. I could see her in me. I couldn't say exactly what it was—our stature, our blue eyes . . . our eyebrows perhaps, our small lips. Mom had inherited Austrian cheekbones, high and sharp, with a strong jawline to match, while I had inherited the softer features of my dad's ancestors. When I was a teenager, I used to suck in my cheeks and wish I had inherited Mom's bone structure.

When I opened the door, Slobber Dog was sitting just outside waiting for me. Her mouth seemed full, so I held my cupped hands in front of her, and she dropped two perfect speckled brown eggs into them. Transferring both into one hand, I pet her and thanked her.

After I put them in the refrigerator, I began to make my way to the hay and horse barn to assess what needed to be done before I hopefully put the estate on the market.

Clouds were already building on the western horizon, two cumulus towers shooting up and leveling off like eagles soaring up into the sky, wings broad and flat on top. Eagles were generally a very auspicious sign, one I had always taken to mean that I was on the right path. But two eagles I had never seen before. Eagles mate for life, but I could not begin to believe Ian was going to track me down and propose. Mating for life was clearly not in my cards.

I sang, "Everyone knows it's Stinky," as I entered the hay barn, but smelled only the faintest hint of skunk, which led me to believe she wasn't there.

The barn was in pretty good order. With a plastic rake that looked like a scoop, I picked up the manure in the two horse stalls and pushed the wheelbarrow to Mom's most recent dumping spot in a small arroyo out behind the paddocks.

As I pushed the wheelbarrow back to the barn, Darrel honked and waved as he drove by on his way home from work, but he didn't stop. He was hoping.

I put away the wheelbarrow and the rake and opened the door to the tack room. The Western saddle, beautifully carved with roses was well-worn. I was quite sure Mom had only used it on a rare trail ride with friends, or when taking a beginner rider for a ride around the property. A small collection of bridles hung near the saddles—

a side pull, a hackamore, two snaffles, and behind the others, one with a curb bit. Some had long reins and some had a single braided rein. One of the snaffle bit bridles had only one rein.

There was something about tack I loved—the smell, for starters . . . the soft, almost sticky texture of well-oiled and well-worn leather. It was both rugged and elegant all at once. Perhaps I could sell it all on craigslist for a hundred bucks. Maybe Darrel could use the brushes, hoof picks, and various ointments.

Before I walked out, I paused in the doorway remembering the warm bliss of brushing Ruby after a good ride, remembering the feeling of her smooth, strong neck as I hugged her, and her velvety muzzle as I rubbed noses with her, remembering bringing Ruby's bridle back in here and hanging it up, setting down the bucket of brushes below it. The tack room had been more or less empty then.

I picked up the bucket of brushes, caught the bay, and went to work polishing him up so that he'd look good for the people who were coming to look at him anytime now. It was hard for me not to think of him as a killer, as a being that robbed me of my mom and robbed my baby of a grandma. He stood nicely as I brushed him even though I did so without much sensitivity, my aggression creeping out inappropriately. He even dropped his head, relaxed. He didn't flinch or pin his ears when I brushed his legs or worked through his mane and tail with a comb. As I brushed his face, I noticed his eyes were very kind. They were not the eyes of a killer. He was not a mean horse. Mom had loved him. She would want me to treat him with kindness and compassion, and not blame him for being a horse and responding to whatever he might have responded to like a horse. She would want me to forgive him. I wondered if he loved my mom to the degree that a horse had the capacity for love or something like it. I wondered if he knew that after whatever happened, she was dead . . . whether her lifeless body in his pasture had been troublesome to him. Who knew what horses understood and how deeply. I knew they had a lot of heart, but that wasn't the same as understanding.

Standing back, I admired my work. He looked almost flashy. I hoped these people would buy him and give him a fresh start. He could go on to his new life where no one had to forgive him for anything, where no one associated him with a fatal accident. He could be someone's good boy again. Mom would want that.

I brushed Spot next. My heart longed to have a horse again. Riding with Darrel a couple days ago had awakened my awareness of that missing part of me. Maybe at some point in my life I'd be able to.

I thought about the arguments Paula made for staying, but I was having a hard time imagining any other life than that of a musician in a city. It had taken so much effort to assert my own dream and my own path instead of getting swallowed up in my mom's dream, and to build a life that a lot of musicians only dreamed of. Would I really just throw that all away and return to a place I didn't like all that much the first time around? I was a musician.

When I put the bucket of brushes down under the bridles, I paused and considered the tack. Side pulls were hard to find and hackamores were expensive. If I went back to L.A., perhaps I'd take them with me . . . just to keep an improbable dream alive, or perhaps just to hang by my bed so their scent would give me sweet, nostalgic dreams.

Just then the prospective buyer I'd been expecting showed up, a woman from Chama looking for a good horse that even her husband could ride. She was pulling a trailer, so she was serious, and this excited me, but shortly after she stepped out and we introduced ourselves, she sized up the bay and determined he would be too small for her husband. She thought the bay was a little short for him but might work if he was stocky enough, but he wasn't; the bay was simply average. My heart sank with disappointment as I watched her drive away. She would have taken good care of the bay. I could not say that for a lot of people who lived in the area. One drive through Coalton, and anyone could see many people here weren't doing such a super job of taking care of themselves.

That's when I heard a noise, a noise that used to make Mom begin to shout with fury and take off behind the dogs. Cows.

The dogs immediately ran for the northernmost part of the vineyard, so I stepped out to see what I already knew was true. In the distance, eight cows feasted on grapes. It was a given that fencing the bottom of arroyos was difficult, and often the soil eroded from under the fence, but still, Mr. Valdez to the north had never seemed particularly upset if his cows had gotten to feed on our land for the day instead of his. For the first six months, Mom pushed his cows back through the bottom of whatever arroyo they came from, but all that did was show him he didn't need to repair his fence because she would continue to solve the problem for him. That was when Mom began to experiment with pushing his cows off her land in the opposite direction—down the driveway and out the gate. She always hoped the cows would find their way onto Cestero Apache land or even all the way to Heron Lake State Park farther to the south because then there would be big fines for Mr. Valdez and incentive to check his fences more often.

Now, there was the same decision to make. On one hand, it seemed unlikely Mr. Valdez was still living there—or even alive for that matter, so it might be some new neighbor's first offense, but it seemed more likely that it would be one of Mr. Valdez's relatives with the same attitude. I didn't know, but figured if all went well, this place would be on the market and I could not have my neighbor's cows destroying my mom's vineyard in my absence. It was one of her few assets. I did not want to lose money on the sale because the vineyard had been thrashed by cows.

So, I slipped a bridle over Spot's head and hopped on bareback, rode down to the driveway to open the right gates and shut the one that would keep Señor Clackers out of the mix, and then I rode up to the winery and down the farthest row of grapes to get behind the cows. I had just begun driving them down the driveway toward the dirt road when I heard a voice from the fence line. "Monica! Monica! Hey, I thought we were past this!"

I stopped, embarrassed. If I tried to get ahead of the cows on the driveway, it would only push them to the road faster. Besides, I'd have to gallop to do that, and I wasn't going to do that while I was pregnant. So, I rode back up the hill at a walk toward the neighbor, self-conscious about riding so slowly, knowing it looked like I didn't care, since a normal person would have trotted over. Behind me, the dogs continued to herd the cows off our land. There was no stopping them. Meanwhile, the neighbor had crossed the fence and was walking downhill in the direction of the barnyard. He wore a brown felt cowboy hat. Mom used to jokingly call cowboy hats "the Western toupee," so I paused to picture him bald underneath it, but it made no difference. He was still remarkably handsome. He had that stubbly look that registered as manly and sexy from a distance. It had appeal until I actually imagined having my own face grated off by that bed of nails. So yes, I did imagine him kissing me within the first five seconds of meeting him. But fortunately, the perfect storm of grief, heartbreak, and a bun in the oven would keep me from getting into trouble. Even if I was in the mood for romance, which I wasn't, nothing repelled a man like my set of circumstances.

I could also see that he was surprised that I wasn't Monica. "Who are you?" he asked.

"Who are you?" I asked back, one of my peeves being men who asked my name without offering theirs. I guessed he was about my age or a little older, and I noticed he wore no wedding ring, so apparently his charms hadn't worked on anyone else either.

"I'm Mark. I bought the Valdez place almost a year ago."

"I'm Willow," I said. "I returned to settle my mom's estate."

His face fell and then froze, his devastation and confusion apparent. It hadn't occurred to me that he and my mom might have been friends until just then. After all, my mom had generally had no small level of contempt for her neighbors—especially the ones whose cows breached the fence on a regular basis. But just looking at his face, I could see he had cared about her. "Monica . . . ?"

I nodded.

He stared at the ground for a moment and then said, "She used to do the same thing to my cows—herd them out there to the road so I'd have to drive all the way around, drive them into a trailer by myself and trailer them back. I invited her over for dinner each time they got through the fence though, grilled some steak, and at some point won her over. She stopped pushing loose cows onto the road and just started pushing them back under the fence in whatever arroyo they'd managed to get through. That's when I knew we were friends. I think she saw me on the fence line a lot and knew I really was doing my level best to prevent escapes. And I think she liked the steaks." He smiled to himself as he remembered. "She's really gone?" he asked, his smile turning back into deep sadness.

I now felt horrible for breaking the news in a way that hadn't been remotely soft, and for pushing his cows out to the road. I nodded that yes, she was really gone. "She came off the bay horse in a bad spot, I guess."

"Charlie?" he asked while looking over at the paddock.

I shrugged. "I don't know his name. The bay."

Mark shook his head. "That makes no sense. Charlie's a good boy."

I looked behind me and beyond to see that his cows had crossed the dirt road and were now spreading out to graze.

"You're welcome to tack him up to go round up your cows. I'm really sorry about pushing them through now. I didn't know you and my mom were friends and they were feasting in the vineyard. I'd help you round them up, but due to a medical condition I have to keep it at a walk. I can't offer you much help."

He looked at me curiously, as if he wanted to ask about that but decided it wasn't his business.

"Thanks," he said. "My horse has an abscess in his hoof right now, so I really appreciate it. Your mom and I put a gate in along the fence line over there." He pointed back behind him and a little to the east. "Would you mind opening it and then maybe coming back around to keep them from going in the vineyard again?"

"No problem," I replied.

I rode on up the hill and then followed the fence until I found the gate. I slid off Spot, unhooked the wire from the top of the fence post, pulled the floppy wires and posts to the side of the opening, and then looked for a good place to mount up again until I found a big rock a little ways away and used that. Looking back down the driveway, I could see that Mark already had the cows rounded up and coming through the driveway. I wasn't sure how I was really going to keep them from scattering through the vineyard again when all I could do was ride Spot at a walk, but as the cows came up the hill toward the fence, it seemed that they did know the drill and were headed for the gate without much argument.

The reason for Mark's speed had become clear—he hadn't bothered to tack up Charlie at all. He had only affixed the lead rope to work like reins on the halter and rode bareback. At the gate, he slid off, handed me the lead rope, and began to pull the fence closed again. "I saw where they got through and will be out to fix it in the next couple hours. I'm really sorry for the inconvenience. And I'm so, so sorry about your mother."

I hated how other people's tenderness chipped away at my shell the way it did, the way I could feel the stinging behind my nose that preceded tears. I was trying so hard to hold it together. No one seemed to understand how much harder it was to hold it together in the presence of kindness. I nodded and looked away, determined not to break.

"If you need anything, I'm just down there." He pointed to the northwest. "Thanks for letting me use Charlie."

"He's for sale," I said.

"How much?"

"Nine hundred."

"Would you take seven?"

"Mom's place is in foreclosure. I'm trying to save it. Every dollar counts."

He nodded. "I'll take him for nine hundred."

I held the lead rope out to Mark. "I'm thinking you could use him now."

He opened the gate, took the horse, and led him through. "Thanks. I'll be back shortly with a check and to fix the fence."

"Sounds good."

"I just . . . I'm just so sorry about your mom," he said before starting off toward home.

"Me too," I said, before doing the same.

52

When I had first arrived in Los Angeles all those years ago, I confess, I was so overwhelmed that I nearly left. From the edge of town, I stopped at a gas station, bought a newspaper, and searched the classifieds for a living situation I could afford. And I needed a job— any job. I didn't know which one I needed first. I unzipped my coin purse where I had twelve quarters for phone calls. Twelve. Twelve chances.

Many jobs said to stop in and get an application, but I didn't know where any of these places were. I drove around looking in vain, but mostly just thinking, *There isn't room for one more person here.*

I had wanted to turn around and go, but I had made such a big deal about coming here, about how my life was going to be so much better—palm trees and the ocean and the music scene. It would have been too embarrassing to return home.

So I did the next best thing. I followed a cloud that looked like a sled dog leading the way north, which is how I found myself in Topanga Canyon, where I felt considerably safer—at least safe enough to curl up into the back of my '76 Volkswagen Rabbit and rest that night. I say "rest" because I couldn't quite call what I did "sleep."

By the grace of God, and I mean truly by the grace of God, I had parked across the street from the small ranch home of Betty Power, a retired secretary who spied me the next morning moving my duffel bag of clothes and my cello out of my passenger seat and into the back of the car. She approached me with a carrot-raisin muffin and a glass of orange juice, and after a short visit, offered to take me in for one month so I could figure out where I was going to live and work without sleeping in my car.

She knew people and made a few calls, which is how I came to work at Canyon Mercantile, an upscale small grocery store just down the hill a bit. I posted a sign on the bulletin board there and a few other places around the area and got a little extra work playing Pachelbel's Canon at weddings some Saturdays. I was happy. And Betty was too, for over muffins and juice in the kitchen one morning, she offered to let me stay on longer for two hundred dollars a month rent, which was nothing. It was charity on her behalf. I think she had liked listening to my stories about life in New Mexico.

But then one day I played at a wedding that Ross, a music producer, was attending. His studio cellist had left, and he thought I was okay, and if he hired me, he wouldn't have to take time out of his recording schedule to listen to auditions and make a decision.

For the first three weeks I commuted, sure I would be fired and find myself back in Topanga Canyon seeking work again. I was so sure I would be fired from this studio job that I wasn't even nervous. I figured I would simply learn as much as I could before this inevitable event. But to my surprise, Ross was pleased with what I added to songs, pleased I didn't try to take them over and show off, pleased I stayed in the background and kept things simple, adding depth but not complexity. Everything I did to hide my weaknesses turned out to be exactly what he wanted.

Occasionally, Ross had the team of studio musicians come in while an artist was recording if he figured out that the artist stepped it up or delivered a different kind or level of energy in some way if there were other people in the room. But usually I came to the studio in the morning when a lot of musicians slept. Ross would hand me some earphones to listen to what the artist had recorded the day before. I listened to it a few times, and gradually began to experiment with what my cello part could be, and then when I was ready, I gave Ross a nod and he pressed record. Sometimes we did this three or four times, with me trying some different things, but usually Ross chose my simplest recording. A few times, he blended all the things I had tried so that it sounded like there had been three or four cellists playing backup. The end product didn't really matter to me. I loved listening to new music every day and I enjoyed the creative process—even if it wasn't complicated, at least most days.

It took an hour and a half to get from the studio to Betty's house in traffic—oftentimes longer, and so when I found a studio apartment just a few blocks away from where I worked, I took it. It had been a motel room at one point in its history, so its kitchen consisted of a mini-fridge and a hot plate. The sink was in the bathroom.

But here is what I remember most about that place: I remember looking out my window at the overwhelming and unfriendly world outside that first night and every day and night that followed, feeling caged like an animal in the pound. That's when my scared and lonely heart would ache like something kicked and bruised, when I would struggle to take a deep breath, and wrap myself tightly in a blanket like a swaddled baby.

53

I still had a couple hours before I needed to get ready to help Grandma Anita, and since Mom's service was in two days, I figured I should pick the perfect place to scatter her ashes. I was drawn to the highest point on the property, a little knoll to the northeast.

L.A. was more or less at sea level, and the ranch was around seven thousand feet in elevation—a huge difference. My body hadn't yet adjusted, so I walked slowly. I didn't know whether I needed to be concerned about the baby getting enough oxygen under these circumstances, but it seemed wise to be safe and cautious.

I wandered through the vineyard on my way up, through the vines I had helped to plant so many years ago. My arms ached just remembering all of the endless hard work—digging through clay soil to plant, pruning, trellising, and harvesting. Every season had involved misery.

I paused and looked all around at the five acres now striped with trellised vines, and thought the vineyard looked like more land than just five acres. Each row was straight. I knew this because Mom and I had taken care to make it so, but I marveled at how something straight could appear wavy just by following curves of the landscape. It struck me as feminine—this influence of the land on all things . . . its ability to soften lines and anything else that was rigid. I tried visually to break up the vineyard into five football fields, but it seemed there was a lot of vineyard left over. Maybe football fields were larger than I remembered. I had planted at least half of all of it with my own two hands, and now it was mature. I was downright impressed with what a woman and her teenage daughter could do.

The grapes looked ready or something close to it, and something about each vine reminded me of fancy ladies—vines with thick green leaves wrapping around the trellis like a feather boa wrapped around outstretched arms, and clusters of indigo berries dripping like jewels. To Mom, they had been jewels. They had been her riches. I picked one and popped it in my mouth, letting the juice sit on my tongue for an extra minute. It still tasted a little green to me, but it was close. It seemed like such a shame to let all of these grapes we had worked so hard to plant and prune just rot on the vine this year, and yet it served no purpose to pick, crush, and barrel when barrels had to be topped off throughout the year to prevent spoilage. It seemed likely no one would be here to do that.

The vineyard, nonetheless, impressed me in a way it never had before—maybe because I had seen the reactions of discerning wine drinkers as they had tasted Mom's Passion. I wondered if she really had known just how much she had, in fact, achieved her dream. It probably hadn't seemed like she'd achieved much with everything she had worked so hard for slipping into foreclosure. Surely that felt more like terror than success.

Only then did I wonder why she hadn't told me anything about her circumstances, or asked me to come help with sales. I supposed she hadn't wanted to impact me living my dream with her inability to live hers much longer. She was so damn independent—independent to a fault.

When I reached the top of the hill, I found myself in a place that seemed rather magical and I knew instantly this was the spot for my mother's ashes. She had created a labyrinth out of rocks—a maze to walk through in a state of contemplation, her footsteps erased by wind and frost heave. On a dead tree, she had hung a collection of bottles—new bottles and antique bottles that had surfaced with the creation of a new arroyo somewhere on this ranch, bottles of all shapes and colors. She had affixed baling wire to them and curled the ends to make spirals, adding a fancy touch. A lawn chair sat on the other side of the tree, and from it, a person could admire the sun shining through the glass. On a low branch of another nearby tree hung some wind chimes. I walked over to it and studied the ground below to see if I was right, picking up a handful of dirt, and carefully sifting through it. Sure enough, I found two BBs. Mom used to blow off stress by shooting at wind chimes with a BB gun. She used to say when she hit her target and it rang, it made her feel like a winner.

For a moment, I just sat in her lawn chair and took in the vista while I caught my breath. There was so much space up here. Large mountain ranges towered in the distance to the north and east, while the tops of other smaller mountains and hills like the one I was on lay before me to the south.

I stood and began to walk through the labyrinth, a rock pathway leading me into the center of a spiral and then back out. *How many times had she walked it?* I wondered. Once out, I slowly walked into the center again, the heel of one foot almost touching the toe of the other one, heavy questions in my heart, praying for guidance.

The clouds had grown into sheep, and if I had to put a feeling to it, I'd say it felt like the sky was shouting that at me. "Sheep!"

Sheep are stupid followers. If one jumps over a line painted on a road, the rest of the flock will all jump over that line. Was I a sheep? Did wanting to remain a musician qualify me as a sheep? I looked up at the sky and threw my hands up in the air as if to let the forces that be know I didn't understand. The clouds roiled until they looked like a huge flock of sheep as seen from above—just heads sticking out of a mass of fluffy bodies. The sky was growing more emphatic every minute.

A low rumble came from far away but still it was a sign to get down to lower ground. The milking barn still needed going through, and then I needed to get cleaned up before three to help Grandma Anita with whatever she needed. There was plenty to do—no need to spend more time up here. I patted the smooth, bare trunk of my mom's bottle tree before heading down the slope, past some junipers, and back into the vines that were laden with the fruits of Mom's labors.

Perhaps after I paid off the debt and put this place on the market, the next owners would buy it quickly enough to harvest. No. The sale couldn't happen that quickly.

Even if they did, they would put a new name on the bottles. My mother's faith in this place, her blind loyalty to it, and her work wouldn't be recognized, and I knew that shouldn't matter but it did. My mom's legacy did matter to me.

Not only did barrels need to be topped off to prevent oxidation and spoilage, they needed to be checked for the perfect moment to bottle. What was I going to do—drive back to L.A. in a rented U-Haul truck full of wine barrels and fill a small apartment with them? I had to let it go.

Clinging to things in grief was a slippery slope. This stirring inside me was just the somewhat crazy grasping that comes with grief. I was rational enough to see that. All of us pass through this world. Some of us leave some ripples behind in our wake. Few of us are ever immortalized. Trying to immortalize my mother with a few bottles of wine was stupid. What was I going to cling to next, the wine itself? Was I going to get so attached to it that I wouldn't be able to stand to sell it or allow anyone to drink it? Would I come to think of that wine as the essence of my mother preserved in a bottle? See, a grieving person could go there to that unhealthy place and I was determined not to.

And anyway, my relationship with wine was as complicated as my relationship with my mother. On one hand, drinking wine was this celebratory thing, this small ritual we still had left in our culture, the sound of a cork popping synonymous with slowing down with dear friends. I had played enough weddings to see wine at its very best. And I remembered days when Betty and I had set out on wine-tasting adventures, visiting the vineyards and wineries of her many friends just a little north of Los Angeles. And on the other hand, wine was this thing that caused so much suffering in so many families, this thing that intensified everything far too much and prevented any conflict from ever being resolved. It was this thing that taught kids and spouses to say whatever it took to keep the peace. While I had learned to appreciate wine, there had been times when I had hated it.

My need to make peace with a ghost would have to take a less tangible form. There was business to take care of. There were decisions to make. There was my life to figure out and resume. Cash from the sale of this estate was step one. With some cash in my pocket, I could afford to take a chance and make a leap. I could start over. It was critical to stay focused on my own dreams and not get sucked into the dream that had been my mom's.

54

"They're here!" Mom had said when I walked up the driveway after school one Friday night in the middle of April in 1989. She was loading tools and gloves in the back up her pickup along with all of the bare-root Cabernet Franc grapes she had spent a small fortune on. "Hurry! Change your clothes. I need your help. There are nearly three thousand of these, and since I spent almost six thousand dollars on them, we can't afford to lose any because we didn't get them in the ground fast enough!" She could hardly contain her excitement, while I could hardly contain my dread. Almost three thousand. My half of that was roughly one thousand, five hundred.

Reluctantly, I did as I was told.

Mom had staked out rows earlier that week, insisting we could build trellises later in the season when they were needed, which meant that she was going to have to wait for the divorce settlement or more child-support money before she would be able to afford materials. The soil was wet when we began, so wet that it was hard to maintain footing in the slick clay, especially on the hillsides, but the digging was pretty easy—especially compared to what it would be later. I remember doing the worst math-story problem ever as I dug hole after hole, carefully setting the roots and then trying to get the clumpy mud to cover the roots without sealing in big air pockets. I had planted about ten in the first half hour. That meant I could plant twenty in an hour. I might plant forty or sixty before it was time to go in for dinner tonight. Forty or sixty out of one thousand, five hundred. However, I slowed down after that first half hour. From time to time, I'd slip and fall down, leaving the front of my jeans covered with cold mud and each evening breeze chilled my legs extra through the wet denim. I had planted about fifty plants before it got so dark that Mom said it was time to go in. By then, temperatures were dropping rapidly below freezing.

We ate chili that night, which is memorable only because it tasted so good after being out in the cold, and I do recall that my hands were a little sore as I held my spoon, but although I thought it was miserable, I had no idea what was to come.

The next morning, we went out while the ground was still frozen and tried to dig through it, and only when that proved to be far too much work for far too little results did Mom lead the way back inside where we ate three scrambled eggs each to fuel us for the day. Three each—not two, also memorable.

The ground thawed around ten, and for the next nearly eight hours we worked solidly. I only planted about one hundred and thirty—less than my one hundred and sixty estimate. Combined with the fifty or so I had planted the previous night, that was one hundred and eighty in all. One hundred and eighty out of one thousand, five hundred.

That night there were blisters on my hands and they hurt when I held a spoon and shoveled two bowls of leftover chili into my mouth. The raw skin hurt when I washed my face and when I held my toothbrush. That night, I woke up once with aching forearms and hands. I thought, well, I'm using new muscles—surely this would get better, but the next day wasn't better at all. My blisters were rubbed off, leaving painful raw spots on my hands that Mom patched up with bandages that refused to stay on. The following week, she used bandages and first-aid tape for reinforcement. The bandages got wet, which made the rest of my existing skin softer and more vulnerable. I only planted about a hundred vines that day, and I looked forward to returning to school the next day for five days. I was terrified of Ramona and Shyla still, but wasn't convinced they could do anything to me that was much worse than this. Besides, another encounter with Ramona and Shyla was a possibility, but another day of this farmwork was a certainty. I was willing to take my chances.

It seemed to me that even if I worked my hardest every day and didn't go to school, it would still take about two weeks to plant all of the grapes. Would the bare-root plants live that long? I talked to Mom about it and we guessed they would in our mostly cold spring temperatures, but we weren't sure. She was making better progress than me, and was hopeful.

After a few more days, plastic bandages weren't enough. Mom wrapped our hands in gauze, and then we put our hands in our knitted gloves before shoving them into the work gloves. Although that was in some respect an improvement, by then it really was too late. Every single contact I made with the shovel hurt.

I wore those bandages to school, and struggled to grip my pencil. The muscles in my hands didn't want to offer any fine motor control. Each day the bandages were a little thicker. Once, a scab cracked and bled through so I had to go to the nurse between history and English to get new dressing. It seemed likely to me that it was she who called Child Protective Services.

The social worker had been unable to make it out the muddy road for a home visit though. I was pulled out of geometry two days later and questioned, and once I figured out what my meeting with her was all about, I thought it might be my ticket out of there.

"Do you feel safe in your home?" she'd asked me.

All I had to do was lie and say I didn't. I wanted so badly to do it. And then I looked up to see Darrel looking through the little window in the door. At first he looked concerned, but then he made a silly face, and it occurred to me that to lie would be to leave him and his grandparents as well. I knew too, how it would feel to tell him I lied to the social worker, or worse, not to tell him.

"Willow, I asked whether you felt safe in your home."

"Yes," I said begrudgingly.

"Does your mom ever spank you with objects?"

I sighed. How cruel it was to be offered opportunity after opportunity to lie. "No," I said.

It went on until she was clear that I was just an overworked farm kid with a struggling mom. I told her I thought it would be over in a couple weeks. That wasn't quite enough to satisfy her. She had me wait while she typed up a letter to my mom on an electric typewriter. It was the first time I had ever seen anyone's fingers move so fast. I found them almost hypnotizing, but snapped out of it when she pulled the paper from the machine, folded it, and sealed it in an envelope to give to my mom when I got home.

Mom's brow furrowed when she read the letter. Rather stoically she said, "Okay," as she tried to contain her anger and her worry. "The State of New Mexico says you get a few days off to heal."

"How many?" I asked, curious.

She shrugged. "Until your hands heal." I could see her concern about what she was going to do, her fear that she would lose thousands of dollars' worth of vines. "You're in charge of all of the cooking and all of the housework for the next two or three weeks. I won't have time for any of that."

I was making three-bean soup with some beans she had started the night before when Grandma Anita and Grandpa Luis pulled up in their pickup that evening. "The soup is not ready yet and I have nothing else to offer," I said.

"That's okay," said Grandma Anita, looking at the thick bandages on my hands. "We have to get back. Darrel is making dinner for us tonight. I just stopped by because Darrel said your hands are bad from so much work."

I nodded. "Mom's too."

"I made you something to soothe them and help them heal." She handed me a jar of green salve. "Put this on your hands at night and then cover them with bandages."

"It works," said Grandpa Luis. "Do what she says. The plants talk to her the way the clouds talk to you. She has a gift."

"Okay," I said, nodding to show I understood. "Thank you very much."

She reached out to hug me. "I brought enough for your mother too."

As I hugged her back, I said, "Thank you very much."

"It's good to help your mother," said Grandpa Luis. "Don't let that lady make you feel like there's something wrong with helping your mother."

"But it's good to heal too," said Grandma Anita, and I loved her for this. "Be careful with your new skin when it comes back."

I thanked them again before they left and finished the soup, which tasted watery and flavorless. Mom ate it without complaint when she came in. I told her about Grandma Anita bringing by the salve and could see from her expression that she wasn't going to try it. I did though. That night after I brushed my teeth, I unwrapped my hands, rinsed them in water I had heated on the stove since it had been a dreary day and our solar-heated hot water didn't work on dreary days, and then I opened the jar of salve, making a face when the smell of it reached me. For a second, I considered not using it, but I knew Darrel's grandma and grandpa would ask me about it and I couldn't lie to them or worse, offend them by not using it—especially after they had driven through more than a half mile of mud to bring it to me. I slathered it on and rewrapped my hands with a new gauze pad and the same gauze wrap.

The next morning, although they still had a long ways to go, my hands were noticeably better, and were completely healed in four days. That was the good news. But the bad news was that it meant I had to return to work helping my mom that following Monday.

Her hands were a disaster as well, so bad that I had to help her brush her teeth two different nights before she finally broke down and started using the salve. That helped with her skin, but not with her pinched nerves and tendonitis.

"I hate this," I remembered saying to her that following week as we planted vine after vine from the seemingly insurmountable pile.

"It will all be worth it in four years when these vines are full of grapes." She put her hands on her hips, looked at all of our work, and smiled with something more than just satisfaction. It appeared she was seeing the future when she looked out at her brand-new vineyard, and she liked what she saw. "Yes, it will all be worth it," she said again, this time quietly, almost as if she was talking to herself.

For two more weeks after that we continued to abuse our bodies trying to get the job done—almost one whole miserable month total. By then the soil was drying out into hard clay, demanding that we use much more force with our shovels, and I confess, when we were done, I felt satisfaction and pride as well. We never did build the trellises that summer. Grapes take four years to mature, and so Mom figured it could wait until the next year, but as it turned out, no trellises were needed the next year or any year after that. Each frigid winter caused the vines to die back to their roots. Each early summer, small shoots would spring from these roots and Mom would feel hopeful again until the following spring when nothing but dead wood stood on them once more.

All of that hard work and misery—for nothing.

The next spring, she talked to other vintners and learned about the hybrids, and after that, at least what we planted didn't die, but still, each of the next five springs, we planted another acre of some kind of hybrid grape or another. Mid-April to mid-May was its own month to me—blister month. And the only thing worse were the following summers when Mom and I used pickaxes to bust through the hard, dry, clay crust until reaching soil that still had enough moisture to be soft enough to use post-hole diggers for the rest of each hole in which we would sink the posts for the trellises. Darn near every day for nearly all of summer break we spent doing that, and I hated every minute of it.

The third spring and summer of that, I had begun cello lessons. After planting was finished and my lessons resumed, Marta would hold my hands in hers as if in prayer for my healing. Having little capacity for the level of control needed to play, she kept herself from wincing when my fingers didn't do whatever I had asked them to do, and said, "Just do the best you can given the constraints of your circumstances today."

I imagined Marta holding my hands between hers and offering me the same advice now.

55

I was taking a minute to lie down on the white couch and watch clouds roll in before I showered and dressed to go help Grandma Anita when Mark rode up on the bay. He had returned in short order.

"Hey," I said, sitting up and waving as he rode down the hill past the winery into the barnyard.

"Hey," he said in return.

"That was fast."

"I didn't want you to have any concerns that I wasn't good for it," he said. I saw something in his eyes that I had not seen in Ian's in all the time we were together—something perceptive, as if he didn't miss much, something like genuine concern, and it struck me that it's what we see in another person's eyes that really makes that person attractive. Mark was handsome, but not remarkable, and yet the more I looked at him, the more attractive I came to find him. But then, consideration is an attractive quality and he was clearly considerate.

He stepped off Charlie the bay and handed me a check. "Best nine hundred bucks I spent in a long time."

"Mom would love it that you have him."

"What about his buddy over there?"

"I'm keeping him until the last minute."

"Mind?" he asked, pointing to an empty seat on the other end of the couch.

"Help yourself."

"So, how long are you here for?"

"I don't know," I answered. "Until I save the farm, and then I need to get back to work."

"In L.A., is that right?"

I nodded.

"I can't remember exactly what she said you did."

"I'm a studio cellist."

"What does that mean?"

"I make background music."

"You mean like elevator music?"

I laughed. "No. When the record label wants some cello on the recordings of the different artists they represent, they send me into the studio to make up parts to go along with their music. It makes songs sound fuller, more polished, sometimes sadder, but usually just warmer."

"Hmm," he said, impressed. "Sounds like a fun job."

"Yeah," I agreed. "Most of the time it is. I get to work with some really great new musicians sometimes, and next month I get to work with Steven Silver."

"Steven Silver? Wow!"

"Yeah, I'm really excited about that," I said.

"So, are you going to sell this place?" I could tell that didn't sit well with him.

"That's the plan. If it's not foreclosed first."

"I suppose this life isn't for everyone," he said sadly.

"No," I agreed gently. "It's not for everyone." Charlie took a step toward him and began to sniff his sleeve and then his face.

"Looks like love," I said, and smiled.

"I have a good feeling about this guy." He reached out and petted Charlie's face. "Well, listen. You know I always invited your mom to dinner when the cows escaped and came over here, so I wanted to invite you to dinner at my house tonight if you're up for it."

"Oh. That's really nice, but I'm actually going up the road to the Vigils' soon and I don't know how long I'll be needed there. And besides, I . . . um . . . don't eat meat."

"Okay. Tomorrow then. I'll make you something vegetarian. Vegetarian or vegan?"

"Wait," I said, confused. "What just happened? You didn't flinch. You didn't even roll your eyes."

He laughed. "I've had vegetarian friends."

"I'm impressed. Sadly, tomorrow is no good either. I have to go to Albuquerque. The day after that, a handful of us are having a very informal memorial service here—up on the hill next to the tree with the bottles, if you'd like to come." I didn't honestly know how I felt about going to dinner at this guy's house. I figured if he had been friends with my mom, he was probably safe, but that didn't mean the experience wasn't going to be painfully awkward.

"I'd like that. Thanks. So, dinner in three days, then."

"You really don't have to."

He looked down at his hands. "I think it would be a nice way to honor your mom," he said quietly. "I mean, I know you're not her, but in a way it would be like getting to do it one more time."

"Okay. Well, preferably vegan, then." Closure looked like different things to different people.

This seemed to make him happier. No man was ever happy about cooking a vegan dinner. He stood to go. "What kind of wine do you like?" he asked, changing the subject back to dinner.

"Oh, at the moment I'm not drinking."

He paused and wondered, but he didn't ask. "You might want to drive," he said. "The sun is setting earlier and earlier. Next road east on the highway. You probably know. Three quarters of a mile down that road. Brown timber house with a blue door. I've got a big red stock trailer in the yard. Six o'clock."

"Okay. Thank you."

He stepped into the stirrup and swung his other leg over the back of the horse. "Looking forward to it."

It was time to go inside and get ready, but I couldn't help but watch him ride up the hill for a moment first. Even if dinner was going to be awkward, it struck me that it might be good for me just to observe a different type of man than Ian.

56

This land had taken a lot of time to get to know—something one might not have expected from land so exposed. I had spent a lot of time walking up and down its arroyos just to be out of the house on days or nights when Mom had chosen wine over me. That probably wasn't a fair way of phrasing it. On nights when mom's resolve and ability to fight her addictive nature was weaker than other nights. I would come out here to this land to get some space, find some peace. And in doing so, I found treasures.

Off to the southwest corner of the three hundred acres, two more cars from the fifties rusted in the bottom of a particularly large arroyo—a DeSoto and a Ford. Farther north up the hill was a dump site full of cans so old they had a dot of solder on the bottom, and nails so old that they were square. I didn't know exactly how old that made either of them, but I knew it made them significantly older than me. The larger brown bottles had all been broken, but sometimes if I picked through the pile enough, I'd even find tiny medicine bottles—clear, purple, and once even turquoise. These I would take back to the house and clean. I wondered what kind of medicine they had held—what ailed the person who had littered here. I wondered who that person was, what ethnicity he was, and whether it had been his land or someone else's when he had dumped the cars, the cans, and the bottles. I wondered what had been in the cans and whether he had enjoyed eating whatever had been in there, or whether he had eaten it just to stay alive.

In the arroyos that carved their way down from the highest spot, gray pottery shards surfaced after rainstorms. I had found scrapers, knives, drills, and small arrowheads made from many types of stone. My favorite was one that had been smaller than the others and made of a glassy, black stone with a red ripple through it—obsidian. And on rare occasions, I'd find manos, metates, stone bowls, or paint pots.

Still farther to the east was a place where I noticed strange rocks—rocks with curvy patterns embedded in them. These soft lines made no sense to me in this rugged place, so I showed Darrel one day and he told me they were fossils of ancient giant octopi that had lived here back when this was the bottom of the ocean. Nearby, we found other fossils of shells.

This land had been many things. It had been Mexico back before the Mexican-American War, a war I had known nothing about until I had moved here. It had been land where the Apaches had hunted. It was likely land other tribes had passed through as well. It had been the bottom of the ocean. Before it was the bottom of the ocean, it had been a forest where dinosaurs roamed. I had never dug deep enough to find any dinosaur remains, but there were paleontological digs at Ghost Ranch and so I believed I had an idea of what might be under the layers of earth I walked on. Maybe.

It had taken time to learn the story of this land, time to discover the clues that told that story. This land had reminded me of my own grandmother, in the way that while I thought I knew her, she would surprise me from time to time by telling a story about sneaking out with my grandfather to dance at a dance hall on Lake

Walker or Wilderness Lake, or of the time she and my grandfather had called up a neighbor with a barking dog and barked on the phone, then hung up and laughed until they cried—things one did not expect of a woman as proper and ladylike as Grandma had been.

And now I was back on this land, land I knew more intimately than anyone still alive, land that had shared its stories with me, land I had listened to. I knew that over the years, it was likely my mom had come to know it far, far better than I ever had, but still, I knew it well. I knew it as well as I had known my own grandmother.

I remembered listening to the sound of my feet as I walked across this land, thinking, *So this is how it sounds when a person walks on the bottom of the ocean.*

In front of me, a multifaceted stone caught my eye, the material shinier than the other stones nearby. I brushed the dirt off the top of it and pulled it from the earth. A spear point of some kind. I knew it didn't belong to me. I knew it belonged to the earth now. It came from the earth and the earth had reclaimed it. I knew I should leave it, that to take it would be like ripping a page out of a library book, or perhaps even stealing a whole book from a library. Other people had a right to read this story too, I knew.

I was still thirteen when my mom drove us to the library in Pagosa Springs so she could look for a Chilton's manual for our old Ford pickup and learn to do a tune-up. While she searched the card catalog and then the shelves, I explored the shelves myself. And maybe because the move had spun me into an emotional regression, I found myself in the children's section looking at the spines of books I had long outgrown. That is when I spotted *The Digging-est Dog.* That book felt like home to me and before I even really knew what I was doing, I had slipped it into my puffy winter coat, letting one corner rest in the top of my pants.

That night, it had felt so indulgent to read it over and over after my mom had gone to bed, and then hug it to my chest like a teddy bear. For almost two weeks it comforted me like that, and then with each passing day, more shame crept into my heart over it. It came to live under my mattress where I supposed I hoped I would forget about it completely, like someone who buried stolen goods deep in the earth, only I didn't forget about it. After Darrel turned sixteen and was given permission to drive his grandfather's truck, I confessed to him what I had done three years prior and he drove me up to Pagosa Springs so I could drop it anonymously in the book-return drop.

I looked at the artifact in my hand, my lesson about taking what was not mine front and center in my memory. But still, I wiped it off and put it in my pocket. Like *the Digging-est Dog,* the artifact felt like home, and when I left here, I wanted to take a piece of the earth, a story it had once told me. I wanted to take it and keep it all to myself, keep it close to my heart. Perhaps before I left here in a few days it would eat at me enough that I would do the right thing and return it, but at the moment, it felt good in my pocket, like kite string that would keep me connected to this piece of earth when the wind blew me far away.

57

I didn't notice any cars going out to the Vigils' place while I was in the shower and getting dressed, and so I was surprised to see a half-dozen cars outside their house. It seemed the Vigils were having a gathering of some kind. Thinking I had been coming to help with something, I didn't make time to get a gift, and suddenly I felt horrified at this breach of etiquette. It was going to be witnessed by many.

Grandpa Luis was outside looking up at the sky, waiting for me when I pulled up. "What have you seen today?" he asked the second I stepped out. He had taken his gray felt cowboy hat off to view the sky, but put it back on so his hands would be free to take mine in his and greet me.

"This morning, two eagles."

"Two?"

"Two."

"A mated pair?"

"Maybe, but it didn't make sense to me either."

"Have you heard from any men today?"

"That guy Mark who bought Mr. Valdez's place last year came

out to the ranch to get his loose cows and then he bought Mom's bay horse. He invited me to dinner at his house. I think it's just a couple miles away as the crow flies."

"I hate crows."

"I know."

"Did you like the guy?"

"Yeah," I said, as if it was no big deal.

Grandpa Luis said, "Hmm . . ." in a way far too knowing.

So, I changed the subject. "A little bit ago, I saw sheep."

"Sheep?" He thought for a moment. "Vulnerable."

"Stupid followers is what I thought. I felt like the sky was telling me I was being a mindless follower."

He smiled, which he rarely did, smiled so big in fact that I could see a couple spaces where teeth had once been. "That's good."

"I was thinking that if I do pay off Mom's debts, that I might move to a smaller city with a music scene. Maybe Austin. Somewhere with cheaper housing than Los Angeles . . . So the sheep thing doesn't really make sense to me. I don't really see how I'm mindlessly following anyone. But you know, maybe I was wrong. Maybe they weren't sheep. I mean, I didn't see their legs. I just saw them from above."

"You saw them from above? Like Great Spirit's view?"

I hesitated while I thought about that. "I guess so."

This interested him greatly. "Hmm . . ."

"Thoughts?"

"I think the sky is telling you that you're not alone and you shouldn't be. You're safer with the flock. Sheep that leave the flock get eaten." He paused and considered the sky. "What do you see now?"

I looked up in every direction. The cauliflower cumulus nimbus had shot up in columns and then leveled off into massive dark clouds that were gradually encroaching on all the remaining blue spaces in the sky. "Mostly I just feel the tension building."

Grandpa Luis nodded. "Tension always builds during a storm. Then it breaks and everything is clear again. Your storm will break too. And after, everything will be clear again."

"Aw, *eheedn, T'soye,*" I said, using the Apache words for thank-you and Grandfather because it always pleased him when I remembered the words he had taught me. I searched the sky one more time and this time I saw a little bear. "Look," I said. "A little bear."

For the second time, Grandpa Luis's smile broke open wide. "A little Apache. The sky is telling you to raise your baby here." He chuckled happily. "All right. You go inside now. *Cho* has some woman business for you."

I knocked and was greeted by cheers. Behind Grandma Anita, Mrs. Jolene Velarde, Mrs. Marian White, Mrs. Sara Vigil, and Paula all stood. Behind them I saw gifts on a table, and some trays of food including cucumber cream-cheese sandwiches with the crusts cut off, speared with toothpicks to keep them together. At first I wondered if it was Grandma Anita's birthday, but then I saw a banner that read, "It's a boy!"

"This is a baby shower?" I asked, confused. On one hand, how incredibly sweet. On the other hand, *Oh my God, was I ready for this?* Was I even at that level of acceptance about this pregnancy?

"This is for you!" Grandma Anita said with so much joy that there was no choice but to open my heart enough to receive it, and so I sat on the couch and imagined the laughter of the women like the music of my cello. I let the sound waves caress my skin and touch my hair. I let their laughter sink deep into me, massage my heart, my lungs, my stomach, even my liver, and my baby. I let it sink all the way into my bone marrow where it seemed to stimulate some life force inside me . . . where it could actually become part of me.

I listened to childbirth war stories and to all kinds of conflicting advice, and although it was cliché, I ate all of the pickles on the relish tray, much to the amusement of the women. I couldn't help myself. They tasted so good. I had a side of finger sandwich with them. And we drank fancy punch with lime sherbet melting on top.

I almost floated above it all, as if the laughter itself had physical properties and could hold me up—up above the storm clouds in my life, up where it was still sunny and clear.

And then the gifts came, but it wasn't just the gifts—it was the look in the giver's eyes, their hopes and wishes for me and this baby, and their expectation that all these wishes would come true. In their eyes, I could see their belief in me—that I could be a good mother, even under these circumstances.

Mrs. Velarde gave me another pair of knitted booties and a blue-and-green hat that matched both pairs she had made. She had used the softest yarn. Mrs. White had actually made my baby little moccasins, beaded on top. I held them to my heart and then held them on my open palm, admiring them. How strange it was to imagine such tiny feet—feet small enough to fit inside of these. Grandma Anita had knitted a red baby blanket with an eagle on it, a symbol of all her wishes for this child. Paula gave me two nonfiction books to see me through pregnancy, childbirth, and the first two years of my baby's life. And Mrs. Sara Vigil gave me three fabric books for babies, books that could take abuse. I was touched, deeply touched by all of it.

Soon after, the party began to wind down. The book-club ladies washed dishes and my former teachers cleaned up wrapping paper and helped me carry my gifts to the truck. As I hugged everyone, and said my heartfelt thank-yous and good-byes, what I realized was that that shower was really an initiation into a tribe of women, a tribe of mothers. I wasn't alone.

58

It was my senior year and my third time at *Go-Jii-Ya* with Darrel and his family. *Go-Jii-Ya* was the most important Cestero Apache holiday of the year, with a big race, feasting, and dancing, and I felt so honored to be welcome among the Vigils. By then, I had figured a lot of things out. I figured out that I really did have friends here—it was just that Apache culture was more subdued and so my girlfriends weren't going to run up to me, hug me, and squeal like my old best friend, Jennifer, sometimes used to do. I had figured out that the attempted genocide that had taken place over a hundred years ago was not forgotten and yet I was not personally being blamed for it. I had figured out I was not the only one with a parent that drank too much—not by any means—and that when my mom had danced at the Christmas concert, she showed many people what we had in common.

I had reached the place where seeing a white person in the community was sometimes startling, and where I could understand how we could be seen as creepy with our ghostly skin and our translucent blue eyes. And I had also figured out that no matter how much I had come to wish I looked like a part of Darrel's family, my physical features weren't going to change. I was what I was.

But Darrel and his grandparents sort of adopted me anyway. I felt like an honorary member of their family perched on their tailgate where Grandma Anita and Grandpa Luis sat in folding lawn chairs in the bed of the pickup behind me. Together, we cheered for Darrel as he represented the *Ollero,* the White Clan, by running down the straight quarter-mile track in the relay race when it was his turn. Only men raced, and so it did not seem odd to me to be on the sidelines with the other girls my age. The Vigils and I cheered for all the runners, while Grandma Anita's older sister, Bernadette, stood in front of me with an aspen branch, and like a handful of elders, whacked *Ollero* runners as they went by if she thought they were too slow, much as she would a lazy horse.

I felt like a part of their family as I hung out under the lattice built of sticks with branches laid on top for shade next to their tipi at their family campsite there on the *Go-Jii-Ya* grounds, where the tribe came out to camp during the festivities each year. Grandma Anita made Apache stew in a kettle and roasted corn on the fire. The same meal was being served in every camp, but I was confident no one's roasted corn was better than Grandma Anita's.

And then as the day grew later, the powwow began. The powwow was a source of mixed feelings for me because on one hand, what a treat it was to watch all the different kinds of dancers in their beautiful costumes, and on the other hand, this was where my skin color mattered. No matter what Grandma Anita and Grandpa Luis taught me about culture and no matter how much they loved me, white people couldn't compete in powwows.

But at the very beginning of the powwow, just after the flags were brought in by veterans, everyone circle danced. Everyone. Everyone was welcome—even me. It was a simple side step around in a circle, all of us facing in. Sometimes a smaller circle formed on the inside facing out where the hosts and the *Go-Jii-Ya* pow-wow royalty court welcomed everyone by shaking their hands as they passed in the opposite direction. I loved circle dancing, this moment of being included.

And right before the circle dance there my senior year, Grandma Anita unfolded a long, rectangular, turquoise traditional shawl with long fringe around the bottom and the two short sides. She placed this over my shoulders with love. "I made this for you," she said.

Surprised and moved, I hugged her, and said thank you. I told her that it was beautiful, and that it meant so much to me.

And then I followed her out to the circle feeling much more beautiful than I had felt just moments ago, my new turquoise shawl around my shoulders, a sign that I belonged. To the degree that I could belong, I did.

The shawl was the same type the women fancy dancers held taut across their back and the backs of their arms as they imitated soaring eagles in their dance. I memorized their moves as I watched them, and that night in my bedroom with no one looking, I fancy danced too. It was inside me—the music, the drums, the movements, and all of these things were deeper and more real than skin color. Our common ancestors had danced to drums too.

59

As my mom's pickup bounced along the bumpy road, a big drop of rain splattered the window, and then another and another. Soon, it seemed there was more water in the sky than air. The windshield wipers barely made a dent in all that water, so I crept along, barely able to see. Thunder clapped nearby. And then, right in front of me, I saw a person. My heart jumped for Darrel if it was who I thought it could be.

He stepped to the side and as I pulled up, I could see it was indeed Quentin. It had been a long time and his hair had grown out long, but still I recognized my old friend, his small frame, his wire-framed glasses, the look on his face as if he hoped the whole world would see how hard he tried to be good. "Quentin! Get in!"

"Willow? Is that you?" He smiled broadly.

"Yes!" Another clap of thunder boomed. "Hurry! Get in!" I moved my beautiful gifts onto my lap.

Quentin ran around to the passenger side and jump in. "I'd give you a hug, but . . ." He was drenched.

I laughed. "A psychic hug will do!" and so we paused and squeezed our eyes shut as if we were squeezing the other one tight, and then laughed about it. *"Gotsaa, shi choni,"* I said warmly. "Welcome home."

"Thank you," he said with a big smile. "Were you just at Darrel's? Is he home?"

"I was at his grandparents'. Darrel is at work. I don't know what time his shift ends, but I know he left his door unlocked for you."

"Well, that's a good sign." He looked hopeful. "I missed him so much. There were so many times I almost came home, but I knew if I did, I would never have an opportunity like this again."

I didn't know what to say. Part of me wanted to ask whether he ever considered he might never have the opportunity for a great love with a man of Darrel's caliber ever again, and wasn't love the whole point of life? And the other part of me understood completely. After all, in some respect, hadn't I made the same choice? Could I have turned my own question back on myself? . . . Had I considered that I might never again have the opportunity to have such a caring community with loving neighbors in which to raise my child? Had I never considered I might never have another best friend like Darrel? I had been away long enough to know a person got one Darrel in her lifetime. Just one. How could I be mad at Quentin for being just as foolish as me?

"Do you think I should wait there? Is that presumptuous? I mean, certainly he must have feelings about me abandoning him for a year to make this other dream come true . . ."

"I am so incredibly not an expert on love or matters of the heart, Quentin. I know almost nothing. But I do know he's probably hoping right this very minute that you'll be there when he comes home tonight or in the morning."

"Yeah?"

"Yeah. I need a good place to turn around. This mud is wicked." I put the truck into gear and looked for a place where I could turn around without getting stuck in the new mud. Quentin pointed to a little road spur that would be perfect.

"How's your mom? What's she up to?"

My heart sank as I realized he didn't know. How would he? "Oh, Quentin," I said softly. "My mom's in heaven now. Darrel saw her horse with one broken rein and then found her body in the bottom of a deep arroyo."

"Oh, Willow, that's terrible. I'm so sorry. I'm so sorry. She was such a nice lady. Sometimes Darrel and I would walk or ride up the road and she'd always smile and wave or even come down to the road to give us some goat cheese and make jokes."

"Yeah, she was a character all right."

"People still talk about the year everyone danced at the Christmas concert. They had so much fun."

I shook my head, smiled, and rolled my eyes. "Yeah, that's my mom."

Quentin put his hand on my shoulder. "Do you need anything?"

"No. Thank you. I'm just . . . cleaning out her things so I can sell her place."

He winced. "Oh, that's a shame. It's such a great place. I was just admiring it as I walked by."

After a heavy-hearted pause, I said, "Oh, also, I might as well tell you before someone else does that I'm pregnant."

"Oh my God!" he exclaimed happily.

"Yeah, it was news to me too. I got here and everyone started congratulating me. Grandpa Luis had had a dream about it."

Quentin laughed. "I can just imagine. Did he dream about whether it's going to be a boy or a girl?"

"A boy, apparently," I said. "How nice that the Grandpa Luis dream test is much more specific than EPT."

"Has he had any dreams about me?" asked Quentin.

"Probably, but no one is talking about it."

"Hmm," he said, looking concerned. And then he said, "You know, Willow, I don't know whether or not Darrel is going to take me back, so maybe I shouldn't say anything. It's just that he and I will never have a baby like you are about to. I don't know. Maybe you love your new life out in L.A. Maybe all your dreams came true. Maybe you have a man that you love very much. If so, I wouldn't want to keep you from any of that. But one important thing I learned on this trip is that there is no better place in this world—at least not for me. And so, it's hard for me not to wish that you would change your mind about selling your mom's place, and just stay here, and let me and Darrel be your baby's uncles."

I gave him another eye-squeezing psychic hug. "Thank you," I said.

We bumped along the muddy road almost blindly for a bit, the rain running off the windshield in sheets. I said, "I hope Darrel is able to get home tonight. This is getting sloppy fast."

Quentin put his hand on his heart, looked up, and took a deep breath. "Ugh," he said, as if the mere thought of waiting that much longer hurt, as if that much more waiting would surely kill him.

When I pulled up in front of Darrel's house, Quentin squeezed his eyes shut tightly and said, "Wish me luck."

"Good luck," I said, and then he ran to the door, opened it, waved at me, and shut it behind him.

What a thing it must be, I thought, *to know what door you wanted to walk through, to know behind which door your heart resided.* I thought about the door to the apartment Ian and I used to have. Nope. Home is a time every bit as much as it is a place. Even if Ian had a change of heart and begged me to come back, that was a home I could never go back to. I could never go back home to the apartment I shared with a boyfriend I trusted.

60

Darrel and I were watching *Pretty in Pink* at his house shortly after school started our junior year. By then I was pining for love like I never had before. It wasn't that I was ungrateful for Darrel, for his love and companionship, for all the ways he blessed my life, but at some point in a person's teen years, the mating imperative hits— that thing that is hardwired, that thing that my mother had warned me about in the thrift store book section, that thing that tells you your number one priority is to find a mate. It didn't even matter whether or not I knew rationally that it was purely biological. It was strong, so strong that it felt like the whole purpose of life.

"I'm so afraid no one is ever going to like me like that," I blurted out near the end of the movie. "I'm white and poor and dumpy."

"I know," Darrel said. "I'm Samoan and fat and gay."

I turned and looked at him. "You're gay?"

"Yeah. I thought you knew."

"No, I just figured you didn't have romantic feelings."

"Willow, come on. Everyone has those feelings."

I stared at him for a minute as it occurred to me for the first time that I could lose him one day to some other love, but I loved him so much that I finally said, "Some boy is going to be so lucky to get you."

He smiled gratefully and asked, "Yeah?"

"Yeah. You're a catch. You're the nicest person I know," I said.

"I *am* pretty nice," he agreed. "But I'm not going to be the right match for most people."

"You don't need most people. You just need one. It will be okay. You will have love," I said.

"You will too," he replied. "We need to get you out of here for a bit. This place is changing how you see yourself. You think there's something wrong with you, but there's not. Go to prom with me."

"Oh, Darrel, that's very nice of you, but the very last thing I want to do is walk into our gymnasium under any circumstances."

"No, we'd only be pretending like we were going to prom. Really, we'd go to Durango all dressed up where we could eat a cheap meal and you could look at other people looking at you and I could look for other gay boys and we could enjoy each other's fabulous company while we did."

"Yes," I said.

And so, three weeks later and unbeknownst to his grandparents or my mom, we headed east toward town and then kept going on the washboard road for an hour and a half. Beyond that, a paved road took us the last half hour of the journey to the worldly college town of Durango where there were other poor white girls like me. It was okay for them, though, because they were in college and expected to be poor. They made it seem hip even. And just like Darrel said, boys looked at me. They didn't stare, but I didn't require that and wouldn't have known what to do with that kind of attention anyway. No, they just looked up at me, as if I existed, as if I was a person, as if I was a young woman who had some attractive qualities maybe. To be acknowledged was such a blessed relief. Truly, going to school in Sweetwater was like being in some bad movie where I accidentally spilled invisibility potion on myself and no one had been able to see me for three years, and then on this day it wore off and people could see me again. I felt so beautifully normal. Just *normal*. And it was wonderful. It was enough.

Darrel had prolonged eye contact with two young men—nothing overly suggestive, but enough that he said to me, "He bats for my team."

"How can you tell?" I asked.

"I just can," he replied. "For one, he looked at me and not you."

"Well . . . good," I said.

All that and an inexpensive vegetarian burrito at the taco place while wearing our secondhand fancy clothes was all it took to make our dreams come true.

We stopped at the photo booth in Walmart before we left town and got our prom pictures for a dollar fifty. There were four. We are making faces in the first two. The third is a moment the camera caught when we were looking at each other, asking with no words whether we should take one nice one, and the last one was us smiling. Darrel let me keep them. His grandparents thought pictures were creepy—some photographer capturing souls and putting them on paper, and so I felt okay about keeping those pictures. I kept them in a box of favorite things so that Mom wouldn't wonder how it was that there was a photo booth in my high school gymnasium at prom. It was that third picture that was my favorite, the one where we were looking at each other. I see how much we loved each other . . . enough to be vulnerable enough to ask, "Should we put our masks down and let this machine capture an unguarded image of us?" That last picture still looks like we're wearing masks—the smiles we knew other people wanted us to have, but that third picture was beautifully authentic.

61

When I got home, I turned on my mom's transistor radio. In addition to local programming, the Cestero Apache radio station also had some enjoyable and interesting NPR syndicates like "Native Sounds, Native Voices" and "AIROS-American Indian Radio on Satellite." When Ian had taught me to stream on my computer back in L.A., this is what I tried first and when the drums came on, I was filled with the feeling of wanting to dance, but Ian was there and even though he was a drummer, I didn't think he would understand, so I didn't.

As I cranked the volume of my mom's radio up loud and found the shawl in my to-keep pile, it struck me as sad, that moment in L.A. when I had reconnected with a part of myself and denied it immediately. Perhaps it was due in part to the fact that I'd had to deny it to some degree here as well.

I picked up the shawl and held it tenderly in my hands. When I had found it while cleaning my closet, I had put it unceremoniously in my to-keep pile, my head too clouded and my heart too heavy with grief in that moment to have stopped and danced. But tonight, I stretched that shawl over my back and down the back of my arms, holding the ends in my hands. Much to the curiosity of the dogs, I leaped and kicked in time to the native music, my outstretched arms tilting one way and then the other like a banking bird with beautiful turquoise wings. I danced and watched the storm roll over the top of me like the waves I used to dive under at the beach. I danced and prayed for strength and guidance. I prayed for a good life for both my child and me. I prayed for a sign. I danced and danced because to the degree that I could, I still belonged.

And when I was exhausted, I collapsed into a chair, listened to the radio, and watched the lighting show a little longer.

Mom's informal service was in a day and a half, and so at some point I turned off the radio and played "The Sound of Music" on my cello a few times even though I was pretty sure I already had it down. When I was positive, I looked at my notes and chose another catchy mistake I had made a few days ago, and worked with these five notes the way a baker works with dough, adding more and more flour, adding more and more notes, waiting for it to take on body and fullness, playing with it, working through it, until at last it was ready.

This lullaby was about enduring storms, about waiting them out. It was about having faith and being brave. It was both a story of this moment when I was doing exactly that, and it was a prayer that my child would do the same when storms came his way. Spending my adolescence here, I knew not everyone was able to wait out the storms in life. Some people broke in storms. Three of my classmates had hanged themselves during those years. I prayed my child would have the strength to endure it all—all of what life would deal him.

I wondered where the best place for both of us would be, what environment would make him the strongest individual he could be. Even if I managed to pay off Mom's debt, realistically it would still be a miracle if a Realtor managed to sell this property. How many people would want to live here? Maybe Paula was right. Maybe staying here for a little while *was* the sensible thing to do.

Outside, the thunderstorm raged.

Standing up, I carried my cello back over to its case, and gently put it away. I looked at my old house from this angle. It was a beautiful house with its large windows perfect for watching lightning storms. I could never afford a house like this in a city. I admired the things that gave it character—the kitchen cabinets, the stone countertops, the rugged old door, the stained-glass window . . .

Just then a bright flash lit up the stained-glass window as a clap of thunder boomed right over us, shaking the house. The dogs cowered on the couch while above the door, Mary and her baby alone with the animals glowed. Again, more lightning lit the window up like a neon sign or a light above an elevator telling me this was my floor. *Here,* it seemed to say. *Stay here with your baby and some animals.* Over and over it illuminated. *Here! Here! Stay here!*

Maybe it was the sign I had prayed for. Maybe.

62

I'd made appointments rather blindly, having not spent much time in Albuquerque at all and certainly not recently, and as I approached the first wine store on my list, I could see I had made a mistake. It was in a part of town that didn't exactly reek of hope. Winos outside looked longingly at the three bottles of wine peeking out of the top of the canvas bag I carried.

Either I had been here before or somewhere like it with Mom back in the day when she was trying to sell wine she didn't have or wine that hadn't aged. She gave a dollar to one of the bums outside—*a whole dollar.* If we'd really had one dollar to spare, I could have used it for more notebook paper at school. Remembering what Dad had said to me on one of our trips to Seattle, I said, "Mom, you shouldn't do that. They're not going to use that for food—they're only going to buy booze and drugs with that."

And she had replied defensively, "So what? If *I* was homeless, *I* would need booze and drugs."

But since I had been well-aware of our poverty, I had feared that might actually happen. And now I wondered whether it might have, had Mom not fallen off of the bay horse. Would she have ended up sitting outside a liquor store, begging for money to buy herself a little comfort?

At the time, I'd found her answer so frustrating. She was missing the point. Didn't she see that the lives of those bums would be so much better if they just got off the hooch? Only now, after walking past the same homeless people in L.A. for years did I understand that some people were so broken that their lives would never be okay. They just didn't have it in them to make it that way. Mom had understood something about offering a little bit of comfort in an otherwise hellish existence, and while I still wasn't sure I completely agreed with her, what I could see and appreciate now was her nonjudgment and her compassion. Many people talked about it, but few really practiced it to that level.

During my senior year when she was drinking a lot, she used to tell me that the problem with alcoholics was that they stopped eating vegetables. That's why they looked so terrible and eventually succumbed to liver disease. *Everything is okay if you eat enough vegetables* was her motto.

While I didn't think that was the only problem with alcoholics, I could not deny that there was truth in vegetables being the great neutralizer and the answer to a lot of life's problems.

When I was halfway from my car to the wine store, I turned around. This wasn't the right place. I didn't want to waste my time and my wine. I drove around the block, called them, and canceled.

The proprietor at the second store I visited was happy to taste Mom's wine and take a price list, but she said she didn't have money for new stock at this time. I supposed it wasn't a waste of time to get the word out about Mom's wine—especially among those in the business, but still, I didn't feel that generous with my time or Mom's wine. I had a ranch to save.

My third stop was at a bistro, where I was informed that the manager's business partner, not wanting the expense and inconvenience of reprinting a new wine list, had vetoed adding another selection to it at this time.

Nothing was flowing easily, and I started having doubts.

But then I sat down at a table with the head chef, the manager, and the four waiters and waitresses at a four-star restaurant on the plaza in the old part of town. I was a little intimidated being outnumbered so greatly. I didn't even bring out Salvation for them. I started with Absolution, which everyone liked well enough, but when we switched to Passion, the head chef went crazy, believing it to be the perfect wine to pair with all chocolate desserts, but especially his chocolate chile torte. In addition, he thought it would pair well with red meats, and emphatically told the waitstaff that he wanted them to push this wine with those items to bring out their flavor. The manager purchased four cases of Passion, and two cases of Absolution. I held the check for $1,320 in my hand. With the $900 from the sale of the bay horse yesterday, I only needed about five thousand more.

A wine store in an upscale business park bought two cases of all three. That was another thousand.

In the business district, I sat down with three young, handsome co-owners of a hip new bar that was closer to L.A. in appearance than New Mexico. In the back, someone was cooking scallops and the smell was about doing me in. Somehow I held it together long enough to sell them two cases of each as well. I was remarkably close to my goal.

I only had one more stop on my list though, just two blocks away, but the odds of it being a twenty-five-hundred-dollar stop was zero. It was a café that primarily served lunch to the business crowd. The owner only took a case of Salvation. One hundred and twenty more dollars.

And so I left, feeling a little disappointed in myself. I had been pretty confident that I'd be able to pull off enough really big sales today to be done, but I hadn't. I'd have to take another day later in the week to go to Los Alamos and possibly Farmington and Cortez. I wanted to be out of here and back in the music studio before that, so before getting back in my car, I figured I'd walk around the area a bit more and look for more establishments that might be a good fit. I passed a couple manly bars where I knew no one was drinking wine, and a couple Mexican restaurants where I knew everyone was drinking margaritas or cervezas. Slightly discouraged, I kept walking.

And that's when Amy from Trader Joe's called and told me both the Albuquerque store and the Santa Fe store would each take three cases of each. I told her I'd deliver today. Three thousand dollars.

I'd done it. *I'd done it! I'd done it!* I mean, I still had to stop at the bank to make deposits, and then send a check to Jerry Schlaich, but I'd more or less done it.

As I drove from Albuquerque to Santa Fe, I called the office of Natalie Garcia, the Realtor whose face I had seen on For Sale signs throughout the county.

She picked up on the third ring. "Natalie Garcia. How can help you?"

"Hello, Ms. Garcia, my name is Willow Davis, and I recently inherited three hundred acres out Monero Canyon near Coalton, with an off-the-grid two-bedroom straw-bale house, a hay barn with horse stalls, five acres of wine grapes, and a small winery, and I'm interested in selling it."

"Have you decided on an asking price?" she asked.

"I don't really know anything about the market around here," I said. "That's a big part of the reason for my call today. I wanted your thoughts."

"Well, I'd have to see it myself, but my first reaction is that it's tricky because it's a unique property in a few ways. It's a winery, which is a bonus to a select few who are looking for that, and it's off the grid, which is something a lot of people don't want to deal with. Banks don't like to finance that kind of thing, so you'd probably have to carry the contract. Three hundred acres at a thousand dollars an acre is three hundred thousand, plus the house, say sixty thousand, and the winery and grapes, maybe another fifty thousand. That's four hundred ten thousand, but truthfully the type of person who is going to want to live off the grid doesn't have that kind of money. Without seeing it, I'd say ask two hundred twenty-five thousand and see what kinds of offers come in. If you'd like to e-mail me some pictures, I can see whether I think it might be worth more or less, but it would be best if I could come out and take a look."

Two hundred, twenty-five thousand dollars. What went through my mind before I could stop it was: *It's worth more than that to me.*

"Would you like to set up a time for me to come out and look at it?" she asked.

"Give me a little time to chew on that," I said. "Tomorrow is my mom's service and . . . I just have a lot to figure out."

"All right. I totally understand. Well, you have my number when you're ready," she said.

As I drove into Santa Fe, I couldn't help but to think about how two hundred and twenty-five thousand dollars—less by the time the negotiating process was complete and sales commissions were paid—would help for sure, but it wouldn't buy a house in a city. It wouldn't even buy us a condo. For a moment, I couldn't breathe.

63

I slipped into the post office with five minutes to spare and sent a check for the balance of what Mom owed off to Jerry Schlaich via certified mail. It seemed strange to me that an act as ordinary as mailing an envelope off could be the difference between slipping through the cracks or not . . . that such an ordinary act could be life changing.

As I was walking back to my car from the post office, Dad called. I don't know why I hadn't expected he would.

"Hello?" I answered.

"Willow? It's Dad. Are you okay?" He sounded worried.

"Hi, Dad. I think I'm okay . . ." I didn't sound certain.

"Do you need anything? Can I help in any way? Do you want me to come out there?"

"That's okay, Dad. If I think of anything, I promise I'll call."

"Okay. You better," he said. "Hey, your sister's here. She wants to talk to you," and with that he passed her the phone.

"Willow? Hey, are you okay?"

"Well, you know," I said. Okay meant something different to

women than men. "It's a tough time for sure. I'm just taking it one day at a time."

"Do you need anything? Do you want me to come out? I know school just started, but I do have bereavement leave I could take . . ." Hailey had grown up to be an elementary teacher with a husband and kids. She never faltered in being a model daughter. "I could leave the kids with Mike and my parents. When's the service?" It never occurred to me that my half-sister might want to be there for me like that. I mean, she didn't even know my mom.

"Oh," I said awkwardly. "Well, about a half-dozen of Mom's closest friends are coming out tomorrow to release her ashes, so no worries. It's going to be really low-key," I explained. "And I'm trying to get back to Los Angeles as fast as possible, so . . . you know, it's okay. Your kids need you and your students need you." I did not want a houseguest at the moment, and Hailey loved being needed, so I knew I could get her to forget about visiting me by appealing to that. It was interesting after all these years to still have the same dynamic. She still came running at me with open arms and I still pushed her back. It was long past time to stop that. I wondered whether people really could change their dynamics. In an attempt to try, I said, "But I appreciate it. I'll come home for a visit as soon as I can."

"Okay. And Mike and I will keep saving as much as we can so we can bring the kids down and spend a day at Disneyland with you. Wouldn't that be fun?"

"It sure would," I replied, because it was easier than opening up a discussion about moving and why I might want to do that. I didn't want to have that conversation yet. "I appreciate you being there for me," I said in that tone of voice that ends conversations.

"Oh, okay. I'll let you go then. I love you, sis."

"I love you too."

"Dad wants to say good-bye." She handed him the phone.

"Baby girl, remember I'm here if you need me," said Dad.

"I will, Dad. Thanks."

"I love you. And I'm so sorry for your loss."

Your loss. "Just mine?"

"I lost her a long time ago, Willow."

I shut my eyes. That was why I hadn't wanted to call him. I didn't want to hear that empty space where our family used to be. I didn't want to feel the chasm between us. "Okay, Dad. I love you."

"I love you too."

64

I was thirty-four and Hailey was twenty when she had taken the Amtrak to Los Angeles to visit me for a weekend—five years ago. She had just finished her second year at UW and wanted to celebrate. I had picked her up and taken her to a taping of *Jimmy Kimmel Live!* and then we had walked Hollywood Boulevard, looking at the names in the stars on the sidewalk, and eating Chinese food out of takeout containers, reaching into the other's box with chopsticks when we needed a little variety.

She had slept on my couch, and the next day we went to Beverly Hills, Santa Monica, and Venice Beach. There, we rented Roller-blades and skated all the way down to Manhattan Beach and back. All of the gorgeous men looked at her and I was invisible once again. Hailey was California beautiful—tall, blond, skinny, and polished. Flawless. I tried not to begrudge her for it.

"It kind of makes me sad," she said, "that other sisters did this when they were growing up, but we never had that chance."

"Well, we're doing it now. That counts for something, right?"

"Yeah," she had said, but I could tell she wanted to say more.

We were in very different places in our lives. There was no getting around that. We were arguably from entirely different generations. And we had very little history together—an occasional Thanksgiving. Years went by without me visiting. And when I did visit, I always felt like I was faking it.

As we skated on, I diverted the subject to the people we passed and things going on offshore—huge cargo containers headed to Long Beach, full of junk made in China, most of which no one really needed. I told her about the studies I had heard about involving the noise levels in the ocean being harmful to wildlife. She pretended to be distracted, but I could tell something was on her mind. I found myself wanting to avoid it, whatever it was. And I did, if I had any control over it at all. We finished our adventure and returned our skates without ever talking about anything deep. We looked at huge men at Muscle Beach and at every walk of life imaginable.

"Wow, this is very different from Enumclaw," she had said. "It must be so fun to live here."

I had trouble not laughing. I think it was only the third time I had come to Venice Beach in all the years I had lived there. "Well, to be honest, I don't leave Hollywood much. It's such a pain to drive anywhere and in L.A., you have to drive everywhere."

"Still . . ." she said in a way that I could tell she had looked up to me.

That struck me as odd. After all, she was the one who was more successful than me in every way. She was the one going to the University of Washington.

The next day, we had plans to go to Disneyland, the grand finale, before I drove her back to the Amtrak station and put her on a train.

And it was there on the Matterhorn, Disneyland's huge rollercoaster, that she attempted to talk to me. Our car moved forward into a dark tunnel and began to tick up a large slope. My heart was in my throat, and I was filled with regret for letting her talk me into this. I hated carnival rides—mostly the ones that spun, but roller-coasters too.

That's when she said, "I wish you would forgive me."

"Forgive you?" I asked. "For what? I'm not mad at you. You didn't do anything."

Just as the roller-coaster crested, she said, "I wish you would forgive me for being born."

She knew. My heart sank. And then the roller-coaster plummeted and whipped around sharp corners. It wasn't quite enough to make us scream, but it was definitely enough to put our conversation on hold for the next two to three minutes. I, for one, was thankful for the time.

As it slowed, I turned to her. "I'm sorry," I said. "I thought I was over it a long time ago. I'm sorry that there's obviously still something inside of me that you're picking up on. I don't know what to tell you except that I will take a look at that and do what I can to get rid of it, because you're a good a person and a good sister and you deserve better."

"Thanks," she said, reserved. As we stepped out of the car and back onto the platform she asked. "Willow, do you like me?"

I looked at her and said, "What's not to like? You're perfect in every way."

The look on her face said, "Gotcha." "You didn't answer my question. I asked if *you* like me."

"I like you," I assured her, feeling my own heart race in a way that would have caused me to flunk a lie detector test. Why? There was no reason not to like her. Except that she'd been born. I had to root out the rest of that feeling and get all of it out of me. It was ugly and inappropriate. And she was a nice sister. Sweet. Enthusiastic. Cheerful. She *did* deserve better.

We didn't talk much as we left the park and drove to the train station. She held on to Pluto, the stuffed dog she had purchased there, making her seem younger to me.

I asked about college and she told me she was going to major in education, like her mom. We made small talk about that for the rest of the drive.

When we arrived at the train station, I felt relieved and ashamed and like I was a hopelessly damaged person. I hugged her and thanked her for visiting. I said I hoped she'd had as much fun as I had. She politely thanked me back and said she had. And then I watched her board the train with her stuffed animal, find her seat, and look at me through the small window. She waved sadly, just a small motion, a look on her face that might have been sorrow at parting ways, but which I suspected was sadness for all she didn't have the power to fix.

I waved back sadly too. I was sorry. I really was.

65

As I drove on home my sense of victory gave way to the big question: *Now what?* There was a decision to make. I had missed a week of work. Two weeks was a pretty normal amount of leave for bereavement so I knew I had a few more days left before I'd start feeling heat from Ross, but my leave was unpaid. I needed to return as soon as possible. It made sense to go back. Besides Alex Mabey, Caitlin Canty, Katya Chorover, and Kate Lynne Logan, the four indie artists I was so excited to work with, I was going to get to record with Steven Silver. I wasn't a rancher or a vintner; I was a cellist. That's what I was.

And maybe Ian's midlife crisis would pass and he would find his way back to me and be a husband and a father. But as soon as I thought it, I knew I was dreaming.

In my mind's eye, I could see Los Angeles spread out before me as I dropped down from the mountains into the chaos, and that sense of being anonymous and invisible washed over me. After my business in Los Angeles was finished, it would feel good to change. I could create a new life where I wasn't invisible, but seen and known. I wanted to live in a community where there were spaces for me. Spaces to live. Spaces to create. Spaces to raise a child. Spaces to walk in nature.

Austin. Austin was smaller, much smaller. The music scene was both prolific and intimate. Most of the music to come out of Austin did not include cello, but maybe what that meant was that there was the opportunity to be innovative with my cello and bring it to a musical genre that had never considered it before. Camper Van Beethoven had brought the fiddle to alternative rock, and that had blown my mind. Nortec Collective had brought a tuba and an accordion to techno music. Again, revolutionary. Certainly I could bring the cello to country, blues, and American rock. Or maybe I would find someone with an even more unique vision for their music and find space to cocreate. Austin was definitely small enough to be seen and known—at least in the music community. It would be hard at first, but I could go back to playing weddings while I got established. Apartments would be cheaper.

If I raised my boy in Austin, he would be a Texan. That was weird to think about. The place I would raise my son would become a big part of who he became. Who did I want him to be?

That thought was interrupted by another. While it was true that I liked the choices the sale of Mom's place would give to me, this was the reality: Even if I put Mom's place on the market tomorrow, it didn't mean it was going to sell this month, or even this year. It didn't mean I was going to have money when I needed to find a place to live in L.A. for a month or two and then move to Austin, or pay bills associated with the birth of the baby.

In the sky was a tiny cloud shaped like a sea star. Sea stars move around a little bit, but mostly they stay.

I thought about the stained-glass window lighting up during the storm, the window that seemed to say, "Stay here."

But Steven Silver. My big chance. Steven Silver and those four indie artists. Work I was going to love. "I'm going to need a bigger sign," I said.

But I would no longer be Willow, the hippie girl who had moved to the big city and made it as a musician. I'd be Willow, the hippie girl that moved to the big city, got knocked up, and came home. I couldn't let that happen, right? I couldn't let myself become that girl.

When I came home, I stood in the doorway, taking inventory of what I had done and what more needed to be done before I put the house on the market. My room, except for the bedding still on the bed, was officially cleaned out, as was my mom's room. And the closet looked good too. That left the bathroom, living room, and kitchen.

Tomorrow, I would host Mom's service, and then as soon as I figured out what to do with the rest of the animals, I could return to work while I still had a job. Hopefully I could sell more wine or more goats before I left so I'd have a little cash in my pocket to relocate. Since Ian and I wouldn't be giving one-month's notice, we would not be receiving our damage deposit back. And being that I got sick every morning, I didn't want to live in the back of my car. I wanted plumbing. And I wanted to be somewhere safe. It would be rude to surf my friends' couches and throw up in their bathrooms. Furthermore, they would figure it out and tell Ian.

I filled a big black garbage bag with clutter from the bathroom drawers—a dried-up bottle of nail polish and some ancient cosmetics I was pretty sure Mom had brought with her from Washington and hadn't used since, and some first-aid ointments in tubes that had cracked or rusted. Then I consolidated four boxes of bandages into one. After wiping down all the drawers and surfaces, I walked back out to the living room, garbage in tow.

As I looked at the house, I still saw so many things that made this my mom's house instead of just another house, and it left me wondering about what I would keep. No single item made this house feel like my mom's. It was the sum total of the collection of meaningless things. My pile of things to keep was tiny—photographs, the shawl that Grandma Anita had made me, a handful of my mom's books, and her reading glasses. I'd take a few bottles of wine, the side pull and hackamore bridles, and the dogs, probably. They were going to hate city life. And they would make finding an apartment much harder. If I did find a place that took dogs, there would be a bigger damage deposit required because of them. Oh God, how was I going to work that?

The small to-give-away pile had been growing since Paula had come and taken so many things away. In moments when my imagination ran away with me, it seemed as if the items were in purgatory, just waiting for me to see their worth and pluck them out, placing them safely in the haven of the to-keep pile. Books I plucked off the shelves that didn't interest me; tattered throw blankets and pillows; dingy, thin sheets; burned pot holders. I felt guilty, and had to remind myself these were inanimate objects. Their feelings were not hurt by being in the thrift-store pile. And they were not my mother. They were just things she had bought at the same thrift store they would be going back to.

I began cleaning out the kitchen. Out of a cupboard I took pots and pans, cake dishes and pie plates, a Bundt pan I was pretty sure Mom had never used, and a colander. These things were big and bulky, but I would need them down the road and it would save me money to keep them. I boxed them up and put them in between the to-keep pile and the thrift store pile since I wasn't completely sure.

What was I going to do? Could I get another credit card and pay it off when the ranch sold? Borrow just enough to get myself established in Austin? I could just play on the streets for change until opportunity found me . . . but change wasn't going to pay for a move. Were goats going to be enough to pay for a move? First, last, and great big deposit?

66

I had this memory that was actually several days blended together into one conglomerate memory. There were moments within it that I could sometimes pick out and date but most of the other moments all blended together, the same every year perhaps. Mom and I had been planting grapes and every single bone in our bodies hurt. Every bone, every muscle, and some of our skin. Sitting up while eating tuna fish sandwiches seemed like too much effort, and every ounce of our energy needed to be conserved for the unfinished task before us, so we lay on our backs and brought our tuna fish sandwiches to our faces while we looked at clouds.

I asked Mom what she saw and she asked me what I saw. I did not tell her the implications of both, that for me this was a conversation with God and a spiritual practice. I just enjoyed having her in my church, in my world, in my reality for a while.

"What do you see?" I asked her.

"Two squirrels," she replied. Preparation. Or, another time, "A beaver." Beavers worked hard to make a home. The last time we did this, she saw a bird flying out of a nest in a lone tree. "What do you see?" she had asked me back.

"A salmon." Salmon migrated downriver from where they were born, went out to sea for years, and then swam back up to the very place they were born. I was preparing to visit Dad. Or, another time, "A whale." Whales lived near the coast and made music. I was near graduation and preparing to move to Los Angeles in another month.

The parts that all blended together were the sun on my face and the sun sinking into my dark clothes while beneath me the ground was still cold from winter. I wasn't sure what felt better, the cold ground icing my sore back or the warm sun soothing my thighs and shoulders. When I factored in all the sun promised about the future, I chose the sun every time.

"Can you imagine how beautiful this place is going to be in a few years when these vines grow into green rows?"

I tried, but I had liked the sagebrush she had pulled out with a tractor and a chain. I had liked the wildflowers that grew in a wet late spring or early summer—the cacti especially, having never seen blooming cactus in western Washington before.

"This land will be covered with green stripes and abundance." Despite her aches and pains, she smiled, her dream in its early stages but moving forward, the outcome within her reach—or so it seemed to her in that moment. "We'll look at all of it and know that we did it together."

One of those years or maybe all of them, I had bought a jar of pickle relish to add to the tuna fish with my Christmas money from Grandma. Pickle relish had no nutritional value, so Mom wouldn't buy it, but oh, how good it tasted mixed in with the canned fish, tart and bright, and it tasted the way Enumclaw had smelled before the Farman's Pickle Factory had closed. Mrs. Farman had lived down the street from us. She'd had a stroke and couldn't speak easily anymore, but if she saw me out riding my bike past her house, she'd come out with a Popsicle and offer it to me, and I'd get off my bike for a bit to stroll through her rhododendron garden with her as I ate it, and in simple terms and gestures we'd discuss which blooms were our favorite color. Lying there in the sunshine eating my sandwich, I understood something about how flavor could transport a person to another place. I had been transported back home by the terroir of Farman's pickle relish.

"When these vines grow and produce, and we harvest and sell, I'm going to buy us both new boots—fancy cowboy boots. And silver jewelry. It's going to be great, Willow. You'll see."

Even then, I doubted this place would ever put enough money in our pockets for fancy new cowboy boots and silver jewelry, but I didn't say so. And I didn't say so ten months later when the snow began to melt off and it became evident the Cabernet Franc had died down to its roots. Mom did not cry as she lifted the small, black vines in her hands then, and not the next year either, but the look on her face was destitute, and in a way, that was more frightening for me.

And so, we had planted cold-hardy hybrids the next four springs, our hands blistered and bleeding each year as we ate tuna fish sandwiches on our backs and looked at clouds until I finally left her here to plant and dream alone. She never bought either of us fancy cowboy boots, and to my knowledge, she had never bought herself silver jewelry, but she had bought me those silver hair ties, and I had known it had meant a lot to her to do so. It had been part of her dream.

67

After I fed the animals and showered, I took pictures of the inside and outside of the house, the barns, the winery, and a few more of the views. I wandered the vineyard, looking for the perfect spot to photograph the house, the winery, and the big barn with rows of grapes in the foreground. The morning light lent the land a magical quality and I thought this is how I wanted to remember this place. I stopped taking pictures for the Realtor and started taking them for me. How unreal it seemed to me that I might never again look down these hills to the canyon that led to the Vigils'. Panic rose in my chest. I might never see *Cho* and *T'soye* again.

Again and again, everything I was weighing spun in my mind—recording with Steven Silver and other artists I loved, raising a baby in a city where no one knew me, getting to make music with Marta, seeing Ian again—maybe with another woman, Darrel. His grandparents. This land that would soon hold my mother's ashes as well as her essence. A house here. A house with room for a child to run and play and discover the wonders of nature. A career that wasn't everything I hoped it would be but had some pretty exceptional moments, several of which were coming up in the next month. Grapes on the vine. The joy of listening to live music after work . . . actually, I wouldn't be doing that once I had a baby, regardless of where I was.

As I made my way back to the barnyard, I passed the tall pile of rocks that marked the place my sweet old horse Ruby was buried, and found myself in a part of the vineyard I didn't immediately recognize—the Cabernet Franc, which Mom and I had planted the first year. The Cabernet Franc, which had died back to its roots every year since. Every year except this one because of the unusually mild winter last year. I examined them closer. Even with an extra year's growth on the vine, the vines still shouldn't have produced as many grapes as they now held. It took four years for vines to reach maturity, not two. I looked around me, as if I might see a fairy godmother or an angel, because this didn't make sense. These grapes were a miracle. Was Mom on the other side somehow able to finally will her dream to come true, or had the growing conditions just been this perfect this year?

This crop certainly would have been my mother's dream come true. I supposed it had been wonderful for her just to see it growing and fruiting, anticipating her big break into the world of respected wines.

Wine critics had turned up their noses at the cold-hardy hybrids Mom had had to resort to—the only vines that could tolerate the harsh winters here at seven thousand feet. Mom attributed their poor attitude to the fact that most of these hybrids were being grown in places with what she called "shitty terroir"—wet places like the Great Lakes region, the Midwest, and the northeast. She argued the wine from her hybrids here in this unique climate, in this place with its exceptional terroir, could rival that of any *vinifera,* those old world classics that everyone was familiar with. Still, wine critics would not give her hybrids the time of day and certainly not a fair chance.

This Cabernet Franc would have put her in a different league of winemakers. In a couple years when this wine matured, she could have taken it to regional wine competitions, hoping to win medals that would recognize her as a wine making talent and put the De Vine Winery on the map. That had been her dream. And here it was, in front of me, all around me—her dream. For a moment, I had this crazy thought—that I could harvest these grapes and make the wine she had always dreamed of making. . . .

Depending on the quality, a Cabernet Franc could bring in forty dollars a bottle or more, largely depending on how many awards it won. If I harvested this crop and did not mess up the wine production part of it, it would bring in a lot of cash. Roughly three thousand bottles of wine came out of one acre. If each bottle sold for forty dollars, this crop was worth one hundred and twenty thousand dollars. *One hundred and twenty thousand dollars.* That was roughly three years' studio musician salary for me. It was highly unlikely these grapes would ever do anything but die back to the roots every year after this, but with global warming, I didn't know. I might get lucky again. Even if I didn't, though, even if this Cabernet Franc phenomenon was just a onetime thing, it was still a game-changer for me.

Sure, the wine would take no less than two years to mature, and so I would not see the money from this for a while, but still, it would support me down the road, likely trickling in over a few years of selling it instead of being a giant windfall. That didn't matter. What suddenly did matter to me was that if I brought in this harvest, it would buy me a few years of being something close to a full-time parent. I wouldn't have to put my baby in day care every day and miss his childhood.

This acre of grapes was my answer, the sign I had been praying for. It was a miracle and a blessing. Everything I needed to meet our basic needs was right here being handed to me—home, community, money to live off of, land to live off of, a job where I didn't have to leave my child. It came with a price. I had to stay here this month and harvest these grapes instead of recording with Steven Silver. I had to let go of my old dream to make room for my new one, give up my old self to make room for the woman I would become. I had to choose motherhood and family over music . . . at least in the capacity I had known music. Steven Silver. Ugh. It was going to hurt to give that up. But I put my hand on my belly and knew what was more important. Yes, it meant giving up a lot. But in that moment of pristine clarity, I knew the truth was that I stood so much more to gain in the big picture. It wasn't just about me anymore.

68

The only thing my mom hated more than a memorial service was a funeral. If Dad went with us, we were stuck going, and Mom would simply fill a flask, which she would take nips off of in the bathroom. But if Dad had to work, which he often did, Mom and I did things her way. We would get dressed to the nines, drive to the church, and walk up the steps, through the front door. Here, we would pause and express our condolences to the bereaved. We would step aside and visit with other people from the community we knew. When a satisfactory amount of time had passed, Mom would sign the guest book, and then it was time for my big line.

"Mommy, I have to go to the bathroom."

"Okay, sweetie," she would always say, guiding me down the stairs or down the hall to the nearest restroom. From here, if no one was looking, we would slip out the back door. If someone happened to walk by while we were in the hall, Mom would say, "Oh, sweetie, wait a minute. You have something on your face." She would then kneel down, lick her thumb, and rub it on my face. This always made me feel like a cat. Only once were we caught in the actual doorway leading out. Fortunately, I was a pro by then, and improvised beautifully. "I'm going to throw up again!" I had called to Mom, and with that the door shut behind us.

We always paused there for a moment. The colors seemed brighter, the sunlight beautifully decadent. We were alive.

From there, we would drive to the garden nursery, where we made no haste choosing something for Mom to plant in a garden that she only added to on these occasions. We would wander the aisles of the outdoor areas even when it was winter and everything appeared to be dormant, but especially in the other seasons when something or everything was in bloom. We wandered the greenhouses, sniffing this flower or that one. I liked the true geraniums best—the ones that were bred to smell like other things—lemons, roses, even chocolate.

For acquaintances, Mom usually picked a blooming ground cover, for an old friend she hadn't seen in a long time, a succulent, and for someone quite dear, a blossoming shrub. I was never certain about whether these plants and shrubs were planted in honor of the deceased or whether they were simply my mom's affirmation of life.

After the funerals for Grandma and Grandpa, which we did attend, Mom and I flew back to Albuquerque and stopped at a garden greenhouse and bought aspen trees. She planted them in a low spot not far from our bedrooms so that we would be able to hear the leaves quake at night, lulling us to sleep.

Looking out the kitchen window, I noticed how those two aspens had become an aspen grove. Their leaves shimmered in the light as the wind teased them.

69

I wanted something pretty to wear at the service, and so I riffled around in my boxes until I found my black motorcycle boots, a light pink crepe sleeveless dress with big bold roses on it, and a black cashmere cardigan sweater to keep warm. I rolled my hair up into a loose bun at the nape of my neck and chose a string of pearls for a touch of formality and elegance.

I was feeling good, so when Slobber Dog brought me two fine eggs, I scrambled them, and then sat sideways in my deep sunny windowsill to eat. In the distance, I saw Darrel and Quentin walking horses up the road, so far away they were little more than specks, and I wondered how things were going. I hoped like crazy they were going well. Darrel had been so lonely before Quentin, and this far out, I wondered whether love would be able to find him again if it didn't work out.

And I wondered if romantic love would be able to find me way out here too. Maybe it already had. I considered Mark. I doubted this was how he wanted to become a father. With a baby, romantic love would be complicated. Truthfully, I didn't know if I wanted it to find me. My heart was feeling pretty weary.

Ultimately I figured, love was love, and love came in infinite forms. It was everywhere all the time, so I could never lack it. It was who I was, who everyone was, so how could I ever lack something I was? I knew this was the truth and I also knew there would be moments I would forget it. That was the nature of life. Regardless of our circumstances, we all had intense moments of experiencing the illusion of separateness. I had been having one for a mighty long time now, and chances were that I would again. It was just part of the human experience.

I would get by. I would figure it out. I would remember the truth from time to time and find my way back to contentment when those hard moments came. But for Darrel, I wanted something more.

From the other direction, I watched Paula's pickup kick up dust as it approached.

"I did it," I told her proudly when she arrived. "I sold enough wine to pay off the farm!"

"Yahoo!" she cried out triumphantly. "That's great! What now?"

"I'm going to stay."

"That's wonderful," she said.

"The Cabernet Franc grew this year. They've died back every year since we planted them."

"Yeah, your mom was so excited about those grapes. She couldn't stop talking about them."

"If I do everything correctly, they'll allow me to stay home with my baby for a few years."

"Every year counts," she said.

I nodded, looking off into the distance, wondering about this great mystery before me, feeling sad my mother wouldn't be here to see it.

As if reading my mind, Paula said, "I have no doubt she's watching over you now and will continue to do so. I have no doubt that she is so very happy about this."

I didn't want to lose composure this early in the day, and fought hard to keep it together.

Seeing me struggle, Paula said, "I like your outfit," to change the subject.

She looked pretty too in a tailored black corduroy jacket and turquoise scarf with her jeans and black Western boots. The scarf was knotted around her neck, cowgirl style. She looked both rugged and elegant—the embodiment of New Mexico. "I like your style too," I said, the intensity of the moment passing.

The dogs barked happily to tell me that Quentin and Darrel were coming up the driveway.

When they arrived, I made introductions. "Darrel was my best friend in the world when I was growing up here . . ."

"Was?" asked Darrel. "What? Have I been demoted? Who is a better friend to you than me?"

"Darrel is my best friend in the whole world," I corrected myself. "And Quentin is also a dear old friend from high school. He just returned from traveling around the world for a year."

I studied both Darrel's and Quentin's expressions for clues about how things were going. I saw no wincing from Darrel, and a blend of enthusiasm and apology in Quentin's eyes.

"I want to hear more about that," said Paula.

I wondered how many times Darrel would hear Quentin's travel stories in the next month, or several months, or even years. I wondered if a day would come when he would not be able to hear them one more time. For the moment, they were holding steady. Simply holding steady counted. It counted a lot.

"I sold enough wine to save the farm," I told Darrel and Quentin.

"Great!" they said.

Darrel looked at me as if to ask the question that Paula had asked earlier.

"Yes," I said.

"Yes?" Darrel asked.

"Yes. I'm staying."

"Yeah!" said Darrel, and then he turned to Quentin and said, "We're going to be uncles!"

"All right!" said Quentin.

"Yeah, you're going to be uncles," I said, moving to stand in between them and putting my arms around them both. "And you're going to be an aunt," I said to Paula.

"That will make me really happy," she said.

Darrel said, "My grandparents want you to know they are thinking of you today. They say if they hear your cello from high on the hill, they will stop what they are doing to dance. But you know, their traditions around this are different."

"Yeah, I know." Apaches were very uncomfortable with death. They didn't cremate their dead, although traditionally they burned the houses of the deceased so the deceased would not try to come back. For this same reason, they did not serve food at funerals. But they loved me, and I knew that, and if the wind was still, maybe they would hear my cello and Marta's from up there and dance.

By the time I went back inside for my cello and the urn, Darrel and Quentin had put their horses in the paddock, and Sara and Dorothy had arrived. Even though I hadn't met Dorothy yet, I knew she was the other woman from my mother's book club. She was older than everyone else by almost a generation. Her curly gray hair was cut short. She wore a black shirt-dress, turquoise jewelry, and black English riding boots.

Sara looked directly at me through her thick glasses and then gave me a big hug. "We all miss your mother so much. She was a dynamo."

While I was still in Sara's embrace, Dorothy extended her hand to me and in a thick Midwestern accent said, "She was. I'm Dorothy." I lifted a hand off Sara's shoulder and shook it.

"Thank you," I said to both women.

"It makes sense that she would want to be sprinkled there—to become part of the terroir," said Sara.

Dorothy added, "Yeah, she would love being part of the grapes."

Marta pulled in next, and I made introductions. It was strange and lovely to see these equally profound but compartmentalized parts of my life come together as I watched Darrel and Marta shake hands.

As I led the way to my mom's spot, Darrel carried Marta's cello, and walked near her in case she lost her footing or her balance, and Quentin stayed near Dorothy, without making it look like that was what he was doing. The hike up seemed longer now that I was responsible for dragging other people up, and despite having been there a little more than a week, I still wasn't used to the thinner air and breathed hard to compensate.

At the top, Mark was waiting beside Charlie.

"Thanks for coming," I said and made introductions while he shook everyone's hands.

Marta and I opened our cello cases, set up our stools, and checked our tuning. And then I stood, realizing that while I had prepared a song, I hadn't really prepared anything to say. There was no choice but to speak from the heart.

"Thank you for coming today . . . for, um . . . for loving my mom . . . exactly the way she was.

"My mother once told me that the mother-daughter relationship was inherently insulting. She said it wasn't that mothers thought their daughters *would* grow up to be just like them—it was just that they assumed their little girls would *want* to grow up and be just like them, and yet daughters generally had their own strong ideas about who they were and who they wanted to be, and they usually wanted to try something else. This, she said, was hard not to take personally. With me, it was never even an option to be like her. She was tougher than me in every way. She was always capable of doing what needed to be done, and she did it . . . usually while I went behind the barn and cried. Mom was bold and brave, smart and resourceful. She was a character. She moved us all the way out here and she stayed. I know she loved this land deeply. I know she would want to be part of it.

"She often said good neighbors were worth their weight in gold, and I know she meant all of you—her community, her fold. Thank you for enriching her life, and thank you for enriching mine as well. Would anyone else like to say anything?"

Paula stepped forward. "When I first moved here just a handful of years ago, Roberto at the feed store asked me if I was Monica's sister, and when I told him I wasn't, he emphatically told me that I had to—*had to*—meet Monica. And you know, the first time I met her, I thought she was my sister too. She was multifaceted for sure. One minute, she might have been reflecting on the principles of the *I Ching* at work in her life, and the next, she was picking up her rifle and blasting a coyote. We spent several hours sipping wine—sometimes on horseback—and discussing philosophy and pragmatic problem solving, like the finer points of hoof trimming. I loved her laughter—this laugh like she could not have been more entertained by life, and I loved what I called 'her winning smile'—that smile she would flash while waiting for my reaction to an outrageous story, as if to ask, 'Can you believe that?' I felt like I had waited my whole life for a friend like her—someone who understood my need to be on the fringes, my need to be free. Indeed, there is no one on this whole earth like her. Life without her seems long. I miss her. She was my soul sister. I loved her."

As I wiped my eyes, Sara stepped forward. "Monica said the things the rest of us only thought. She had no filter." She laughed. "That's what I loved about her most—her honesty. God, she was funny. And you know, so right-on."

Darrel laughed. "She always made me laugh."

"Me too," Quentin added quietly.

"She saw the humor in everyday life," said Darrel.

Quentin nodded his agreement, and said, "She had a lot of gusto."

"Gusto" was the perfect word. I smiled.

"She was not someone you messed with," said Mark with a smile. "She made every attempt to hide her affinity for me even after I won her over, but I could always see right through it. I always knew she had a heart of gold."

"Thank you," I mouthed to him, and he nodded back.

Dorothy read a short poem by Hafiz about death being a false notion.

And then, since it was breezy, I knelt down and poured the contents of the urn near the base of the bottle tree, for I could think of no better memorial marker than that.

Finally, I picked up my cello and said, "Well, I understand this was my mom's last wish. This one's for you, Mom." With that, Marta and I played "The Sound of Music." The book-club ladies and Darrel and Quentin twirled, arms wide open, and then proceeded to do something like a slow-motion square dance, hooking arms and spinning, twirling one person and then the next, even pulling Mark into the dance, despite the fact he didn't know what this was all about. He smiled and went with it. All of them dancing together . . . it was lovely, unspeakably lovely. Lovely and perfect.

There was a moment when, overcome by emotion, I stopped playing, and Marta carried the song until I was collected enough to resume again. The guests danced and danced. Mom would have loved it. At times I thought I saw her out of the corner of my eye dancing with them all.

70

We had descended together and gathered at the winery for food and for those who wanted it, wine. People told stories that I absolutely loved hearing and I thought, *Wow, I almost missed out on this,* thinking I needed to do this alone.

". . . That's when Señor Clackers broke through the fence and made a break for it. He came running down the street toward a place where Monica was enjoying lobster tacos. People all around her were scrambling. She said that she and the bull made eye contact and something magical happened . . ." Sara was telling the story I'd never gotten to hear my mom tell.

Mark interjected. "She told me that the bull said to her in plain telepathic Spanish, *'¡Salvame!'* Save me!"

Darrel and Quentin nodded as if this was completely reasonable.

"The story got better every time she told it," said Sara. "So she walked right up to the bull, who sniffed her. She had one of those purses with clips on the end of the strap, so she unclipped one end from her purse and clipped it to the bull's nose, and walked it down the street to her pickup truck, which thankfully had rails on it."

"She told me that the morning before she left, she was looking at the stained-glass window on her way out the door and noticed the livestock behind the Madonna, and then she heard a woman's voice in her own mind but not her own, tell her to put the rails on the truck and be ready," said Mark.

Again, Darrel and Quentin nodded, and I could tell by their expressions that they liked this part of the story very much. But who was I to question it? Hadn't lightning flashing through that very stained-glass window spoken to me just two nights ago?

"Excellent," said Sara. "That really takes the story to a new level for me."

"Me too," said Paula.

Sara continued, "She claimed the bull hopped up into the back of her pickup by its own free will," and that as she pulled away, a mob of angry rodeo men began to chase her with sticks."

"She told me they were on horseback with guns," said Mark.

Sara just smiled and went on. "Up ahead was a checkpoint with *Federales* who appeared to be in communication with perhaps the rodeo people, and concerned about the bull. She feared there would be trouble, so, according to her, she kissed one of them on the mouth twice—passionately, and then drove on through while he was still too stunned to stop her."

At this point, Marta, who had never heard anything of this story before, began wiping tears from her eyes. "Your mother was something else!" she said to me.

"She was that," I said.

Paula said, "She was definitely tenacious and resourceful."

Mark nodded and smiled like someone who had been on the receiving end of that tenacity and resourcefulness in the worst way, but with a sense of humor about it.

"She bribed the ag inspector in Tecate to give her proper documentation for one thousand pesos, and then she drove on through the American inspection point at the border with no problem. She drove on through the night, stopping just once to buy a bucket and two gallons of water at a grocery store in Roswell. And that, Willow, is how Señor Clackers came to live on the De Vine Winery and Goat Ranch."

We all laughed and the loveliness of being surrounded by my history keepers touched me. This was exactly what I wanted for my son. "You know," I began, "it just really hit me how lucky I am to be able to raise my son in a place where people can tell him these stories about his grandmother. It's important."

The book-club ladies and Darrel and Quentin all nodded, while Mark looked something between surprised and confused.

Marta broke from the crowd and loaded her cello into her car, and I took this as my cue to stay good-bye for now and thank her very much for her support today. Then I waved as she drove off down the driveway, past Señor Clackers, and out the dirt road.

Mark approached me, away from the others. "You're going to have a baby, huh?"

I nodded. "Yep," I said, matter-of-factly, trying to hide my feelings about it.

Smiling broadly, he gave me a heartfelt congratulations. "So when are you due?"

I had to think about that, and I think that surprised him. "Gosh, April, I guess."

"And you're staying?"

I shot him my best winning smile. "Howdy, neighbor."

"By yourself?"

I shrugged.

"Are you going to be okay out here with a baby all by yourself?" he asked.

I looked back at the gathering, and pointed to them with my lips, as was the custom here. "Look around," I said. "I'm not all by myself," and with that, I led him back to the gathering, which had begun to break up.

"No, I suppose you're not," he said.

People collected their serving dishes and carried wineglasses back into the winery where Paula washed them. We said our good-byes and then one by one they drove or rode away.

After everyone left, I unpacked. I put my mom's kitchenwares back in the cupboards along with my own mismatched china. With the clothes I loved, I filled the hangers in my closet where the ugly clothes of my youth had hung just days ago, and something about that specific act made me realize something with even greater clarity—that living here again did not by any means mean regressing. I didn't have to go back to a time when I was an earlier version of myself. I could be the best me I had ever been. I was bringing with me the best of all I had learned, experienced, and acquired, both in this physical way and in ways less tangible. I could be more empowered this time. I could still have style and live a creative life like I more or less did in L.A. I could write and perform music with Marta.

I called the studio back in L.A. and left a message for Ross, who I expected would not be able to be interrupted. I dreaded breaking the news to him, and wished I could offer him an explanation that made more sense without risking that Ian would get the news. To my circle in L.A., it was going to look like I'd lost my mind. But life went on.

After I hung up, I changed into Mom's overalls before I stopped in the winery for a few plastic bags and a refractometer. With dogs in tow, I wandered the vineyard to get Brix readings. If Mom was here, it was what she would do. She would be checking these vines that we had planted so long ago. Wandering through the rows of vines, I remembered all the mornings I watched my mom do just this. I popped an occasional berry in my mouth, not only tasting the flavor but feeling its texture—whether the skin was soft, whether it still tasted a little green. The illustrious Cabernet Franc needed more time, but despite the recent rain, the Marechal Foch was ready, with the Baco Noir and Frontenac close behind.

There was work to do. With Mom's tractor, I loaded a picking bin on the trailer, and hooked the trailer up to her pickup. I found her C-shaped knife and her clippers, work gloves, a couple buckets, and a cassette tape of Spanish baroque that Marta had given me long ago. I'd found it while cleaning out my chest of drawers.

With that, I drove out to the vineyard, parked the pickup truck near the first row of Marechal Foch, and cranked the music. And with buckets in my hands and the knife and clippers in the handy pocket of my mom's overalls, I took my first step into my new old life and started my first day of my new job.

How delicious it was to work in the sun, especially my favorite sun of all—the September sun. This was the time of year I most hated to stay inside, and now, I didn't have to. I had awareness of birdsongs, which I knew I should equate with grape robbers, but I could not begrudge any musician for needing to eat. Whatever they ate through the nets seemed like a reasonable price for their songs. I listened to the wind in the leaves blending into the orchestra so beautifully that it simply sounded like part of the percussion section.

Each cluster I cradled in my left hand while I cut its stalk with my right, and then gently dropped the cluster into the bucket. The work was meditative. I paced myself by pausing to stretch and drink plenty of water. In the past, Mom and I had rushed the harvest, but the rain two days ago had surely lowered the sugar content of the grapes, and so if I picked slowly today, it would actually be a good thing. It would give the sugars time to rise in the rest. An acre took about four days to pick, and with five acres ahead of me,

I needed to move steadily ahead. Farming required a delicate balance of will and surrender. And it required a sense of perfect timing. I supposed life in general did as well.

As I picked bucket after bucket under the shade of my mom's broad straw hat, the cassette tape ran out of music, and rather than flip it over, I savored the birdsongs and the wind in the leaves alone. In the moments when the wind quieted, I enjoyed something close to silence. How truly indulgent silence struck me. I remembered the times I had felt assaulted by a trendy pop singer belting out the high note, a note like a smack in the face in case the listener hadn't been paying close enough attention. I'd heard a lot of great music, but I'd also heard a lot of sounds that I hadn't found pleasant and when I could, tuned out. But out here, there was no need to tune anything out. I was not being assaulted by sound. In fact, listening even closer was pleasant, and that struck me as a good thing—for a musician to want to listen closer.

When at last the bed of the pickup was full, and it was time to crush, I flipped the tape and drove back down just behind the winery, unloading the grapes through a chute that led directly into the crusher.

Inside, I pushed a wine tote into the spot where I wanted it, hooked up the hoses, and flipped on the crusher.

Outside, I poured bucket after bucket down the chute.

Then back inside, I turned off the crusher until my next load, and paused to look at the juice in the bottom of the large open plastic box where it would go through its initial fermentation. Here it was. The first of my future wines. My future.

I returned to the vineyard to pick some more, and then just as I was almost finished crushing my second load, Darrel and Quentin rode up the driveway.

"*Daanzho!*" I called out to them.

"*Daanzho,*" they called back.

321

Darrel said, "Ride with us!"

"Do you have time now?" asked Quentin.

I looked back at the grapes. *I shouldn't,* I thought, but I did anyway. It was, after all, the first day of my new life and my new life involved riding horses with my friends. An hour of working wasn't something I was going to remember decades from now, but this hour with my friends on the day of my mom's service, on my first day of my new life, I quite possibly would. I slipped a bridle on Spot, and hopped on.

We stayed on the road at a walk like Darrel had promised his grandmother, the three of us talking not exactly like old times but something close. Quentin told a few stories from his travels—of seeing the northern lights, his first elephant, of the best meals of his life.

And the topic of food led into the topic of *Go-Jii-Ya,* which was coming up in a week. Darrel and Quentin were still debating about whether or not to run in the race this year. On one hand, they were getting old. On the other hand, sometimes the *Ollero,* the smaller of the two clans, needed all the runners they could get.

I would be around for *Go-Jii-Ya* this year, I thought happily.

Although all in all relatively unremarkable, it was a nice ride. Usually, it was the unremarkable things that counted. Riding with Darrel and Quentin made me think of the times I had poured sugar or flour out of a bag into a canister and had tapped the canister to shake it just enough to make its contents settle, to make room for more. The ride felt like that, like the horse beneath me shook me just enough to cause all these transitions inside me to settle, to make room for more.

And when it was over, I rode up the driveway as Darrel and Quentin continued on down the road. I slipped off Spot's back and led him to the corral and stall that had been Ruby's. He was mine now. While I waited for the trough to fill with water, I brushed him and hugged him. And then I sat on a nearby bale of hay, looking at my new horse, my new buddy, and I felt fifteen again, like a girl whose dream had just come true. In a few moments, it would be time to turn off the hose, find a headlamp, and get back to work picking and crushing, but in this moment, it was okay simply to sit, to sit and savor the smell of a good horse, to sit and feel grateful, to sit and feel good. It was so dang nice to feel good again.

71

I had never really been back on this road. There had never been cause to. But sure enough, I spotted the stock trailer and his timber house, similar to a log house in how it was constructed, but made with large timbers that had been milled. It was small but not tiny, and might have looked quaint had it not been for the skeletons of old cars, trucks, and tractors that littered the yard nearby. Two black-and-white border collies ran down the driveway to greet me, seemingly euphoric to have an important job at the moment—security. Mark opened his door and called the dogs back as I parked and stepped out.

"Welcome!" he called. "Come in!" As I approached, he gestured toward the junk in his yard and said, "I'm still dealing with the archaeology that came with the house."

I laughed. "New Mexico is rich in archaeology. You might just try putting a 'Free' sign on those things and one at the end of the road and see if anyone comes out and takes them away for you." I greeted his dogs, who wagged their tails.

Mark appeared to consider that idea as he led the way inside where the scents of coconut and ginger hung heavily in the steamy air of the kitchen. I smiled. It seemed likely that this dinner was not going to be rich in the Top Ten Cheap and Nutritious foods. Small culinary luxuries like ginger still filled me with happiness. I inhaled deeply.

"I thought the ginger would help your stomach. When Darrel and I were visiting after your mom's service, he said your stomach has been upset lately."

A little embarrassed, I simply said, "That was thoughtful of you." He shrugged as if to say it was nothing.

"So, I don't believe you told me the story of how you ended up way out here," I said, changing the subject and turning the focus back onto him.

"I just couldn't do it anymore, you know? The corporate thing . . . My wife and I worked all the time—even when we were at home. I just . . . wanted more out of life than that. At some point she changed her mind about having a family and decided she didn't ever want to have kids. I thought having a family was kind of the whole point of marriage and life, or at least a mighty big part of it, so anyway, I filed for divorce and looked for a place where I could get the most acres per dollar. I grew up on a ranch up in northeast Colorado and after living, if you can call it that, in the city, I just wanted to return to my ranching roots. I still do some consulting work to supplement my income, but I don't let it take over my life, you know?" He stood in front of a pan, and stirred its contents and then peeked under the lid of another pan.

I nodded. "But if family is something you valued so much, weren't you worried about essentially moving to a monastery? I mean, surely you've figured out that it's slim pickins' out here."

He laughed. "Nah. I believe in God and that through Him, all things are possible."

A part of me was terrified that I had just stumbled into a religious conversation, but another part of me thought of how nice it would be to believe like that. It wasn't that I didn't believe that to some degree, but I'd simply had plenty of experiences where the outcome I wanted seemingly hadn't been possible.

"Sometimes the answers to my prayers don't always look the way I expected them to, but . . ." and again, he shrugged as if to say it was okay. "I figure God knows what's best for me. I knew He would send me someone."

He turned back around and began dishing up food onto plates, and thank goodness he did so that he missed the look on my face as I wondered whether his last comment was purely a thought he'd had a year ago, or whether he was saying that voilà, here I was, the answer to his prayers. I chose to leave it alone. *This could go a lot of ways,* I thought. He might become a brother spirit like Darrell, or simply a helpful neighbor. He might be the one, or I might need to slap a restraining order on him at some point in the future. It was too soon to tell.

"Stir-fry with vegetables, ginger, and coconut milk on basmati rice. Will it nauseate you or offend you if I mix some meat in with mine? I can eat meat later if it would." Wow. That was courteous.

I shook my head. "It's fine. Thanks." He handed me a plate and then I followed him to the table, which seemed far too large for a bachelor. "I never thought a rancher would make me coconut ginger stir-fry," I said with a smile.

"*With* tofu," he added.

"Don't you get stripped of your rancher status if you serve tofu?"

"Only if someone finds out. Promise me you won't tell."

"Your secret is safe with me," I said.

He waited with animated anticipation for me to taste what he had prepared, and so I was prepared to fake enjoyment if necessary when I took a bite, but it was wonderful. I may have made noises that bordered on inappropriate and then caught myself and stopped, but not before he laughed with satisfaction. "It tastes all right?" he asked.

"Mmm!" I nodded emphatically. "Believe it or not, my mom was not a great cook by any means, perhaps because we didn't have money for anything that would give a meal flavor. Other people take flavor for granted, but I do not."

"Have you had any cravings?" he asked.

I thought about it. "No, not really. At least not yet. But animal crackers tasted especially delicious when I had some about a week ago." We ate in silence for a moment and then I joked, "Was that a pregnant pause?"

"Yes," he answered and smiled. "Actually, I was wondering about the father of your baby, but I didn't want to be too nosy, so I was deciding not to ask. But look what I did. I managed to ask indirectly without looking like I was asking." He gave me a winning smile that reminded me a bit of my mom's winning smile, the smile she shot me when she was especially proud of herself and waiting for a reaction.

I wondered if Mom had taught Mark to smile like that with such similar timing, or whether it was something many people did. Regardless, I said, "Brilliant. Well done." I figured I might as well answer since in a small town everyone but him probably already knew anyway. "My boyfriend broke it off with me before I knew," I said.

"How long were you together?"

"Three years."

He seemed surprised. "That's a long time. So are you going to tell him?"

"I don't know. He dumped me so he could pursue his new band. He moved out of the apartment we shared and into his friend's closet to save four hundred bucks a month. If a girlfriend was too much baggage to carry into the next era of his life, it stands to reason that a baby would be too. So, I'm quite confident he doesn't want to be a parent. And I'm quite confident that I don't want to share custody with him. I mean, maybe it's wrong, but I just can't imagine handing a helpless baby over to him every other weekend, you know? But I figure I don't have to make any decisions about that today. I have time."

"Yeah. You do. That's a tough position to be in." He was quiet for a bit and then he said it. "I know there must be something greater at work, but still, sometimes it just seems like it's not fair that the people who don't want babies get them anyway."

"I want this baby," I said even though I had wavered.

"I meant your ex-boyfriend."

"Oh," I said and paused before I added, "yeah, it's not fair to anybody. I guess we just play the hands we're dealt." I stared at my plate as I stabbed at a piece of broccoli.

"I'm sorry," he said. "I didn't mean to bring the conversation down."

"That's okay." I took another delicious bite, finished chewing, and then said, "Let me ask you something. If you had the ability to have a baby by yourself, like say there was such a thing as a man uterus so you were able to be in my shoes but it was only good until your fortieth birthday . . ."

"Where would the baby come out?"

"Uh . . . You'd have to have a C-section, I guess. It doesn't matter. My question is, would you do it? Would you do it by yourself? I mean, go out and make it happen?"

"Wait, what would I have to do to make it happen?"

"I don't know, Mark, it doesn't matter. The question is would you intentionally have a baby all on your own if you could?"

"I'd rather not do that on my own if I had a choice."

"Who would?" I asked. "You've got, say, one month to use your man uterus before your fortieth birthday—what are you going to do?"

"You know this conversation is a little creepy, right? Man uterus and all."

"Yes. Answer the question," I said.

He took a deep breath. "Yeah, I suppose I would. And then I suppose I would hope that God would send me my wife after the fact and that she had a heart big enough to let both of us into it."

That was when it seemed to me his eyes twinkled in a way that suggested that he wondered and even hoped if he might be a husband like that to me one day. It was too much, too fast, too close. I wasn't ready to flirt with someone new or even consider the possibility of another romance. Flustered, I quickly looked down at my plate and concentrated on my last two bites.

"More?" he asked.

"No, that was perfect," I answered.

He took our plates to the kitchen and I thought I might be able to excuse myself in short order. I could always play the pregnancy card. But he returned with a pot of herb tea and a small plate of lemon bars.

"My mom said she craved these when she was pregnant, so I made them for you. Do you have to watch your sugar intake though? I know there's such a thing as gestational diabetes . . ."

"I don't know."

"What does your doctor say?"

"Uh, I haven't been yet. I just . . . I haven't known that long, and I was busy trying to save Mom's farm . . ."

"Oh." I could tell he thought I should go. He was right. I'd have to figure that out. "So, it's about time to harvest grapes, right?"

"Yeah. I started already. In fact, I should be out picking now. Timing is everything."

"I'll come help you tomorrow so you don't have to feel guilty about tonight. How's that?"

"Not necessary," I said. "Really."

"Hmm," he replied, as if he'd already made up his mind.

"These are delicious," I said, finishing my lemon bar while I wondered if I had wolfed it down too quickly. He had really gone the extra mile.

"There's more. Help yourself. I don't judge."

"I'm good," I said, and sipped my tea. "So you and my mom used to have dinners like this?"

"Yeah, I'm pretty sure she may have lifted up the fencing at the bottom of a couple different arroyos so that my cows would cross over onto her land and I'd feel obligated to cook for her again, but I didn't mind. I needed a little entertainment and she was a hoot." He smiled as he stared at a random spot on the floor and remembered.

"Well, if you had left it at just the stir-fry, I might have left your fences alone in the future, but after the lemon bars, I can't say I won't do the same. But I'll wait until after harvest."

He nodded and played along. "That sounds like a good plan."

Wait, I thought. *Did I just flirt?* I didn't mean to flirt. I had to get out of there before I locked in a new boyfriend. "Okay, well, sadly I have an early morning tomorrow, so I should go," I said.

"Oh," he said, sounding disappointed, but he walked me to my car nonetheless. "You know, you don't have to wreck my fences if you want to come to dinner again. You can just call and invite yourself over." He handed me a piece of paper. "I enjoyed your company."

"Thanks," I said, putting the paper in my pocket. "And thanks again for a truly lovely dinner. It was delicious."

"My pleasure," he said as I stepped back into my mom's old pickup.

"Okay, good night," I said awkwardly.

"Good night," he replied in a way that wasn't awkward at all, in a way that seemed to suggest that he was looking forward to seeing whether his destiny might involve me.

What the heck? I thought as I drove away. *Who does that? Who hopes some woman who is pregnant with another man's baby will be his destiny?* Maybe one day years from now when we were still just good neighbors and good friends, we would laugh about this night, this night when we came dangerously close to flirting at times, this night when neither of us really knew what was possible.

72

When I finished being sick and drove out to the vineyard the next morning, Mark was either really repairing a section of fence, or else he was pretending to while he waited for me. Charlie the horse was tied to a fence post nearby. "I helped your mom a little bit last year. She paid me in wine."

I did need help. That was a fact. I was not in a position to turn down help just because it was potentially awkward. "Fair enough," I said, and with that, he crawled between two strands of barbed wire and made his way over to the truck, pulled out two buckets from the back, and followed me down the row where I had left off the day before. "Clippers or knife?" I asked, pulling both out of my pocket, hoping he would choose the clippers.

"I brought my own," he said, pulling some clippers out of his pocket and working on the opposite side of the row from me, carrying my buckets back to the truck before I could when they were full, and bringing new buckets back.

We told stories from the past—his about growing up on the ranch, mine about life in Washington before and after my parents' divorce and about visits with my grandma. We talked about old dogs and old horses. I told him about Ruby. Time passed quickly that way, and by the end of the day I was confident that I wouldn't be slapping him with a restraining order ever. Instead, I thought he was a pretty darn nice new friend and neighbor.

Sometime after lunch, Paula showed up and helped for a bit. Like Mark, she explained, "I helped your mom a little bit in previous years. She paid me in wine and goat cheese."

"You got goat cheese?" asked Mark. "I guess I jumped too quickly at her first offer."

"I'll pay you in goats," I said. "How's that?"

"I'll totally work for goats," said Mark.

"I'll work for goats too," said Paula.

"One goat for every eight-hour day?" I asked, and they both nodded as if that was more than reasonable. Oh, this was wonderful. I got help picking grapes *and* I was going to get rid of the goats, which I did not want to milk, eat, or have to feed.

With Mark and Paula's help, I brought in the rest of the Marechal Foch grapes over the next three days. My hands ached at the end of each day, but I couldn't help but play my cello for just a little bit each night. An idea was developing. I hadn't felt creatively inspired like this since . . . well, ever. I had already written two lullabies this week, and they were good. I was proud of them. And they were mine. When was the last time I had written a song? Had it been years? It had. Many years. And now this child was inspiring me.

I wanted to make a CD of cello lullabies. Just thinking of this project made my heart sing out a resounding yes. In this digital age, I could market the CD even from here. And while it wasn't likely that it alone would support me, it would help.

But really, it would be a musical accomplishment for me— something that would turn me from someone who made background filler into a composer, a higher level of musician. A musician who made the world a slightly better place by creating such lovely songs that babies who heard them would fall asleep. What a lovely thing to do. I put my hand on my belly. What a lovely way to let my love for this baby go out and touch the world.

73

A little more than a week after my mom's service, Mark, Paula, and I all needed a day to rest our hands, and so I took the opportunity to wander the aisles of the Pagosa Garden Nursery, looking for the perfect thing to plant in honor of my mom. I had my heart set on a tree because sometimes bigger was better. A tree seemed enduring. But the De Vine Winery and Goat Ranch wasn't an easy place to be a tree. I could plant another aspen . . . perhaps in a new location where it might start a new grove, but I had to be careful. Aspen trees could really mess up the drain field if I planted it on the other side of the house. Their runners were far-reaching.

I considered an apricot tree. It might survive. If it did, it would help feed us. Mom would like that. If it didn't survive, I feared I might take it hard. I wasn't sold.

There were some hardy rose varieties. Mom had beauty and Mom had thorns, but somehow a rose didn't seem quite representative of her . . . I supposed because Mom was more practical, more pragmatic. If something was going to get water on the farm, it had better be practical.

I considered herbs for an herb garden—still a great idea, but maybe not as her memorial. Maybe better to buy and plant them in the spring.

Returning to the apricot tree, I thought apricots were sunny. Apricots were happy. I supposed I could even make apricot wine. Certainly the apricots would have a positive effect on the terroir of our wine. The tree looked fresh and young despite its autumn colors. I wanted it, but maybe for me. Maybe for my own affirmation of life. Would it make it through the winter if I planted it this late in the season? I didn't know. It wouldn't have time to establish deep roots before the ground froze, but it might simply go dormant and be ready to go next spring.

Then I looked down low behind me and that's when I saw grapes. Their vines were complicated and gnarled. I looked at the tag—Concord. And I imagined these grapes growing on a trellis over the door. She loved grapes. They would feed her grandchild and me. She would love that. I could build a trellis out of willow branches so that the two plants that best represented us would come together and hold on.

74

Later that afternoon, I approached the Vigils' house on my way to Darrel's and sure enough, Grandma Anita and Grandpa Luis came outside, and laughing, said that watching me ride down the road made them feel twenty-five years younger.

"Have you seen any clouds lately?" asked Grandpa Luis.

"I saw a small frog this morning," I answered.

"Rain," he said. "That's good."

"Not for me at this particular moment," I told him. "It makes the sugars in the wine go down. I need those sugars for good wine."

"Well, it was a small frog," said Grandma Anita, "so maybe it will just be a little rain."

"A gentle mist," said Grandpa Luis, and then he and Grandma Anita looked at each other and laughed. "When has there ever been a gentle mist up here?"

"Maybe it will be beautiful downdrafts that never quite reach the ground," I said hopefully.

"Now don't be selfish," joked Grandpa Luis.

"Have you had any dreams lately?" I asked him.

"It's going to be a winter with lots of snow," he said. "Much more than usual."

"Really? That's good!" I replied.

"When we need to go to the store, Darrel and Quentin might have to pull us on the horses while we sit on the sled," said Grandma Anita.

"Oh, do you have a sleigh?" I asked, envisioning an image more reminiscent of New England, a Grandma Moses painting of horse-drawn sleighs adorned with jingle bells. How romantic.

"Not a sleigh," said Grandpa Luis. "A sled. One of those round plastic ones with the handles . . ."

I started laughing. "You're both going to fit in it?"

"Oh, I don't know . . ." laughed Grandma Anita. "Have you seen signs of winter coming at your place? Have the mice been coming into your house?"

"There was mouse poop in her house when I arrived, but I haven't heard any noises or seen any new mouse poop. It's just a matter of time though. You know how it is."

"Wait a minute," she said shuffling into her house and calling back, "I have something for you."

Sure enough, she returned with two calico kittens. "They're lucky kittens," said Grandpa Luis. "We figure anyone who is expecting a baby could use a little luck. They're a gift. You have to keep them because they're a gift."

I started laughing. "Wait a minute. I think I'm getting déjà vu!"

"That can happen to us sensitive types," said Grandpa Luis, playing along. "Here now, you put these in your coat . . ."

By then Darrel and Quentin had caught their horses, bridled them, and ridden up. I watched them closely and it seemed to me that they were beginning to get their bearings with each other, beginning to find their rhythm.

"There are kittens in my coat!" I called out as they approached, grateful that the front panel of my mom's overalls was protecting me from their claws.

"They're lucky kittens," said Quentin.

"Anyone who is going to have a baby could use all the luck she can get," said Darrel.

"No, I didn't mean they were lucky kittens because they have four colors," said Quentin. "They're lucky kittens because Willow's adopting them."

I laughed more. "*Eheedn* for the lovely gift," I said to Grandma Anita and Grandpa Luis.

"*Aoo, nzhugo,*" said Grandpa Luis.

"Make sure she keeps that horse at a walk!" Grandma Anita told Darrel and Quentin as we started off toward my house.

"We will!" called back Quentin.

As I rode back to the house with my friends, my coat full of kittens and the September sun on my face, I felt happy, really happy, happier than I had been in a long, long time—maybe ever. I had a baby growing inside me, family-of-choice all around me, and a steady horse under me. I had cello lullabies cooking in my mind and spirit, grape juice fermenting in the winery, friends to help me harvest, a bull to protect me, and I'd still have a handful of goats left to make milk if I wanted it. I had a warm, safe home, two loyal dogs, and fresh eggs every morning brought right to my door. I had the music of birds, of wind in the leaves, and occasionally the sound of rain on the roof. I had a shawl to wear at *Go-Jii-Ya* in a couple days, and people in the community I loved to circle dance with. I had a good life. And my baby would too.

In the sky to the south, clouds began to blow in and take the form of birds flying in every direction. I couldn't tell exactly what kind of birds, but they seemed joyful to me somehow and the feeling I got from them was that of freedom. They were happy and free together.

75

Spring brought new kids—mostly goats but a human one as well. He was swaddled and strapped to my front as I tied a mama goat to a post and held her back end still so her black baby could nurse. Mom had been right. Goats were racist bastards.

Smelling skunk, I began to sing, "Everyone knows it's Stinky" until I spotted her. She looked at me and walked on by.

When the baby goat had had its fill, I untied the mama, and picking up my pruning shears, went to work in the vineyard, funneling my excitement and anxiety into the tedious work.

Darrel and Quentin rode up before my dad, stepmom, and half-sister arrived, slid off their horses, and tied them so their hands would be free to hold Kai.

Grandpa Luis wouldn't give me his blessings to name my son *Kla ya ii,* the Apache word for "bear" because he said white people needed something less complicated and most of all the first part of *Kla ya ii,* "*Kla*" meant "butt." It was the part of a bear most often seen since they mostly ran from people, he explained. He thought Kai would be a better name. It meant "willow" in Apache and Navajo. He joked I could call him "Junior," which I sometimes did.

The dusting of snow that had fallen early that morning had melted as the spring daytime temperatures rose. I unzipped my jacket the rest of the way, freed Kai, and handed him over to Quentin. Darrel slapped his belly like a big drum and then both and he and Quentin began to sing a powwow song. Kai kicked vigorously. Then Darrel and Quentin stopped singing at the exact same moment and Kai stopped kicking and furrowed his brow. Before he started to cry, Darrel and Quentin began drumming and singing again, and again, Kai kicked wildly. This was their favorite game—one they could play for hours.

It made me laugh too. Kai did the same when I played my CD of cello lullabies and rocked him, or when I laid him next to Mr. Lickers and Slobber Dog on a folded-up blanket of his own and attempted to play my cello for a moment. It was as if he could hardly wait until he had enough coordination to participate in all things music. Until then, all he could do was kick and wiggle.

"Do you have time for a ride today?" asked Darrel.

Grandma Anita had given me her blessings to ride with the baby only if I used a saddle and kept the horse at a walk, but I knew freak things happened and wasn't quite comfortable with that risk yet, and so a few times Darrel and Quentin had come over, taking turns playing with Kai while I went for a short ride.

"I think they'll be here soon," I replied. "But thanks!"

"A new chapter," said Darrel. Quentin handed Kai to him.

A new chapter. Yes. I was hopeful. Babies had a way of breaking a person's heart wide open in the best way. Now, in retrospect, I knew something about what Dad had hoped when Hailey was born, how he had hoped I'd be as happy as he was. Now they were coming. And I felt as if there was a new opportunity for unity.

"Is Mark going to meet the family?" asked Quentin.

I smiled. "Yeah," I said, a little shy.

Darrel handed Kai back to me, and I swaddled him again, and

slipped him back inside the Moby Wrap, a long piece of fabric that held him to my front.

"*T'soye* had a good dream about it." *T'soye*. Grandpa.

"Well then, and so it is," I replied.

They walked to the mounting block, hopped on, called out good-bye and good luck, and then kicked their horses into a canter. As I watched them, something caught my eye off to the right—a white rental SUV slowly coming up the muddy road. I waved and waved as the SUV with my dad, my stepmom, and my half-sister approached, smiles on their disoriented faces growing clearer and clearer as they neared. It had already begun. My new chapter.